MISTRESS

Amanda Quick

MISTRESS

BANTAM BOOKS
New York Toronto London
Sydney Auckland

A Bantam Large Print Edition

MISTRESS

A Bantam Book

PUBLISHING HISTORY

Bantam hardcover edition published July 1994

Bantam large print edition / July 1994

Library of Congress Cataloging-in-Publication Data

ISBN 0-553-09663-X

Published simultaneously in the United States and Canada

Bantam Books are published by Bantam Books, a division of Bantam Doubleday Dell
Publishing Group, Inc. Its trademark, consisting of the words "Bantam Books" and the
portrayal of a rooster, is Registered in U.S. Patent and Trademark Office and in other
countries. Marca Registrada. Bantam Books, 1540 Broadway, New York, New York
10036.

PRINTED IN THE UNITED STATES OF AMERICA

BVG 0 9 8 7 6 5 4 3 2 1

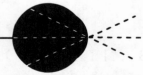

This Large Print Book carries the
Seal of Approval of N.A.V.H.

To Alberta Castle,
MOTHER AND FRIEND,
WITH LOVE FROM A GRATEFUL
DAUGHTER

$\mathcal{P}$ROLOGUE

$\mathcal{Y}$our latest mistress is creating a sensation back in London, Masters. Society finds her vastly entertaining." Charles Trescott, seated before the fireplace, downed a swallow of brandy and eyed his host with a sly expression. "As you've taken a notion to rusticate here in the country at the height of the Season for some odd reason, I thought you'd better know what's going on back in Town."

"Very thoughtful of you to go out of your way to give me the latest gossip."

"Least I could do, especially since it's your name that is on everyone's lips at the moment. I know how that sort of thing annoys you." Trescott, bored and dissolute at thirty, paused with a barely concealed air of anticipation.

"You are mistaken, Trescott. I do not give a

bloody damn what the *ton* chooses to gossip about over tea."

Trescott was disappointed but undaunted. In the manner of a willful child intent on provoking a lion in a cage, he made another stab at eliciting a reaction. "Must admit, I'm as curious as everyone else to know why you're letting her get away with her outrageous conduct. Whole world knows that you always insist on discretion from your paramours. Thought that requirement was one of your infamous rules."

Marcus Valerius Cloud, Earl of Masters, turned the crystal brandy glass slowly between his large, callused hands. He studied the reflected glow of the flames imprisoned within the heavily cut glass.

Several months ago he had grown interested in the curious properties of light and glass. He had undertaken extensive experiments with prisms and mirrors.

Those studies had led him to his current passion for telescopes. Astronomy had proven so fascinating that he had left London at the height of the Season this year in order to pursue his experiments at one of his more remote estates. The night skies here in Yorkshire were pristine and clear, unlike the smoke-filled air of the city which impeded the view through his new telescope.

It had always been thus for him. Ever since he had been a lad growing up on his family's farm in Yorkshire, he had been endlessly enthralled with matters of a mechanical, technical, or scientific nature.

From carriage springs to clocks, from music boxes to the stars, he had a passion for discovery, invention, and a need to comprehend the rules and laws that dictated the way things worked.

Marcus liked rules, especially his own. He had a personal set which he had formulated several years ago and from which he never deviated. They were simple and straightforward:

Never remarry.
Never discuss the past.
Never explain his actions to others.
Never retreat from an objective or alter a decision.
Never get involved with virgins or other men's wives.

Marcus looked up from his contemplation of the brandy glass. He had never particularly cared for Trescott. The man was typical of so many of the self-indulgent, licentious rakes of the *ton*, men whose own personal rules allowed them to prey on the innocent and those whose social ranking was lower than their own.

"Tell me what the lady has been doing to cause such comment," Marcus said in a deliberately disinterested tone.

Trescott's gaze glittered with malice. "Rumor has it that she has dismissed you and is trolling for a new lover. All of London is agog."

"Indeed."

"Mrs. Bright descended on the *ton* a fortnight ago and has taken it by storm. No one can believe that you have actually allowed your mistress to hand you your congé. Really quite extraordinary, given your, shall we say, notorious reputation?"

Marcus smiled slightly but said nothing.

Unsatisfied with that reaction, Trescott recklessly tried another sort of prod. "You know very well that you are considered to be the most mysterious and quite possibly the most dangerous man in all of London."

"As is the case with beauty, Trescott, mystery and danger are in the eyes of the beholder."

"The rumors about your past guarantee that you qualify as a full-fledged legend, Masters. Naturally any woman who has the nerve to throw you over is bound to excite comment and speculation."

"Naturally."

Trescott narrowed his eyes. "I will allow that the lady is unusual, even for you, sir. Where did you ever discover such a charming widow?"

"You have seen her?"

"Of course." Trescott chuckled. "Mrs. Bright is seen everywhere. No soiree or ball is a success without her. Your mistress is by far the most fascinating creature Society has viewed in years."

"Do you find her fascinating, Trescott?"

"Certainly. Everyone does. They call her Lady Starlight, you know."

"Do they?"

Trescott shrugged. "Not that she's a great beauty, of course. But then, you would know that better than anyone. Still, there's something about her that draws the eye, is there not? Expect her nickname was derived from her choice of attire."

"Ah, yes. Her gowns."

Trescott grinned malevolently. "Imagine, the recent paramour of the most notorious lord of the *ton* going about in purest white as though she were a bloody virgin. Utterly outrageous."

Marcus stopped rotating the brandy glass in his hands. He looked at Trescott. "She still favors white?"

"Never wears anything else," Trescott assured him. "A genuine Original. By the bye, that ridiculous little white and gilt carriage of hers is the envy of every woman in town. I'll wager it cost you a packet. Mind if I ask how much of the ready you put out for it?"

"I do not seem to recall at the moment." Marcus glanced into the fire.

"I expect you bought her so many expensive trinkets and baubles that the white carriage and those excellent white mares that go with it went unnoticed, hmm?"

"I pay very little attention to such matters."

Trescott groaned. "Must be pleasant to be as rich as Croesus. Well, no offense, sir, but it's obvious that she got her little claws rather deeply into you before she decided to look for another lover."

"Widows frequently inherit vast sums from their late husbands."

"Word is that the late Mr. Bright was quite elderly and lived a reclusive life somewhere in Devon." Trescott gave Marcus a shrewd glance. "He may have left her some money, but the whole world suspects that she did very well out of you, Masters."

"You know how these things are. A man must pay for his pleasures."

Trescott smiled thinly and then boldly stuck his hand all the way into the lion's cage. "How does it feel to have been well and truly fleeced by a scheming mistress who is now determined to find another man to replace you in her bed?"

"The sensation I am experiencing at the moment is somewhat difficult to describe, Trescott."

"I vow, there's scarcely a man in Society who would not give a fortune to take your place in her boudoir."

"Indeed."

"Certainly all of your acquaintances, especially those with whom you occasionally play cards, are seen in her vicinity on a nightly basis," Trescott continued. "Lartmore, Darrow, Ellis, and Judson are usually clustered around her. And there are several fops and dandies such as Hoyt, who contrive to amuse her so as to be seen in her company."

"Some men will go to any length to be in fashion."

"Speaking of fashion," Trescott added, "her knowledge of classical antiquities has drawn a number of ladies into her circle of associates. You know how it is these days. Every female in Society is anxious to redecorate her house in the classical style. Each wants her decor to be more authentic than anyone else's."

"Antiquities," Marcus repeated softly.

"All the rage right now and your Mrs. Bright

seems to know a remarkable amount about the subject. Apparently she spent a year touring antiquities in Italy." Trescott shook his head. "Must admit, I'm not overly fond of females endowed with intellectual natures."

"Understandable, given your own nature."

Trescott did not notice the insult. "Does her outrageous behavior mean nothing to you?"

"I find it . . ." Marcus paused, searching for the right word, "interesting."

"*Interesting*. Is that all you can say? Devil take it, man, at this very moment you're being humiliated by a former mistress in some of the best drawing rooms in London."

"It may not be all I can say, but it is most certainly all that I intend to say. Have you finished delivering your news, Trescott?"

Trescott scowled. "Yes. Should think it would be enough."

"It is. Quite enough. You will no doubt wish to be on your way." Marcus glanced at the clock. "It will be growing dark soon and the nearest inn is some distance from here."

Trescott's mouth tightened. If he had expected an invitation to spend the night at Cloud Hall, he was sorely disappointed. He got to his feet.

"Good evening to you, Masters. I trust you will have a great deal to mull over tonight. Rather glad I'm not in your place just now.

Damned embarrassing to have one's mistress make a fool of one."

Trescott turned and strode out of the library.

Marcus waited until the door had closed behind his visitor. Then he rose and crossed the room to stand at the window.

The sky was clear and cloudless, aglow with gold and peach, the fading hues of a spring day. It would be a good night for viewing the stars through his new telescope.

He had intended to spend the rest of the month here in Yorkshire. But now it appeared he would have to make arrangements to return to London earlier than he had anticipated.

His curiosity, a force that in him was as powerful as sexual desire, was deeply aroused.

In truth, in spite of what the London gossips believed, he did not have a current mistress.

He had not been involved with a woman for over four months. He and his last paramour, a strikingly beautiful widow in her late twenties, had gone their separate ways some time ago. The break had occurred after the lady had finally accepted the fact that Marcus did not intend to violate his rule against remarriage. The lovely widow had decided to pursue less elusive game.

Marcus could not help but wonder who the mysterious Mrs. Bright was. But he was even more intrigued by her daring.

Any woman who possessed the breathtaking courage to masquerade as his mistress at the highest levels of the *ton* promised to be interesting, indeed. Almost as interesting as the stars.

ONE

The Earl of Masters was alive.

Iphiginia Bright nearly fainted for the first time in her life when the earl entered the glittering ballroom. Her surroundings went into a slow spin as she struggled with the staggering shock.

The last thing she had expected to discover that night or any other night was that Masters was not dead after all.

He was alive.

The shock receded as a dizzying sense of joy soared through her. Although she had never met him, she had spent a feverish fortnight learning everything she possibly could about the earl before she had gone into Society to masquerade as his mistress.

The most shattering thing that she had discovered during the course of her study was that he was the man of her dreams; a man she could have loved as she had never loved anyone else; the right man for her.

She had fully expected him to remain a figure of her most intimate fantasies forever. But here he was, a living, breathing reality.

And when he learned who she was and what she had done, he would surely despise her.

"Good God, I don't believe it," Lord Ellis muttered. "Masters is here."

Iphiginia gazed, speechless, at the tall, powerfully built man who was descending the blue-carpeted staircase with such casual arrogance. A part of her was stunned to realize that he was just as she had imagined him to be: dark-haired, coldly proud, a man who lived by his own rules. She could not believe her eyes.

Neither could anyone else, apparently.

The scene in the ballroom froze into absolute stillness for a single heartbeat. A stunned hush fell upon the crowd.

It seemed to Iphiginia as though the brilliantly gowned ladies and elegantly dressed men were all caught in a drop of liquid amber that hardened instantly, imprisoning them. Even the flames of the massed candles in the huge crystal chandeliers appeared to still for an instant.

In the next heartbeat the amber turned to liquid once more and released its captives.

Freed from their frozen state, the sparkling creatures began to flutter like so many brilliant insects. Shimmers of excitement ruffled their gaudy wings. Greedy anticipation lit their hard, faceted eyes.

Iphiginia knew what prompted the anticipation in those around her. A scene was expected —a scene that would generate gossip for days.

She also knew that the astonishment of the crowd stemmed from the fact that Masters had not been expected to put in an appearance tonight. He was presumed to be out of Town on a lengthy visit to one of his estates. Certainly no one had thought that he would show up here to confront his former mistress.

Only Iphiginia and those closest to her had believed him dead. They had been told as much in the blackmailer's horrid note. That missive had made it clear that Iphiginia's Aunt Zoe, Lady Guthrie, would be next to die if she did not meet the villain's demands.

But here was Masters in the flesh and there was no denying that he was not only alive, he appeared quite fit. He radiated the dangerous vitality of a large beast of prey.

Obviously the blackmailer had lied. He had cleverly taken advantage of Masters's disappearance from London in order to terrify Zoe.

Torn between euphoria and despair, Iphiginia watched Masters's relentless approach and realized that all her carefully laid plans had suddenly been plunged into utter chaos.

An entirely new sort of disaster threatened, one that would affect her and those near and dear to her. Masters would not be pleased to learn that he had a mistress whom he had never even met. A mistress, moreover, who had allowed the *ton* to believe that she was shopping for a replacement for him.

He would surely make quick work of the trappings of her masquerade, she thought. He would shred them to ribbons, leaving her exposed to Society as the fraud she was.

Iphiginia's heart raced as she listened to the low-voiced conversation that broke out among the group of gentlemen standing nearby.

"Masters always did have incredible nerve." Lord Lartmore, specter-faced and cadaverously thin, jerked his champagne glass toward his mouth and emptied it in a single swallow. "Never thought he'd show up in any ballroom where Lady Starlight was holding court, though. Too bloody humiliating."

"By Jove, this should prove interesting." Darrow, a middle-aged man whose paunch was not well concealed by the poor cut of his coat, cast a speculative eye at Iphiginia.

Herbert Hoyt leaned closer to Iphiginia in a touchingly protective manner. His normally cheerful blue eyes were troubled. "I say, this could prove a trifle awkward. The generals did not invent the extremely useful tactic known as strategic retreat without good reason, m'dear. Would you care to employ it? I stand ready to assist you, as always."

Iphiginia fought to compose herself. It was difficult to draw a complete breath. This could not be happening. There must be some mistake.

Her fingers, which were lightly resting on Herbert's sleeve, trembled. "Don't be ridiculous, Mr. Hoyt. Masters is not about to create a scene for the entertainment of the *ton*."

"Wouldn't count on it." Herbert studied the rippling wake in the crowd that marked Masters's progress across the room. "One never knows what he'll do. Man's an enigma."

Iphiginia flushed. In spite of her own desperate situation, she felt the urge to defend the earl. "He's not an enigma. He happens to prefer to maintain his privacy, that's all. Perfectly reasonable."

"Well, you've gone and made a spectacle of him and robbed him of his precious privacy, haven't you, m'dear? He won't appreciate it, that's for certain."

Herbert, unfortunately, was right, as usual.

Iphiginia slanted her new friend an uncertain glance. Herbert was far more familiar with the treacherous ways of London Society than she. He had been swimming in these unpredictable waters for the past two years.

Since making his acquaintance a fortnight ago, she had learned to value his judgments. Herbert seemed to know everyone who was anyone. He comprehended all the nuances of behavior in this elite world, from the simple snub to the cut direct.

In terms of social rank, Herbert was a small fish in the London pond. But he was one of a number of charming, gallant males of indeterminate age who made themselves indispensable to hostesses and anxious mamas alike.

Men such as Herbert were willing to dance with wallflowers or sip tea with elderly matrons. They fetched champagne for wives whose husbands were occupied in the card rooms. They chatted easily with nervous young ladies who were being launched into Society. In short, they were eminently useful and therefore they always managed to obtain invitations to the best balls and soirees in town.

Herbert was in his middle thirties. He was a pleasant-faced, slightly plump man with ruddy cheeks, pale blue eyes, and a good-natured, inoffensive manner. His thinning, light brown hair was cut and curled in the latest style. His yellow waistcoat, which fitted a trifle too snugly at the waist, as well as his elaborately tied cravat were in the very forefront of fashion.

Iphiginia liked Herbert. He was one of the few men who seemed to have no interest in trying to take what everyone imagined to be Masters's place in her life. She could be at ease in his presence. He enjoyed discussing matters of art and architectural fashion. And she respected his advice in social matters.

But even Herbert, rarely at a loss for the proper response to any given social situation, appeared to be floundering tonight. Obviously he did not know how to handle the impending catastrophe.

Iphiginia unfurled her white lace fan as she collected her wildly scattered thoughts. The only thing that would see her through this disaster was her own intelligence. She reminded herself that she had her fair share of that commodity.

"Masters is, above all, a gentleman. There is no reason for him to embarrass either me or himself."

"Whatever you say, my dear." Herbert arched one bushy brow in a knowing fashion. "I assure you, there's no need to go into the details of your connection to Masters with me. Everyone in Town is well aware of just what sort of friends you and Masters were."

"Indeed." Iphiginia's tone held the repressive note that she employed whenever someone grew too bold on the subject of the earl. She rarely needed to use that tone with Herbert. He was usually more discreet.

She could hardly complain about the assumptions Herbert and the members of the *ton* had made concerning the nature of her relationship with Masters. Society had arrived at precisely the conclusions that she had wanted it to reach.

Such assumptions and conclusions were part of the grand plan to gain entrée into Masters's exclusive circle of acquaintances. The scheme had worked until tonight.

"Regardless of your past association with Masters," Herbert said, "the question everyone is asking tonight is, what happens next? We have been led to believe that you and he had come to a parting of the ways, m'dear. But his presence here this evening indicates otherwise."

Iphiginia ignored the questioning note in his voice. She could hardly provide him with an answer when she did not have one.

Unable to think of anything else to do in the midst of the crisis, Iphiginia determined to do the only thing possible. She stuck to the story she had concocted when she had embarked on her perilous adventure.

"Masters knows very well that our connection is finished unless he chooses to apologize for the quarrel he caused," she said smoothly.

"One never uses the word *impossible* when one is discussing Masters," Herbert said. "But in this instance, I think it is permissible. It's safe to say that no one in this room tonight can conceive of the earl apologizing to a lady who has humiliated him in front of the whole of Society."

Iphiginia was horrified. "But I have done no such thing, Mr. Hoyt."

"No?"

Iphiginia fanned herself rapidly. She felt much too warm. "I merely indicated that he and I were no longer in charity with each other."

"And that it was all his fault."

"Well, yes." Iphiginia swallowed. "It certainly was all his fault. But I did not seek to humiliate him in front of his friends."

Herbert gave her an odd look. "Come now, my dear. Let us be honest here. You have hinted that you and Masters had a violent quarrel, one that shattered your close *friendship*. You cannot tell me that you were not looking for a bit of revenge when you descended on Society. Everyone believes you to be searching for a suitable replacement for him."

"That is not true." Iphiginia cleared her throat. "I mean, the earl does owe me an apology, but I never intended to, uh, obtain one from him." *One did not get apologies from dead men.*

"Whatever your intention, you have made certain that everyone understood that you were the one who severed the connection. They believe that you actually had the temerity to give Masters his congé."

It had all been part of her scheme to transform herself into an instant rage in the eyes of the *ton,* but Iphiginia could hardly explain that to Herbert. "As to that slight misunderstanding—"

"Misunderstanding?" Herbert gave her a pitying look. "For the past fortnight, Society has not been able to decide if you are the most daring lady in London or simply a candidate for Bedlam."

"I am beginning to wonder myself," Iphiginia muttered under her breath. She must have been mad to get herself into this situation.

"You know that the *ton* has been waiting on tenterhooks to see how Masters will respond to your notion of vengeance."

"I have told you, Mr. Hoyt, that I have absolutely no interest in vengeance. There was a small tiff between us, that's all. It requires an apology, nothing more."

"So now it's a minor tiff, is it? Heretofore you have termed it a major quarrel."

"These things get enlarged out of all proportion under the influence of gossip, do they not?"

"They certainly do, m'dear." Herbert patted her hand reassuringly. "But fear not. I shall remain by your side, ready to assist you if Masters turns unpleasant."

"A reassuring thought."

But it was not reassuring at all. Masters had somehow come back from the dead and there would be the devil to pay.

Herbert's reaction to the situation confirmed everything Iphiginia had learned thus far about the notorious earl. Society thought him deliciously dangerous and unpredictable.

There were rumors of a duel years ago in which he had very nearly killed his opponent. Worse yet, it was whispered that he might have actually been responsible for the murder of his former business associate, Lynton Spalding. It was certainly a fact that after Spalding's death Masters had assumed control of the profitable investment pool his associate had once managed.

Many claimed that the lucrative pool was not the only thing Masters had seized following Spalding's demise. It was said that he had indulged in a long-standing affair with Spalding's

widow, Hannah, and that the affair continued
to this day even though she had remarried and
was now Lady Sands.

No one would ever know the truth about
those incidents or any others because Masters
never spoke of them. Indeed, he had a rule
against discussing his past and another against
explaining his actions. He was an intensely private man.

Masters was definitely not the sort who
would tolerate humiliation of any kind.

Iphiginia reminded herself that she had been
in other precarious situations. Her recent year
abroad during which she and her cousin
Amelia had toured the ruins of Italy had not
been without incident. There had been that
rather nasty confrontation with a street thief in
Rome and another equally dangerous encounter with a bandit on the journey to Pompeii.

Still, Iphiginia was only too well aware that
she had never dealt with a man whose reputation was of the legendary proportions that
characterized the earl's.

The trick was to stay calm and in control,
Iphiginia thought. She was dealing with a potentially dangerous adversary, but she knew
from her research that Masters was a highly
intelligent man. With any luck, he would
choose to approach the coming confrontation
in a rational, cool-headed manner.

From what she had learned about him, she was almost certain he would not allow his emotions to govern his actions during the next few minutes.

Almost certain.

Iphiginia saw Herbert's brow furrow with uneasiness as he watched the crowd. She heard a sharp, distinct crack. She glanced down and saw that she had accidentally snapped the delicate spokes of her fan.

At that moment the knot of people directly in front of her unraveled. A woman's nervous laugh rang out and then was cut off abruptly. Men edged out of the way. Even Herbert stepped back a pace or two.

Iphiginia suddenly found herself standing quite alone in the middle of the crowded ballroom.

Marcus, Earl of Masters, came to a halt directly in front of Iphiginia. Because she had been looking down at her broken fan, the first thing she noticed about him was his hands.

He was the only man in the room not wearing gloves.

In a world where soft, elegant, graceful hands were much admired in a man, Marcus had the hands of a seasoned warrior. Large and powerful, they were the hands of a man who had made his own way in the world.

Iphiginia suddenly recalled that he had come

into his title a mere five years earlier. It had been a bankrupt inheritance. He had not been born into wealth and power. He had created those attributes for himself.

Iphiginia tore her gaze away from the riveting sight of his muscular hands and looked up quickly. Marcus possessed a face that could have been etched on an ancient gold coin. Strong, relentless and bold to the point of being harsh, it was the face of an ancient conqueror.

He watched her with amber eyes that glittered with a fierce intelligence. His hair was very dark, almost black. There was a flash of silver in the curving swath that was brushed back from his high forehead.

Iphiginia met his brilliant eyes. A shock of deep awareness and recognition flashed through her. Something that had been smoldering deep inside her for weeks suddenly leaped into full flame.

This was the man she had fallen in love with, never dreaming that she might one day meet him. He was exactly as she had imagined.

Iphiginia knew that the crowd was waiting breathlessly for her reaction.

"My lord," Iphiginia whispered so softly that only he could hear. "I am so very glad to see that you are alive."

With a heartfelt prayer that she was correct

in her assumption that the earl's curiosity would govern his reaction, she closed her eyes and sank gracefully into a mock swoon.

Marcus caught her before she reached the floor. "Very clever, Mrs. Bright," he muttered for her ears alone. "I wondered how you would extricate yourself from this tangle."

Iphiginia did not dare to open her eyes. She felt herself swept up high against Marcus's chest. His arms were strong and firm. She felt oddly secure and safe in his grasp. The scent of him aroused a curious sensation within her. She was startled by the unexpected, deeply sensual pleasure she felt.

She had never known anything quite like the feelings that were thrumming through her at this moment. She raised her lashes just far enough to see that the frothy skirts of her white silk gown cascaded over the black sleeve of his coat.

Marcus carried her effortlessly across the ballroom floor toward the door.

"Step aside, if you please," he ordered to those in his path. "My very good friend needs fresh air."

The crowd melted away in front of him.

Murmurs of astonishment and speculation followed Iphiginia's grand exit from the crowded ball.

Marcus carried her out of the large mansion.

Without pausing, he strode down the wide front steps to where a gleaming black carriage horsed with two black stallions waited.

The door of the carriage was opened by a footman garbed in black livery. Marcus carried Iphiginia into the cab. The door was closed.

The black carriage set off into the midnight streets of London.

*T*WO

I expect you have a few questions, my lord."
"Several, as a matter of fact." Marcus settled into his seat. He watched Iphiginia sit briskly upright, straighten a white plume in her hair, and shake out her skirts.

"Only to be expected and I shall be pleased to answer them," she said. "But first I want to thank you for not giving away the game a moment ago. I am well aware that you must have found the entire performance a bit awkward."

"Not in the least, Mrs. Bright. I assure you, I found it quite fascinating."

She gave him a glorious smile. Marcus was momentarily transfixed. He suddenly realized how she had managed to captivate the majority of his acquaintances.

"I knew you would play along with me until

you discovered precisely what was afoot."
Iphiginia's vivid hazel eyes held more than a
hint of satisfaction. "I was certain of it. I knew
you would be too clever, too perceptive, too
coolheaded, too intelligent to do anything rash
until you had investigated the matter thoroughly."

"I appreciate your confidence in me. I assure
you, however, that I also possess enough wit
not to be completely distracted from the matter
at hand by your very charming flattery."

She blinked in surprise. "But I was not flattering you, sir. I meant every word. I have
made an intense study of your nature and I
have concluded that you have a very fine
brain."

Marcus gazed at her, briefly at a loss for
words. "You admire my brain?"

"Yes, indeed," she said with what was, to all
appearances, genuine enthusiasm. "I have read
all of your papers in *The Technical and Scientific Repository* and I was most impressed. The
one on the potential of the steam engine was
particularly inspiring. Not that your proposal
for a mechanical threshing machine was not
also extremely exciting."

"Bloody hell."

She blushed. "I confess I am not well versed
in technical and mechanical matters. Person-

ally, I am a student of classical antiquities. Most of my time has been spent in that field."

"I see."

"But I am pleased to say that I was able to comprehend most of the mechanical principles you discussed in your articles. You write quite clearly, my lord."

"Thank you." He had spoken too quickly when he had told her that he possessed too much wit to fall victim to flattery, Marcus thought wryly. He was momentarily enthralled. He had never had a woman compliment him on his scientific and technical writings, let alone on his intelligence.

"You also wrote a quite instructive piece on building construction techniques which was of considerable interest to me," Iphiginia continued. She launched into a recital of the significant points of the article.

Marcus listened with a sense of dazed wonder. He lounged back into the corner of the black velvet seat cushion, crossed his arms, and studied Iphiginia's face in the glow of the carriage lamp.

Whatever it was he had expected to find when he finally cornered his new "mistress" in the Fenwicks' ballroom, he reflected, Iphiginia Bright was not it.

Charles Trescott had been wrong when he'd

implied that the adventurous widow made a mockery of chastity and purity with her choice of virginal white attire.

Iphiginia Bright somehow managed to give the impression of being the real thing, a lady of pristine, unstained virtue. It was really quite astonishing.

The effect was not achieved solely by her angelic white gown, gloves, and shoes. It seemed to emanate from the very depths of the woman herself.

There was something about her clear, intelligent, forthright gaze, arresting nose, and soft, gentle mouth that spoke of virtue. Her hair was the color of dark honey. She was striking in some ways, subtle in others. Although she was no great beauty, she was the most interesting female Marcus had ever encountered.

There was also an alluring air of very feminine sensuality about her, yet she had not chosen to emphasize it with her clothing. The cut of her gown was surprisingly demure. Another clever touch, Marcus conceded privately. A man's imagination was a powerful tool and she knew how to employ it.

The curves of Iphiginia's small, high, delicately rounded breasts did not overflow the bodice of her dress. They were discreetly covered by white silk ruffles. Such breasts were not meant to be crudely fondled, Marcus thought.

They had been fashioned for a connoisseur of fine things, a lover endowed with an artist's slender, sensitive fingers.

He absently flexed his own sturdy, callused fingers. The fact that he possessed the hands of a farmer did not mean that he did not enjoy touching fine, soft things.

Iphiginia was small and slender. The skirts of her high-waisted gown drifted airily down over what was clearly a very narrow waist. The wispy silk barely hinted at the enticing shape of womanly hips and rounded thighs.

No wonder she had captured the fancy of the *ton,* Marcus thought. She certainly had his full attention.

He was intrigued by the mysterious Mrs. Bright, more so than he had been with any other woman for longer than he cared to recall.

He was also half-aroused, he realized abruptly.

He could feel the dull ache of awakening desire in his loins. Perhaps it was not so surprising. It had been four months since he had last been intimate with a woman and Iphiginia had been on his mind constantly for the past two days. He had speculated on nothing else except his unknown paramour during the entire journey back to London.

It occurred to Marcus that if he had deliberately set out to find an interesting new mistress, he could not have done better than Iphiginia Bright.

"I beg your pardon, my lord," Iphiginia said, obviously embarrassed by her lengthy commentary on his journal article. "I expect I am boring you. It is not as though you are not perfectly familiar with your own theories on the use of timber pilings in foundations."

"Perhaps we should get back to the main topic," Marcus said smoothly. "But first you must give me your address so that I can convey it to my coachman."

Iphiginia cleared her throat. "My address?"

"It would be useful, considering the fact that I am attempting to escort you home at the moment."

"You are?"

"Given the role you have led everyone to believe that I play in your life," Marcus said, "it is only natural that I take you home after the ball."

"But—"

"It is expected," Marcus emphasized. "People will wonder if I do not claim the privilege."

"You're quite certain that is the normal thing to do?"

"Quite certain."

"Oh." Iphiginia caught her soft lower lip between her very white teeth, apparently contemplating the matter. She came to a decision.

"Very well. I have a town house in Morning Rose Square. Number Five."

Marcus was briefly interested in that bit of news. "Morning Rose Square was only recently completed, was it not? The architect did a superb job of combining classical elements with a design that is comfortable and suited to the English climate. The houses were well constructed and sold quickly, as I recall."

Iphiginia looked surprised. "You seem to know a great deal about it."

"The project aroused my curiosity because it made money." Marcus rose and knocked on the trapdoor of the carriage. "A great many speculation investments of that sort do not. I have known any number of people involved in such financial arrangements to go bankrupt."

The trapdoor opened. "Aye, m'lord?" the coachman called.

"Morning Rose Square, Dinks. Number Five."

"Very good, m'lord." Dinks allowed the trap to fall back into place.

Marcus dropped back into his seat. "Perhaps we should get on with your explanations, Mrs. Bright."

"Yes, of course." Iphiginia straightened her shoulders. "Where to begin? First, let me tell you how excessively relieved I am to discover that you are alive, my lord."

He considered her through half-closed eyes. "You mentioned something to that effect back in the Fenwicks' ballroom. There was some doubt in your mind?"

"Oh, yes. A great deal of doubt. We assumed you had been murdered, you see."

"*Murdered?*" He wondered if he had gotten involved with a madwoman.

"Yes, my lord, murdered. It was the reason why I decided to take the desperate measure of masquerading as your mistress."

"And just who did you believe was responsible for my demise?" Marcus asked coldly. "One of your other *intimate* friends?"

She gave him a shocked look. "Of course not, my lord. Oh, dear, this is all so complicated. I assure you that I do not have the sort of friends who would even dream of resorting to murder."

"I am relieved to hear that."

"Aunt Zoe is a bit theatrical by nature and my cousin Amelia can be rather grim at times, but I believe that I can safely say neither of them would ever murder anyone."

"I shall take your word for it, Mrs. Bright."

She sighed. "I realize that this must all be extremely confusing to you."

"I shall do my best to muddle through. Perhaps my excellent brain will assist me."

She gave him a glowing smile of approval. "You are doing very well under the circumstances, my lord."

"I had come to the same conclusion."

She winced at the sarcasm. "Ah, yes. Yes, indeed. Well, then, to get on with it. We thought the blackmailer had done you in, you see."

"Blackmailer? This grows more absurd by the moment. What blackmailer?"

That gave Iphiginia pause. "You mean to say that you are not being blackmailed, sir?"

The question irritated him. "Do I appear to be the sort of man who would pay blackmail, Mrs. Bright?"

"No, my lord. And that is precisely why we believed you had been murdered. Because you refused to pay, you see."

"Continue, Mrs. Bright," Marcus ordered evenly. "You have a long way to go before any of this becomes clear."

"My aunt received a note from the villain informing us that you had been dispatched as a lesson to others who refused to pay. The note implied that it was only a matter of time before Society realized you were not spending the month at one of your estates, but had, instead, disappeared for good."

"Good Lord."

"Well, you must admit that you had vanished from Society at the height of the Season, sir. Most unusual."

"I was at my estate in Yorkshire," Marcus retorted. "Not in a shallow, unmarked grave. Madam, this is ridiculous. I have had enough of this game. I want the truth and I want it before we reach Morning Rose Square."

She frowned. "I am attempting to relate the truth, sir. There is no call to be rude. Now, kindly cease interrupting me. As I said, my aunt had every reason to believe that you had been murdered and that if she did not meet the blackmailer's demands, she would be next."

"She paid the blackmail?" Marcus demanded.

"Naturally. She was quite frightened. I learned all this the day after she had paid. I had just arrived here in London after a year on the Continent. My cousin Amelia was with me. We called upon Aunt Zoe and discovered her dire straits. I immediately devised a plan to find the blackmailer."

Marcus was beyond amazement now. "You hoped to find him by pretending to be my mistress?"

"Exactly." Iphiginia gave him another bright, approving smile. "At the time, I believed that I was hunting not only a blackmailer but a great villain who was capable of murder. You can imagine my concern."

"I am not dead, Mrs. Bright."

"Yes, I can see that," she said patiently. "It does confuse the issue, does it not?"

"Not unduly, I trust."

"I became your mistress in the eyes of the world so that I could mingle with your associates and acquaintances. My plan was to make discreet inquiries of them in an effort to decide who might have murdered you."

"Very thoughtful of you to try to hunt down the villain who had murdered me."

"I must admit that I did not undertake the deception in order to avenge you, my lord."

"I'm crushed."

Iphiginia's eyes widened with dismay. "I do not mean to sound uncharitable or unfeeling, sir, but you must recall that when I first learned of this villainy, I did not even know you. I had not yet had a chance to study your nature."

"That would explain your lack of feeling, I suppose."

"But I didn't lack feeling, sir," she said quickly. "On the contrary. I assure you, I was exceedingly sorry that you had come to such a dreadful end." She hesitated and then added in a small burst of honesty, "In a rather general way, if you see what I mean."

He restrained a smile with effort. "I'm grateful for whatever compassion you were able to spare. There are those who would not have been the least bit sorry to learn of my demise, not even in a rather general way."

"Nonsense. I'm quite certain that once Society had learned that you had been murdered, everyone would have been properly horrified."

"I'd advise you not to place any large wagers on that. What the devil did you think you'd learn as my mistress?"

Iphiginia leaned forward. She was bubbling over with enthusiasm now. "I reasoned that the blackmailer had to be someone close to you, my lord. Someone who knew a secret so dreadful that he expected you to pay blackmail rather than allow it to be revealed."

Marcus raised one brow. "And that same person would also have to be privy to some grave secret of your aunt's. Is that what you thought?"

"How very perceptive of you, sir. That is precisely what I concluded. But I went one step further. I realized that whoever knew such intimate secrets about both your past and my aunt's also had to know of your plans to be out of Town this month." Iphiginia paused meaningfully. "The last blackmail note arrived the very day you disappeared, you see."

Marcus felt the old, familiar twist of curiosity. It temporarily swamped common sense in a way that he would never have allowed physical passion to do. "You reasoned that there could not be too many people who would have links to both me and your aunt, is that it?"

"Precisely." Iphiginia gave him an unabashed look of admiration. "You are, indeed, very quick, my lord, just as I had suspected."

This time Marcus flatly refused to be seduced by her glowing respect for his brain. He stuck to the issue at hand. "So you posed as my mistress in order to gain entrée to my circle of acquaintances."

"It seemed the only thing to do under the circumstances, although I admit that I was somewhat daunted by the task I had set myself."

"I find that hard to believe, Mrs. Bright," Marcus said dryly. "I cannot conceive of you being daunted by anything or anyone."

"In most cases, you would be correct," she agreed without a trace of humility. "But in this instance, I knew that I could not possibly hope to live up to the expectations people would have of me."

"Expectations?"

"You know very well what I mean, sir. From what I could gather, your previous mistresses have been remarkably lovely widows who possessed a certain, shall we say, flair?" A wistful expression appeared in Iphiginia's eyes. "They were all very dashing, everyone said."

"Everyone?"

"My Aunt Zoe is up on all the latest gossip. It was not difficult to unearth a considerable number of details concerning your previous paramours."

"That is the sort of news that could keep a man awake nights."

Iphiginia gave him an embarrassed look. "I was not certain that I could compete, if you see what I mean."

He surveyed her pristine white attire. There was no need to inform her that gossip had always exaggerated both the number of his affairs and the exotic qualities of his mistresses. "So you set out to create an illusion that would take Society by surprise and thereby create an entirely new set of expectations."

"I wanted to create an image that was so outrageous it would cause your friends and acquaintances to use their imagination to turn me into a far more mysterious and dashing creature than I actually am."

"My compliments, Mrs. Bright. It appears you were successful."

"Thus far, my little deception has worked rather well," Iphiginia admitted with obvious pride.

If she was exerting any effort at all to appear modest, she was failing spectacularly, Marcus decided. "I'm certainly impressed. Even awestruck."

Iphiginia must have heard the cool amusement in his tone. Her brief flash of pride dissolved at once into a disgruntled look. "I realize that, in your eyes, I am a complete failure in my role as your new paramour."

"I wouldn't say that."

She glanced down at her demure white silk gown. Red stained her elegantly sculpted cheekbones. "I know that I do not appear to be at all the sort of woman with whom you usually consort."

"My dear Mrs. Bright, as anyone will tell you, I have never favored the usual. I much prefer the unusual."

"You're certain that you should be taking me home like this?" Iphiginia asked with another uneasy glance out into the night.

"You know very well that it is quite the thing for a gentleman to escort his paramour home after an evening's round of social affairs. In our particular situation, it would be considered strange if I did not."

"I suppose so."

"Now, if you were an unmarried young lady in the market for a husband, it would be quite a different matter, of course." He watched her face closely. "But you are an unattached widow, are you not?"

"Don't be ridiculous, sir." She concentrated on the view of the night-darkened streets. "What else would I be?"

"Exactly." No innocent or respectable spinster intent on guarding her reputation would have dared undertake such an astounding masquerade, Marcus thought. "Even if you were not already posing as my mistress, there would be nothing to stop me from escorting you home tonight."

"No, but—"

"The widows of the *ton* are the most privileged of ladies, are they not? Financially independent, free of the encumbrance of a jealous husband, they may form whatever liaisons they wish, so long as they are reasonably discreet."

"I realize that a widow has a great deal more freedom than an unmarried female, sir. Indeed, I am not arguing that point. But the thing is—"

"Yes? What is the thing?"

She turned to face him once more with a resolute expression. "The thing is, I have put a great deal of effort into creating an image, if you will. Part of the illusion consists of a certain air of elusiveness."

"So I have been told."

"My lord, until tonight I have not allowed any gentleman to see me home."

"Ah." He wondered why he was so pleased to learn that small fact. "A nice touch."

"I have kept to that habit during the entire time that I have been posing as your mistress."

"Lady Starlight."

She scowled. "I beg your pardon?"

"I am told that they call you the untouchable and unobtainable Lady Starlight. You are seen as a glittering midnight star who lures and entices but remains just out of reach while she searches for a replacement for me in her bed."

Iphiginia opened her mouth, closed it again, and then opened it once more. Her voice, when she finally spoke, sounded breathless, as though she had been running a great distance. "You know how Society is when it comes to sticking labels on people, sir. Calling me Lady Starlight was a bit much, I'll grant you. Nevertheless—"

"Nevertheless, in this case the appellation is apparently quite appropriate."

She looked briefly disconcerted. "It is?"

Marcus realized that he was enjoying himself. They were playing a cat-and-mouse game and he got to be the cat. "Definitely. Furthermore, you are in luck. As it happens, I have recently made a study of elusive, untouchable stars. There are ways to capture the light. If a man is very clever, he can hold it in the palm of his hand."

"I do not understand, sir."

"No, I don't suppose you do yet. But you soon will. In the meantime, you must allow me to retain some air of mystery, Mrs. Bright. I am known for it, you see."

She eyed him speculatively. "You are going to be difficult, aren't you?"

"We shall see."

"I was afraid of this. Would you mind telling me if you are truly very angry about my impersonation, my lord?"

"You cannot determine that for yourself?"

"No, actually, I cannot. They say you are a deep one. I begin to understand what everyone means by that. Even after my extensive study of your nature, I still find there is much I do not know about you."

"I suppose I should be grateful for that small favor," he muttered.

"There is no need for sarcasm," she said with an injured air.

In the golden glow cast by the coach lamps, Marcus could tell that, although she was putting a remarkably good face on the situation, she was really quite anxious.

Iphiginia sat very stiffly. Her huge, shadowed, sea-green eyes flickered frequently to the coach window. Marcus had a hunch that she was surreptitiously checking their location in order to verify that she was, indeed, being driven straight home. She had a death grip on her white fan.

Marcus was satisfied that Iphiginia was not nearly as cool and composed as she tried to appear. He refused to feel any sympathy for her. Considering what she had put him through earlier this evening and what was yet to come, she deserved to suffer a bit. She had made certain that the pair of them would be the choicest morsel of conversation at every breakfast table tomorrow morning and in every club in St. James tomorrow afternoon.

"I congratulate you again, Mrs. Bright." Marcus inclined his head in a small gesture of mocking respect. "It is not every woman who could have duped Society into thinking she was my latest paramour."

She bit her lip. "Thank you."

"Quite a fascinating accomplishment, actually."

He would never forget his first glimpse of her in the Fenwicks' ballroom. In his view, Iphiginia had succeeded in making every other woman in the room appear either overdressed, underdressed, or gaudy. Marcus could not put his finger on why she looked so *right,* but he had been in the world long enough to recognize a woman with an intuitive artistic sense of style. It had nothing to do with her gowns or her accessories. It had everything to do with how she wore them.

"The choice of virginal white for your attire was a brilliant notion," Marcus continued. "Outrageous, but brilliant."

She hesitated, as if uncertain whether he was mocking her. Then she smiled tremulously. "One of the reasons I chose to go about in white is because you are said to favor black in your own attire and in many of your personal possessions." With her gloved hand she indicated the elegant black carriage with its ebony fittings. "The rumors were accurate, I see."

"Were you working on the hypothesis that I would be attracted to my opposite?"

Iphiginia considered that very seriously. "I do not subscribe to that particular theory myself. I believe like-minded people are drawn together, not true opposites. But I knew Society would jump to the wrong conclusion. Most people think that those of opposing natures are attracted to each other."

"And it was Society that needed to be convinced."

"Aunt Zoe feared my plan would not work, but I assured her that it was our only hope."

"Ah, yes. Your little scheme to catch a blackmailer. I had almost forgotten about it."

She glowered at him. "You do not believe a

word I have said, do you, sir? I knew that you were very intelligent and everyone said you were quite arrogant about the fact, but I had not realized that you would be so stubborn."

He chose to ignore the observation. "Tell me about your Aunt Zoe."

"What do you wish to know?"

"There are a number of Zoes in Society. Which one is your aunt?"

Iphiginia's brows snapped together. "She is Lady Guthrie. I must warn you that she and I have kept our family connection a secret, however. I felt it would be easier to carry out the masquerade if no one knew the truth. If people knew that I was her niece, it might give rise to too many questions about me, you see."

"Of course," Marcus murmured. "It was essential that you remain a mystery to the Polite World."

"Extremely essential, sir. One question would soon lead to another and I might have been unmasked before I had accomplished my goal. At the very least the blackmailer might have realized that I was not your mistress."

"I see."

"Society believes Zoe and I to be friends, but nothing more. That explanation provides an excuse for us to be seen together rather frequently."

Marcus mentally ran through a list of the

people who moved in his world. His memory
was excellent. He was quite certain he had
never met Zoe, Lady Guthrie. "I seem to recall that a certain Lord Guthrie belonged to
one or two of my clubs. I believe he died a year
ago."

"Aunt Zoe is Guthrie's widow."

"I do not believe that I have had the pleasure of meeting her."

"No. That is the curious thing about all this,"
Iphiginia said quickly. "Aunt Zoe told me that
the two of you had never been introduced. She
has seen you from a distance at parties and
balls and Guthrie had mentioned your name in
a casual way, but that was all."

"Yet your blackmailer claimed that we were
both on his list of victims?"

"Yes. Rather odd, don't you think?"

"I find this entire situation rather odd."

"My lord, I swear to you, this is not a joke or
a game. There really is a blackmailer out there
somewhere and he is threatening my aunt. I
concluded that there must be some connection
between your circle of acquaintances and that
of my aunt's."

"You're forgetting one thing here, Mrs.
Bright," Marcus said calmly. "I am not being
blackmailed."

She scowled. "You're quite certain of that,
my lord?"

"It is not the sort thing that would slip one's mind."

Iphiginia's soft mouth firmed. "No, I suppose not. But why would the blackmailer make reference to you when he threatened my aunt?"

Marcus glanced out into the busy night streets. "The reference, if it was made, was obviously a ruse designed to terrify your aunt and convince her to pay the extortion money."

"The reference was indeed made, sir," Iphiginia insisted.

"Tell me, just how far did you get in your investigation?"

"Well, as to that, I was making considerable progress," she said eagerly. "I have already succeeded in searching Mr. Darrow's and Lord Judson's studies."

"You *what*?"

She tilted her head and gave him a quizzical glance. "I said I have had opportunities to search Darrow's and Judson's studies. I took advantage of invitations that I received to soirees that were held in their homes. I managed to slip into their studies in the course of the evening and search their desks."

She was serious, he realized. "Damnation, woman, are you mad? I don't believe this. Why would you want to search their studies in the first place? What did you hope to discover?"

"Black wax and a seal engraved with a phoenix," she said succinctly. "Both were used to
seal the blackmail notes that Aunt Zoe received."

"Bloody hell." Marcus was too stunned by
her audacity to think clearly for a few seconds.
He finally collected his thoughts. "Black sealing wax is not uncommon. I use it myself."

"I know, but you are unusual in that you use
it for your routine correspondence, my lord.
Most people employ black wax only for mourning. And you must admit that a phoenix seal is
uncommon. In fact, the use of a seal, any sort
of seal, is, in itself, distinctive. One would think
that the average blackmailer would use a simple wafer to seal his letters."

"Is there such a thing as an average blackmailer?"

"I am serious, sir. Black wax and a seal engraved with a phoenix would constitute strong
evidence against the blackmailer."

"So you went looking for both?" It was simply too outrageous to be believed. The lady was
surely lying, which he had suspected from the
start. That was the only explanation, Marcus
concluded.

And he had thought he was an inventor of
some talent, he thought wryly. Iphiginia Bright
could give him lessons.

"Unfortunately, I have not yet had a chance to search the studies or libraries of the others."

"Which others?"

"The men with whom you frequently play cards, of course."

"You intend to search the libraries or studies of every man with whom I have played cards?" Marcus was curious to see how elaborate her tangle of lies would prove to be.

"No, only those who were also in the habit of playing cards with Lord Guthrie when he was alive," Iphiginia said crisply. She held up a hand and ticked off familiar names. "Lartmore, Darrow, Pettigrew, and Judson. They are the four men who link your household and that of my aunt's."

"Because they were known to play cards at one time or another with both me and Guthrie?"

Iphiginia sighed. "It was the only link I could discover between your circle and that of my aunt's. I concluded that someone who knew Lord Guthrie had somehow learned Aunt Zoe's secret. Perhaps from a servant. That same person also knew a great deal about you."

"But not a secret worthy of blackmail," Marcus pointed out. "I told you, I am not being blackmailed."

"Perhaps not, my lord, but the blackmailer

was sufficiently well acquainted with you to know that you intended to be out of Town for a considerable length of time."

"That was not a secret, either."

"No?" Iphiginia gave him a challenging look. "Virtually everything you do is a secret to most people, sir. Think back. How many people actually knew your plans to go to your estate for a month?"

"Any number of people," Marcus replied easily. "My man of affairs, for example. My servants."

"And the men with whom you played whist shortly before you left London?" Iphiginia asked blandly.

"Hell and damnation." Marcus experienced a grudging sense of admiration. The lady was clever, indeed. "You really did make a thorough study of me, did you not?"

"Yes, sir, I did. I am very good at research. Among the things I discovered almost immediately was that you had played cards with Lartmore, Darrow, Pettigrew, and Judson at one of your clubs the day before you left London."

"And Lady Guthrie confirmed that they had also played a few hands with her late husband."

"Not only that," Iphiginia said with great satisfaction, "but they had played cards quite regularly with him for nearly twenty years before he died, sir. That number is important because my aunt's great secret dates back eighteen years."

Marcus smiled slowly. "Brilliant, Mrs. Bright. Absolutely brilliant. You have concocted a truly amazing tale to explain your astonishing behavior. I am consumed with admiration for your inventiveness and originality."

Her face fell. "You believe that I have invented the entire thing?"

"Yes, madam, I do." Marcus held up a hand. "But don't let that stop you. I assure you, I am enjoying the play to the utmost. You are a captivating actress of exceptional talent. I feel privileged to have a minor role in the performance."

Confusion and a deep wariness flickered in her eyes. "You do not believe me, but you are not angry?"

"To be perfectly truthful, I'm not yet certain just how I feel about the entire affair. I am still pondering the matter."

"I see," she muttered. "Do you generally take a long time to consider matters before you decide how you feel about them?"

He smiled at the note of asperity in her voice. "You sound like a governess demanding a response from a slow pupil. The answer is that I have a rule against altering a decision once I have made it. But the corollary to that rule is that I gather all the facts first before making my decision."

She brightened. "I am well aware of your famous rules, sir. May I take it that you are still gathering the facts in this instance?"

"Why not?"

"That is a great relief, sir." She gave him her shatteringly brilliant smile. "I have faith in your intellectual nature. I know that once you realize that I am telling the truth, you will be only too happy to assist me in my efforts to discover the blackmailer."

Marcus felt the carriage rumble to a halt. "Rest assured, Mrs. Bright, I shall take pleasure in learning everything there is to know about this entire situation."

"Of course." She seemed blithely unconcerned now. "That is your nature."

"Do you know," Marcus observed as his footman opened the carriage door, "I do not believe that anyone has ever before set out to study my nature. Did you find the task interesting?"

"Oh, yes, my lord." Her eyes glowed as she allowed herself to be assisted down onto the pavement. "It was every bit as fascinating as the ruins of Pompeii."

"Nice to know I can hold my own with a classical ruin." Marcus got out of the carriage and took her arm. He glanced up at Dinks. "I shall be a while."

Dinks, who had been with him for years, nodded with an air of cheerful complacency. "Aye, m'lord. We'll be waitin' for ye."

Iphiginia glanced sharply at Marcus as he walked her up the steps of Number Five, Morning Rose Square. "What did you mean by that? You won't be but a moment."

"Come, now, my dear. Surely you intend to invite me inside for a brandy?" Marcus glanced with approval at the new gas lamps that had been installed in front of each town house on the street.

"Inside?" Iphiginia's voice rose in astonishment. "Do not be ridiculous, sir. I have no intention of allowing you into the house at this hour."

"We have much to discuss, Mrs. Bright, and I can think of no more convenient time or place for our conversation." Marcus raised his hand to give the brass knocker a sharp rap.

"No, wait, do not knock," Iphiginia said hurriedly. "I have instructed my housekeeper not to wait up for me. I have my key in my reticule."

Marcus held out his hand for the key. She hesitated and then handed it to him. He took it without a word and opened the door.

Iphiginia stepped quickly ahead of him into

the dark hall. She grabbed a candle that had been left on a nearby table, lit it quickly, and swung around to confront him. "Sir, I really do not think that you should come inside."

He deliberately put one booted foot over the threshold and smiled. "If you wish your illusion to continue to withstand Society's scrutiny," he said very softly, "then I fear you must allow me to stay here for a time tonight. It is expected, you see."

"Expected?" She stared at him with dawning hope. "Do you mean that you're willing to allow me to continue posing as your mistress?"

"Why not?" Marcus moved through the door and closed it with a solid thud. "You can hardly carry out your inquiries if your identity is revealed at this point. If you are unmasked, you will be cast out of Society and there will be no way to reenter it."

"Very true. Sir, I cannot tell you how grateful I am. I realize that you do not yet believe my explanations. I want you to know that I find your open-minded consideration of the situation extremely admirable. It confirms everything I have learned about you."

"It's quite all right, Mrs. Bright. I am willing to go along with the masquerade for a while, at least until I have satisfied all of my questions. Is this your library?" Marcus walked through the doorway on the left side of the hall.

"Yes, it is." Iphiginia picked up her skirts and hastened after him. "My lord, this is really most generous of you."

"I know." Marcus could see nothing but dark, looming shapes. He aimed for what he assumed was the fireplace.

"As you are apparently not one of the blackmailer's victims after all, you really do not have any obligation to assist me in my inquiries."

"I ceased doing anything out of a sense of obligation years ago. I found it rather pointless. However, occasionally I do things because I am cursed with a deep sense of curiosity about the oddest . . . Damnation." Marcus winced as his booted toe rammed a large, unyielding object.

"Do be careful, my lord." Iphiginia held her candle aloft. "This room is a bit crowded at the moment."

"So I see."

The taper threw dancing shadows across a chamber full of broken statuary, sepulchral masks, strangely designed urns, and huge vases.

The furniture was even more bizarre. Chairs with clawed feet and griffin-headed arms were arranged near the windows. A massive Grecian-style sofa finished in green velvet and gold fringe sat grandly in front of the fireplace. It looked sensual and pagan in the candlelight.

The tables placed on either side of the sofa were decorated with lions' heads and sphinxes.

"I told you that my cousin and I have only recently returned from a most educational tour of the Continent," Iphiginia said. "I purchased a great many antiquities during our journey."

Marcus peered down at the jagged chunk of marble which had marred the glossy polish on the toe of his black Hessian boot. There was just enough light from Iphiginia's candle to see that it was a portion of a statue of some mythical winged beast. "What the devil is this?"

"I bought it in a shop in Rome." Iphiginia set the candle down on her desk. There was a scratching sound as she lit a lamp. "Fascinating, is it not? I made several other equally interesting purchases at the same shop. I'm especially fond of this Roman centurion."

The centurion, Marcus saw, was nude, except for his helmet, sword, and shield.

"It looks as though you've transported a complete archaeological ruin into your library," Marcus said.

"Yes, I am rather pleased with the effect." Iphiginia glanced around with satisfaction. She drew her gloved fingertips lovingly along the arm of the naked centurion. "It both excites the senses and stimulates the intellectual faculties at the same time. Don't you agree?"

Marcus could not take his eyes off her fingers as they glided over marble muscles. He felt an instant and dramatic effect on his already stirring manhood. Unlike the centurion, he reflected, he was not made of stone.

"What do you intend to do with all of this, Mrs. Bright?"

She leaned pensively against the statue, one elbow propped on the warrior's shoulder. She rested her chin on the heel of her hand. "I'm not entirely certain yet. At the moment I am merely studying these items and making sketches."

"Studying them?" Marcus watched her skirts drift over the statue's bare thigh. He could almost feel the silk on his own skin.

"My goal is to produce a pattern book of ancient motifs and designs that can be used as a guide to decorate both the interior and exterior of houses," she confided. Her eyes sparkled with enthusiasm. Oblivious to the effect she was having on Marcus, she nestled one hip intimately against the statue.

"I see." An almost overpowering restlessness came over Marcus. In a vain attempt to alleviate it, he untied his cravat and inhaled deeply to clear his head.

He promptly caught a whiff of Iphiginia's rose-scented perfume and his senses became more clouded than ever.

"So much of what passes for accurate

archaeological design these days is quite mis-
guided and frequently wrong," she said.

"I've noticed."

"Have you?" She gave him a pleased look.

"Yes." His gaze slid over the gentle swell of
Iphiginia's thigh where it fit warmly against the
cold marble of the statue. He had not been
pushed this close to the edge of his control in
years.

"My pattern book of classical designs will be
inspired directly from actual observations and
sketches of genuine ruins such as these."
Iphiginia waved a graceful hand to indicate the
jumble of artifacts around the room. "That way
fashionable people who wish to decorate in the
antique manner will be assured that their architects and decorators adhere to the original ver-
sion of whichever classical style they choose,
whether it be Greek or Roman, Egyptian or
Etruscan."

"It sounds an ambitious project, Mrs.
Bright."

"Yes, it is. But I am quite looking forward to
it. I have spent the past year collecting these
items and as you can imagine, I am very eager
to get to work on my pattern book."

"Naturally." He studied the creamy color of
her skin in the lamplight and wondered how it
would taste. He started toward her.

"But first things first." Iphiginia straightened

away from the centurion. "I must deal with my aunt's blackmail problem before I can begin my project. You're quite certain that my impersonation will not cause you any undue problems?"

"On the contrary. I'm certain it will cause me no end of trouble." Marcus reached out and took hold of her bare shoulders. Her skin was incredibly warm and soft beneath his hard, callused hands. She did not flinch from his touch. Indeed, she seemed momentarily mesmerized.

"Marcus? I mean, my lord?" She touched her lower lip with the tip of her small tongue. "I do not wish to cause trouble for you, sir." She sounded breathless again. Her eyes were deep and enticing whirlpools in a bottomless sea.

"I stand ready to put myself at your disposal, Mrs. Bright."

"That is very kind of you, sir. May I ask why you are willing to be so helpful if you do not entirely believe my explanations about the blackmailer?"

"As it happens, I am in need of a mistress."

He lowered his mouth to hers and kissed her as he had been aching to kiss her since he had first seen her in the Fenwicks' ballroom.

THREE

*S*hock lanced through Iphiginia with the force of lightning shooting through a cloud.

She could not have been more startled if the marble centurion had suddenly sprung to life and taken her into his arms.

She was so astonished by the feel of Marcus's mouth on her own that she went absolutely rigid for a few disbelieving seconds.

Marcus was kissing her. His strong, powerful hands rested on the naked skin of her shoulders, sending small shivers of excitement down her spine.

This notorious man whom she had come to know so intimately and whom she admired so much, this man who had stridden through her dreams every night for nearly a month, was making love to her right here in her own library.

Marcus had occupied her every waking moment since she had returned to London. She had spent her days studying him so that she could turn herself into a believable illusion of a woman to whom he might conceivably make love.

She had garnered rumors, tales, and a few real facts from every available source. She had read everything that he had written that she was able to find. She had spent hours contemplating the smallest details that she had learned about him in an effort to comprehend him and make him seem more real.

In the process she had created a very private fantasy for herself, one she had not shared with anyone, not even Amelia or Aunt Zoe.

Late at night, after a long, tension-filled evening of playing her role, she had lain awake imagining how it would feel to actually be Marcus's mistress, to be the woman he took to his bed, to be the woman he loved.

The woman he loved.

A long time ago she had quietly concluded that she was not the sort of female who could experience great passion or inspire it in a man. She had come to terms with that knowledge, accepted it. She had told herself that she was too levelheaded, too practical, too intellectual to fall in love.

Nevertheless, in spite of her own self-knowledge, she had woven a web of fantasies around Marcus.

It had all seemed harmless enough because the man was safely dead.

But tonight he had walked out of her dreams straight into her life. And he was far more fascinating in the flesh than he had ever been in her dreams.

"You are most unusual, Iphiginia. Not at all what I expected." Marcus's voice was dark and shadowed with heavy sensuality. "Yet you are exactly what I seem to want tonight."

She could not answer, not only because he captured her mouth again, but because she was quivering from head to toe. His arms tightened around her as he nibbled gently at first, then persuasively, and then more insistently. His hands tightened on her shoulders.

She gasped, parting her lips. He responded by invading her mouth with his tongue.

The momentary stiffness created by her initial surprise evaporated, leaving Iphiginia feeling incredibly warm and pliant. Heat pooled in her lower body. It was an extraordinary sensation.

She gave a muffled moan which seemed to please Marcus. His fingers flexed on her skin.

Another wave of delicious shivers went through her.

She lifted her hands and gripped the dangling ends of his long, white cravat. "This is really most astounding, my lord."

"Yes, it is, is it not?" He kissed her jaw and the tip of her nose. "And I promise you that you are no more astonished than I."

"My lord."

"My name is Marcus."

"Oh, Marcus." Consumed in the fires of her excitement, she released his cravat and wound her arms snugly around his neck.

The movement instantly brought her body into closer contact with his. She was pressed tightly against him now. Her breasts were crushed against the wall of his broad chest. She could feel the shockingly hard bulge of his manhood straining beneath his breeches.

His long fingers brushed against the nape of her neck.

She cried out softly in response. The place between her legs began to grow damp. Her head tipped back against his arm, and his lips found her throat.

"Marcus. Dear heaven." She clenched her fingers in his hair. Her senses were whirling now. She could not seem to think.

"I believe you will make me a most excellent mistress, my sweet." Marcus took a step back toward the wide green and gold Grecian sofa. He tugged Iphiginia with him.

She heard a dull thud as his boot came up against one of the broken chunks of marble.

"Bloody hell."

"Oh, dear." Iphiginia started to pull back. "Do be careful, my lord. You'll do yourself an injury."

"No doubt, but I trust it will be worth it." Marcus sidestepped the stone and fell back onto the sofa.

He kept one foot on the floor and tumbled Iphiginia swiftly down on top of him. She spilled across his hard, muscled body and lay captive between his thighs. Her airy skirts fluttered delicately for a moment or two as if in protest. Then they settled across Marcus's legs with a soft whisper of surrender.

The heat that poured from Marcus threatened to burn Iphiginia. She had never felt anything so intense.

He caught her face between his hands and brought her mouth to his.

The spell was broken by a horrified exclamation from the vicinity of the door. "*Iphiginia. What is going on in here?*"

Dazed from Marcus's lovemaking, Iphiginia started to raise her head. "Amelia?"

"Damnation," Marcus growled. "What in the bloody hell?"

"Let her go at once, you damnable man. Do you hear me? In the name of heaven, release her."

"Amelia, wait. Stop." Iphiginia pushed herself up on her hands and turned her head toward the shadowed doorway. She saw Amelia, dressed in a chintz wrapper, her dark hair unbound, racing forward through the maze of statuary and furniture.

"Amelia, it's all right." Iphiginia struggled to sit up.

Amelia paused, but only long enough to grab a poker from the hearth. She hoisted it in a threatening fashion and glared at Marcus. "Let her go this instant, you bastard, or I'll brain you. I swear I will."

In one swift, startlingly efficient movement, Marcus pushed Iphiginia out of the way, rolled off the edge of the sofa, and got to his feet. He reached out and jerked the poker from Amelia's hand before she had even realized what he was about.

Amelia's shriek of dismay was a high, keening wail.

"Amelia, calm yourself." Iphiginia stumbled to her feet, slipped past Marcus, and ran to her cousin. She put her arms around the distraught woman. "Calm yourself, cousin. I am all right. He was not hurting me, I promise you."

Amelia raised her head and looked at

Iphiginia uncomprehendingly. Then she turned to stare at Marcus. "Who is he? What is he doing here? I knew this plan of yours was dangerous. I knew that sooner or later some man would seek to take advantage of you."

Iphiginia patted her soothingly. "Amelia, allow me to present the Earl of Masters. My lord, this is my cousin, Miss Amelia Farley."

Marcus raised one brow as he set the poker aside. "A pleasure, I'm sure."

Amelia gazed at him, slack-jawed. "But you're supposed to be dead."

"So I have been told." His mouth quirked slightly at the corner. "But evidence to the contrary continues to crop up."

Amelia swung around to confront Iphiginia. "The blackmailer did not murder him, after all?"

"Apparently not." Iphiginia blushed and hastily straightened her gown. She noticed that one of her plumes was lying on the floor next to Marcus's boot. "It is a great relief to know that we are not dealing with a murderer, is it not?"

Amelia narrowed her gaze suspiciously at Marcus. "I'm not so sure of that. What, precisely, *are* we dealing with here?"

"An excellent question. Certainly not a ghost." Marcus reached down and scooped up the white plume. He held it out to Iphiginia. "I shall enjoy helping you answer the question in greater detail, Mrs. Bright. But as it grows late and the mood of the evening has been dispelled by the events of the last few minutes, I believe I shall take my leave."

"Yes, of course, my lord." Iphiginia snatched the plume from his hand. "But you did mean it when you said that you would allow me to continue to masquerade as your paramour, did you not?"

"I meant every word, my dear Mrs. Bright." Marcus's eyes gleamed in the lamplight. "I shall do everything in my power to help you create a deception that is so true to life that one cannot distinguish it from the real thing."

"That is very kind of you, sir." Iphiginia felt a rush of gratitude. "Is it your intellectual curiosity that persuades you to indulge me, my lord, or your natural gallantry?"

"I strongly suspect that it is not gallantry which persuades me to assist you, madam."

"Then it must be your intellectual nature," she said complacently.

He gave her an amused glance as he made his way toward the door. "You know me so well."

"She should." Amelia glowered at him. "She has made an extremely thorough study of you, my lord."

"I am honored." Marcus walked out into the hall. He paused, his eyes resting thoughtfully on Iphiginia. "Be sure to lock your door after I leave."

Iphiginia smiled. "Of course, my lord."

Marcus stepped out into the night and closed the door very quietly behind him.

There was a short, taut silence in the library. A moment later the wheels of the earl's black carriage rumbled on the paving stones.

Amelia swung around to face Iphiginia. She had herself under control, but her soft brown eyes were still haunted with traces of the old fear.

She was twenty-six years old, a year younger than Iphiginia. In many ways she was far prettier, with her finely wrought features, glossy dark brown hair, and excellent eyes. But there was a starkly remote quality to her that made her seem austere and unapproachable.

"I thought he was forcing himself on you," Amelia whispered.

"I know you did. I understand your concern. But, in truth, he merely kissed me, Amelia."

Iphiginia was the only person in whom Amelia had ever confided the details of the hellish experience that she had endured eight years earlier as an eighteen-year-old governess.

Amelia's mother had died giving birth to her daughter. Amelia had been raised by her scholarly but poor father, who had given her the one thing he had in abundance, an education.

When he had died, the small stipend on which he and Amelia had depended abruptly ceased.

Faced with the task of making her own way in the world, Amelia had done what countless other young women possessed of a good background but no funds did: She had applied for a post as a governess.

She had been raped by her employer's houseguest, a man named Dodgson.

The lady of the house had walked in on the scene only moments after Dodgson had finished the assault. The woman had been scandalized. Her immediate response had been to dismiss Amelia.

The rape had not only cost the penniless Amelia her much-needed position, it had made it impossible for her to secure another one. The agency which had sent her into the household where she had been attacked had refused to find her another post.

The head of the agency had informed her that she was no longer sufficiently respectable to work for a firm which prided itself on its exclusive clients and the unblemished character of the governesses and companions it supplied to the best families.

Iphiginia knew that deep inside Amelia the deep scars of that terrible night had faded but had never entirely healed.

"You *allowed* him to kiss you?" Amelia

shook her head in wonder. "But he is a stranger. Indeed, by rights, he is supposed to be a dead stranger."

"I know." Iphiginia sank down slowly onto a Roman-style chair. She gazed at the plume in her hand. "But he does not feel as though he were a stranger. Do you know what my first thought was tonight when I saw him in the Fenwicks' ballroom?"

"What was that?" Amelia asked warily.

Iphiginia smiled. "I thought that he looked exactly as he was supposed to look."

"Rubbish. You have spent far too much time dwelling on what you suppose to be his nature."

"Very likely."

Amelia scowled. "He just appeared at the Fenwicks' ball?"

"Yes. He knows nothing about the blackmail situation, by the way. He says that he is definitely not a victim."

"Good lord. And he did not give you away?"

"No. He obviously had heard all the rumors that we have contrived to put about. You could say that he and I patched up our quarrel in front of the entire *ton*."

"I wonder why he went along with the thing," Amelia mused.

"Masters is a very intelligent man with a keen sense of curiosity and a marvelously open mind. Obviously he made the very sensible decision not to unmask me until he discovered what I was about."

Amelia snorted. "Hmm."

"A man of his wide-ranging intellect would naturally possess a rational, coolheaded nature. He is not the sort to jump to conclusions."

"It makes no sense," Amelia snapped. "I do not like this business. I'll wager he's got another reason for being so cooperative."

"What reason would that be?"

"I wouldn't be surprised if he has decided that it would be amusing to turn you into his real mistress."

Iphiginia caught her breath. "Oh, I really don't think—"

"Precisely." Amelia gave her a grim look. "You have not been thinking properly since this affair started. Bah. Why the devil isn't the man dead as he was purported to be?"

"He has been away at one of his country estates and only returned to Town because he heard about me."

"So the note Aunt Zoe received claiming that Masters had been murdered because he would not pay blackmail was merely a ploy to frighten her."

"Apparently. This is all very odd, Amelia."

"This entire plan has struck me as decidedly odd from the beginning."

"I know you have not approved," Iphiginia said. "But I thought it was working rather well."

"Until Masters came back from the dead. Some people have no consideration. What are you going to do now?"

"I have no choice but to continue posing as Masters's mistress." Iphiginia tapped her gloved forefinger against her pursed lips. "My original plan is still the only one we have and I believe that it is still a good one. If my true identity is revealed, I will lose my entrée into Masters's social circle."

"No great loss, if you ask me," Amelia grumbled.

"I disagree. As the mysterious Mrs. Bright, paramour of the Earl of Masters, I can go anywhere and talk to anyone."

"But as Miss Bright, spinster, bluestocking, and former proprietor of Miss Bright's Academy for Young Ladies, you will be confined to a much more mundane circle of acquaintances. Is that it?"

Iphiginia made a face. "I'm afraid so. It's true that I now have ample funds, thanks to our very good fortune with our property investments—"

"You mean thanks to your very shrewd knowledge of architecture and Mr. Manwaring's talents as a businessman," Amelia corrected.

"And your skills in financial matters," Iphiginia added. "Do not forget your contribution."

"Yes, well, that is not the point."

Iphiginia smiled wryly. "As I started to say, regardless of the status of my finances, as Miss Iphiginia Bright, I lack the social contacts and the cachet I need to move in Masters's circles."

"And you are still convinced that whoever is behind the blackmail threat moves in Masters's world as well as your aunt's."

Iphiginia stroked the white plume. "I am certain of it. It is clear that whoever he is, he knew a great deal about the earl's plans for the Season. He was able to time the delivery of his threat to Aunt Zoe very precisely."

"Yes, I know, but—"

"And he knows the secret from Zoe's past. The only connection between Masters and Aunt Zoe are those men who played cards with Guthrie and who now play occasionally with Masters."

"But Guthrie, himself, never knew Zoe's secret."

"Guthrie was so drunk most of the time that he couldn't even win at cards, let alone perceive what was happening right beneath his nose. But someone who was close to him might well have guessed what was going on between Zoe and Lord Otis and put two and two together when Maryanne was born."

"And tried to blackmail her with the facts eighteen years later?"

"Yes. Do not forget that the news that Maryanne is actually Lord Otis's daughter, not Guthrie's, was not worth much until the Earl of Sheffield asked for her hand in marriage a few months ago."

Iphiginia did not have to go into the details. They both knew that if there was a scandal connected to Maryanne's name, Sheffield would no doubt retract his offer.

The Sheffield family was notoriously high in the instep. They very likely already had doubts about the wisdom of the heir marrying someone such as Maryanne. True, she had a respectable portion to recommend her, but it was not a great fortune. And she was quite lovely, but there was no denying that her family was somewhat undistinguished.

Sheffield could have looked much higher and everyone knew it. His alliance with Maryanne was a love match and love was considered a frivolous reason for marriage in the *ton*.

"I don't know, Iphiginia," Amelia said after a moment. "This whole scheme was dangerous enough when we thought the earl was dead.

But now that he is alive, I have a feeling that matters could get considerably more complicated."

"Yes." Iphiginia glanced at the nude centurion. "But I must tell you that I am very glad that he is alive, Amelia."

"I can see that." Amelia's mouth thinned as she rose to her feet. "It comes as no surprise. You have been falling in love with him for weeks.

Iphiginia felt her face turn very warm. "You exaggerate."

"I know you better than anyone. Even better, I believe, than your sister or your Aunt Zoe. I have never seen you react like this to any man. Not even Richard Hampton."

Iphiginia grimaced at the mention of her sister's new husband. "I assure you, I never found Richard as . . ." She strove for the appropriate word, "as *interesting* as Lord Masters."

"Not even when he was courting you?" Amelia asked gently.

"Richard never actually courted me," Iphiginia said briskly. "I completely misread his intentions for a time. It was all a terrible misunderstanding. The mistake was soon sorted out."

To Iphiginia's acute chagrin it had been her sister, Corina, whom Richard had really loved.

"You were not the only one who misread his

frequent visits," Amelia said. "We all did. I am still convinced that he did fix on you in the beginning, if you want to know the truth. And then changed his mind as he watched Corina bloom into a great beauty."

"That is unfair, Amelia. Richard is not shallow."

"Don't be too certain of that. And I'll tell you something else. He would never have offered for Corina, either, if you had not settled a large portion on her. His parents would never have given their approval if they had not believed that she could bring some money into the family."

"You are right on that point." Iphiginia wrinkled her nose in disdain. She had never liked Richard's parents.

Iphiginia had known Richard most of her life. They were the same age. The Hamptons and the Brights had been neighbors in the small Devon village of Deepford.

Squire Hampton and his wife had never fully approved of Iphiginia's parents. People with uninhibited, artistic natures were always suspect in small villages dominated by unspoken rules of decorum and behavior.

Iphiginia had always liked Richard, however, and he had always been kind to her, especially during the difficult time after her parents had been lost at sea.

When she recovered from the impact of the first dreadful shock of their deaths, Iphiginia had found herself left with her nine-year-old sister and herself to support.

Unfortunately, the Brights had left very little in the way of an inheritance. Iphiginia's mother had never made much money from her paintings. Her father, a gifted architect, had lacked the business acumen to turn his elegant, classical designs into reality.

The unexpected hidden costs of construction, a poor talent for selecting his business associates, and the myriad problems inherent in building houses on speculation had combined to make most of Bright's profits evaporate.

In any event, both of Iphiginia's parents had been far more interested in renewing their artistic spirits with frequent trips to the ruins of Egypt, Italy, and Greece than they had been with making money.

The Brights had traveled widely, with little concern for the shifting theaters of the war that had raged at various points on the Continent for years. Iphiginia and her sister had usually accompanied them on their travels.

But Iphiginia and Corina had been left behind when the indomitable Brights had set out on their last journey. News of their deaths at sea had come as a devastating blow to their beloved daughters.

Faced with the responsibility of providing for herself and Corina, Iphiginia had taken a bold step. She had scraped together every available penny she could get from the sale of her mother's paintings and a pattern book that her father had created.

She had used the small sum to open her academy for young ladies. It had been an immediate success.

Richard had assisted Iphiginia by persuading his father to rent her a suitable house for her academy. He had made certain that the rent was reasonable. He had gone out of his way to perform other small acts of kindness as well. He had even convinced his mother to recommend Iphiginia's academy to her friends.

She would always be grateful to Richard, Iphiginia thought. And she would always feel a certain fondness for him. He was a handsome, amiable man with a likable manner.

But she knew now that she would not have been the best choice for a wife for him. He, apparently, had comprehended that better than she had at the time.

The truth was, she would have been quite miserable if she had been forced to spend the remainder of her life in Deepford. She had not realized just how much she had been obliged to repress her naturally exuberant, independent, adventurous, intellectual nature until she had left the village last year.

She had felt as though she had shed a cocoon and become a creature with wings.

Iphiginia had discovered this past year that she had inherited a full measure of her parents' unconventional, artistic sensibilities. She would have had a very hard time behaving in a manner suited to the wife of a staid country squire.

Her sister, on the other hand, was entirely comfortable with the strictures of life back in Deepford. Corina even seemed to like her new in-laws.

"Iphiginia?"

Iphiginia surfaced from her brief reverie. "Yes?"

"I am very concerned about this new development."

"Whatever do you mean?"

"This situation is dangerous."

"Nonsense. We shall find the blackmailer and all will be well."

"I am not talking about the blackmail situation." Amelia gave her a searching glance. "I am talking about your personal situation. This business of masquerading as a notorious widow entails far too much risk. Look at what happened in here tonight."

Iphiginia's cheeks burned. "Really, Amelia. It was just a kiss."

Amelia watched her with worried eyes. "For your own sake, I pray you will take great care not to indulge in any more such reckless embraces. Masters is not some harmless country squire whom you can control with a word or a frown. He is a powerful man, accustomed to getting what he wants."

"He is a gentleman," Iphiginia protested.

"Men of his stamp seize what they desire and do not care whom they hurt in the process."

Iphiginia could think of nothing to say in response. She was only too well aware that Amelia spoke from painful experience.

In the perilous days ahead, she must bear in mind that she was not really Mrs. Bright, the exciting, exotic widow, mysterious paramour of the most notorious earl in the *ton*.

She was Miss Bright, spinster, scholar, student of classical design.

And she had a blackmailer to catch.

She was fascinating, Marcus thought as he walked up the front steps of his town house. Intelligent, passionate, and so delightfully different from the usual run of females. She would make him a most interesting mistress for the remainder of the Season. Perhaps longer, if he was fortunate.

Marcus experienced a surge of what could only have been hope. It would be an enormous relief to settle into a comfortable, stable, long-term affair with an intelligent woman.

One who accepted his rules and did not pester him for marriage or subject him to childish tantrums and irritating emotional scenes.

One who understood the demands of his assorted intellectual interests.

One who did not constantly seek to divert his attention from whatever book he was studying or whatever project he was working on at the moment.

One with whom he could actually converse after the demands of passion had been temporarily satisfied.

Lovelace opened the door just as Marcus reached the top step. "Good evening, sir. A pleasant night, I trust."

"An interesting evening, Lovelace." Marcus stripped off his coat and handed it to his butler along with his hat.

Lovelace's expression, usually as impassive as an Egyptian sepulchral mask, registered momentary surprise. "I am pleased to hear that, sir. You do not usually return from an evening's round of social affairs with such, ah, enthusiasm."

"I am well aware of that, Lovelace. Tonight's affairs were of a somewhat unusual nature."

Marcus crossed to the library. His boots rang on the gold-veined black marble floor. "You may go to bed. I shall see to the lamps."

"Thank you, sir." Lovelace paused delicately. "There is one item of news to relate."

"And that is?"

"Your brother arrived here earlier this evening. He left an hour ago. I believe he went out to his club."

"Bennet is here in London?" Marcus frowned. "He is supposed to be visiting friends in Scotland."

"Yes, m'lord. I know."

"Well, I shall talk to him in the morning." Marcus went into the library. "Good night, Lovelace."

"Good night, sir." Lovelace quietly closed the door.

Marcus crossed the room to the small table in the corner. The rich French brandy inside the crystal decanter glowed a mellow shade of amber.

Marcus poured himself a glass of the brandy and settled into the large, comfortable wingback chair. He absently inhaled the heady fumes that emanated from his glass as he contemplated the fact that he was about to become involved in another liaison.

The astounding thing was that he was filled with a deep sense of anticipation this time.

Most unusual.

He had always disliked the customary un-
pleasantness that accompanied the inevitable
ending of an affair. Lately, however, he had
actually found himself resenting the investment
of time and effort that it took to form a new
connection.

It was difficult to work up enthusiasm for the
project when one knew precisely how it was all
going to end. He had even gotten very good at
predicting exactly when it would all terminate.

He had been allowing the periods between
affairs to stretch out longer and longer, until
the pressure of his physical needs grew too
strong to ignore.

The difficulty was that he was burdened with
a full complement of the usual masculine
desires. When he was in a particularly melan-
choly frame of mind, he sometimes wondered
what it would be like to be freed of his passions. He would then be able to abandon the
murky world of romantic entanglements in
favor of devoting himself to the satisfactions of
his intellectual endeavors.

The thought made him grin briefly. If there
was one thing he had discovered tonight, it was
that there was no immediate likelihood that his
body would allow him to ignore his lust. The
talons of unsatisfied desire still gripped his
loins.

But the most interesting aspect of the situation was that he was not dreading the work of seduction that lay ahead. In truth, for the first time in a long, long while, he was looking forward to it.

All his instincts told him that with Iphiginia things were going to be new and different.

For starters, he could not see the inevitable conclusion to the affair.

For once he would be going into a liaison without knowing when and how it would end. That alone was enough to whet his appetite.

Marcus sipped the brandy and contemplated the pleasures of a passionate attachment that held the promise of surprise and unpredictability.

He wondered how long she would stick to her outrageous tale of a plan to catch a blackmailer.

He gave the lady high marks for creativity. She had hit upon a brilliant way to thrust herself into Society at the highest levels.

She had no doubt expected him to remain away from London for the full month, which would have given her time to entice a wealthy paramour. Or perhaps she had been out to capture his attention all along.

That last was an intriguing notion. And rather flattering.

Marcus turned the brandy glass lazily in his

hands. He would allow her to continue her pretense of hunting a blackmailer as long as she pleased. It did no harm and it would be amusing to see how long she could keep up the charade.

But in the meantime he had other, more interesting games to play with Iphiginia Bright.

An unpleasant sensation of dampness made Marcus glance down at the front of his coat. He groaned when he saw the dark, spreading stain that marred the expensive fabric.

He got to his feet, removed his coat, and reached into the inside pocket. He withdrew the metal object there and regarded it with some dismay.

Clearly his latest design for a reliable hydraulic reservoir pen that contained its own supply of ink and could be carried about in one's pocket needed more work.

This was the third coat that he had ruined in the past two weeks.

$\mathcal{F}$OUR

$\mathcal{M}$arcus had just helped himself to a portion of eggs from one of the trays on the sideboard when Bennet sauntered into the breakfast room the next morning.

" 'Morning, Marcus."

"Good morning. Lovelace said you had returned to London. I wasn't expecting you." Marcus glanced at his brother, started to smile, and then blinked in astonishment. "Bloody hell. What happened to your hair?"

"Nothing happened to my hair." Bennet's handsome face twisted into an offended scowl. He went to the sideboard and busied himself lifting the lids of various serving trays. "This style is all the rage."

"Only among Byron and his crowd." Marcus

surveyed his brother's elaborately tousled curls. Bennet's dark hair was normally quite straight, just as Marcus's was. "Remind your valet to be cautious with the crimping iron. He'll set fire to your head if he's not careful."

"That is not amusing. Are there any muffins?"

"Last tray on the end, I believe." Marcus carried his own heavily loaded plate back to the table and sat down. "I thought you intended to spend the entire month in Scotland with your friend Harry and his family."

Bennet kept his attention focused on the muffin tray. "I thought you were going to spend the month in Yorkshire."

"I changed my mind."

"Well, so did I."

Marcus frowned. "Did something happen to cause you to alter your plans?"

"No." Bennet concentrated intently on ladling eggs out of another tray.

Marcus eyed his brother's back with an uneasy feeling. He knew Bennet all too well. Bennet had never kept secrets from him. Something was wrong.

Marcus had single-handedly raised Bennet since their mother's death eighteen years ago. True, Marcus's father had still been alive at the time, but George Cloud had taken no more interest in his youngest son than he had in his eldest. George preferred his hounds, his hunting, and his friends in the local tavern to the bothersome burdens of family life.

There had been no one else to see to the rearing of Bennet, so Marcus had taken on the responsibility, just as, at an even earlier age, he had assumed the responsibility of working the family farm.

The profits from the farm improved steadily over the years, thanks to Marcus's successful experiments with tools, fertilizers, plows, and breeding techniques.

George had used much of the increased income to purchase better hounds and jumpers. When Marcus's mother had timidly suggested that Marcus be allowed to attend Oxford or Cambridge, George had squashed the idea immediately. He was not about to deprive himself of the income produced by the best farmer in the district.

Occasionally George clapped Marcus on the back and chortled about having produced such a useful son. Once in a great while he thought to hoist Bennet aloft in a gesture of casual affection.

Cloud frequently observed with some satisfaction that it was fortunate both of his sons had inherited his own excellent constitution.

He pointed out that chronic ill health, such as Mrs. Cloud suffered, was a damnable nuisance. But that was the limit of his paternal involvement in his sons' lives.

Marcus's mother, whose medical complaints were generally of a vague nature and featured such symptoms as melancholia and fatigue, contracted a very real fever the year Marcus turned eighteen. She succumbed to it within a matter of hours. Marcus had been at her bedside, his two-year-old brother in his arms.

His father had been out fox hunting.

Cloud had lived for nearly a year after his wife's death, an event he had noticed more because it had interfered with his hunting plans than because of any great sense of loss. But eleven months after his long-neglected spouse had succumbed to the lung fever, he managed to break his own neck in a fall when his newest jumper failed to clear a fence.

Marcus was at work in the fields with his men the morning the vicar came to tell him that his father was dead. He had been studying the effectiveness of the modifications he had recently made in a new reaping machine.

He still recalled the curiously detached sensation he had experienced while he listened to the vicar murmur words of condolence.

A year earlier he had wept alone after his

mother's death. But on the morning of his father's demise he could not summon a single tear.

His principal emotion beneath the sense of detachment had been a brief, senseless anger.

He had not understood the reason for the inner rage, so he had quickly buried it somewhere deep inside himself. He had never allowed it to resurface.

Young Bennet seemed virtually oblivious to his father's absence. He'd focused all his attention and affection on the one person who was a true constant in his life, his older brother Marcus.

Marcus pushed the memories aside and watched Bennet wander over to the breakfast table.

"Harry and I got bored in Scotland," Bennet offered. "We decided to return to London for the Season."

"I see." Marcus spread jam on a slice of toast. "I thought you had declared the Season a dead bore."

"Yes, well, that was last year."

"Of course."

Last year Bennet had been barely nineteen. He'd just come down from Oxford, full of a young man's enthusiasm for politics and poetry. He had been disdainful of the frivolousness of the Season. Marcus had gotten him into a club populated by other young men who were passionate about the new poets and the latest political theories. Bennet had seemed content.

Marcus had been quietly pleased to see that his brother was not the type to be swept off his feet by the superficial entertainments of the *ton*.

Oxford had done its job.

Marcus had not sent Bennet to Oxford for an education. On the contrary, he had seen to his brother's schooling at home with the assistance of an excellent tutor and his own ever-expanding library.

A young man did not go off to either Cambridge or Oxford in order to study. He went there to obtain a social polish and to mingle with the young men with whom he would later do business for the rest of his life. He went there to form friendships with the scions of the best families, families from which he would eventually select a suitable wife.

Marcus had been determined that his brother would not be like him, a naive, rough-edged country squire who knew nothing of the world beyond life on a farm.

Marcus had paid a high price for his own lack of worldliness. He did not want Bennet to suffer the same fate. A man needed to shed his illusions and dreams as quickly as possible if he was to avoid becoming a victim in this life.

Marcus took a large bite of his toast. "Where did you go last night?"

"Harry and I both went to our club," Bennet said vaguely. "Then Harry suggested that we drop in on a few of the more interesting soirees."

"Which ones?"

"I don't remember precisely. The Broadmore ball, for one, I believe. And I think we stopped briefly at the Fosters' levee."

"Did you enjoy yourself?"

Bennet met Marcus's eyes for an instant and then his gaze slid away. He shrugged. "You could say that."

"Bennet, I've had enough of this evasiveness. If something is wrong, tell me."

"Nothing is wrong." Bennet glowered at him. "At least not with me."

"What the devil is that supposed to mean?"

"Very well, Marcus, I shall be blunt. I understand you made a spectacle of yourself last night."

"A spectacle?"

"Hell and damnation. They say you carried your new paramour out of the Fenwicks' ballroom in your arms, for God's sake. Talk about causing a scene."

"Ah, so that's the problem." Marcus's hand tightened on the handle of his knife. He cut into his sausage with grave precision. "Did I embarrass you?"

"Marcus, are you going to spend the rest of your life titillating Society with your bizarre behavior?"

"I did embarrass you." Marcus forked up a bite of sausage and chewed meditatively. "Try not to take it to heart, Bennet. Society has seen worse."

"That's hardly the point, is it?" Bennet slathered butter on his muffin. "The thing is, a man of your years should behave with some sense of propriety."

Marcus nearly choked on his sausage. "A man of my years?"

"You're thirty-six. You ought to have remarried years ago and settled down to the business of filling your nursery."

"Bloody hell. From whence springs this sudden concern with my nursery? You know full well that I do not intend to remarry."

"What about your obligation to the title?"

"I'm quite content to see the title go to you."

"Well, I don't particularly want it, Marcus. It's yours and it should go to your son." Bennet scowled in obvious frustration. "It's only right and proper that you should see to your responsibilities."

"I perceive that my actions last night have, indeed, humiliated you," Marcus said dryly.

"You must admit, it's a trifle awkward to have an older brother, a thirty-six-year-old unmarried earl, no less, who has no compunction about becoming the latest *on dit*."

"This isn't the first time."

"It's the first time that you've caused a scene in the middle of a fashionable ballroom."

Marcus cocked a brow. "How would you know? You've hardly spent any time at all in Society."

"Miss Dorchester told me as much," Bennet retorted, clearly goaded.

Marcus stilled. "Juliana Dorchester?"

"I had the great privilege of dancing with her last night," Bennet muttered.

"I see."

"Whenever you say 'I see' in that particular tone, it generally means you disapprove. Well, you had best not say anything unpleasant about Miss Dorchester to me, Marcus. She is a beautiful young lady with extremely refined sensibilities who would never dream of getting involved in a scandalous scene."

"This is Juliana Dorchester's second Season," Marcus said grimly. "She has to secure a husband this time around because the Dorchesters cannot afford a third Season for her. Do you comprehend me, Bennet?"

"You're trying to warn me off her, aren't you? Well, it won't work. She is an unrivaled paragon of womanhood and I shall be forever grateful that she allowed me into her presence last night."

"She is no doubt thanking her lucky stars right this minute that you took notice of her. She'll be plotting to appear in whatever ballroom you happen to show up in this evening."

"Damnation. She's not the type to plot anything. She's too innocent, too gentle, too sweet-natured to *plot*."

"She's plotting right this minute. Trust me."

"How would you know?"

"She's Dorchester's daughter and I know Dorchester. He's desperate to marry Juliana into money. And her mother wants a title in the family so badly she can taste it." Marcus pointed a fork at Bennet and narrowed his eyes. "You're a prime catch on the Marriage Mart, Bennet. You're rich and there's every expectation that you'll inherit the title. You must be on your guard."

Bennet flung down his napkin. "That's outrageous. Miss Dorchester is not the type to concern herself with money and titles."

"If you really believe that, then you are infinitely more naive than I thought."

"I am *not* naive. But neither am I as cold-natured and rigid and set in my ways as you are, Marcus. And I certainly don't hang about with outrageous females such as your Mrs. Bright."

"You will speak of Mrs. Bright with respect or you will not mention her name at all, is that understood?"

"She's your mistress, for God's sake."

"She is my very good friend."

"Everyone knows what *that* means. You have some nerve criticizing Miss Dorchester. Your Mrs. Bright could take a few lessons in decorum from her, if you ask me."

Marcus slammed his coffee cup down onto the saucer. "No one asked you."

The door of the breakfast room opened. Lovelace loomed. He had a small silver tray in one gloved hand.

"A message for you, m'lord. It just arrived."

Marcus frowned as he took the note from the tray. He read it quickly and silently.

M:
I must see you at once. Very urgent. The park.
Ten o'clock. The fountain.
Yrs.
H

Marcus glanced at Lovelace. "Have Zeus saddled and brought around at nine-thirty. I believe that I shall ride in the park this morning."

"Yes, my lord." Lovelace backed out of the breakfast room.

"Who sent you the note?" Bennet asked.

"A friend."

"Mrs. Bright, I expect."

"No, as a matter of fact, it's not from Mrs. Bright."

Bennet's mouth tightened. "I've never seen you quite so touchy about one of your paramours."

"She is my *friend*." Marcus tossed down his napkin and rose to his feet. "Do not forget that, Bennet."

At five minutes before ten, Marcus rode Zeus, his heavily muscled black stallion, into the park. He took the graveled path that led toward the center of the vast wooded swath of green. It was the least traveled of the many paths.

Hannah, Lady Sands, was waiting for him in a small closed curricle. She was dressed in a dark maroon carriage gown. The high, fluted collar accentuated the graceful line of her throat. Her lovely face was concealed beneath the veil of her stylish maroon hat.

"Marcus. Thank God you have come." She lifted her veil and gazed at him with stark, anxious eyes. "I have been beside myself for days. This morning, when I learned that you were back in Town, I sent my note at once. I feared you would not be free to see me on such short notice."

"You know that I am always available to you, Hannah." Marcus did not like the tense set of her delicate features or the shadows in her gray eyes.

Hannah was twenty-nine, married to the wealthy, likable Lord Sands and recently blessed with an infant son.

She had been widowed seven years ago. Her new marriage, which had taken place three years previously, had appeared to be a happy one. Marcus had been glad for her. He had thought her days of fear were behind her, but this morning he recognized the old haunted expression in her eyes.

"What is it, Hannah?"

"I am being blackmailed," she whispered. Her face crumpled in despair. "Oh, Marcus, someone knows *everything*."

Marcus did not move. "That's impossible."

"No, it's true." Tears formed in her eyes. "Oh, God, he *knows,* do you comprehend me? He knows how Spalding died. He knows that I killed him."

"Hannah, get hold of yourself. Are you telling me that someone has demanded money from you?"

"Yes. Five thousand pounds. I have already paid it. I was forced to pawn some earrings."

"Bloody hell."

"I fear there will be more demands."

"Yes." Marcus tapped his riding crop against his boot. "I think we can safely assume that there will be more demands. There always are when one is dealing with a blackmailer."

"Dear heaven, I am so afraid, Marcus."

"Hannah, listen carefully. When did you get the first demand?"

"Six days ago. I would have sent a message to you at once, but I did not know where you had gone. I only knew that you were out of Town for an extended period of time."

"I was at Cloud Hall."

"I have been absolutely desperate. I haven't slept in days. Sands is becoming very concerned. He keeps asking me what is wrong. He wants me to summon a doctor. What am I going to do?"

"Nothing for the moment," Marcus said gently. "I shall deal with this."

"But what can you do? Marcus, did you hear me? This person knows that I . . . that I am a murderess."

"Hush, Hannah. Calm yourself. You did not

murder Lynton Spalding. What you did was done in self-defense. Do not ever forget that."

"No one will believe it. What will Sands say if he ever learns the truth?"

"I suspect that your husband would be far more understanding about this than you believe," Marcus said. It was not the first time he had tried to talk Hannah into telling Sands the truth about her first husband's death. But Hannah was adamant in her refusal to do so.

"I dare not tell him, Marcus. He would never be able to accept the knowledge that he is married to a woman who had actually killed her first husband. How would you deal with such a revelation if you were in his shoes?"

Marcus shrugged. "Knowing what I do about Spalding and his treatment of you, I would congratulate you on being such an excellent shot."

Hannah gave him a stricken look. "Please, I beg you, do not tease me."

"I'm not teasing you. It's the truth. I think you underestimate your new husband."

"I know him better than you do. He thinks I am a paragon. I simply cannot tell him the truth."

"Apparently the blackmailer knows that, too," Marcus observed. "Interesting."

"What are you going to do?"

"I believe that I shall have a long talk with

someone who appears to know more about this situation than I had realized."

"What on earth are you saying?" Hannah wailed. "Marcus, you must not tell anyone about any of this."

"Do not concern yourself. I shall not give away your secret. But I do intend to seek a few answers to some questions I neglected to ask last night."

"I don't understand."

"It appears I was somewhat hasty. I did something I rarely do: I leaped to a conclusion." Marcus steadied the prancing Zeus. "I thought I was being treated to a very inventive banbury tale, you see."

"What are you talking about?"

"Never mind. It's a long story and I do not have time to tell it at the moment. Rest assured that I shall look into this matter at once, Hannah. And do not pay another penny in blackmail without consulting me first, do you understand?"

"Yes." Hannah's elegantly gloved fingers tightened on the reins. "I am so relieved to be able to talk to you about this. I was going mad."

"It will be all right, I promise you."

Hannah smiled mistily. "That is what you said the night you helped me dispose of Spalding's body."

"And I was right, was I not?"

She gave him an odd look. "You kept my secret but at a great cost to yourself. You know very well that there are still those who say that you murdered Spalding in cold blood in order to gain control of the investment pool."

Marcus smiled. "No one could ever prove that he was not killed by a footpad, and that was all that mattered. Gossip does not bother me, Hannah. I am accustomed to it."

Her mouth curved wryly. "Sometimes I think that nothing bothers you." She hesitated. "I read the morning papers. I could not help but see the gossip about a certain exhibition at the Fenwicks' ball last night."

"Did you?"

Hannah gave him a quizzical look. "Come now, Marcus. You and I are old friends. You can confide in me. We both know that you are not the type to become besotted with any female. Did you actually carry Mrs. Bright out of the ballroom in your arms?"

"She fainted."

"You have never gotten involved with anyone who made scenes, Marcus. You are infamous for demanding absolute discretion from your paramours."

"Mrs. Bright is not my paramour," Marcus said coldly. "She is my very good friend. She fainted and I made certain that she got some fresh air so that she could recover. That was all."

Hannah sighed. "You're in a strange mood today." She reached up to tug her veil down over her face. "Forgive my intrusion. Your connection to Mrs. Bright is entirely your affair."

"Yes."

"I must be on my way. I told Sands that I was shopping this morning."

Marcus gentled his tone. "Try not to worry unduly about the blackmailer, Hannah. I shall look into the matter."

"Thank you." She gave him another sad smile. "I am very fortunate to count you as my friend." She flicked the reins and drove off down the graveled path.

Marcus studied the sparkling fountain for a long while and then he turned Zeus's head and rode back toward the western entrance of the park.

"But he's supposed to be dead," Zoe, Lady Guthrie, wailed. "Why isn't he?"

"Hush, Aunt Zoe." Iphiginia cast a quick glance about at the uncrowded showrooms of Hornby and Smith, Upholsterers. Fortunately, no one appeared to have overheard Zoe's lament. "I cannot say, but it's an encouraging development, don't you think?"

"It confuses the issue, if you ask me," Zoe declared.

Amelia, dressed in one of the dull bombazine gowns she favored, nodded in agreement. "Your aunt is quite right. This whole thing is a great tangle. I do not like it."

"Please keep your voices down, both of you. Someone will hear you." Iphiginia glanced anxiously around the showroom again.

The proprietors hovered behind a counter at the rear of the shop. Mr. Smith was a broad, plump man garbed in a shocking pink waistcoat and the latest style of pleated trousers. Hornby, gaunt, stooped, and balding, was wearing a paisley printed waistcoat. It contrasted sharply with his purple coat.

Hornby gazed longingly down the length of the shop at where Iphiginia, Zoe, and Amelia stood together around a pattern book. He was clearly waiting for an opportunity to pounce. He had been rebuffed twice already, but Iphiginia knew that he was on the verge of making another attempt to offer his assistance.

The walls of the long room were lined with drawings and designs that purported to offer suggestions for decorating one's residence in the latest fashion. Samples of the newest styles in chairs and tables were arranged in a row down the center of the room.

Pattern books containing drawings of lavishly decorated interiors for every room in the home were set out on several tables.

Iphiginia, Zoe, and Amelia were making a show of studying a design for a combined library and statuary hall. But the real reason they had all met at Hornby and Smith's this morning was to discuss the latest developments in the crisis.

"Obviously the blackmailer was lying about having murdered Masters," Iphiginia said. "He was attempting to frighten you, Aunt Zoe, so that you would meet his demands."

"He succeeded. To the tune of five thousand pounds," Zoe muttered. "It is really too much. I finally regain control of my own money after all these years of watching Guthrie fritter it away on horses and women, and what happens? Some nasty blackmailer happens along and tries to take it away from me again."

"I understand, Aunt Zoe. We shall identify him and put a stop to this, I promise you," Iphiginia murmured sympathetically.

She was very fond of her aunt and had every intention of doing her best to free Zoe from the blackmailer's clutches.

At forty-five, Zoe was an energetic, vivacious woman with a flair for the dramatic. Her hair, once the same tawny shade as Iphiginia's, was

attractively streaked with silver. She had the
cleanly etched profile that characterized all the
women on the Bright side of the family.

Twenty-five years earlier Zoe had not only
been quite striking, she had also been an heiress. The handsome portion her doting parents
had settled on their only daughter had attracted the eye of Lord Guthrie. No one had
discovered until too late that Guthrie was
nearly penniless. By then Zoe was married and
her husband had gained legal control of her
portion.

Having secured the money he had coveted,
Guthrie promptly lost interest in his new bride.
Fortunately, he had not been a complete idiot.
He had managed to avoid squandering all of
Zoe's inheritance. He had, however, gone
through the income and had started to make
serious inroads on the capital before conve-
niently suffering a stroke.

As Zoe had once said to Iphiginia, it was
typical of Guthrie that, even in the act of departing this mortal plane, he had managed to
humiliate her. He had died in a brothel.

Zoe let it be known far and wide that the
only benefit she had ever received from marriage was her lovely daughter, Maryanne. She
was thrilled with Maryanne's recent betrothal
to the handsome and, as Zoe had taken care to
ascertain, wealthy Sheffield.

During the long years of her unhappy marriage to the obnoxious Guthrie, Zoe had taken comfort in her liaison with Lord Otis. Otis had been devoted to her from the moment they had been introduced. He had never married. The fact that he was Maryanne's real father, however, had been a deep, dark secret until the blackmailer had somehow discovered it.

Maryanne, a charming, warmhearted young lady, was exceedingly fond of Otis. She treated him as though he were a favored uncle. Otis doted on her.

After the death of her husband, Zoe had, in the manner of so many of Society's widows, finally come into her own.

The first thing she had done was gather together what remained of her inheritance. She had invested the whole of it in Iphiginia's first property speculation venture, Morning Rose Square.

When the initial income from that investment had been realized last year, Zoe had promptly settled a handsome portion on Maryanne. She and her daughter had both set about replacing all the drab, unstylish gowns in their wardrobes with new clothes fashioned by elegant modistes who possessed French accents. When all was in readiness, Maryanne was launched on Society. The offer from Sheffield had come shortly after Maryanne's first ball.

Zoe's mouth tightened as she studied the illustration of the combined library and statuary hall. "Otis says there very likely will be more demands, and soon. He claims blackmailers are like leeches. They usually return time and again until they have succeeded in bleeding their victims dry."

Iphiginia shuddered. "What a ghastly analogy. From what I have heard, he is right." She frowned over the illustration in the pattern book, her mind on her aunt's problem. "It is unfortunate that Masters thinks the entire matter is merely an amusing jest."

"Are you certain that he did not believe you?" Zoe asked.

"He made it quite clear that he thinks I invented the tale in order to explain my masquerade to him."

Zoe groaned. "What a disastrous affair this is. I still cannot credit that he has actually agreed to allow you to continue posing as his paramour."

"Well, he has agreed to it and we must be grateful. It will allow me to continue searching the studies and libraries of the suspects."

"I'm beginning to think that it is all a waste of time," Zoe said. "Thus far you have learned nothing."

Iphiginia tapped one gloved finger lightly against the illustration. "I wouldn't say that. I have eliminated both Darrow and Judson from the list of those who might be the blackmailers."

Zoe sighed. "I don't know. It all sounds so vague."

"We have nothing better to go on at the moment." Iphiginia broke off when she caught a flash of purple out of the corner of her eye. "Oh, hello, Mr. Hornby. We are still studying this illustration, as you can see."

"Of course." Hornby, unable to resist the temptation to encourage potential clients, sidled closer. "Perhaps I can be of some assistance?" He gave Iphiginia, Zoe, and Amelia an unctuous smile.

Iphiginia thought quickly. "This is a most unusual decoration above the fireplace in this design, Mr. Hornby."

Hornby beamed. "It is an exact copy of an ancient sepulchral ruin, madam. It gives the library a serious, weighty sort of atmosphere, quite suited to the characteristic use of such a chamber."

"I see," Iphiginia said.

"Very interesting." Zoe peered more closely at the illustration. "What on earth are those odd creatures that support the lamps?"

"Sphinxes, madam. All the rage at the moment, you know. They go rather well with the Egyptian hieroglyphic wallpaper."

"Yes, of course."

Amelia frowned. "What is all this drapery hanging from the ceiling, Mr. Hornby?"

"Turkish tent hangings, madam. They provide an exotic air that will astound visitors."

"It certainly will," Iphiginia murmured. She surveyed the picture quite closely. "The room appears to contain a somewhat mixed collection of antique vases."

"All are exact copies of antiques in the Etruscan style, madam. Exceedingly fashionable."

Iphiginia elected not to point out that the vases were no more Etruscan in design than his paisley waistcoat. "Where do you plan to put the books?"

"The books?" Mr. Hornby looked baffled.

"It is a library, is it not?" Iphiginia said.

Hornby assumed a politely superior air. "Madam perhaps is not aware that few people of fashion actually use a library for the purpose of reading these days."

Iphiginia concealed a smile. "Of course. I do not know what I was thinking to even mention books."

"Quite all right, madam," Hornby said. "It is precisely the wish to avoid such decorating mistakes that brings persons of taste to a firm such as Hornby and Smith."

Amelia frowned. "Mr. Hornby, you are obviously not aware that Mrs. Bright is accounted an expert in matters of antique design."

Hornby's eyes widened. "Uh, no. No, I was not. Forgive me, madam. I had not realized."

Iphiginia waved aside his stammered apology. "Quite all right."

Her expertise in antiquities had been one of the most useful elements of her masquerade. Zoe had quickly fed the rumor mill with the news that the mysterious Mrs. Bright had a scholar's knowledge of the antique style, the latest fashion in home decoration.

Iphiginia had been an immediate success at every ball, as there was no shortage of people who wanted to discuss their decorating schemes with her. Maintaining a fashionable home was as essential as being *au courant* in one's dress.

Before Hornby could apologize further, the small bells over the shop door tinkled discreetly. A short round woman of middle years bustled into the showroom. She was a vision in several yards of flounced and ruffled white muslin.

Her gown was trimmed with a white spencer and she wore a massive white hat trimmed with huge white flowers. She carried a lacy white parasol and a snowy white reticule.

"Good grief," Zoe muttered as she gazed in awe at the newcomer. "Lady Pettigrew looks like a giant snowball."

"It is not my fault," Iphiginia whispered.

Amelia raised a brow. "It certainly is. They are calling it the Lady Starlight fashion. Any number of ladies are determined to wear it."

"Oh, Mrs. Bright," Lady Pettigrew sang out. "I thought I saw your carriage in the street. How fortunate. I have been most anxious to speak to you. Do you have a moment?"

"Good morning, Lady Pettigrew." Iphiginia had encountered the plump, vague, eccentric Lady Pettigrew at a number of social affairs. Although the woman's husband was on Iphiginia's list of potential blackmailers, Iphiginia was rather fond of Lady Pettigrew. "Allow me to introduce you to my friend, Lady Guthrie, and my cousin, Miss Farley."

"Delighted." Lady Pettigrew smiled benignly at Zoe and Amelia. "I assume you are seeking Mrs. Bright's opinion on a matter of classical taste and fashion, Lady Guthrie? That is precisely what I wish to do."

"As a matter of fact, I have asked Mrs. Bright to give me her advice on how to use antique vases to the best effect in my town house," Zoe said smoothly.

Lady Pettigrew beamed enthusiastically. "It is well known that Mrs. Bright is an authority on the archaeological style. I, myself, wish to consult with her about my Temple of Vesta."

That piqued Iphiginia's interest. "Are you constructing an antique temple, Lady Pettigrew?"

"Actually, I already possess one," Lady Pettigrew said, not without a touch of pride. "It is a wonderful old ruin located in a charming grove on the grounds of our country house in Hampshire."

"How old is it?" Iphiginia asked.

"It was built about thirty years ago by Pettigrew's father. The thing is, I am not entirely certain it is accurate in every detail. I should very much like to restore it properly."

In spite of her more pressing concerns, Iphiginia was captivated by the prospect of examining the Pettigrew ruin. "As it happens, I made careful measurements and sketches of the ruin of a genuine Temple of Vesta while I was in Italy. I would be happy to compare them with your ruin, Lady Pettigrew. I might be able to offer some suggestions on how to produce a more precise copy."

"Wonderful, wonderful. I am giving a small house party next week. I shall send you an invitation. Our estate is only a day's journey from London."

"That is very kind of you. I should love to come."

It was a perfect opportunity, Iphiginia thought jubilantly. The house party would give her a chance to search through Lord Petti-grew's country house library to see if he had black sealing wax and a phoenix seal concealed there. At the same time she would be able to view the Temple of Vesta. *Two birds with one stone.*

The shop chimes banged suddenly and with such force that one tiny bell shuddered, bounced, and fell to the floor. It emitted a tiny, stricken clang and then fell silent.

Everyone turned toward the door as it opened.

Marcus strode into the showroom. He was dressed for riding in a black coat, breeches, and gleaming ebony Hessians. He was bareheaded and his dark hair was windblown.

His amber eyes fixed instantly on Iphiginia with an expression of chilling intent. He started toward her, moving like a raw, dangerous force of nature through the samples of dainty draw-ing room furniture and the displays of fashion-able drapery.

A deep sense of unease snaked through Iphiginia. Something was decidedly wrong, she realized. This was not the indulgent, casually amused man who had kissed her last night.

It was Lady Pettigrew who broke the taut, tense silence that had settled on the shop the

moment Marcus appeared. She fluttered cheerfully.

"Masters," she exclaimed. "How good to see
you. I was just chatting with your close friend,
Mrs. Bright."

"Were you, indeed?" Marcus did not take his
eyes off Iphiginia. "I am about to have a chat
with her myself."

Iphiginia blinked at the tone of his voice. She
saw Amelia's eyes narrow.

Heedless of the undercurrents, Lady Pettigrew smiled brightly at Marcus and gave him a
shrewd, knowing look. "I have invited her to
attend a small gathering at my country house
next week. Perhaps you would also care to
visit? I know you are not overly fond of house
parties—"

"No, I am not."

"But you may be quite interested in this one,
my lord." Lady Pettigrew arched one brow.
"I'm certain you and Mrs. Bright would thoroughly enjoy a stay in the country. So much
privacy available, you know."

It took Iphiginia a few seconds to comprehend Lady Pettigrew's subtle emphasis on the
word *privacy*. When she did, she felt herself
turn pink. Lady Pettigrew was making it clear
to Marcus that he and his mistress would have
ample opportunity for dalliance at her country
house party.

Marcus's eyes moved reluctantly from Iphiginia to Lady Pettigrew's bouncy little snowball figure. "Very kind of you, Lady Pettigrew. I shall consider your invitation carefully."

Lady Pettigrew glowed with triumph. "I am delighted to hear that, my lord. I am most anxious to have Mrs. Bright examine my Temple of Vesta, you see. I wish to obtain her opinion on the archaeological exactness of my ruin."

Marcus gazed at Lady Pettigrew as though he had suddenly discovered that she were a rather curious archaeological object herself. "Temple of Vesta?"

"Surely you are acquainted with the style, my lord," Iphiginia murmured helpfully. "There is a very fine example in Tivoli. It is a lovely circular structure. The Vestal Virgins are said to have tended the sacred flame there."

"Virgins," Marcus said, "have never been a subject that was of much interest to me."

*F*IVE

I will see Mrs. Bright home," Marcus said as he escorted Iphiginia, Zoe, and Amelia outside the premises of Hornby and Smith. "She and I have one or two matters to discuss in private."

Zoe and Amelia glanced at each other and then looked at Iphiginia.

"Do not concern yourselves," Iphiginia said quickly. "Take my carriage. I shall see you both later."

"You're quite certain?" Amelia gave Marcus a stony stare.

"Yes, Amelia." Iphiginia did not care for the rough edge in Marcus's voice any more than Amelia or Zoe did. She thought it best, however, not to make an issue out of it right there in the middle of Pall Mall.

"Very well." Zoe gave Marcus one last uneasy look and then nodded at Amelia. "Let us be off."

Marcus watched Amelia and Zoe walk toward Iphiginia's small, delicate white carriage. The airy, graceful equipage was trimmed with gilt and horsed with two white mares. The animals' braided manes were adorned with white plumes. The gleaming harness sparkled in the spring sun. The coachman wore white livery trimmed with gold buttons.

"Your carriage, I presume?" Marcus said to Iphiginia.

"How did you guess?"

"It looks like something out of a bloody fairy tale."

"I thought it appropriate. From the description I was given of your equipage, I understood it to look like something a wicked troll might drive. I wanted to provide a counterpoint."

"A wicked troll, eh? What does that make you, my dear Mrs. Bright? A fairy princess?"

"I assure you, I am no fairy princess."

"Thank God for that much." Marcus tightened his grasp on Iphiginia's arm. He started to stride swiftly along the broad promenade of the fashionable shopping street. "I have enough problems at the moment."

Iphiginia dug in the heels of her white kid half boots. "If you wish to discuss your problems with me, which I presume is your intention, you'll have to slow your pace, my lord. I do not intend to gallop the length of Pall Mall with you."

Marcus scowled, but he shortened his stride. "Enough of this nonsense. Who are you and what the devil do you think you're about?"

"I beg your pardon?" Iphiginia busied herself with the act of unfurling her lacy white parasol. "I do not comprehend your tone or your meaning, my lord. I explained everything to you last night."

"Last night," Marcus said, "I believed you to be playing some clever game in order to make a place for yourself in Society."

"Yes, I know you did."

"This morning it was forcibly brought to my attention that you are involved in something other than an amusing masquerade. I wish to know precisely what it is you are about."

Iphiginia tried to be patient. "I told you, sir. I am attempting to discover the person who is blackmailing my aunt. Nothing has changed. What has overset you so this morning?"

"I am not overset. You make it sound as though I were having the vapors. I am bloody furious."

"Oh."

He shot her a frozen look. "Is that all you have to say for yourself?"

Iphiginia thought about it. "If it would not be too much trouble, my lord, I would like to know what it is that has, ah, outraged you."

He hesitated, as though debating how much to tell her. "I have just learned that a close friend of mine is being blackmailed."

Iphiginia stared at him, astonished. "Good heavens. Someone other than my aunt is also being blackmailed after all? This is very interesting news, indeed, my lord."

"Is it not?"

"Sir, I do not understand your sarcasm. I should think you would be alarmed to learn that the tale I told you may well be true and that a friend of yours is also a blackmailer's victim. Why are you angry with me?"

"I suggest that you construct a reasonable hypothesis to explain my irritation."

"I beg your pardon?"

"A guess, Mrs. Bright. Make a guess."

Iphiginia's mouth dropped open. Now he was being more than sarcastic. He was becoming impossibly rude. She swiftly composed her expression when she noticed three lounging dandies gazing raptly at her. She blocked their view with her parasol.

"This is ridiculous, Masters. Why are you annoyed with me?"

"Because I have come to the obvious conclusion that you are very likely the blackmailer."

"What on earth?" Iphiginia came to a complete halt. She yanked her arm free and whirled about to confront Marcus. "You go too far, sir. What do you think I am?"

"A clever, scheming little adventuress who has gone one step beyond the pale." Marcus's voice was soft, but it was weighted with steel. "Last night I found your silly masquerade amusing."

"My lord, please—"

"I was even willing to go along with the charade for a while. I will admit that you are far and away the most interesting female who has crossed my path in some time. However, this morning when I learned the truth, I decided that you were no longer nearly so amusing, madam."

"No longer amusing? Of all the stupid, idiotic, offensive things to say. You clearly do not know what you are talking about. I will not stand here and listen to your accusations, sir." Iphiginia turned on her heel. She could hear the tittering laughs of the lounging dandies.

Marcus put out a hand and caught her arm. "Not so fast. I have one or two questions to put to you, Iphiginia."

"I have better things to do than answer your insulting questions."

"Such as?"

"Such as find the blackmailer," Iphiginia

hissed. "Let me go, my lord, or I promise you, I shall scream."

"Devil take it, we are not in Drury Lane. Kindly cease the theatrics." Marcus brought her forcibly around so that she was once again obliged to face him. "Unless, of course, you want news of this little scene to be all over Town this evening?"

"Why should that concern me? Everyone in Town is already talking about us, my lord."

"You must believe me when I tell you that the gossip can get a great deal worse than it already is. If you persist in quarreling with me in the middle of a public thoroughfare, I promise you that it will."

Iphiginia flushed. "Is that a threat, Masters?"

"It is. If you do not maintain at least the pretense of being a lady, I am not going to continue acting the gentleman. I swear, if you try to walk away from me, I shall put you over my shoulder and carry you off to someplace where we can continue this discussion without an audience."

Iphiginia was seething. "You would not dare."

"Would you care to place a wager on that, Iphiginia?" he asked much too softly. "It was one thing for me to carry a swooning lady out of the Fenwicks' ballroom last night. It will be quite another if I haul you off as though you were a sack of coal this afternoon."

Iphiginia contemplated her options for a few seconds. She was acutely aware of the growing number of stares aimed in her direction. More than one head had turned. More than one ear was discreetly cocked in an attempt to overhear the fascinating exchange that was taking place between Masters and his new paramour.

It was obvious from the ruthless set of his jaw and the unyielding line of his mouth that Marcus was in a dangerous mood. He was apparently willing to stage a humiliating quarrel for the entertainment of the fashionable shoppers in Pall Mall if Iphiginia did not accede to his wishes.

"Very well, my lord." She gave him a brittle smile as she placed her gloved fingertips lightly on his arm. "If you insist on playing the role of the wicked troll, so be it."

"An excellent decision. I have often been cast in the role of the troll and I assure you, I am capable of giving a truly electrifying performance."

"I do not doubt it for a moment. I would have you know, sir, that during my travels on the Continent this past year I was never once obliged to deal with this sort of ungentlemanly conduct. There was a nasty little street thief in Rome who had better manners."

"Perhaps one day I shall have the opportunity to take lessons. They do say that travel is broadening. Come, we have drawn enough attention." Marcus's fingers closed more tightly around her arm. He resumed the brisk pace along Pall Mall.

"People are staring at us."

"I should think you would be accustomed to it by now. Tell me why I should not conclude that you are the blackmailer."

"First tell me why you came to the conclusion that I was."

Marcus slanted her an unreadable glance. "You are an exceedingly clever female. You have made a study of me that was so astute it enabled you to fool the *ton* into believing that you are my mistress."

"We all have our little skills."

"Your particular skills convince me that you could have delved just as deeply into the background of others and perhaps come up with suitable material for blackmail."

Iphiginia nearly choked on her outrage. "Material such as that which is being used to blackmail your friend?"

"Precisely."

"I would never do such a thing." Iphiginia

realized that she was hurt as well as angry and she did not know quite why. Marcus's alarming conclusions about her were not unreasonable under the circumstances. Nevertheless, she felt wounded by them. "If you knew me better, my lord, you would not make such accusations."

"Ah, but I do not know you very well at all, do I? Not nearly as well as you appear to know me. And that, madam, has finally begun to worry me."

"I do not see how I can persuade you of my innocence, nor will I lower myself to even attempt to do so."

"Then we have a problem on our hands, my dear." Marcus inclined his head a bare half inch at an acquaintance who nodded from the doorway of a snuff shop.

Iphiginia pretended to focus on some gloves that were displayed in a shop window. She could feel the avid curiosity in the gaze of the man who stood in front of the snuff shop. Indeed, she could feel a dozen pairs of eyes boring into her.

There was very little privacy here in Town. Anonymity was impossible, especially for any woman whose name was linked with that of the Earl of Masters.

It was almost as bad as living in Deepford, Iphiginia thought resentfully. But at least here in London she would not be subjected to lectures on propriety from the vicar or from the parents of her sister's in-laws-to-be.

She merely had to listen to such lectures from Marcus.

"You are making a much more difficult problem out of this affair than is necessary," Iphiginia said forcefully. "But then, something tells me that you are a very difficult man."

"Regardless of how unpleasant this problem is for you, madam, you may rest assured that until it is resolved, you and I are going to be spending a great deal of time in each other's company."

"What is that supposed to mean, my lord?"

"It means that until I am convinced that you are not involved in this blackmail scheme, I intend to keep you very near at hand." Marcus smiled without any trace of amusement. "Where I can keep an eye on you. How fortunate for me that you have chosen to masquerade as my mistress. It provides the perfect excuse for me to stay very close to you."

Iphiginia bristled. "What if I decide that I no longer wish to continue the masquerade?"

"It is far too late to change your mind about your role in this charming little play." Marcus acknowledged another acquaintance with a faint tilt of his head. "You are too deeply into the part."

"If that is the case, I give you fair warning that I fully intend to proceed with my inquiries. I am determined to discover the identity of the blackmailer."

"What an odd coincidence. I have set myself precisely the same goal."

Fulminating, Iphiginia studied him in silence for a moment. "We are going to carry on with our pretense, then?"

"Yes." Marcus responded to the greeting of an elderly woman who was emerging from a bookshop. "Mrs. Osworth."

"Masters."

Iphiginia recognized the beady-eyed lady. She managed a civil smile. "Good day, Mrs. Osworth."

"Good day to you, Mrs. Bright." Mrs. Osworth turned her sharp gaze on Marcus. "Lovely day, my lord, is it not?"

"Indeed," Marcus said.

"I trust we shall be seeing you both at the Lartmores' ball this evening?" Mrs. Osworth murmured.

"Doubtful," Marcus said flatly.

"I certainly plan to attend," Iphiginia said briskly. Out of the corner of her eye she saw Marcus's mouth thin with disapproval. She deliberately brightened her smile. "I understand that Lord Lartmore has a very extensive collection of statuary."

"Yes, I believe he does," Mrs. Osworth said. "My husband mentioned it once. I have never seen it myself. I'm not terribly interested in antique statuary. Oh, dear, you must forgive me. I must be off."

"Yes, of course," Iphiginia said.

"I have an appointment to interview a woman who is being sent over from the Wycherley Agency. I am seeking a new companion, you know."

"No, I did not know," Iphiginia said.

"My last one—a flighty little thing if you must know the truth—ran off two days ago with a young man of absolutely no background. Can you imagine? After all I'd done for the girl. Ungrateful wretch. This time I shall hire someone older. And a good deal plainer. Until this evening, then, my dear."

"Good day, Mrs. Osworth," Iphiginia said.

Marcus was silent until Mrs. Osworth was out of earshot. "Why do you wish to go to the Lartmore ball? Bound to be a dead bore."

"Two reasons," Iphiginia said crisply. "The first is that I would dearly love to see Lord Lartmore's statuary collection."

"He allows only his closest acquaintances and certain, ah, connoisseurs to tour it."

"I hope to prevail upon him to show it to me."

"You wouldn't be interested. Rather poorly executed copies, for the most part."

Iphiginia momentarily forgot that she was annoyed with Marcus. "You've seen it?"

"Yes, and you may take my word for it. There is nothing to interest the scholar in Lartmore's statuary hall."

"How disappointing. I was so looking forward to viewing his antiquities."

"Save your time. What was the other reason you wished to attend?"

"To pursue my inquiries, of course. His name is on my list of men who connect your world with that of my aunt's. And you did play a few hands with Lartmore at your club that night before you left for Yorkshire."

Marcus eyed her speculatively. "You really have done a most thorough investigation of my activities, have you not?"

"I told you that I had made a close study of your habits."

"Lartmore is no blackmailer."

"How do you know that?"

"He's extremely wealthy. He has no reason to resort to blackmail."

"Perhaps he has recently suffered some serious reverses in his fortunes."

"Unlikely," Marcus said. "As it happens, however, I intend to dine at my club this evening. Afterward I shall arrange to play some cards. One can learn a great deal at the card tables. I shall see if there is any hint of gossip concerning Lartmore's finances."

Iphiginia pursed her lips. "I wish I could arrange to play a few hands at some of the gentlemen's clubs. There is no telling what I might learn."

"Do not even think about it," Marcus said. "It's impossible and well you know it. I shall look for you at the Richardsons' ball sometime around eleven. I can give you my report."

"You are attempting to dissuade me from attending the Lartmore ball, are you not?"

"Mrs. Bright, so that you are quite clear on this point, allow me to make it plain that I am ordering you not to go to Lartmore's."

"Hmm. My lord, I have a question for you."

"Yes?"

"Would you care to tell me precisely why your friend is being blackmailed?"

"No, I would not," Marcus said bluntly. "Surely you do not expect me to divulge a confidence."

"No, of course not. I merely thought that if I knew the nature of your friend's secret, I might be able to compare it to the sort of secret information that is being used against my aunt. I cannot help but wonder if there might be some similarities."

Marcus narrowed his eyes. He looked intrigued in spite of himself. "I don't suppose you would care to tell me the nature of the secret material that you claim is being used to blackmail Lady Guthrie?"

"No."

"So I am left to wonder if she really is being blackmailed."

Iphiginia gave him a lofty smile. "You cannot expect me to trust you with my secrets when you have made it clear that you are not prepared to trust me with yours."

Marcus's powerful hand clamped more firmly around her arm. "Your lack of faith in me is going to make it somewhat awkward for us to work together."

"It certainly will," Iphiginia agreed. "And your lack of trust in me will have an equally chilling effect on our efforts."

Marcus gave her a disturbing smile. "It is clear that if we are to break down the barriers of distrust between us, we must become more intimately acquainted, Mrs. Bright."

"How do you suggest we go about becoming more closely acquainted, sir?"

"To begin, why don't you tell me what happened to Mr. Bright?"

"I beg your pardon?"

Marcus raised one brow. "I was referring to your late husband."

"Oh, him."

"Obviously you no longer grieve for the departed."

"He wouldn't have wanted that." Iphiginia swallowed uneasily. She must learn to think of this man as an adversary, she warned herself. "He believed that one should put unhappy events behind one. After a suitable mourning period, of course."

"Of course. And was there a suitable mourning period after his death?"

"A reasonable one, considering the circumstances. Mr. Bright was considerably older than I," Iphiginia murmured.

"I see."

"He lived a very full and active life."

"I imagine it got considerably more active after he married you."

Iphiginia gave him a repressive look. "I do not wish to pursue this topic of conversation. I'm sure you comprehend, my lord. Much too painful."

"I understand," Marcus said.

"And so you should. I believe you have a rule of your own against discussing the past, do you not?"

"Yes, Mrs. Bright, I do have such a rule."

"Personally, I am not overly fond of rules, but I believe that I shall adopt that particular one myself." Iphiginia caught sight of a dis-

creetly painted sign hanging at the corner of a
small street off Pall Mall. "Oh, look, there's Dr.
Hardstaff's museum. Mr. Hoyt mentioned the
establishment the other evening."

"I cannot imagine why."

"He said something about Lord Thornton
having recently taken a treatment from Dr.
Hardstaff." Iphiginia studied the sign.

Dr. Hardstaff's Museum of the Goddesses
of Manly Vigor
Learn the Secret and Authentic
Invigorating Powers of
the Goddesses of Antiquity

Marcus glanced at the sign. "You would have
no interest in Dr. Hardstaff's museum,
Iphiginia."

"But I am always deeply interested in antiquities." Iphiginia turned her head to look back
at the sign as Marcus urged her forward. She
frowned. "I do not believe that I know which
classical goddesses are particularly associated
with manly vigor."

"You astound me, madam. I thought you
knew all the answers."

Shortly after ten that evening Marcus left the
card room at his favorite club. He was in a

dark, unpleasant mood, although he had won, as he so often did when he played whist.

He took no particular satisfaction in the victory. There was no serious challenge to be found in a game when one's opponents were so deep in their cups that they could scarcely hold their cards.

The restlessness that gripped him had nothing to do with the recent game of whist. He had been feeling this way since he had met with Hannah in the park. The sensation had intensified after the conversation with Iphiginia.

Logic told him that he could not trust her, but his growing desire for her was undeterred by reason and common sense.

He wanted her.

Marcus glanced at the stately tall clock and saw that it was nearly time to hunt Iphiginia down at the Richardsons' ball. He wondered what she had been doing all evening. Had she been innocently pursuing what she termed her inquiries or had she been setting snares for other potential blackmail victims?

One could only pity the late Mr. Bright, Marcus reflected. Any man married to Iphiginia would no doubt find himself growing old before his time.

"I thought I might find you here, Masters."

Marcus glanced over his shoulder. It took an

act of will to avoid swearing aloud when he saw Hannah's husband, Edward, Lord Sands.

Marcus had often thought that under other circumstances he might have gotten along very well with Sands. There was a solid, substantial feeling about the man. Sands radiated a sense of unflinching integrity. He was the sort of man one would wish at one's side in the heat of battle. A man with whom one could do business.

Marcus knew that there was no chance for genuine friendship between himself and Sands, however, as long as Hannah and her secret stood between them.

"Good evening, Sands." Marcus nodded politely. "What brings you here? You rarely bother to put in an appearance at this particular club."

"I came here to find you." Sands's pleasant, open features were set in such rigid lines that they could have been carved from stone.

Marcus told himself he was not surprised. Nevertheless, he had hoped to avoid this confrontation. "What can I do for you?"

Sands's gloved hands clenched and unclenched at his sides. "You can stay away from Hannah, damn your eyes. I know that you met her in the park this morning. I will not have it."

"Hannah is an old friend," Marcus said gently. "You know that."

"Listen to me, Masters, and listen carefully. Whatever happened between the two of you before I met Hannah is your affair. But she chose me, by God. She is my wife and I will not let you play your games with her, do you comprehend?"

"If you knew anything at all about me, Sands, you would know that I have an ironclad rule against involving myself with innocents and other men's wives. And I never break my own rules."

"I have heard of your so-called rules," Sands said roughly. "The gossips claim that you have always made it a point to form your connections with the most interesting and attractive widows of the *ton*. But they also say that Hannah is the one exception."

"You should know better than to listen to gossip," Marcus said.

"If I hear that you have met privately with my wife again, I vow, I shall call you out. I am not bluffing, Masters. I am accounted a good marksman."

"I believe you," Marcus said calmly.

"I have heard that you once very nearly killed a man on the field of honor, but that does not frighten me."

"I have no intention of keeping a dawn appointment with you, Sands."

"Then stay away from Hannah."

"Did Hannah tell you that I had met with her this morning?"

"She did not have to tell me. I heard about it from an acquaintance, who had been told by someone else that you both were seen entering the park at an early hour."

Marcus shrugged. "You have my word of honor that I have no designs on your lady. Since you pay attention to rumors, I trust you will have heard by now that I am presently spending a great deal of my time in the company of a charming widow named Mrs. Bright."

"I have heard about your so-called Lady Starlight. She sounds just your sort. If you are wise, you will confine your attentions to her."

"I fully intend to do just that." Marcus glanced once more at the clock. "If you will excuse me, I shall go in search of the lady herself. She and I have arranged to meet at the Richardsons' ball. Good night, Sands." Marcus inclined his head in a pleasant fashion and walked past Sands toward the door.

Iphiginia Bright had complicated his life no end, he reflected a few minutes later as he vaulted into his black carriage. Now, on top of everything else, he was being hounded by a jealous husband.

Half an hour later, Marcus stalked back down the steps of the Richardson town house.

He was no longer brooding over the difficulties Iphiginia presented. He was furious.

It had never occurred to him that she would ignore his instructions to rendezvous with him at the Richardsons'. Marcus was not accustomed to having his orders brushed aside. But that was not the worst of it.

What really annoyed him was that he had a strong suspicion that she had gone to the Lartmore mansion.

Marcus hesitated just as he was about to get back into his carriage. The London streets were choked with vehicles of all descriptions. It was midnight at the height of the Season and everyone who was anyone was in motion, traveling from one soiree to another. It could easily take a good forty minutes for his coachman to forge a path to the Lartmore mansion.

"I'll go on foot," Marcus called up to Dinks. "Meet me at the Lartmore house."

"Aye, my lord," Dinks muttered from the box. "Watch yer back. All kinds out on a night such as this."

"I'll be careful."

Marcus paced swiftly along the crowded thoroughfare. His path was dimly lit by the gas lamps that had recently been installed in this section of Town.

He moved through clumps of drunken dandies on their way to the gaming hells off St.

James, clusters of brightly garbed fops en route to heckle the actors at the theater, and young men consumed with Byronesque ennui who were headed for adventure in the stews. Marcus sincerely hoped that Bennet was not among the last group.

Here and there prostitutes solicited passersby from shadowed doorways. A surly-looking individual dressed in a cap and baggy pants eyed the cut of Marcus's finely tailored clothes, but he did not attempt to leave the shelter of an alley.

A bare fifteen minutes later Marcus walked up the wide steps of the Lartmore mansion. The footman on duty in the hall bowed and did not ask to see his invitation. He headed straight for the balcony that overlooked the crowded ballroom.

Marcus planted both hands on the railing and looked out over the glittering scene. He searched the crowd for a glowing figure dressed in virginal white.

"I believe you'll find her in the statuary hall, Masters. Lartmore invited her to, ah, survey his antiquities." Herbert Hoyt chuckled as he came up behind Marcus. "I wouldn't worry about it, if I were you. She assured me that she can handle Lartmore."

Marcus turned to study Herbert's amused face. He did not know the man well, but he knew the type. Hoyt was a harmless sort. "How do you know where Mrs. Bright is at this particular moment?"

Herbert lounged his well-padded thigh against the railing and took a sip of champagne from the glass in his pudgy hand. "Because I was with her when she asked Lartmore for a tour."

"I see."

"Mrs. Bright is an authority on classical statuary and architectural design, you know."

"Yes, I know."

"She and I have had numerous enthralling discussions on the subject of ancient architecture. She recently loaned me her copy of Grayson's *Illustrations of Classical Antiquities*. Have you read it, sir?"

"No, I have not." Marcus was in no mood to listen to another man, even harmless Herbert Hoyt, as he chattered on about his close friendship with Iphiginia. "Excuse me."

Herbert gave him an apologetic look. "I did try to hint to her that she might not want to view Lartmore's statuary collection, but she was adamant. In my experience it's almost impossible to stop Mrs. Bright from doing exactly as she wishes."

"So it would seem." Marcus made to move past the other man.

"I congratulate you, sir. Mrs. Bright is a most

fascinating lady. But then, I am always captivated by a female who gives one the impression that she is not quite what she appears to be."

Marcus stopped and turned back. "What the devil do you mean by that, Hoyt?"

Herbert held up a hand and hastily swallowed his mouthful of champagne. "Beg pardon. No offense intended, I assure you. It's the element of mystery she projects, you see. Gives the lady an enticing elusive quality, don't you think?"

"Mrs. Bright is a mystery only to some," Marcus said very softly. "To me she is an open book. We understand each other very well."

"I see." Herbert's brow wrinkled in a perplexed expression. "Then you were no doubt already aware of her keen interest in Lartmore's statuary. I must admit, it came as something of a surprise to me."

Whether Herbert Hoyt was harmless or otherwise, Marcus had an almost overpowering urge to toss him over the railing. He told himself that it would be a futile exercise. Hoyt had not stated anything that everyone else who knew of Iphiginia's visit to Lartmore's statuary hall was not already thinking.

Marcus turned on his heel and walked away without a word. He knew where to find Iphiginia. Lartmore's collection of erotic statuary was famous among the males of the *ton*.

SIX

"This one is called *Ecstasy*. You will notice the boldly modeled curves of the female form, my dear Mrs. Bright." Lord Lartmore stroked the extraordinarily large breast of a stone figure with his skeletal hands. "Only the ancients could invest their work with such lush power." He tweaked a nipple. "What a pity that today's artists have lost that vitality."

Iphiginia swallowed and stared at the statue. She fought to conceal her shock. She had more than a passing familiarity with the work of the ancient sculptors. But she had never seen anything to compare with the figures in Lartmore's statuary hall.

It was not that the large-bosomed statue which Lartmore fondled with such a lascivious touch was nude that startled Iphiginia. She had

seen any number of unclad classical statues. It
was the odd pose of the figure that left her
momentarily speechless.

The stone female sat astride the naked loins
of a reclining male figure. Her thighs were
splayed wide, emphasizing the cleft in her buttocks. Her spine was arched, her head was
thrown back, her eyes were closed, and her
mouth was open in an expression of what could
only be acute agony.

The male figure looked to be suffering equal
torment as he jutted his hips upward. It was
apparent that his stone shaft was buried deep
within the marble woman.

"Most unusual," Iphiginia managed weakly.
She hoped the lamplight concealed her hot
face.

"And so provocative to the passionate
senses, don't you agree?" Lartmore gestured
with a limp hand to indicate the dimly lit room.
The eyes in his skull glittered. "My collection is
filled with the unique and the unusual, as you
will see. I insist that every piece of statuary I
collect be imbued with true antique sensibilities."

Iphiginia debated whether to inform him
that none of his statues were in the true antique mode as far as she could see. She tried to
study some of the nearby figures with an objective eye.

It was not an easy task. The faintly glowing lamps revealed a room full of stone and marble statues that appeared to have only one thing in common. They were all images of men and women posed in astonishingly intimate and exceedingly odd positions.

A buxom female crouched on her hands and knees, her buttocks arched high. The male figure positioned behind her gripped her hips as he thrust into her.

"That one is called *Unbridled Passion,*" Lartmore murmured. "One of my favorites."

"Indeed." Iphiginia could not think of anything else to say.

"Over there is *A Taste of Delight.*"

Iphiginia gazed at the figure of a woman seated on a rock. A man crouched between her widely spread knees. His face was buried between plump stone thighs.

"I see."

"And this one I call *The Elixir of Life.*" Lartmore touched a stone leg and smiled at Iphiginia.

She frowned as she studied the figures. At first Iphiginia thought the female was praying. She blushed furiously when she saw that in actuality the nude had a very long length of marble manhood in her mouth.

"Good heavens," Iphiginia whispered.

"I am especially fond of my newest acquisitions." Lartmore led the way toward the far end of the hall to where a series of sculptures had been arranged. He beamed with pride. "I should dearly love to have your opinion on them, Mrs. Bright. Everyone knows that you are an expert in these things."

Iphiginia's initial reaction to the series of statues was relief. The first few pieces appeared to be much more decorous than the others. These figures were at least clothed.

Relaxing slightly, Iphiginia took a step closer to get a better look at the shadowed statues. In the first of the series a young woman wearing a prim gown sat on a stone bench. A properly attired man sat beside her. They appeared to be conversing politely.

Then Iphiginia noticed that the man's hand was on the woman's leg beneath her skirts.

"What do you call this?" Iphiginia asked uneasily.

"The entire series is called *The Breaching of the Virgin's Maidenhead*. You will notice that with each succeeding statue in the collection the figures become increasingly more intimate until, in the last one, the deed is done. Amusing, is it not?"

Iphiginia cast him a sidelong glance. She noticed that the expression in Lartmore's colorless eyes had become a hard gleam. A sheen of sweat had appeared on his balding skull. Even as she watched, he edged closer to her. His cadaverously thin body was touching her white skirts.

It was definitely time to return to the ballroom. As much as she hated to admit it, Marcus had been right. Clearly it had been a mistake to come in here. There had to be another way to get into Lartmore's library tonight.

Iphiginia cleared her throat authoritatively. "As you have asked for my opinion on your statuary, my lord, I fear I must tell you that these examples are extremely poor imitations of the antique mode."

"My dear Mrs. Bright, how can you say that?" Lartmore looked grievously wounded.

"To be perfectly blunt, the style is not at all in the manner of the ancients. I see no indications of either Roman, Grecian, or Etruscan motifs in any of these statues."

"But, Mrs. Bright, surely you are mistaken."

"No, sir, I am not mistaken. I assure you, I have examined a great deal of genuine antique statuary and none of it bore any resemblance to these pieces."

Lartmore put a hand to his chest in a gesture of anguish. "I am crushed." He took a step closer to Iphiginia.

"I trust you did not pay a great deal for any of these statues." Iphiginia sidestepped deftly and moved quickly around Lartmore. "If you did, you were fleeced."

"Mrs. Bright, allow me to show you the rest of my collection." Lartmore put out a long-fingered hand to detain her.

"Unfortunately, I do not have the time to linger." Iphiginia managed to avoid his groping hand with a quick move to one side.

"But I insist." Lartmore lunged, claws outstretched to seize her.

Iphiginia picked up her skirts and fled.

She nipped around the stone figure of the man braced on his knees behind the crouching female, sprinted past a man and woman engaged in sexual congress on top of a pedestal, and plowed straight into a very large, very immovable object that loomed in her path.

This male figure was definitely not made out of stone, but it was as unyielding as any of the sculptures in the hall.

"*Marcus.*" Her reaction was instantaneous and instinctive. She smiled brilliantly as she staggered and clutched at his arm to catch her balance. "I cannot tell you how very happy I am to see you, my lord."

"I've been searching for you, Mrs. Bright." But Marcus did not look at her. His eyes were on Lartmore. "I was under the impression that we had arranged to meet at the Richardsons'."

"Yes, well, I planned to go there immediately

after I left here, sir." Iphiginia checked her hair to see if the white roses were still in place. "Lord Lartmore kindly offered to show me his statuary hall, so I was somewhat delayed."

"I see. How unfortunate."

Iphiginia winced at the unmistakable menace in his voice. She hurried to defuse what was clearly about to become a very awkward situation. "Well, then, as you are here and I am ready to leave, I do not see why we should not be off."

"In a moment," Marcus said absently. "There are one or two matters that should be clarified first."

Lartmore rushed to his own defense. "Masters, I assure you, there was nothing objectionable about this little tour of my gallery of statues. I sought Mrs. Bright's intellectual opinion on my collection. Nothing more."

"Nothing more?" Masters repeated ominously.

"Absolutely not." Pinned by Marcus's cold eyes, Lartmore appeared to grow thinner and even more cadaverous. He stuck one bony finger beneath his cravat and tried to loosen the heavily starched fabric. "We were just finishing the tour, Masters. I was about to escort Mrs. Bright back to the ballroom."

"There will be no more such tours," Marcus said.

"No, no, of course not." Lartmore cast a desperate glance at Iphiginia.

"I have given Lord Lartmore my opinion of his statuary collection," Iphiginia said coolly. "I'm afraid I found it all of rather poor quality. Completely lacking in true antique sensibilities."

"Fascinating," Marcus said very gently. "I believe I had already warned you that it was not of the best quality and would be of little interest to you."

"Ah, yes." Iphiginia rallied quickly. "Yes, you did, my lord, but I am the sort of person who prefers to form her own conclusions."

"Perhaps it would be wise if you learned to take sound advice when it is offered."

Iphiginia scowled but decided not to say anything. Something told her this was not the best time to inform him that she rarely took other people's advice these days. She'd been obliged to endure far too much of that commodity back in Deepford.

"If you will excuse me." Lartmore slithered between two copulating statues and headed for the door. "I must get back to my guests."

Iphiginia glowered at the retreating Lartmore. When he had vanished like a wraith, she swung around to confront Marcus.

"I do not recall that your advice was *offered,* precisely, my lord. I believe it was put a bit more strongly. Some would say that your so-called advice was more in the nature of an extremely autocratic command."

Marcus took a single step closer. His face was ruthless in the shadowy lamplight. "It was your choice to go about London disguised as my paramour, was it not?"

Iphiginia blinked and took a wary step back. "Well, yes, initially I suppose one could say it was my idea. However—"

"Let me make something plain to you. So long as you are gallivanting about Town masquerading as my mistress, you will bloody well act the part."

Alarmed by the dangerous softness of his tone, Iphiginia took another discreet step backward. "Now, see here, my lord, you must understand that this is merely a role I am playing. One could say that I am your mistress-in-name-only."

"If you expect me to allow you to continue playing this part, you will follow my *advice* to the letter."

She lifted her chin. "You mean your commands, do you not?"

"Aye, madam. I mean my commands."

Iphiginia took another cautious step back. Her leg came up against a cold marble statue of two writhing figures. "I am not accustomed to obeying any man's commands, sir."

"That much is clear. The late, lamented Mr. Bright obviously let you take the bit between your teeth and run wild. But if you think that I will allow you to make a complete fool of me in front of the *ton,* you are sadly mistaken."

Iphiginia was momentarily stricken with guilt. "My lord, there is no denying that you were put in a somewhat unfortunate position by my masquerade, but I assure you that I never meant to humiliate you."

"Only because you were proceeding on the mistaken assumption that I was safely dead."

"Well, yes, granted. However—"

"Last night I found your audacity mildly entertaining. Tonight, however, you have stepped over the line and I am no longer amused."

Iphiginia's brief flash of guilt evaporated. Anger took its place. "I am not doing this to amuse you, my lord."

Marcus took another menacing step toward her. "Until such time as you and I are finished with this charade, you will stay in character, madam."

"In character?" She could not retreat any farther. She was trapped by the stone limbs of the couple copulating behind her. "Sir, I shall play this part as I see fit."

"No, madam, you will not." Marcus reached out and grasped a foot and a shoulder on the statue behind her, effectively caging her between his arms. "I am the authority on this role. If it weren't for me, the part would not even exist. Is that not correct?"

"I suppose one could make such an argument, but—"

"I *am* making the argument. I created the role. Therefore I shall direct you in it."

He brought his mouth down on hers and pinned her against a stone thigh.

What should have been a small, breathless gasp emerged from Iphiginia as a silent sigh. She clutched at his shoulders, more to steady herself than to push him away. The weight of him as he crushed her against the marble was intoxicating.

Just as it had last night, excitement showered through her, an incandescent rain that made all her senses bloom at once.

She heard Marcus groan. It was a rough, dark sound that came from deep in his chest. He leaned closer. His body was as hard as the statue's but infinitely warmer.

She was supposed to be acting out a role, Iphiginia reminded herself. But everything suddenly felt very real.

She shivered and wrapped her arms around his neck, just as she had done last night. Now she could feel every inch of him pressing against her. He felt so good, so strong, so right.

She was enthralled, consumed by a deep longing that dazzled her with its intensity.

Iphiginia realized that she had been yearning for this sensation all of her life.

Marcus lifted his mouth from hers. His eyes were brilliant with desire and wonder. "You're going to drive me mad, aren't you?" He threaded his fingers through her elegantly styled hair, gripped a handful, and forced her head gently back. He kissed her throat.

Iphiginia trembled beneath the sensual assault. And then she was kissing him with a passionate ferocity that seemed to have sprung from nowhere. She strained to taste him, touch him, feel him.

She loved the feel of his skin beneath her lips. The scent of him filled her head. The strength in his hands thrilled her.

"Marcus."

"I told you last night that I am in need of a real paramour."

He slid one hand down to her waist and then he spread his fingers over her hip. He squeezed gently, crushing her white silk skirts. When she moaned, he moved his palm lower, took a handful of silk in his fist, and raised it to her thigh.

Iphiginia was startled by the feel of stone directly against the back of her leg. She opened her eyes, confused and disoriented.

"I do not—"

"Hush." Marcus covered her mouth with his own, sealing her halfhearted protest behind her lips.

He braced her against the statue behind her. He slid his hand up along her stocking-clad leg past her garter and wrapped his fingers around her bare thigh.

Iphiginia flinched in reaction.

To her astonishment, he stilled. "Does my touch offend you? Do you find my hands rough on your soft skin, Mrs. Bright?"

"No," she managed in a thin voice. She clung to him. "I love your hands, sir." She kissed his jaw. "They are so . . . so . . ." Words failed her.

"Yes?" He stroked his rough palm along the inside of her leg.

Iphiginia gasped and buried her face against his shoulder. "So very exciting," she whispered.

He seemed to relax. "I'm pleased that you are excited." He dropped a small kiss on her ear. His fingers flexed on her leg.

Iphiginia could hardly breathe. No man had ever touched her so intimately. She was stunned by the sensations roiling within her.

She reminded herself that Marcus believed her to be an experienced widow, not a naive innocent. She must not allow him to notice that she was close to being overwhelmed by love-making.

"Sir, I am not at all certain this is either the time or the place for this sort of thing. Someone might walk in on us." Iphiginia knew that she did not really want him to stop. What she wanted was for him to go more slowly. But she could not explain to him that she needed time to adjust to the new and disturbing demands of passion.

"Calm yourself, Iphiginia. We are alone in this chamber. No one is likely to walk in on us."

Without any warning, Marcus raised her leg and hooked it over a stone arm. Her skirts fell back along her thigh, exposing her completely. Marcus's palm went straight to the hot, damp place between her legs.

Iphiginia shrieked very softly in astonishment. *"My lord."*

Marcus kissed her deeply, cutting off the soft, startled sound. He stroked her deliberately.

Iphiginia froze. Her fingers locked on his shoulders. *She was an experienced widow, a woman of the world. . . .*

"My God, you feel good," Marcus whispered thickly. He sounded pleased and somewhat awed. "Do you always respond this readily?"

Iphiginia tried to answer, but she could not speak. She kept her hot face pressed against his shoulder and shook her head quickly.

"No? The late Mr. Bright did not have this effect on you, then?"

Iphiginia could not lift her head. Frantically she shook her head again. "No."

Marcus drew one finger slowly between the soft, plumped folds of feminine flesh. "And your previous lovers? Did you grow this moist and this hot this swiftly for any of them?"

Iphiginia was nearly beside herself now. Her fingers bit so deeply into the fabric of his coat that she was surprised she did not poke holes in it.

"Did you, Iphiginia?" Marcus touched an unbelievably sensitive spot.

"*No,*" Iphiginia yelped, her voice muffled. "No, my lord. Indeed, I do not—"

"Have there been many?"

Iphiginia could barely think. "Many what?" she asked distractedly. Oh, God, he was doing something to that special place. Rubbing it, tugging gently, circling it with his finger. Everything inside her lower body was twisting into a knot.

"Have there been many lovers since your husband went to his reward?" Marcus eased a finger a very short distance into her feminine passage.

"*No*. Oh, *no*."

"That explains why you are so very snug." He tested her gently with his finger. "Very tight, indeed. You are going to fit me more closely than a new pair of breeches."

Iphiginia knew that if he were not supporting her, bracing her against the statue, she would have crumpled to the floor as though she were made of melted wax.

"Dear heaven," she whispered.

She had never felt so wicked, so sensually abandoned in her life. Clearly she was at last on the verge of surrendering to the ungoverned artistic sensibilities everyone had always assumed that she had inherited from her parents.

During her years in Deepford a great many people had warned her that such inclinations were in the blood and that she must be constantly on guard against them. But until Marcus had come into her life she had been disappointed to discover that she'd had no such interesting inclinations to guard against.

"I am glad that you have not had a string of lovers since your husband's death." Marcus took her earlobe between his teeth. "I have no use for inexperienced females, but I confess to a strong preference for those who have been somewhat discriminating in their choice of lovers."

"I have been extremely discriminating, sir."

"Something tells me that the late Mr. Bright was not very demanding."

"Uh, no." She lost her breath entirely for an instant as he began to stroke her more quickly. "No, he was not. He was a . . . a most considerate gentleman." *Whatever that meant.*

"What a waste." Marcus eased his finger back inside her and probed deliberately. "I assure you I shall not make the same mistake."

Iphiginia cried out. Her whole body seemed to clench around Marcus's hand. She clung to him for dear life and pushed her face deeper into his shoulder as the most inexplicable sensation she had ever known soared through her.

"Bloody hell," Marcus breathed as she quivered in his arms. "So this is how it feels to touch starlight."

Iphiginia could no longer speak. She fought for breath as she went limp.

Marcus's soft laugh held a husky note of masculine satisfaction. He removed his hand slowly from between her legs, steadied her carefully, and began to unfasten his breeches.

Iphiginia barely realized what he was about. She was too busy marveling at the delicious tremors of release that were already swiftly receding into the distance.

"That was really quite astonishing, sir."

"Yes. Quite remarkable. And it will be even

more interesting to be inside you when it happens the next time."

"Inside me?" Iphiginia tried to focus on what he was saying.

"Do not concern yourself, madam. I brought along a condom. French, of course. They do make the best ones, do they not? It is designed to my precise specifications. After some study of the subject, I elected to modify the original design somewhat in order to—"

"For heavens' sake, sir."

Marcus winced. "Forgive me. This is neither the time nor the place for such technical discussions, is it? Sometimes my interest in mechanical and scientific matters gets the better of me. Rest assured that I shall take very good care of you."

Iphiginia was speechless. She had heard of condoms. A charming countess in Italy had once described them to her and Amelia over tea. They were fashioned of sheep gut and secured with little red strings.

A small sound came from the shadowed doorway. It was followed by a woman's giggle. A man hushed her and then chuckled drunkenly.

"Damn it to hell." Marcus hastily refastened his breeches.

"What is it?"

"We are no longer alone." Marcus lowered her skirts and shook them out for her.

"Someone is here? In this chamber?"

"Yes. Are you all right?" He glanced down at her with some concern.

"Yes, of course." Iphiginia felt strangely languid, almost uncaring about the possibility of being discovered in such an embarrassing position.

Reality and the memory of why she had initially encouraged Lord Lartmore to lead her into the statuary hall returned in a rush. She hesitated and glanced toward the far end of the shadowed room.

"There is no need to hide." Marcus sounded amused. "You look quite untouched." He drew his finger along the curve of her bare shoulder and smiled. "Not at all as though you had only recently been imitating one of these statues."

"But I came in here for a reason."

Marcus's expression darkened. "Did you?"

"Yes. I cannot miss the opportunity. I may not get another. This way, sir. Hurry."

More drunken laughter sounded from just inside the doorway. The newcomers had paused to examine the first of the erotic statues.

"What the devil are you up to, Iphiginia?"

"There is another door at the end of the hall.

Lartmore told me that it opens directly onto his library."

"Why in the name of the devil do you—" Realization appeared to dawn on him. "No. Absolutely not. We are not going to pursue your ridiculous plans tonight."

"I may never get another chance."

"Damn it, Iphiginia, this is nonsense. Let's get out of here and find a quiet place where we can finish what we started."

She blushed and glanced at him in surprise. "Do you mean there is more?"

Marcus grimaced. "That is not amusing, madam. I am suffering mightily."

"You appear to be quite fit, sir. Come, this way." Iphiginia grabbed his hand and started through the maze of statuary.

Marcus allowed himself to be dragged toward the rear of the statuary hall. "I am going to regret this, aren't I?"

"Don't be silly." She found the door just as the other couple burst into another bout of raucous laughter and then fell silent.

"Here we are," Iphiginia whispered. She twisted the doorknob. It turned readily enough.

Lartmore's small library—no more than a study, really—was shrouded in darkness. There was just enough moonlight to see the candle on his desk.

A man's hoarse groan echoed down the length of the shadowed hall. "I say, just like the bloody statue, by God. Just like the *statue*."

"Damnation," Marcus muttered. "We cannot go back that way."

He pushed Iphiginia into the library, followed her inside, and quickly closed the door, cutting off the woman's loud moan.

"It's all right, Marcus. They do not know we are here."

He swung around. "Very well, madam. You have got us in here. Now what?"

"I merely want to take a quick look at Lartmore's desk." Iphiginia lit the candle and held it aloft.

Marcus's face was grim. "Are you searching for black wax and a phoenix seal, Iphiginia, or merely looking for something of value to filch?"

She stared at him, stung by the accusation. "You do not think very highly of me, do you, sir?"

"You must admit this situation appears somewhat questionable."

"And you, of course, would immediately question it."

"Given the, ah, unusual nature of our association, I think I have a right to scrutinize your actions."

"You are willing to make love to me, but you do not trust me, is that it?"

"Iphiginia—"

"Never mind, my lord." Iphiginia lifted her chin proudly. "I quite understand. Put your mind at ease; I am not here to steal the silver. I am pursuing my inquiries."

"I told you that Lartmore is highly unlikely to be the blackmailer."

"Yes, I know you expressed your opinion, sir, but I have my own opinions." Iphiginia surveyed the desk, searching for the wax jack. She spotted it at once.

"I see." Marcus propped himself on the corner of the desk and folded his arms across his chest. He watched intently as she studied the design of the seal and the remains of once-molten red wax. "Do you always ignore the opinions of others?"

"I was forced to listen to the opinions of others for years, my lord. I was also obliged to submit to them. But I am an independent woman now."

"An independent woman, eh?"

"Yes. Damnation. There is some sort of flower engraved on this seal, not a phoenix."

Marcus glanced disinterestedly at the seal. "What did you expect to find? Only a fool would use his own distinctive seal and wax on a blackmail note. People would recognize them."

Iphiginia glowered. He had a point. She did not want him to think that she hadn't already considered every possibility. Marcus was too bloody arrogant as it was.

"It has occurred to me that the blackmailer may have two seals, one of which he uses exclusively for his nasty notes," she informed him. "He may even have two different colors of wax, one for his regular correspondence and one for blackmail letters."

"So?"

"So I am hoping to either find the second seal, which he no doubt keeps hidden, or to discover traces of the black wax in his wax jack."

"The jack. Of course." Marcus gave her a look of grudging respect. "Highly unlikely that he would have two jacks to melt wax."

"Precisely. Even if he uses two different colors of wax, he would no doubt melt both in the same jack." Iphiginia examined the wax jack on Lartmore's desk. She could see only traces of red wax.

"Well?" Marcus asked blandly.

"I do not see any bits of black wax."

"I believe I indicated earlier that you would not. Lartmore has his idiosyncrasies, but he is no blackmailer."

Iphiginia set down the wax jack. "Nobody likes a person who is always saying 'I told you so,' my lord."

His mouth curved slightly. "I'll bear that in mind."

"You do that."

Marcus studied her. "Have you got anything else to go on besides the color of the blackmailer's sealing wax and a phoenix design?"

"No." She shot him a disgruntled look. "And even if I did, I'm not at all certain that I would share the information with you, now that I know you do not trust me."

"It is obvious that our association is going to be of a somewhat tricky nature, Mrs. Bright."

"It all seems quite simple to me."

"Does it, indeed?"

"Yes, it does," Iphiginia said coldly. "We are bound by a single mutual interest. We both wish to discover the identity of the blackmailer, although in your case I believe you are merely seeking proof that I am guilty."

"On the contrary, Iphiginia. There is something else that binds us together as surely as the search for the blackmailer."

She gave him a wary glance as she tried one of the desk drawers. "What is that?"

"Passion, my dear Mrs. Bright. Pure, unbridled, honest passion. Or have you already forgotten what happened out in the statuary hall?"

She blushed. "I have not forgotten. I will admit it was a very interesting experience."

"Thank you." He inclined his head with mocking grace.

"I have, however, begun to think that it might be best to avoid such experiences in the future."

Marcus's eyes gleamed in the candlelight. "What makes you think you will be able to avoid them?"

"You will find, my lord, that I am a woman of exceedingly strong willpower. I generally accomplish what I set out to accomplish." She put out the candle. "Come, let's be off. There is nothing of interest here."

"I disagree." Marcus's voice was soft with challenge as he straightened away from the desk. He took her arm. "My interest has been well and truly whetted, my dear Mrs. Bright. And as is the case with yourself, I generally accomplish what I set out to accomplish."

SEVEN

*T*wo days later Iphiginia sat at the desk in her library and studied a sketch of a design she was creating for the first level of a house. It was one of a series of designs that she was completing for the new construction project that she and Amelia were organizing.

The square of town houses was to be known as Bright Place in honor of her parents. The name of the project was still a secret known only to those in Iphiginia's small circle of relatives and to her trusty man of affairs, Adam Manwaring. Until her masquerade was concluded, Iphiginia did not want the name of the square to become widely known. She feared the rumors. At the very least, she would be hounded to death at parties by potential investors. At worst, questions might be raised which could, in turn, invite inquiries into her past.

The houses in Bright Place would be unlike so many of those being built in English towns these days. She had not set out to re-create any one particular classical design. Rather, Iphiginia wanted to produce a harmonious blend of the best of ancient and modern designs.

She was concerned with both exterior and interior elements. Her efforts took into account such factors as the English temperament and the climate. Quality of the building materials would be excellent. In terms of technical design, she planned to incorporate some of the things that she had learned from her perusal of Marcus's theories on building foundations.

She would not be a slave to the classic tradition the way her father had been, she vowed. But neither would she make a mockery of it by allowing the extremely daring artistic impulses that she had inherited from her mother to run wild.

The trick was to create a graceful synthesis. She called upon the skills her father had taught her, of course: perspective, architectural detail, and a knowledge of classical elements. But she also utilized some of the bold style her mother had bequeathed to her.

The secret of her success with Morning Rose

Square, she knew, was that she had never allowed herself to forget that everything she created had to work against an English landscape. She was determined not to make the mistake so many architects made. She would not try to impose buildings designed for the hot, dry climates of Greece and Rome onto the English countryside. Potential purchasers needed homes that could withstand the damp weather and the chill of cold winters.

She eyed her newest design with a critical eye. All of her rooms had high ceilings and stately, well-proportioned windows. Those elements were a legacy from her father. He had been much enamored of the Palladian tradition.

Her new design incorporated classical features as well as graceful staircases and a light, airy feeling which owed nothing to the weighty antique tradition. Iphiginia's artistic instincts told her that the mixture of effects blended well together.

She put down her pen and glanced out the window into the street.

Usually when she concentrated on her designs her thoughts became clear and organized. She often resorted to sketching a library or a drawing room whenever she needed to think about some other, unrelated matter. But this morning the technique was not working.

Her thoughts were in a jumble.

It had been the same yesterday morning.

In fact, it irritated her to realize that she had been suffering from this inability to concentrate properly since Marcus had stridden into the Fenwicks' ballroom and carried her off into the night.

She propped her elbow on the desk and rested her chin on her palm. She had dealt with a great many problems in her life, from those related to raising Corina to the difficulties she and Amelia had encountered on their journeys. But she had never been obliged to deal with anyone quite like Marcus.

She still burned deep inside whenever she recalled the intimate way he had touched her in Lartmore's hall of erotic statuary. Iphiginia wondered if Marcus thought about that encounter at all or if it was such a normal event for him that he had already forgotten about it.

He certainly had not mentioned it during the past two days. Indeed, he had been a paragon of gentlemanly behavior since he had reduced her to that quivering, boneless creature who had gone limp in his arms.

Perhaps he'd had second thoughts about making love to a woman he did not trust.

She scowled at a vegetable seller's cart that was rumbling down the street. She had absolutely no intention of allowing Marcus to touch her in that shatteringly intimate manner ever again.

Not unless he developed true trust, respect, and, yes, some degree of affection for her.

She did not think that she was asking for too much. After all, she was in love with the man. The least he could do was demonstrate some warmth of feeling.

Unfortunately, she did not think that Marcus recognized love when he saw it.

His experience of life had obviously made him too wary, too cynical, too self-controlled to enable him to surrender easily to love. He would be extremely cautious about opening himself to any emotion that he feared would render him vulnerable.

Thus far she had not discovered the precise events in his past which had influenced his temperament, but she could not deny the facts. Marcus had been badly scarred.

She was willing to be sympathetic and understanding up to a point. She was even willing to make a few allowances. But if he thought that she would accept him as a paramour when he had made it plain that he did not even trust her, let alone love her, he was very much mistaken.

Iphiginia wondered if he recognized her determination on that point. He was a very intelligent man, after all. Perhaps that was the reason he had not attempted to press his attentions on her since the other night.

He was the sort of man who would think matters through carefully before making his next move.

The library door opened.

"Iphiginia?" Amelia, dressed in a gray high-necked gown that made her look considerably older than her twenty-six years, came into the room. "Mrs. Shaw is bringing tea."

"I could use a cup. I need to collect my thoughts before Mr. Manwaring arrives."

"He will be here shortly." Amelia glanced at the clock. "He is a punctual person. By the bye, I have made a preliminary list of widows and spinsters who might be interested in participating in our new venture."

"Are they all from the investment pool we formed for Morning Rose Square?"

"Most of them are, but two of them are new. A Miss Sanders and a Miss Crest. I met them at the museum last week. They are both paid companions who have managed to set aside a small amount to invest."

"Excellent." A thought struck Iphiginia. "That reminds me, I ran into Mrs. Osworth in Pall Mall the other day. She mentioned that she was interviewing a new companion. The woman was from the Wycherley Agency."

Amelia grimaced. "I'm not surprised. The Wycherley Agency caters to families such as the Osworths. Very exclusive."

"I thought the name rang a bell. That was the agency which employed you, was it not?"

"Yes." Amelia's mouth tightened. "It's been in business for years."

A discreet knock sounded on the library door. Iphiginia glanced at it. "What is it, Mrs. Shaw?"

Mrs. Shaw, as solidly built and very nearly as stately as a classical ruin, opened the door. "Mr. Manwaring to see you, Mrs. Bright."

"Please send him in."

Mrs. Shaw stepped aside to usher the visitor into the library. Iphiginia and Amelia greeted him with welcoming smiles.

"I did not hear your carriage, Mr. Manwaring," Iphiginia said.

"It's such a fine day that I chose to walk." Adam Manwaring smiled at both women. His eyes lingered warmly on Amelia, who appeared to be oblivious.

Adam was an earnest, sober-minded man of twenty-seven years. He was the youngest son of a country squire who owned lands in the north. With no hope of inheriting his father's property, Adam had been obliged to forge a path for himself in the world. He had an excellent head for numbers and details and it had led him to his present career as a secretary and man of affairs.

Three years ago Iphiginia and Amelia had become his exclusive employers. He was devoted to them. His allegiance had been based initially on the fact that the two had hired him after he had begun to despair of ever finding a good position. His youth and lack of connections had made it difficult for him to secure clients.

Adam's unwavering loyalty to Iphiginia and Amelia was now cemented by considerably more than gratitude. It was also based on a solid financial interest. He had scraped together every penny he could put his hands on to join them in the Morning Rose Square venture. A year ago Adam had taken his hefty profits together with the widows and spinsters who had formed the investment pool.

Although Iphiginia had complete trust in Adam, she had not told him about her scheme to catch a blackmailer. He had been instructed to be absolutely discreet concerning her identity. Adam assumed she merely wished to remain anonymous and to keep her connection to the investment pool a secret so that she would not be pestered by interested parties.

Adam did not move in social circles and had little interest in gossip. He was very aware of

who was who in the *ton,* however, and, more
important, he knew a great deal concerning
their financial affairs.

"Please have a seat, Mr. Manwaring."
Iphiginia pretended not to notice the tinge of
red in Adam's cheeks as he fixed his wistful
attention on Amelia.

Iphiginia wanted to give her cousin a shake.
Could not Amelia see that she and Adam were
perfect for each other? she wondered.

Iphiginia had recognized instantly that the
two were well suited a few weeks ago, directly
after she and Amelia had met Adam in person
for the first time. Until then, their transactions
with him had been conducted through the post.

Adam's honest, open countenance made it
easy to read his reactions. There was no doubt
that he had developed a tendre for Amelia, although he had not yet worked up the courage
to make an overture.

"How are things progressing with Bright
Place?" Iphiginia asked as Adam sat down on
the other side of her desk.

"I am happy to say that the initial plans are
almost complete." Adam's expression became
very intent. He leaned forward to spread out
his neatly penned papers on Iphiginia's desk.
"Final arrangements have been made to secure
the property. I have also drawn up an agreement with the same builder that we used on

Morning Rose Square. It remains only to complete our list of investors."

"I have drawn up a preliminary list of interested people," Amelia said.

"Excellent." Adam's cheeks became slightly more ruddy. "The usual names, I presume?"

"Yes, and two new ones."

Adam glowed with admiration. "Very good. By the bye, rumors are abounding now that we have secured the property. I have had some inquiries from wealthy gentlemen who have heard about the profits that were made by the investors in Morning Rose Square. They have expressed an interest in our new venture."

Iphiginia gave him a sharp look. "They do not know that Miss Farley and I are the principals in the venture, do they?"

"No, no, of course not," Adam assured her swiftly. "You know that I would never abuse your confidence in that regard. Whenever I have had inquiries on the subject, I have always explained that the two people who organize the ventures prefer to remain anonymous."

Iphiginia relaxed. "Good. I do not want to be hounded by potential investors at various social affairs. Most unpleasant."

"I quite understand," Adam said.

Amelia tapped a quill pen against the sheet of foolscap that she held. "Who are the gentlemen who wish to invest in our new project?"

"I have the names with me." Adam picked up a sheet of paper from the pile he had put down on Iphiginia's desk. "Let me see. Matthews, Conklin, Jenerette, Dodgson . . ."

Amelia froze.

Iphiginia stared at Adam. "Dodgson, did you say?"

Adam glanced up with a puzzled frown. "Yes. Mr. Anthony Dodgson. Rumor has it that he's got his finances in something of a muddle and is anxious to repair them through some profitable investments. Do you know him?"

"No." Iphiginia was careful not to look at Amelia's white face. "I have never met him. But I have heard of him. He is not the sort of person with whom we wish to associate ourselves, is he, Miss Farley?"

"No." Amelia's voice was almost inaudible. She swallowed visibly and tried again. "No, indeed not."

Iphiginia gave Adam a direct look. "You may inform Mr. Dodgson that he is not welcome to invest in our venture. We shall give some consideration to the other names on your list, but, personally, I prefer to keep wealthy and influential men out of the pool. That type has a tendency to try to take charge. We do very nicely on our own."

"Very well." Adam glanced at Amelia's stricken face and then he turned back to

Iphiginia with a worried expression. "May I ask why Dodgson is to be excluded? He will surely ask for an explanation."

Iphiginia centered one of the pages containing architectural elevations for Bright Place in front of her. "You may inform Mr. Dodgson that the majority of investors involved in the project are widows and spinsters."

"Yes, I have already told him as much," Adam said.

"You may also remind Dodgson that many widows and spinsters have been obliged to work as paid companions and governesses. As Mr. Dodgson has a reputation for treating such female employees in a thoroughly unprincipled manner, they do not wish to do business with him."

"I see." Adam's clear eyes narrowed. "I had not realized that the man was a cad. I shall take great pleasure in telling him that the members of the investment pool do not want him in their number."

Amelia sagged slightly with evident relief. The paper she was holding trembled in her fingers.

"That is settled, then." Iphiginia bent over her drawing. "Let us get down to work."

Marcus drew the sleek black phaeton to a halt in front of Iphiginia's town house with a stylish flourish. He tossed the reins to his groom and leaped down onto the pavement.

"I shall return in a few minutes."

"Aye, m'lord." The groom steadied the fresh, eager stallions.

The door of the town house opened just as Marcus started up the steps. A soberly dressed, serious-faced man emerged.

"I beg your pardon." The man paused when he saw Marcus. He blinked once or twice in the sunlight. Then his gaze went briefly to the crest etched in gold on the black phaeton. "My lord." He inclined his head politely and then hurried down the steps.

Marcus paused with one booted foot on the top step. He turned to watch the other man hurry off down the street. His jaw tightened.

Damnation, he thought. This was not jealousy he was experiencing. He never allowed himself to feel jealous. He was merely annoyed to find himself tripping over another man on Iphiginia's front steps.

It was a perfectly normal reaction, Marcus assured himself. Any male in his situation would feel irritated in such circumstances. Assuming, of course that there was any other male in Town who found himself in such a unique situation.

Highly unlikely.

The odds were that he was the only man in

the whole of England who possessed a mistress-in-name-only.

Marcus absently stripped off his York tan
driving gloves. The only time he ever wore
gloves was when he rode or drove. Otherwise
he ignored the fashion. He supposed that it was
a perverse streak in his nature that made him
refuse to conceal his very unfashionable, work-
roughened hands from the eyes of polite society.

"May I help you, sir?" the housekeeper inquired from the open doorway.

Marcus turned slowly around to face her.
"Please inform Mrs. Bright that Masters has
come for her."

"Yes, m'lord. Please come in. Mrs. Bright is
in the library."

Marcus glanced at the closed door to the left
of the hall. "On second thought, don't bother
to announce me. I'll take care of it."

"But yer lordship—"

Marcus ignored the fluttering housekeeper.
He opened the library door himself and strode
into the room. Iphiginia was seated at her desk,
a vision in white muslin and a little white lace
cap. Her cousin sat across from her. Both
women glanced up in surprise.

"Masters." Iphiginia's eyes lit briefly with a
warm welcome. A second later, her expression
altered to one of sudden alarm. She hastily

thrust several sheets of foolscap that were lying on her desk beneath a large pattern book. "I heard a carriage in the street, but I did not realize it was yours. I was not expecting you until one."

"Good day, ladies." Marcus shut the door and walked straight to the desk. Unfortunately, he was too late to get a look at the papers Iphiginia had hidden under the pattern book. "I thought it would be a good idea to get an early start so that we will have plenty of time at the museum."

"Yes, of course." Iphiginia looked at Amelia. "Would you mind entertaining his lordship while I go upstairs to fetch my pelisse and bonnet?"

"Not at all," Amelia murmured.

Iphiginia rose and hastened out of the room.

Marcus and Amelia exchanged assessing looks. There was no point being subtle, Marcus decided. The woman already disliked him.

"Who was that gentleman who was leaving just as I arrived?"

"Mr. Manwaring."

"I see. I don't believe I know him."

"I doubt that he moves in your circles, my lord." Amelia gave him a repressive look. "Would you care for tea while you wait?"

"No, thank you. He seemed in something of a hurry."

"Who?"

"Mr. Manwaring."

"Oh, did he?" Amelia picked up a sheaf of papers and straightened them. "Perhaps he had a business appointment."

"He had the look of a secretary or a man of affairs."

Amelia hesitated. "No doubt that is because he is a man of affairs. Are you certain you won't have some tea, my lord?"

"No, thank you." Marcus perused the titles of some of the volumes on the library shelves. Such respected and oft-reprinted works on classical architecture as Desgodetz's *Les Edifices Antiques de Rome* and Langley's *Ancient Architecture Restored & Improved* sat side by side with Hope's *Household Furniture and Decoration* and Halfpenny's *The Art of Sound Building*. "How long have you lived with your cousin, Miss Farley?"

"Nearly five years." Amelia spoke cautiously, as if weighing every word.

"You lived with her while her husband was alive, then?" Marcus said easily.

"Ah, yes. Yes, I did."

"I have a vague recollection of having known a Bright family at one time." Marcus paused briefly as though reflecting on a very distant memory. "From the Lake District, I believe."

Amelia scowled. "I doubt if there is any connection. Mrs. Bright's husband had no relatives
in the Lake District."

"Then he must have been connected to the
Yorkshire Brights," Marcus said smoothly.

"No," Amelia said swiftly. "They were a
Devon family."

"I see. I knew some Devon Brights. They
lived near Plymouth."

"There is no connection, then," Amelia assured him. "Mr. Bright's people were from the
northern part."

"Barnstaple, then."

"No, Deepford," Amelia said quickly. "A
very tiny village."

"I do not believe I know it."

Amelia looked relieved to hear that. "The
Deepford Brights were a very small family,"
she said in a determinedly chatty manner. "Mr.
Bright was the last of his line."

"How unfortunate. Then there are no
heirs?"

"No."

"Are you enjoying London, Miss Farley?"

"I find it very interesting." Amelia looked almost pathetically grateful for a change of topic.
"Quite educational."

"Very different from the country."

"Indeed."

"I take it that you and Mrs. Bright were not able to come to Town very often while Mr. Bright was alive?"

"Mr. Bright was infirm. He did not care to travel."

"I see." This was not getting him anywhere, Marcus decided. He would have to try a different tack. "Perhaps I'll have some tea, after all."

Amelia jumped to her feet. "I'll ask Mrs. Shaw to bring a fresh pot."

Silence descended on the library as Marcus and Amelia waited for the tea to be brought in.

When it arrived, Marcus accepted a cup, picked it up, and paced to the window beside Iphiginia's desk. He studied the sunny street scene.

"A fine day for an outing." Marcus surreptitiously tilted his cup and casually spilled tea on a copy of the *Morning Post* which was lying on the end of the desk.

"Oh, dear," Amelia gasped.

"Damnation. How very clumsy of me."

Amelia started to her feet. "It will mar the wood."

"Fetch your housekeeper," Marcus ordered in the tone of voice he reserved for those occasions when he wanted instant obedience. It always seemed to work and he had grown to expect the results he invariably got. Except with

Iphiginia, he reflected wryly. She was not very good at following orders.

"I'll call Mrs. Shaw." Amelia hurried toward the door.

Marcus yanked a large handkerchief out of his pocket and began blotting up the tea. "I do not believe there will be any great harm done if you hurry."

"I hope not." Amelia threw him a disapproving look over her shoulder. "Iphiginia is very fond of that desk. Her father designed it." She opened the door. "Mrs. Shaw? Please come quickly. Some tea has been spilled."

Marcus casually lifted the edge of the pattern book and glanced at the top sheet of foolscap. He realized that he was looking at what appeared to be an architectural elevation for a row of town houses. The words "Bright Place" were inscribed beneath the picture.

He lowered the pattern book back into place just as Amelia turned around.

"Mrs. Shaw is on her way," Amelia said.

"I believe I have blotted up most of the tea. The newspaper has absorbed the rest." Marcus folded his tea-stained handkerchief.

Mrs. Shaw bustled into the room. She carried a cloth in one hand. "Here, now, where's the tea spill?"

"Over here." Marcus stepped back from the

desk. "My fault entirely, I fear. I think I got most of it, however."

Iphiginia appeared in the doorway. She was wearing a white pelisse over her white muslin gown. She carried a white straw bonnet in one hand and a large apron in the other.

She frowned in concern at the commotion in the library. "What happened?"

Marcus stared at her for a few brief seconds. She looked as pure and chaste as new-fallen snow. What a pity that there was nothing so deceiving as innocence.

He quickly recovered himself. "A small disaster. I spilled some tea. There is no damage to your desk."

"I'm relieved to hear that." Iphiginia put on her bonnet and tied the strings. She smiled cheerfully. "Well, then, shall we be off, my lord? I am eager to see the museum's collection of Greek vases."

"By all means," Marcus said. He glanced at the apron she carried. "What is that for?"

Iphiginia grimaced. "White is a very effective color for some purposes, but it has its disadvantages."

Half an hour later Marcus stood with Iphiginia in the gloom of a vast tomblike museum hall.

The high-ceilinged chamber was crammed

with broken statuary, chunks of stone, and assorted bits and pieces taken from old ruins.
Dust motes danced in the shafts of sunlight fil-
tering through the upper windows. The hush of
antiquity blanketed the scene.

Iphiginia, clad in her apron, moved through
the sepulchral atmosphere with cheerful disre-
gard for her oppressive surroundings. Her enthusiasm was contagious, Marcus realized.

Although he had once made a superficial
study of the more intriguing construction details of the classical style, antiquities had never
been a subject of particular interest for him.
He was a man of the modern age. Generally speaking, he preferred to devote his attention to such things as astronomy and steam
engines.

Today, however, he found himself consumed
by a rare fascination with archaeological matters.

He watched as Iphiginia studied the designs
on a row of ancient vases. She was beautiful
when she was absorbed in intellectual contemplation, he realized. Almost as beautiful as she
had been the other night when she had found
her release in his arms in Lartmore's statuary
hall.

If he had not known better, he would have
thought it was the first time she had ever been
brought to such a sensual peak by a man.

Without any warning, desire, hot, sweet, and urgent, whipped through him. It left him shaken and half-aroused. And ruefully annoyed.

These abrupt, fiery rushes of passion were coming upon him with increasing frequency of late. Each time they crashed through him, they seemed stronger. This morning he had awakened at dawn to discover himself as hard as any marble statue.

This afternoon he was growing heavy with arousal just watching Iphiginia in a museum. It would have been ludicrous if it were not so bloody uncomfortable.

The anticipation growing within him was almost unbearable in its intensity. Soon, he thought. Very soon he would have to make love to her.

It had to be soon or he would become a candidate for Bedlam.

He forced himself to contemplate the large vase that had caught her attention. "Etruscan, do you think?"

"No. Definitely Grecian." Iphiginia glanced up at another row of dust-laden vases. "Quite spectacular, are they not? The forms are so perfect, so exquisitely right. There is such an impressive combination of intellect and art in the designs."

"Most impressive," Marcus agreed, his gaze riveted to the gentle curves of her breasts.

She turned her head and saw him studying her bosom. Her face grew very pink. "Have you learned anything useful yet, my lord?"

"About Greek vases?"

"Of course. That is what we are discussing, is it not?"

Marcus lounged against a rubble of old stones, folded his arms across his chest, and contemplated a vase. "I have learned a great deal, my dear Mrs. Bright, but not nearly enough."

She smiled with glowing approval, as though he were a precocious student. "It is your nature to constantly thirst for more, my lord. The passions of the intellect are difficult to satisfy, are they not?"

"Indeed. Fortunately not all passions are impossible to assuage, Iphiginia. Some merely require the proper time and place."

Barclay, Marcus's stout, bespectacled man of affairs, hurried into his employer's library shortly before four o'clock that afternoon. He was out of breath. Sweat beaded his balding head.

"You sent for me, sir?"

"I did." Marcus looked up from the notes he

had been making. "Thank you for coming so quickly."

"Not at all, m'lord." Barclay sat down gratefully, pulled out a handkerchief, and mopped his brow. "You know that I am always pleased to assist you. What do you wish me to do for you?"

"Two things. First, I want you to make inquiries about a property called Bright Place. I do not know much about it, but I believe that it may be a new speculation venture."

"This is a property here in London?"

"I'm not certain. I suppose it could be in Bath." Marcus recalled the elevations he had seen on Iphiginia's desk. "One of the two places, most likely, although I suppose the property could be located in some other large town. The drawings I saw were of buildings that were clearly designed for a city, if you know what I mean."

"I see." Barclay stifled a small sigh, adjusted his spectacles, and made a note.

"Second, I want you to discover whatever information you can about a certain Mr. Bright."

Barclay raised suddenly wary eyes. He cleared his throat cautiously. "Ah, would that be the *late* Mr. Bright?"

"It would."

"The deceased husband of a certain Mrs. Iphiginia Bright of Morning Rose Square?"

Marcus smiled coolly. "One of the things that makes you so invaluable to me, Barclay, is that you are always possessed of the latest gossip and rumor."

Barclay ignored that. He scowled. "You wish me to discover whatever I can about a dead man, m'lord?"

"Precisely." Marcus leaned back in his chair. He picked up his newly modified hydraulic reservoir pen and examined the steel nib with care. There was no sign of a leak. "You will be discreet, naturally."

"Naturally." Barclay mopped his forehead with his handkerchief once again. "Where would you suggest that I start looking for information on the late Mr. Bright?"

"I believe that you will want to begin your quest in Devon."

"Devon is a rather large place, m'lord. Have you any notion of precisely where in Devon I should look?"

"You might try a little town called Deepford."

EIGHT

*I*phiginia swept into Zoe's drawing room at
ten minutes after three the following afternoon. Amelia was right behind her.

"We came as quickly as we could." Iphiginia
glanced first at her aunt, who was ensconced on
her new red velvet Roman sofa. Then she
looked across the room at Lord Otis, who was
helping himself to a glass of brandy.

"Thank God you're here," Zoe said in a
voice that held elements of a Greek tragedy.

Otis, a short, stocky, kindly faced man with
thinning gray hair and bushy brows, gave
Iphiginia and Amelia a look of grim despair.
"Disaster has struck again."

"What on earth is wrong?" Iphiginia untied
the strings of her ruffled, high-crowned white

bonnet. "Your note said something dreadful had occurred, Aunt Zoe."

"I have received another blackmail demand," Zoe said. She picked up a folded sheet of foolscap and handed it to Iphiginia. "See for yourself."

Iphiginia took the note. She glanced at the broken black wax seal with its all-too-familiar phoenix emblem and then read the contents aloud.

Madam:
If you wish for continued silence on a certain very personal matter you must bring five thousand pounds to the new sepulchral monument constructed for Mrs. Eaton at Reeding Cemetery. Come on the stroke of midnight tonight. The money must be placed on the stone in the center of the monument.
Come alone, madam, or the price will double the next time.
Yrs.
The Phoenix

Amelia sat down heavily on a chair. "So we were right. The first one was only the beginning."

"I told you this would happen," Otis muttered darkly. He went across the room to where Zoe sat and put a comforting hand on her shoulder. "Blackmailers always come back for more. It's the nature of the beast."

"What am I going to do?" Zoe wailed. "I could handle the first payment and I suppose that I can handle a second. This blackmailer seems to be shrewd enough to keep his demands within reason. But I cannot continue to pay blackmail for the rest of my life. Sooner or later he will surely bleed me dry."

"We'll find the bastard," Otis vowed. "And when we do, I'll personally wring his neck."

Zoe lifted one hand to touch Otis's fingers in a grateful gesture. She looked at Iphiginia. "Have you discovered anything at all?"

Iphiginia sank down slowly onto a claw-footed chair. "I believe I have eliminated three of the men who played cards regularly with Guthrie eighteen years ago and who also move in Masters's circle."

"Which ones?" Otis demanded.

"Lartmore, Judson, and Darrow. I have managed to get into all of their studies or libraries and examine their wax jacks and seals. None of them appear to use black wax. Nor did I discover any seals engraved with a phoenix."

"They may have hidden both the seals and the wax," Amelia pointed out.

"Yes, I know," Iphiginia said. "Masters remarked upon that possibility also. But I searched their desks very carefully. In any event, we have no choice but to continue along this line of inquiry. The black wax and the phoenix seal are the only clues that we have."

"They have got us nowhere thus far." Zoe slumped back against the curve of the sofa and heaved a theatrical sigh. "I am lost. What are we going to do?"

"There, there, do not take on so, m'dear." Otis patted her shoulder. "We'll find a way out of this."

Iphiginia refolded the note and contemplated the seal. "I wonder if Masters's friend has also received a second blackmail note."

Amelia frowned. "An excellent question."

"I know nothing of the demands his acquaintance may have received," Zoe muttered. "But I can tell you that I must act immediately. The note said that the money is to be delivered to the appointed place at precisely midnight tonight."

"A cemetery at midnight," Iphiginia mused. "How very melodramatic. It would seem our blackmailer has been reading some of Mrs. Radcliffe's gothic novels."

"Either that or he enjoys amusing himself in this strange manner," Zoe muttered.

"Yes." Iphiginia made her decision. "I shall deliver the money this time."

Zoe, Amelia, and Otis stared at her in amazement.

"Absolutely not," Zoe said. "Otis will handle it, just as he did last time."

"You cannot possibly undertake such a dangerous task, Iphiginia," Amelia said.

"Quite right," Otis announced. "I'll deal with it."

Iphiginia raised a hand for silence. "The note specifically instructs Zoe to bring the money. That means the villain will no doubt be watching from the shadows to see that his orders are carried out. He will expect to see a woman. If he does not, he may very well ask for ten thousand pounds next time."

"Ten thousand pounds." Zoe looked as though she were about to faint.

Otis produced her vinaigrette. "Here, m'dear."

"Thank you." Zoe took a gentle whiff of the smelling salts.

Otis scowled at Iphiginia. "You cannot make the delivery. Someone is bound to recognize that little white carriage of yours and wonder what you are about visiting a cemetery at midnight."

"Do not concern yourself. I shall be perfectly safe." Iphiginia frowned in thought. "I'll use a hackney coach and I shall pay the coachman to wait for me. I shall dress anonymously and wear a cloak with a hood that will conceal my features. If the villain sees me, he will assume it is Zoe."

"But Iphiginia"—Zoe looked horrified— "it's a cemetery, for goodness' sake. At midnight, no less."

"After a year traipsing about the ruins of Italy, I am quite accustomed to sepulchral ruins."

"This is hardly the same thing as a visit to Pompeii," Amelia muttered. "Zoe is right. It is much too dangerous."

"Cannot allow it," Otis said authoritatively.

"Nonsense," Iphiginia said. "There is no danger. The blackmailer is hardly likely to murder the person who leaves the money. That would be rather like killing the goose that laid the golden eggs."

Zoe looked aghast. "*Murder*. Dear heaven. I thought we'd at least established that the villain is not a murderer."

"A poor choice of words," Iphiginia said quickly. "What I meant to say was that there is no reason the blackmailer would want to hurt me."

"I'll come with you," Amelia said.

Otis's brows jiggled up and down. "So will I."

"I must come, too," Zoe said.

"No, no, no." Iphiginia shook her head impatiently. "Impossible. The blackmailer might see the three of you and decide to make good on his threat to increase the demands. No, we must obey his instructions to the letter."

Amelia frowned. "Why are you so determined to make the delivery this time, Iphiginia?"

"I am hoping to learn something useful," Iphiginia admitted.

Zoe's eyes widened. "Never tell me that you are going to try to observe the blackmailer as he picks up the money. I cannot possibly allow you to take such a risk."

"No, of course not," Iphiginia said. "I would not do anything so rash."

But that was precisely what she intended.

Tonight's visit to Reeding Cemetery might well be an opportunity to discover a useful clue to the villain's identity.

At ten minutes to midnight the hackney carriage clattered to a halt at the fog-shrouded gates of Reeding Cemetery.

Iphiginia, dressed in an old nondescript gray gown and a long gray cloak, peered out into the darkness.

Tendrils of cold mist coiled around the tombstones and monuments that dotted the small cemetery. The pale glow from the hackney's lamps penetrated only a short distance into the fog. Iphiginia shivered as she collected the canvas bag full of banknotes and a lantern and prepared to descend from the carriage.

The blackmailer could not have chosen a more unnerving setting than this, she thought as she opened the door. It had clearly been a deliberate ploy to frighten his victim. She wondered if he had even been clever enough to predict the fog.

She stepped down from the carriage, hoisted the lantern, and looked up at the coachman.

"I shall return very shortly."

The coachman's face was heavily shadowed by the broad brim of his hat. "Ye certain ye want to pay yer respects to the dear departed at this unholy hour, ma'am?"

"I promised," Iphiginia said. "It meant a great deal to the poor woman to know that I would carry out her last request."

"She's long past knowin' if ye fulfill her bloody stupid request, if ye ask me. Well, go on, then. I'll wait 'ere for ye."

"Thank you."

Iphiginia walked to the gates of the cemetery. She was not certain what she would do if they were locked.

But the heavy iron gates swung slowly inward when she pushed against them.

Iphiginia stepped into the graveyard. She

held the lantern aloft and tried to peer through the mist. The light illuminated the first row of tombstones.

Iphiginia pressed on deeper into the cemetery. She read the names on the stones as she went past.

John George Brindle, aged three years,
    one month.

Mary Alice Harvey, beloved wife and
    mother.

Edward Shipley, b. 1785, d. 1815. A brave
    soldier. A good friend.

An oppressive weight settled on Iphiginia. It sent an icy shudder through her soul.

Amelia had been right. This was a considerably different experience than a tour of the ruins of Pompeii.

But there had been no choice. Iphiginia knew that Zoe would not have lasted two minutes in this ghostly place. Her dramatic imagination would have been overcome by the atmosphere. She would not have been able to make the delivery and the result would have no doubt meant steeper demands from the blackmailer.

The yawning entrance of a large stone grotto loomed in the fog directly in front of Iphiginia.

The twin halves of an elaborately designed iron gate stood open. The dark, shadowed interior beckoned.

Iphiginia caught her breath and held the lantern higher. She had never thought of herself as possessing melodramatic sensibilities or an impressionable temperament, but this was very nearly too much, even for her.

The flaring lantern light picked out the name that had been carved above the arched doorway.

Elizabeth Eaton, b. 1771, d. 1817
Ill-treated in life, may she rest in peace

Iphiginia hesitated on the brink of the monument's threshold. The lantern illuminated only the first few feet of the stone passageway.

A cold, damp draft seemed to emanate from the depths of the sepulchral grotto.

Iphiginia's pulse raced so swiftly that it made her feel light-headed. Her stomach churned. The urge to turn and flee back to the waiting hackney nearly overwhelmed her.

She clutched the bag of banknotes tightly, took a deep breath, and walked a few paces into the grotto.

It was as though she were walking into a cave.

The darkness was so deep that even the lantern light appeared to weaken in the face of it. Iphiginia could see that whoever had built and dedicated the monument had spared no expense. The stone walls were heavily carved. The design was a strange combination of twisting vines and open books.

Iphiginia raised the lantern to read the words that had been engraved on one of the stone books:

The path of vengeance takes many twists and turns but it is sure and certain.

The terrible groan of iron hinges sounded from the open mouth of the grotto.

Iphiginia spun around, a scream on her lips. *"No."*

She dropped the sack of money and ran for the entrance.

She was too late. A cloaked figure appeared briefly in the mist. The iron gates slammed shut. The ominous rasp of a key in a lock echoed down the passageway.

Iphiginia fought back terror as she raced toward the gate. "Wait. Please, wait. I'm in here."

She reached the sealed gates just in time to see the cloaked figure disappear into the fog. She gripped the iron bars of the gates and shoved with all her strength. They did not budge.

She was trapped in the sepulchral grotto.

She opened her mouth to call for help. Surely the coachman who had brought her here would be able to hear her. But even as the thought occurred, she heard the receding clatter of carriage wheels and steel horseshoes on the pavement.

The hackney was leaving.

"Help me," Iphiginia shouted into the dark mist. "I'm here, in the grotto. Please come back."

There was no sound from the graveyard. The mist seemed to thicken at the gates of the grotto as though preparing to invade the interior.

A rush of anger overcame Iphiginia's panic. *"Bloody hell."*

Then she noticed the small piece of paper lying at her feet. She bent down and picked up the note. The lantern light revealed that the missive was sealed with black wax.

You have been warned. The next time you interfere, the penalty will be far more serious.

"Bloody hell." Iphiginia glanced at the lantern. She wondered how much longer it would continue to burn.

And then she wondered what Marcus was doing and whether or not he had noticed that she had not turned up at the Sheltenhams' ball.

Marcus stopped pacing the length of Iphiginia's library when he heard the door open. He swung around to confront Amelia. She was wearing a nightcap and a chintz wrapper. Her face was pale and strained.

"Where the devil is she, Miss Farley? And before you answer, you had better know that I am in no mood for lies. Iphiginia was to meet me at one o'clock at the Sheltenhams'. It is now nearly two."

"My lord, I will not claim to be your greatest supporter, but I do believe I am rather glad to see you tonight." Amelia closed the door and walked into the room. She glanced at the tall clock. "I have been growing increasingly anxious since midnight."

"Anxious about what?" Marcus clenched his fingers around the edge of the marble mantel. The disturbing sensation he had begun to experience sometime during the past hour was riding him hard now. Something was wrong.

"It is Iphiginia, my lord. I am very worried."

"What is she about this time? If you tell me that she has taken it into her head to explore some other man's study in search of black wax and a phoenix seal, I vow I will not be responsible for my actions. I have had enough of her reckless ways."

Amelia clutched the lapels of her prim wrapper and regarded Marcus with somber eyes. "She is at Reeding Cemetery."

Marcus stared at her, dumbfounded. "A cemetery? At this hour? For God's sake, why?"

"Lady Guthrie received another blackmail note."

"Damn it to hell."

"The instructions were to leave the money at a new sepulchral monument in Reeding Cemetery. Iphiginia undertook to carry out the task in her aunt's place."

Marcus felt as if he had just stepped off a cliff. For an instant raw fear gripped his gut. And then rage swept through him. "How did she dare to do something like this without telling me?"

"Iphiginia knows that you do not trust her. Why should she trust you with all of her secrets?"

"She goes too far this time." Marcus strode toward the door.

"My lord, where are you going?"

"Where do you think I'm going? Reeding Cemetery."

"Thank you," Amelia whispered. "I have been so concerned."

"Save your thanks. I doubt that Iphiginia will

be glad to see me. In my present mood, I am bound to prove even less amusing company for her than the ghosts in the cemetery."

The gates of Reeding Cemetery stood open. The gravestones and monuments beyond were barely visible in the mist.

Marcus got out of the carriage, a lantern in one hand and a pistol in the other. He glanced up at Dinks. "Wait here."

"Aye, m'lord. Would ye be wantin' any assistance?"

"No. Watch the gates. If anyone tries to leave before I do, stop him."

"Aye, m'lord." Dinks reached under his box for the pistol he kept hidden among his carriage tools. "I'll take care o' the matter for ye."

Marcus walked into the graveyard and contemplated his surroundings for a moment. The swirling gray mist was so thick that he could not see much farther than the nearest rows of headstones.

He glanced down. The flaring light of the lantern revealed crushed damp grass between a row of stones. Someone else had come this way quite recently. It was impossible to tell whether the person had been entering or leaving the cemetery.

Marcus went forward swiftly, following the

trail of matted grass. He ignored the smaller tombstones, searching for the larger, more imposing monuments that various people had erected in honor of the dear departed.

The dark mouth of a grotto loomed up suddenly in the fog. The deep sense of foreboding that plagued Marcus grew abruptly more intense. The footsteps he followed went right up to the gate and disappeared on the other side.

A dim glow of light from deep within the monument indicated the presence of a fading lantern.

"Iphiginia."

Marcus strode to the gate and discovered at once that it was locked. He put the lantern down on the ground but kept the pistol in his hand. He shook the iron bars with the fury of a caged beast. The heavy gate rattled on its hinges. "Iphiginia, are you in there? For God's sake, answer me."

"Marcus." The lantern light drew closer. Footsteps sounded on the stone floor of the grotto. "Thank heavens, it's you."

"Bloody hell." Marcus watched as Iphiginia appeared at the end of the passageway. "I'll kill whoever is responsible for this, I swear it."

Iphiginia rushed toward the gate from the depths of the grotto. She stumbled to a halt on the other side of the iron bars. Her heavy gray cloak swirled around her. Her eyes were huge in the shadows of the hood.

Marcus's stomach clenched when he saw the stark expression that drew her delicate face taut. Her soft mouth trembled. She was breathing much too quickly. It was clear that fear had come close to tearing her apart, but she had somehow managed to retain her self-control.

Marcus knew that only sheer willpower had kept Iphiginia from succumbing to panic. Intense admiration for her courage surged through him.

"I saw the lantern light." There was a tremulous quality in Iphiginia's voice, but her words were astonishingly steady. She gripped one of the iron gate bars. "I prayed it would be you, but I could not be certain, so I stayed back inside the grotto."

Marcus put his hand through the bars and caught her chin. "I shall fetch my coachman. He will likely have something among his carriage tools that I can use to open this lock. Stay right where you are. I shall be back in a moment."

Iphiginia smiled weakly. "I am not going anywhere."

"No," Marcus agreed grimly. "And I do not believe that you will be going anywhere again at night without me."

.   .   .

It took nearly fifteen minutes for Marcus to break the lock on the monument gate. When it finally came apart in his hands, he tossed the hammer and chisel to Dinks.

"Here, take these."

"Yes m'lord." Dinks took charge of the tools.

Marcus jerked open the gate. He started into the passageway but halted abruptly as Iphiginia flew out of the grotto.

He braced himself when he realized that she was heading straight toward him.

"Marcus."

Deep satisfaction swept through him when she hurled herself into his arms. He caught her and held her very tightly until she stopped shivering.

"Hell and damnation, woman. Do not ever, *ever* do this to me again," he growled into her hair. Then he looked at Dinks over the top of her head. "Let us be off."

"Ye won't get any argument from me, m'lord." Dinks wrinkled his nose as he surveyed the sepulchral grotto. "Don't much fancy hanging around a graveyard at any time, let alone at three in the mornin'."

Iphiginia raised her head and looked at Marcus and Dinks. "Thank you both," she whispered. "I shall always be grateful."

"Not at all, m'lady." Dinks tipped his hat. "Not at all. I've been in his lordship's employ for nearly ten years now. Don't generally see this sort of excitement. Kind o' livens things up a bit."

"Come." Marcus took a firm grip on Iphiginia's arm. "We have wasted enough time in this damnable place."

He hurried Iphiginia down a long row of brooding tombstones, out through the cemetery gates, and into the carriage. When he had her safely seated inside, he looked up at Dinks.

"Number Five, Morning Rose Square."

"Aye, m'lord."

Marcus got into the carriage and sat down across from Iphiginia. He reached out to close the curtains and then he leaned back to study Iphiginia's face in the lamplight. Her eyes were still too shadowed, but other than that, she appeared to be surprisingly fit, considering the ordeal she had just endured.

For an instant he allowed himself to savor again the good feeling he'd experienced a few minutes earlier when she'd flown into his arms. Then his anger blossomed once more.

"Iphiginia, your activities tonight constitute, beyond a doubt, the most inexcusably reckless, thoughtless, brainless adventure I have had occasion to witness in longer than I can recall. You claim to be an intelligent female. Pray tell, what intellect was involved in this night's work?"

"Marcus—"

"Damnation, what the devil did you think you were about?"

She winced. "Do you make a practice of lecturing all of your mistresses in such an unpleasant fashion?"

"No, madam, I do not," Marcus said through his teeth. "But then, I have never had a mistress such as yourself."

Her lips curved slightly and some of the sparkle reappeared in her eyes. "You mean you have never had a mistress-in-name-only?"

"No, I have not. And considering that you are merely masquerading as my mistress, I think I have a right to feel somewhat imposed upon. Christ, Iphiginia, you gave me a bad time tonight. How in God's name did you wind up locked in that bloody monument?"

"I assume that you have spoken to Amelia?"

"Miss Farley was the one who told me where I would find you."

"Then you know that the instructions in the blackmail note were clear. I was to leave the money inside the grotto."

"Yes."

"Someone came to the gates and locked them after I had gone inside," Iphiginia said quietly.

Marcus stilled. Then he leaned forward. "You actually saw this person?"

"For all the good it did. He wore a hooded cloak, just as I did. I saw nothing of his face. I'm not even certain that it was a man." Iphiginia reached inside the pocket of her gray cloak. "Whoever it was left this on the floor of the grotto."

Marcus took the note from her hand and read it quickly. "A threat."

"Yes. Obviously he or she knew I was not Aunt Zoe."

"Then the bastard knows far too much." Marcus refolded the note. He glanced up, frowning, as a belated thought occurred to him. "What did you do with the money?"

Iphiginia's eyes widened. "Good grief, I left it in the grotto."

"Bloody hell." Marcus stood up and pushed open the trapdoor in the carriage ceiling. "Turn back, Dinks. To the cemetery. Quickly."

Dinks shrugged. "Aye, m'lord."

Iphiginia frowned. "Do you think we'll get there in time to see the blackmailer pick up the money?"

"I doubt it. Not with the way my luck has been running lately."

Marcus leaped out of the carriage the instant the cemetery gates came into sight. He ran down an aisle of tombstones, straight to the grotto. Iphiginia's cloak swirled out behind her as she followed close at his heels.

They were too late. In the few minutes that it had taken to drive away from the cemetery, turn around, and return, someone had managed to get into the grotto and retrieve the five thousand pounds.

Iphiginia stared out into the foggy mists that surrounded the monument to Mrs. Eaton. "He must have been watching," she whispered. "And waiting. All the while I was in there, nearly going out of my mind, he was out here."

"He suspected someone would come to rescue you," Marcus said softly. "But how the hell did he know it?"

Iphiginia pulled her cloak more tightly about herself. "You are right, my lord. Whoever he is, he knows too much. About all of us."

$\mathcal{N}$INE

$\mathcal{M}$arcus leaned against the mantel in Iphiginia's library and contemplated his next move. "We will start with the sepulchral monument. The site was obviously chosen with careful consideration. There may be a connection between it and the blackmailer."

"Perhaps." Iphiginia set her teacup down onto its saucer. "Or he may have selected it merely because it was remote and atmospheric and bound to create an extremely unpleasant effect on the sensibilities of whoever brought the money." She shivered. "He was not wrong on that last point, I assure you."

Amelia gazed into the fire that Marcus had lit. "Whoever is behind this enjoys frightening people, first with threats of murder and now with ghosts. But what possible connection could the monument to this Mrs. Eaton have to do with the thing?"

"I don't know," Marcus conceded. "But it's worth making a few inquiries in that direction."

"I agree," Iphiginia said quietly.

Marcus glanced at her. He was still brooding on the notion that someone had gone out of his way to terrify her tonight. His hand knotted into a fist on the mantel top.

He deliberately dampened the fires of anger that burned in his blood and tried to take a more rational, objective view of the situation and of Iphiginia.

He was relieved to see that she was showing no obvious ill effects from the three hours she had spent sitting alone in the funeral grotto. He did not know any other female who would have come through the experience in such fine form. For that matter, he did not know many men who would have come out of it in such good spirits.

His mistress-in-name-only had great courage, he thought. Nevertheless, when he finally got his hands on whoever had locked her in the grotto, he was going to take great pleasure in avenging her.

"How do you intend to proceed?" Amelia asked.

Marcus considered the question closely. "To begin, we must try to discover who Mrs. Eaton was and, more important, who built such an elaborate monument to her."

"Our man of affairs, Mr. Manwaring, can look into it," Iphiginia said.

Marcus recalled the man he had seen leaving Iphiginia's town house the previous day. Manwaring enjoyed much too casual an entrée into the household, he decided.

"I'll have my own man of affairs handle the matter," he said, and then broke off as a thought struck him. "Devil take it. That will not be possible. At least not immediately."

"What's wrong?" Iphiginia asked.

"Barclay is, ah, out of Town on a business matter at the moment." Marcus drummed his fingers on the mantel. He could hardly explain that Barclay was in Devon looking into Iphiginia's past. "But he will not be gone long. He'll deal with the problem when he returns."

"Are you certain that you don't want us to ask Mr. Manwaring to handle it?" Iphiginia said. "He's really very good at obtaining detailed information, is he not, Amelia?"

"Yes," Amelia said. "Very good."

"No," Marcus said grimly. "Barclay can manage." He glanced from Iphiginia to Amelia and back again. "You have employed Mr. Manwaring for some time?"

"Three years," Iphiginia said. "He's an excellent man of affairs. Why do you ask?"

Marcus shrugged. "No particular reason. It just occurred to me that one's man of affairs knows a great deal about one's personal life."

Iphiginia scowled. "I assure you, Mr. Manwaring is entirely trustworthy. Surely you do not suspect him of being involved in this blackmail business?"

"Not at the moment. I was merely thinking aloud." Marcus paused. "Is it conceivable that, having been in your employ this long, your Mr. Manwaring could have learned enough about your aunt to blackmail her?"

"Absolutely not," Amelia said with unexpected fierceness. "Mr. Manwaring is a gentleman, sir. His character is quite above reproach. He would never do such a thing."

"Amelia is correct." Iphiginia's fine brows snapped together in a withering frown. "Mr. Manwaring is a decent, entirely honorable man."

Marcus could see immediately that there was no point in explaining that some men wore a facade of honor in order to hide a lack of integrity.

"Very well, he is your man of affairs," Marcus said gently. "I shall accept your opinion of him."

"I should think so," Iphiginia muttered.

"In any event," Marcus continued, thinking it through carefully, "even if he were the one blackmailing Lady Guthrie, I do not see how he could possibly know my friend's closest secret."

"Of course not." Iphiginia suddenly smiled a little too sweetly. "My lord, does this newfound suspicion of Mr. Manwaring mean that you are prepared to consider someone other than myself as the villain?"

"I suppose it's possible that you staged the entire play tonight for the express purpose of causing me to believe that you are innocent, but I think it unlikely."

Iphiginia's smile vanished. "Thank you very much, sir. Does it occur to you, my lord, that I could interpret the entire chain of events in such a manner that you would appear to be guilty?"

That irritated him. "Don't be ridiculous."

"What is so ridiculous about it?" she challenged. "You could very easily be the blackmailer."

She was serious. Marcus was stunned.

He knew full well that there had been a great deal of gossip about him over the years. Rumors concerning the duel and the death of Lynton Spalding were legion. But no one had ever voiced such speculations to his face. No one dared.

"You are either very foolish or very bold, Iphiginia. In any event, you go too far."

"Or not far enough," she retorted, undaunted.

Amelia cast her an uneasy glance. "Really, Iphiginia, I do not think this will get us anywhere."

"On the contrary." Iphiginia kept her stern gaze fixed on Marcus. "I wish to make a point. Pray consider the facts. We are told that you are quite ruthless, my lord, and I know that you are extremely intelligent. You are certainly clever enough to have learned all sorts of secrets over the years."

"Enough, Iphiginia," he warned very softly.

She acted as though she had not heard him. "You could have sent the blackmail notes. You could even have been the person in the cloak who locked me inside the grotto tonight."

Marcus was coldly furious. "That is a damned insult, madam."

"You have insulted me just as unbearably during the past few days."

"Your actions have been suspicious from the beginning. Parading about London as my mistress. Sneaking into gentlemen's studies to peruse the contents of their desks. Touring Lartmore's statuary hall. Dashing off to a cemetery at midnight with five thousand pounds that have since disappeared."

"Please," Amelia whispered. "This will accomplish nothing."

"Oh, yes it will," Iphiginia said. "It will prove to his lordship that his actions can be made to look every bit as suspicious as my own."

Marcus scowled. "Damn it, I am not the blackmailer."

"I never thought you were," Iphiginia said airily. "I was merely making a point."

Marcus moved very deliberately away from the mantel. He crossed the room to where Iphiginia sat on the Grecian sofa and halted directly in front of her. "Men have died making points such as yours."

"Perhaps, but I do not believe they have died by your hand, sir. You are much too intelligent to go about issuing challenges over such trivial matters."

"You think a man's honor is a trivial matter?"

"No, of course not. And neither is a woman's honor. But one cannot prove one's honor on a dueling field, can one? The truth is not established by lodging a bullet in someone else."

Marcus leaned over her, one hand on the arm of the sofa, the other braced on the curved back. She was trapped in the corner. "Be that as it may, a well-lodged bullet has a remarkably quieting effect on gossip."

"I doubt it. It merely drives it underground. But who gives a fig about gossip? You and I have the luxury of being virtually immune to gossip, do we not, my lord?"

"There are limits to everything, Iphiginia, and you have reached the limits of my indulgence. A mistress-in-name-only can tread only so far and no further."

"How would you know, sir? You have already admitted that you have never had a mistress-in-name-only before."

Amelia held up a hand. "I think it would be an excellent notion to put an end to this nonsense before your quarrel grows any more ludicrous."

Marcus glanced at her. "You're quite right, Miss Farley. Thank you for injecting a note of reason into the situation."

"You're welcome."

Marcus straightened and started to prowl the room. "Now, then, let us get back to more important matters. Another interesting possibility has just struck me."

Iphiginia sat forward and fluffed her skirts in the manner of a small cat grooming herself after she had been rudely disturbed. "What is that, sir?"

"I have been thinking about the statement that started our argument."

"Your observation that one's man of affairs is often in a position to gain a great deal of private information?" Iphiginia gave him a curious look. "What of it?"

"It occurs to me that such men are not the only ones who have access to extremely personal information. There are other people stationed in many of the best households who come to know things that are very private."

Amelia studied him intently. "You refer to servants? I do not believe this blackmail is the work of a servant."

"I agree," Iphiginia said quickly. "Whoever is behind this feels at home in Society. Do not forget he was aware of your personal plans for a month in the country, sir."

"And that business with the phoenix seal indicates some familiarity with classical subjects," Amelia added. "A servant would be unlikely to make such associations."

"The notes are written with a fine, well-trained hand," Iphiginia put in. "We all agreed in the beginning that the writing is well formed and the language of the notes indicated an educated intellect."

Marcus looked at her. "A governess or a companion would have such a background."

Iphiginia and Amelia stared at him with startled expressions.

"Good lord," Amelia whispered. "He's right, Iphiginia. Governesses and companions occupy a place somewhere between the servants' quarters and the drawing room. They are as well educated as their employers and yet they remain as unnoticed as the servants in most households."

Iphiginia leaped upon the possibilities. "And while she would not go to balls and soirees, a governess or companion would have access to the most intimate details of the lives of her employers. She would hear things and see things."

Marcus frowned. "My hypothesis would mean that we are searching for a woman who would know the most intimate secrets of at least two households."

"Someone who worked in Aunt Zoe's household at one time and then in your friend's household." Iphiginia looked at Marcus. "How old is your friend's secret, my lord?"

Marcus hesitated, debating how much he could divulge without betraying Hannah's confidence. "The events for which she is being blackmailed occurred seven years ago. I believe you mentioned that your aunt's secret dates back eighteen years?"

"Yes." Iphiginia moved one hand back and forth along the scrolled arm of the sofa. "It is an interesting theory, my lord, but I doubt that we shall discover that the same woman worked in both households."

"Still, it's worth looking into," Marcus said. "My hypothesis is a good deal more sound than your own. That business of rummaging through gentlemen's desks in search of a black wax and seal never did make much sense to me."

Iphiginia glared at him. "I disagree, sir. My theory is infinitely more reasonable and logical than yours. And unlike yours, it has some supporting evidence. After all, we have established that there are a handful of men who are connected to both your circle and Guthrie's. Your notion, on the other hand, is pure conjecture."

"It may be unproven," Marcus said, "but it has a great deal more to recommend it than yours does."

"That's not true. Furthermore, I would like to point out—"

Amelia held up a hand for silence. "Once again, may I request that we avoid these useless squabbles? They do not do us any good."

Marcus smiled coolly. "Miss Farley, you are the voice of common sense. Iphiginia is not thinking clearly tonight. Only to be expected, considering what she has been through."

"I resent that," Iphiginia said. "My thinking is every bit as clear as your own, Masters."

"You must admit that our areas of expertise differ somewhat," Marcus said politely. "Yours is in the field of classical antiquities, a subject far removed from what we are dealing with here. My own interests, on the other hand, have always been of a scientific and technical nature. In the pursuit of those interests I have obviously had occasion to develop the skills of reason and logic more fully than you have."

Iphiginia bounced up off the sofa. "Of all the arrogant, condescending, presumptuous things to say."

"Please," Amelia begged. "If the two of you do not stop this idiotic quarreling, we shall never get anywhere."

"I could not be more in agreement," Marcus said smoothly. "We shall proceed in a logical fashion. As I said, I'll have Barclay make inquiries into the ownership of that sepulchral grotto in Reeding Cemetery as soon as he returns to Town. In the meantime, you will ask your aunt if she had a companion in her employ several years ago who might have suspected her secret. I shall ask my friend the same question."

"Hmm," Iphiginia muttered.

Marcus ignored her fulminating gaze. "We shall see what we learn from that avenue of inquiry. In the meantime, I think it would be best to remove you from London for a few days, madam."

"Certainly not." Iphiginia was outraged. "Why would I wish to leave London? I have far too much to do here."

Marcus shook his head. "The blackmailer is obviously becoming more dangerous. His actions tonight indicate that he is not above harming you."

"He didn't harm me. He merely gave me something of a scare."

"His lordship is right." Amelia clasped her hands together in her lap. "His note says quite clearly that locking you in the grotto was a warning, Iphiginia. Who knows what he will do next?"

"Precisely," Marcus said. "I think it would be best for me to keep a close eye on Iphiginia until Barclay has had an opportunity to make a few inquiries."

"Rubbish," Iphiginia said.

Amelia ignored her. She gazed intently at Marcus. "And just how do you propose to do that, my lord?"

Marcus ran through the very short list of possibilities in his head. "I suppose Iphiginia could return to her home in the country for a while."

"*Absolutely not,*" Iphiginia said very loudly. "Utterly impossible. I will not go home and that is final."

Marcus made a private note of her vehemence on the subject. It would be interesting to see what Barclay learned in Devon. "Then in that case, I suggest that we take Lady Pettigrew up on her invitation to spend a few days at her country house in Hampshire this week."

Iphiginia considered that. "It would give me an opportunity to search Pettigrew's library."

Marcus stifled an oath. "I will handle that matter. You will examine Lady Pettigrew's Temple of Vesta, as you promised to do."

"Are you certain that you will know how to search a man's library properly?" Iphiginia asked dubiously.

"I think I can manage the task. I watched you search Lartmore's library, did I not? How can I fail after watching an expert such as yourself?"

Iphiginia pursed her lips. "Very well, my lord. We shall go to Hampshire, as planned."

Marcus exhaled with a sense of relief. At least Iphiginia would be safe under his careful eye while they were in Hampshire. By the time they got back to London, Barclay would have returned. Marcus intended to set him to investigating the ownership of Mrs. Eaton's monument as soon as possible.

Something told him that there was a connection between the funeral grotto and the blackmailer. He could almost feel it. He intended to explore the problem until he had the answers he wanted.

The blackmailer had become more than a nuisance. Tonight he had gone too far. He had threatened Iphiginia.

Marcus would not stop until he had caught him.

Three days later, Marcus strolled over to one of the shelves in Pettigrew's library and studied the titles with keen interest. "Cicero, Virgil, Newton. *Philosophical Transactions of the Royal Society*. I commend you on your excellent and extremely varied collection, Pettigrew. I had not realized that you were interested in so many different subjects."

Pettigrew, a dour man whose gloomy, withdrawn temperament was the exact opposite of his lady's, scowled even more ferociously than he usually did. "A man's got to read something besides the newspapers if he doesn't want his mind to rot."

"Well said." Marcus took down a recent volume of the *Philosophical Transactions* and leafed through to the table of contents. "Would you mind if I borrowed this?"

"Help yourself." Pettigrew poured claret into a glass. "Mind if I ask you how long you intend to stay with us, sir?"

Marcus pretended to ignore Pettigrew's lack of hospitality. It had become evident immediately upon arrival yesterday that the house party was entirely Lady Pettigrew's notion. Her unsociable husband had no interest in entertaining visitors.

"I believe we shall be here for only a few days, no more. Your wife has requested Mrs. Bright's opinion on your Temple of Vesta. It will no doubt require my friend some time to make all the measurements and compare them with those of the original ruin that she saw in Italy."

"Perfectly good Temple of Vesta." Pettigrew tossed the claret down his throat. "Don't see why we need Mrs. Bright's opinion." He slid a quick sidelong glance at Marcus. "No offense, sir. I realize that she's a very close friend of yours."

"Yes. She is." Marcus idly examined the table of contents of the copy of the *Philosophical Transactions*. The volume was over a year old. He spotted an article on astronomical observations that caught his interest.

He had, of course, read this issue of the *Transactions* months earlier when he had received his own copy. He always perused the latest issue of the Society's papers as soon as they appeared. But nine months ago he had glanced only cursorily at the paper dealing with astronomy. At that time he had confined his inquiries

into the properties of light and reflective sur-
faces and had not yet taken an interest in the
stars.

"Known her a long time?"

"Who? Mrs. Bright?" Marcus looked up.
"As it happens, I have not known her nearly
long enough."

"I see. Rather an unusual female."

"Yes. Very. She and I have discovered that
we have a great deal in common."

Pettigrew furrowed his brow in some confusion. "You're interested in antiquities and
such?"

"I am these days." Marcus closed the *Transactions*. "By the bye, my valet neglected to pack
my writing box, for some inane reason. Would
it be a great imposition for me to borrow some
paper? I have a few letters to write."

"What? Oh, no. No, not at all." Pettigrew
waved a hand at his cluttered desktop. "Help
yourself."

"I'll need to borrow your wax jack, too. I
trust you don't mind?"

"Over there near the globe."

"Very kind of you."

"You may as well use my desk to write your
bloody letters." Pettigrew heaved a glum sigh.
"God knows I won't have much of a chance to
use it while this crowd is in residence. Don't
know why my wife has to have so many people

down here from London during the Season.
I've told her that if she wants to socialize, she's
free to do it at our house in Town."

"She has a right to be proud of this house.
It's not every estate that can boast a Temple of
Vesta."

"Be different if one could boast of a few virgins to go with it," Pettigrew said. "But these
days they're as rare as unicorns and phoenixes,
ain't they?"

Marcus studied the rolling lawn outside the
library window. "Phoenixes?"

"You know, mythological bird that's supposed to be reborn from its own ashes."

"I lost interest in mythological creatures at
about the same time I lost interest in virgins,"
Marcus said.

"What a lovely evening." Iphiginia gazed up
at the night sky.

She had dragged Marcus out onto the terrace on the pretext of admiring the tranquil
summer evening before they retired. In truth,
she intended to quiz him on what he had
learned in Pettigrew's library this afternoon.
She had been eager to speak to him in private
all day, but there had been no opportunity to
do so.

Now that she had him to herself out here
under the stars, she was no longer in such a

rush to question him about his discoveries. She realized that all she really yearned to do was share a few quiet, private moments with him.

It was nearly midnight. After an evening of dinner and cards, most of the Pettigrew guests had drifted upstairs to their bedchambers.

Although it was the height of the Season in Town, here in the country there was no endless round of balls and soirees to keep one up until dawn. Spending a few days in the country was considered a good way to refortify oneself for the hectic pace of Town life.

A soft, balmy breeze stirred the leaves of the nearby trees. The scent of flowers floated on the air. Iphiginia took a deep breath, savoring the fragrance of the night.

"It certainly is clear." Marcus leaned against the ornate balustrade. His gaze was fixed on the heavens. "I'd give a great deal to be at my estate in Yorkshire."

"Why do you wish you were in Yorkshire?"

"Because that's where my new telescope is."

"Telescope? You are interested in astronomy?"

"Yes."

Iphiginia was intrigued by the revelation. No matter how much she discovered about this man, it seemed that there were always new depths waiting to be explored. "I had no notion, my lord."

His mouth curved faintly. "Did you think that you had learned everything there was to know about me when you studied for your role as my mistress?"

"No, of course not." She felt herself grow warm. "But I thought I had made a rather thorough inquiry into your past and present interests."

"Do not concern yourself." Marcus kept his attention on the night sky. "It was only a small oversight. You no doubt missed my interest in astronomy because it is a rather new one. I was led into it by my studies of the properties of light and mirrors."

Iphiginia pushed her questions about Pettigrew's wax jack and seal aside for the moment. She was far more curious to learn new things about the man she loved. "How did they lead you into the subject of astronomy?"

"Very easily." Marcus glanced briefly at her before returning his attention to the skies. "When one studies the stars, essentially one studies light. Mirrors can be used to focus light in such a manner that one can see a great distance into the skies."

"You mean the sort of mirrors which are used in telescopes?"

"Yes. Mirrors can also be used to concentrate the light itself so that it can be studied. I have been working on just such a project." He gave her an oddly hesitant, sidelong glance. "I have devised a small machine which allows me to study light."

"How does it work?"

"It utilizes a prism and a small telescope—" He broke off with a rueful expression. "Forgive me. As a student of antiquities, I expect you find this topic rather a dull one."

"Oh, no, not in the least," she assured him. "As it happens, the ancients were very concerned with studies of the heavens. Indeed, the very stars and planets are named after the heroes and heroines of antiquity."

"True."

"Tell me, what do you hope to learn from an investigation of starlight?"

"I'm not certain." Marcus shrugged. "But something Mr. William Herschel wrote a couple of years ago intrigued me greatly."

"What was it?"

Marcus reached out, took her hand, and led her toward the wide stone steps that descended into the gardens. "He pointed out that in some sense when we look at the stars we are looking into the past."

"I do not understand."

"The light from the stars takes thousands of years to reach us, by all modern calculations."

"Yes, of course. I see what you mean. The light we see must have been originally emitted eons ago," Iphiginia whispered. "I never thought of it in that fashion. What a fascinating notion."

"I find it so." Marcus smiled at her. "But I have learned that few people outside of a small group who are interested in such matters care to listen to a detailed conversation on the topic."

"I understand." Iphiginia savored the feel of his big hand wrapped around her own smaller fingers. She felt as though she and Marcus were linked together mentally as well as physically tonight. It was good to know that he no longer suspected her of blackmail. "I have often been accused of being something of a bore myself, sir."

"I find that difficult to believe."

"Oh, but it's true. I'm afraid I was obliged to live a very quiet life until last year."

"Due to your husband's age and infirmities, I expect."

"Uh, yes. Mr. Bright did not get out much."

"And therefore, neither did you."

"No."

"Tell me something, Iphiginia," Marcus said very softly. "Were you faithful to your Mr. Bright?"

Iphiginia gasped and somehow managed to stumble over a small stone buried in the grass. "What a ridiculous question, my lord."

He steadied her. "What is so strange about it? You have been in Society long enough to know that faithful wives are few and far between."

"From what I have observed, the number of unfaithful wives is exceeded only by the number of unfaithful husbands," Iphiginia retorted.

"I suppose that is true."

Having won the point and neatly changed the topic in the process, Iphiginia grew suddenly more daring. "Were you a faithful husband, my lord?"

Marcus was silent for a moment. "I have a rule against discussing my past. Most particularly, I do not discuss my marriage."

The rebuff chilled Iphiginia. "Yes, of course. How could I forget your infamous rules? Tell me, do you enjoy living by such rigid rules, sir?"

"They have served me well."

"Life is short," Iphiginia whispered. "I find that too many rules can make one's existence seem very dull and confined."

"I find that they protect one's privacy."

"But one misses out on so much of life's excitement when one lives by the overly strict rules of Society," Iphiginia protested.

"I do not live by Society's rules, Iphiginia. I live by my own."

They wandered into a more heavily wooded

portion of the extensive Pettigrew gardens. The lights of the big house were far behind them now. When Iphiginia glanced over her shoulder, she realized she could not even see the stately home any longer. A stand of trees stood in the way.

The night was lit only by starlight and the glow of the nearly full moon.

"It is as if we were alone in the world," Iphiginia said.

"A very pleasant sensation." Marcus glanced at a large structure looming in a nearby grove. "What have we here?"

Iphiginia saw the tall, elegant columns of the Temple of Vesta. "That is the ruin. I finished my measurements of it this afternoon while you were in Pettigrew's library. By the bye, did you discover anything of interest there?"

"No. Pettigrew uses red wax. There was no sign of any black wax in his jack and his seal bears the emblem of a hart."

"How very disappointing. Did you examine his desk with great care?"

"Yes, I did. Trust me, Pettigrew is not the blackmailer." Marcus changed course to stroll over to the circular structure. "Did you find this Temple of Vesta to be a good copy of the original in Tivoli?"

Iphiginia heaved a small sigh of regret over the news that Pettigrew had been removed from the list of suspects. She surveyed the graceful, airy antiquity. Moonlight cascaded down through the open roof, lending an enchanting, mystical quality to the ruin that had not been present earlier in the day.

"Not bad, actually," she said judiciously. "It conveys the lightness of feeling that one encounters in the original. You will note the fine proportions of the columns. The circle in which they are constructed is quite precise in measurement."

"Indeed."

Iphiginia realized that Marcus was looking at her, not at the temple. His eyes gleamed in the shadows. Something in his low, deep voice turned her insides to warm pudding.

She took a breath and tried to sound suitably casual and erudite. "One can almost imagine the Vestal Virgins tending the sacred flame within such a classical setting."

"Your imagination is considerably more vivid than mine." Marcus led her between two of the tall stone columns. He drew her to a halt in the center of the round floor and stood gazing about with amused interest. "I cannot seem to conjure up any virgins here, but I find the setting inspiring nonetheless."

Iphiginia felt her mouth go dry. "Do you?"

"Yes." He framed her face with his strong

hands. "The name Lady Starlight suits you, Iphiginia. You were born to walk in starlight."

She shivered. *I was born to love you,* she thought. A haunting sadness swept through her. She would very likely never be able to say those words aloud to him because he would not want to hear them.

"Have you enjoyed playing my mistress, Iphiginia?"

"Oh, yes. Enormously. As your paramour, I am considered absolutely riveting by all and sundry. In truth, I shall be a bit sorry when the whole thing is over."

"Will you?"

"Well, not entirely," she confessed. "The thing is, it would be a great nuisance to be the focus of so many eyes all of the time. But I must admit that it has been something of a grand adventure. Almost as exciting as my recent journey to Italy."

Marcus's brows rose. "Almost as exciting? I am devastated to hear that being my mistress has not been quite as entrancing as your tour of antiquities."

Iphiginia was horrified at the realization that she might have insulted him. "I did not mean to offend you, my lord. In truth, I have found playing the part of your mistress vastly interesting."

"But not quite as interesting as, say, touring the ruins of Pompeii?"

"Well, Pompeii is Pompeii, after all, my lord," she chided gently. "Few things on the face of the earth can compare with that."

"No, I suppose not. But allow me to try to add some additional excitement to your current adventure."

His mouth closed over hers. Iphiginia did not know whether it was the moonlight or the heat from Marcus's body that set her senses on fire.

TEN

This was the right place, the right time, the right man.

Iphiginia was utterly lost in the glorious wonder of that realization. It was as though everything she had done since she had cast off the shackles of her quiet, proscribed life in Deepford last year had been done in preparation for this moment.

She was free. Free of her obligations to her sister, free of the suffocating rules of her small village, free from the beady, prying eyes of disapproving neighbors.

During the past year she had come into her own and now she was truly free to love for the first time in her life.

She must seize the moment, she thought. She would worry about the consequences later.

This was the grandest adventure of all, one she had begun to fear that she would never have an opportunity to experience.

She stood on tiptoe and wrapped her arms tightly around Marcus's neck.

A shudder went through him. He gave a low, rasping sound and deepened his kiss. He gripped her fiercely, holding her still while he explored her mouth.

Iphiginia sighed softly and leaned closer, her senses thrilling to his warmth and strength.

"My sweet Lady Starlight." Marcus slid his big hand slowly down Iphiginia's throat. He eased her delicate white shawl aside, exposing her bare shoulders. "You cannot know how I have ached to touch you again."

"Yes. Please touch me. Please, Marcus." Iphiginia turned her head to kiss his hand. She felt the soft cashmere shawl fall from her shoulders and drift down to pool at her feet.

She was dazed by the moonlight and his touch. Nothing seemed quite real and yet her senses had never been more acutely alive. His fingers probed gently, seeking the fastenings of her gown.

A small, distinct shock went through her when Marcus found the tapes, undid them, and slowly, reverently lowered the bodice. The soft, scented air wafted over her bare breasts.

She buried her face against his cravat.

"Beautiful." Marcus covered her nipples with his palms. "So beautiful."

Iphiginia felt her breasts swell and become incredibly sensitive beneath his warm hand. She shivered at the realization that, although he had touched her with dazzling intimacy the other night in Lartmore's statuary hall, Marcus had never actually seen her nude.

Until tonight no man had ever seen her naked.

She should have been mortified, Iphiginia thought. But the sensual admiration in Marcus's voice was having just the opposite effect. He made her feel exquisite and irresistible.

The urge to explore him as he was exploring her swamped any lingering hesitation. She reached up and began to untie his cravat with trembling fingers.

"Yes," Marcus whispered.

A moment later the ends of the long neckcloth hung loose.

Iphiginia looked at him. The hard planes of his face were etched in moonlight and shadow. His eyes were brilliant. His mouth curved slightly in a small smile of unmistakable sensual hunger.

"Marcus?" She did not know how to ask the unformed question. She only knew that she wanted more than a kiss out here in the moonlight.

"Why not?" he said, as if he had read her mind. He drew his thumb slowly along the line of her jaw. "I had thought to wait until we had returned to the privacy of your bedchamber, but some things cannot be put off."

He bent his head and kissed the curve of her shoulder. She shivered in his arms and thrust her hands beneath the edges of his shirt. Deliberately she flattened her palms against the strong, sleek muscles of his chest.

"You feel wondrously fine, my lord," she breathed, awed by the feel of him. "Altogether magnificent. You remind me of a statue of Hercules that I once viewed in Venice."

Marcus gave a muffled laugh that quickly turned into a groan. "Be warned, I am no statue, madam, although at the moment a certain part of me is certainly as hard as stone."

"I am aware of that," she whispered. She could feel the bulge of his manhood pressing against her. It both intrigued and alarmed her.

He released her reluctantly to shrug off his coat. He spread the garment out on the floor of the ruin. Iphiginia glanced and then raised her eyes to meet Marcus's gleaming gaze. She knew without being told that he was going to lower her down onto the coat and make love to her.

All the great mysteries of the cosmos were about to be explained. She knew that if she wanted to stop this from going any further, she must speak up now.

She smiled at Marcus and said nothing at all.

Marcus appeared momentarily mesmerized by her smile. For an instant he did not move.

Then, with a hoarse exclamation, he caught her up in his arms and lowered her to the coat.

Iphiginia reached for him as he came down on top of her. She drew him to her, holding him tightly as if she could keep him with her always.

"Iphiginia."

Marcus's touch was no longer deliberate or restrained. He rained rough, urgent kisses across her breasts. His powerful hands trembled as they moved over her body. He caught one of her nipples between his teeth and bit gently as he pushed his hands up beneath her skirts.

A thrilling sense of anticipation poured through her when she felt his fingers on her inner thigh. He was going to touch her again the way he had in Lartmore's statuary hall. She could barely wait for the fascinating sensations to sweep through her.

"You're ready for me, aren't you?" Marcus sounded as though he were running a great race. "You turn to liquid starlight when I touch you like this."

"Oh." Iphiginia squeezed her eyes shut. Her legs closed tightly around his hand.

Marcus probed gently, penetrating just enough to make her tremble with eagerness.

"Marcus. Oh, my God, *Marcus.*" She wanted more from him. She had to have more. But she did not know how to describe what she needed. She lifted her hips, arching against him instead.

"Hotter than the sun itself." Marcus opened her gently.

Iphiginia cried out. Her fingers sank into the fabric of his shirt, biting into the muscles of his shoulders.

She was dimly aware of him removing his hand from between her legs. She realized he was fumbling with the fastening of his breeches.

She knew what would follow. After all, she had seen those statues in Lartmore's hall. Iphiginia tried to prepare herself. The problem was that she did not know quite what to expect.

"Kiss me," Marcus ordered against her mouth.

"Oh, yes. Yes, of course." She clutched at him eagerly. This part was easy. She knew exactly how to kiss him, how to hold him close.

"My God," Marcus muttered into her mouth. "You take my breath away."

She felt him move between her legs and then she felt an object that was far larger than his finger start to enter her. She could tell at once that it would never fit.

"Marcus, I fear something is amiss here."

"You are so amazingly tight." He sounded half-strangled.

"Sir, you seem to be somewhat larger than the statues in Lartmore's hall," Iphiginia said desperately.

"This is no time to make me laugh." Marcus withdrew slightly.

Iphiginia started to draw a sigh of relief. But without any warning he refitted himself to her soft passage and forged back into her in one long, powerful movement.

"*Marcus.*" Iphiginia's eyes flew open in stunned shock. She went absolutely still. She could not breathe.

But her reaction was nothing compared to Marcus's. Buried to the hilt inside her, he went rigid.

"Bloody hell. *Bloody damn hell.*"

A terrible silence gripped the Temple of Vesta.

"Is it always like this?" Iphiginia finally managed to inquire. "I had rather hoped it would feel the way it did the other night when you touched me."

Marcus raised his head and looked down at her with glittering, accusing eyes. "You're a virgin."

Too late Iphiginia recalled her carefully crafted tale of widowhood.

"Oh, no. No, indeed." Iphiginia licked her lips. "It's just that it's been a very long time since Mr. Bright passed on. And even when he was alive he was not what you'd call enthusiastic about his husbandly privileges. And he was not nearly so, ah, well-proportioned as yourself, my lord, if you take my meaning."

"You're a damned virgin. You lied to me."

With a sinking heart, Iphiginia realized that he was furious.

Despair shot through her. She was not sure what to say next. Obviously he had guessed the truth. She sought for a way to moderate his anger.

"But no one knows that except you, my lord. Surely it does not signify? In the eyes of the world I am a widow."

"How many roles are you playing, Iphiginia?"

Tears filled her eyes. "I am not playing any role at the moment."

"For God's sake, do not cry." He braced his elbows on either side of her and caught her face between his palms. "I will not tolerate tears. Not after what you have done."

Anger and outrage stormed through her. "I am not crying." She sniffed. "And if you are going to use that tone of voice with me, sir, you can bloody well get off and let me up. I do not have to lie here and listen to you make nasty, hateful comments."

"Iphiginia—"

"I said, get off me." She braced her hands against his shoulders and shoved as hard as she could. It was like pushing against a mountain.

"The damage is done, you little fool."

"I do not consider myself to have been damaged, my lord." She glowered up at him. "I wanted you to make love to me. At least, I thought I did."

"Why? Tell me why, damn it. Was this to be another of your grand adventures? Something akin to a tour of the ruins of Pompeii, perhaps?"

"Yes, it was," she flung back furiously. She tried once again to shove him off her. "But you have ruined it."

"Why did you have to choose me?" Marcus's voice was raw. "Why didn't you pick Hoyt or Lartmore or someone else to take you on this particular tour for the first time?"

"Because I chose you, you great, half-witted idiot. *Get off me.*"

Marcus looked thunderstruck. "Iphiginia—"

"Off, I said."

He flinched as though she had struck him. In the moonlight, Iphiginia saw the sheen of sweat on his forehead. His dark hair was damp with it. His jaw was locked. Every muscle in his body was as hard as though it had been carved from marble.

Marcus gritted his teeth and slowly began to withdraw from her body. Iphiginia wriggled impatiently.

"Hold still," Marcus said urgently. "*Damnation*." He wrenched himself free of her with shocking suddenness.

"Ouch." Iphiginia yelped in dismay. "That hurt."

Marcus did not pay any attention. His features were contorted in an expression of what appeared to be unbearable anguish. He sucked in his breath, shuddered heavily, and collapsed, facedown, alongside her. A terrible groan shuddered through him and then he lay absolutely still.

"Oh, my God. *Marcus,* are you all right?" Iphiginia forgot about her own discomfort. She levered herself up onto her elbow, horrified by Marcus's sudden and mysterious collapse.

A terrible, soul-destroying fear shook her to the core. *Marcus was dead and it was all her fault.*

Iphiginia scrambled to her knees. Frantically she shook his shoulder. He did not stir.

She leaned over him to see his face, which was turned away from her. His eyes were closed.

She recalled the expression of agony that had twisted his features.

"Dear heaven, what have I done? My lord, are you alive? Speak to me, please speak to me."

She struggled to pull him into her lap. It was not easy. He was impossibly heavy. She managed to get his face onto her knee. She stroked his hair back from his forehead.

"I am so very sorry, Marcus." Tears ran down her cheeks. "I never meant to hurt you. That is the last thing I would ever do. Please, Marcus, you must not die. Not now after I have finally found you. I could not bear it. I love you, Marcus."

Bloody hell.

He'd lost his self-control for the first time since his wedding night.

He'd spilled his seed like some clumsy, untried youth with his first woman, just as he had that first time with Nora. Somewhere in the darkest reaches of his memory he thought he heard her angry, jeering words.

You've got the hands of a farmer, you great oaf.

"Marcus, Marcus, please forgive me. Open your eyes. You cannot die."

Marcus opened one eye.

"You're alive." Iphiginia's face glowed with hope and relief. "Thank God." She started to ease his head off her lap. "Wait right here, my lord. Do not move. I shall go back to the house and fetch help."

Marcus opened his other eye, reached out, and caught her wrist. "No."

"But it is obvious that you need a doctor. You have suffered some sort of seizure."

"For better or worse, I do believe that I am going to survive. My compliments, *Miss* Bright." Marcus grimaced with self-disgust. "You have the ability to make a thirty-six-year-old man feel like a young blade of twenty again."

She peered at him anxiously. Her fingertips were astonishingly gentle on his cheek. "Are you quite certain that you are not in need of a doctor?"

"Absolutely certain. I may, however, be requiring a new coat." He thought of how he had pumped himself ignominiously into the expensive superfine of one of his tailor's more expensive creations. "I do not know if my valet will be able to salvage this one."

"I shall pay for a new coat for you," Iphiginia said very earnestly. "This is all my fault. I am very much aware of that, my lord."

Marcus swallowed an oath. "I should have guessed that you would prove to be as much of an Original in the role of the outraged innocent as you were in the part of the notorious widow."

"But Marcus, I am not outraged. Nor am I a green chit fresh out of the schoolroom. I am quite old enough to make my own decisions."

"You were a virgin." Marcus sat up wearily. "I never get involved with virgins. I have a rule against it. I have never broken that rule until tonight."

"You must look on the positive side, my lord." Iphiginia smiled brightly. "I am no longer a virgin, therefore you are no longer in violation of your own rule."

Rage flickered through him. "Damnation, woman, this is not a jest. I vow, there are times when your mouth would drive any sane man to the edge. If I had not already just taken your virginity, I would be strongly tempted to put you over my knee for that stupid remark."

Iphiginia's smile vanished. "Sir, I comprehend that you are angry because you have broken one of your precious rules. But truly, you must not blame yourself."

Marcus concentrated on refastening the front of his breeches. "A virgin masquerading as a widow." He felt as if his fine intellect had turned to mush. "I should have known."

"That is ridiculous. How could you possibly have known?"

Marcus got to his feet and stood looking down at her. For a moment he was transfixed by the sight of Iphiginia sitting in the center of the ruin, bathed in moonlight. Her white skirts frothed around her as she clutched the bodice of her gown to her graceful breasts. Her hair was in disarray and one of her small white shoes had come off. The aura of innocence still enveloped her, just as it had done the very first time he had seen her.

"I think that I did know," he said quietly. "But I refused to acknowledge the truth because I did not want to see it."

Iphiginia scowled. "Are you always this hard on yourself when you break one of your own rules, sir?"

"I don't know." Marcus reached down to pull her to her feet. "This is the first time that I have ever broken one. Come."

"Where are we going?"

"Back to the house." Marcus helped Iphiginia adjust the tapes of her dress. "We must take care that no one sees us."

"Why must we be careful, my lord?" Iphiginia gave him a thoroughly exasperated look. "In the eyes of the world nothing has changed. Everyone is convinced that I am a widow and they all believe that I am your mistress. There is no way that anyone in the house can know the truth."

"I know the truth." The truth was that he'd broken his own rules and he would pay the price.

Well, at least marriage to Iphiginia would make a change, he thought wryly. His first wife had been a woman of experience who had pretended to be an innocent. This time he would marry an innocent who had masqueraded as a woman of experience.

He ought to take Iphiginia's advice and look on the bright side, Marcus told himself. This time he would be marrying his own mistress rather than one who had belonged to another man.

Marcus scooped up his coat and eyed it glumly. He'd ruined several expensive coats during the past few weeks, thanks to his experiments with his new hydraulic reservoir pen. This was the first one he'd soiled in this particular fashion, however.

He'd completely lost his self-control.

He had not even remembered to employ the specially designed sheep-gut condom he had brought along in his pocket.

Marcus ignored Iphiginia's searching gaze. He took her hand and led her out of the ruin of the Temple of Vesta.

The night fell softly around them as Marcus walked Iphiginia back to the great house. The stars appeared clear and bright in the sky.

Marcus considered how his life was about to change. He wondered how Bennet would react to the news of his impending nuptials.

At least Iphiginia was unlikely to object to the amount of time he spent in his library and laboratory, he thought philosophically. She would understand.

There might be children. Perhaps even a son to inherit the title. Odd, he had never before cared about having an heir of his own blood. Tonight, however, the prospect of Iphiginia carrying his babe gave him a strange sensation of possessiveness, an awareness of the future that he had not been conscious of until now.

It was a troublesome concept.

"Marcus?" Iphiginia's voice sounded breathless.

Marcus realized that he was walking so swiftly she was obliged to skip to keep up with him. "Yes?"

"I realize that you are very angry, my lord. I want you to know that I sincerely regret my actions."

"Hush, Iphiginia."

"I should not have misled you about my past."

"We will talk of this tomorrow. I must think on the matter tonight."

"Yes, my lord. I understand. You are vastly

annoyed and no doubt wish to abandon your pretense of being my lover."

"I do not see any alternative." He was going to replace the role of lover with that of husband.

"On the contrary," Iphiginia said swiftly. "There is every reason to continue on with our masquerade."

"That is no longer possible, Iphiginia."

"Come now, sir. You are a very intelligent man."

"Do you think so? I, myself, am having some doubts on that particular point."

"Nonsense," Iphiginia said bracingly. "You are really quite clever. There can be no question about the powers of your intellect."

"Hmm."

"And although you are angry, I know you will not allow your emotions to dominate your keen sense of reason."

"I appreciate your confidence in my brain," he said gravely.

"Yes, well, the thing is, I would like to remind you that I had a very good excuse for pretending to be both a widow and your mistress."

"This is not the best time to remind me of your talent as an actress." They were almost back to the terrace. Marcus saw that most of the lights on the upper floors were out. The guests were abed. It should not be difficult to get Iphiginia back to her bedchamber unseen.

"Sir, I must ask you to keep in mind that my reason for undertaking the role of your mistress-in-name-only still exists. We must maintain the pretense until we discover the identity of the blackmailer. I trust you will not do anything rash?"

"Rash?"

Iphiginia's eyes were wide and luminous in the shadows. "I pray you will not terminate our liaison so far as Society is concerned. You will allow our pretense to stand, will you not?"

Her obvious failure to comprehend the ramifications of what had just happened on the floor of the Temple of Vesta caused Marcus to lose what was left of his patience.

"Miss Bright, I would like to remind you that you have a new and potentially far more significant problem on your hands than you had an hour ago."

She blinked uncertainly. "I beg your pardon?"

"You are no longer a mistress-in-name-only."

She looked blank for an instant. Then realization dawned. "Oh, I see what you mean."

"Do you, Miss Bright?"

"Yes, of course." She lowered her eyes, apparently fascinated with the pleats of his shirt. "But I do not see that one extremely brief little interlude that did not amount to much need alter the nature of our association in any way."

"Damnation, Iphiginia—"

"Marcus, please." She raised a hand as though to touch his cheek and then apparently changed her mind. "I know that you did not enjoy what happened back there in the ruin."

"My pleasure or lack of same is the least important element in this situation," he said roughly. "I do not believe that you quite grasp the enormity of the problem."

"But I do, my lord. I mean, I realize precisely how unnerving, indeed, how very alarming your collapse must have been for you. Heavens, for a moment there, I believed that you had died or at the very least had suffered a fit of apoplexy."

"*Apoplexy*. Christ. I am going mad. There can no longer be any doubt."

"You must believe me when I say that I had no notion that your discovery that I was a virgin would have such a debilitating effect on you. I am truly sorry, my lord."

Marcus reached the balustrade that surrounded the terrace. He came to a halt and looked at Iphiginia. Her conversation had become riveting in some strange, demented fashion. He was literally fascinated.

"Quite right," he agreed. "How could you have known just what your virginity would do to my delicate sensibilities?"

"Precisely." She smiled her brilliant smile. "But you have assured me that you are all right now. You were being truthful, were you not?"

"I do seem to have made a rather remarkable recovery, considering the circumstances."

"Excellent. I know the entire affair must have given you quite a shock."

"A shock." He nodded once. "Yes, that describes it very well."

"And it no doubt frightened you. But set your mind at ease, sir. I can assure you that there is no cause for further concern."

Marcus put one hand on the balustrade and gripped it very tightly. "Why not?"

"Because you have my word of honor that I will make no further demands of an, ah—" she paused to gently clear her throat, "of an amorous nature upon you."

He contemplated her expectant face for some time. He could not recall another female who had robbed him so thoroughly of speech.

"That is very thoughtful of you, Miss Bright."

"Think nothing of it," she said graciously. Then she leaned closer and lowered her voice to a more confidential tone. "To be perfectly frank, I did not find our little interlude all that pleasant, either, and I assure you that I am in no great rush to repeat it."

Marcus went cold inside. The "interlude," as she termed it, had been a debacle. On top of everything else, he had ruined her first experience of passion for her.

In spite of his initial anger and the devastating knowledge that his life had been irrevocably changed by her deception, Marcus felt a rush of guilt. His only goal tonight had been to give her pleasure even as he took his own. He had failed.

"Iphiginia, I regret the unpleasant nature of the experience. If I had known—"

"No, please." She put her fingers over his mouth to silence him. "You must not apologize. Had I truly been what I pretended to be, a widow well acquainted with the intimacies of the marriage bed, I would have been better able to make the calculations."

"What calculations?"

"Why, the sort I make when I am analyzing the perspective and elevations of a fine ruin," she explained. "I would have realized that everything about you would be in, er, equally majestic proportion, if you see what I mean."

"Proportion?"

"I fear that I was somewhat misled by my

previous experience with classical statues." She frowned. "And even by those in Lartmore's collection, now that I think of it."

"Iphiginia—"

"In my own defense, however, I must tell you that in all my studies of ancient statuary, I have never come across an example which was constructed with precisely your proportions."

Marcus interrupted deliberately. "This is undoubtedly one of the most interesting conversations I have ever had. However, it is getting quite late and I am determined that we shall deal with this matter at a later time."

"After you have regained your composure, you mean?"

"That is one way of putting it. Let us go upstairs to our bedchambers, madam. I have some thinking to do." He took her arm and started her toward the door.

"Marcus." She clutched at his sleeve. "Promise me that you will not tell anyone that I am not really your mistress."

"Calm yourself, Iphiginia." Marcus opened the door and ushered her into a darkened hall. "Your little fiction is no longer a pretense, as we had agreed. There is no secret to keep. Tonight you really did become my mistress."

She gave him a sharp glance. "You will not tell anyone that I am not really a widow, either, will you?"

"Believe me, I am no more eager for Society to learn the truth than you are."

"No, of course not." She appeared to relax slightly. "You would not want anyone else to know that you had broken one of your own rules, would you?"

"No," Marcus said. "Things are going to be awkward enough as it is."

"What do you mean by that?"

"Never mind, Miss Bright. I shall explain it all to you at a more convenient time."

"Mrs. Bright," she corrected urgently. "We must maintain the masquerade in private or we might become careless in public."

"I beg your pardon. Mrs. Bright."

Marcus braced his hands against the windowsill of his bedchamber and looked out at the stars.

He had never thought to wed again.

He was about to break another of his own rules. Tonight, with the scent and the feel of Iphiginia still so fresh in his mind, he could not seem to think rationally on the subject of marriage.

The only thing that was transparently clear in his mind was the memory of Iphiginia bending over him, terrified that she had somehow murdered him with her virginity. Her words still rang in his head.

I love you, Marcus.

She had been hysterical, of course, frantic at the thought that she'd accidentally killed him. That was the only reason she had said such a thing.

The next morning after breakfast, Lady Pettigrew regarded her departing guests with sincere regret. "I do wish the two of you could stay another day or so. We so enjoyed your visit, didn't we, George?"

"Visit was fine," Pettigrew muttered. He was having a hard time disguising his relief that at least two of the unwelcome guests were about to leave.

Lady Pettigrew turned to Iphiginia, who waited on the front steps as Marcus's black phaeton was readied. "Mrs. Bright, I cannot tell you how thrilled I am to learn that my Temple of Vesta is indeed a proper sort of ruin. Thank you so much for taking the time to study and measure it for me."

"You're quite welcome." Iphiginia was terribly conscious of Marcus standing next to her. His impatience was palpable.

"You do feel that our ruin is quite accurate?" Lady Pettigrew pressed.

"Yes, indeed," Iphiginia murmured. She could feel Marcus's laconic gaze resting on her.

"It is amazingly accurate in every detail,"

Marcus said. "I toured it myself last night. I vow, with very little imagination, one could imagine the presence of a genuine temple virgin."

Lady Pettigrew glowed with pride. "Really?"

"Not bloody likely," Pettigrew muttered. "And you cannot tell me you'd have wanted one to actually put in an appearance, Masters. Whole world knows that you have a rule against getting involved with virgins."

Iphiginia was annoyed. "Some rules are made to be broken, so far as I am concerned."

ELEVEN

*T*he following morning Barclay was ushered into the library of Marcus's town house. He sat down with a weary sigh, fumbled his spectacles into place, and withdrew several sheets of paper from a leather case.

Marcus leaned back in his chair and tried to restrain his seething curiosity while Barclay consulted a page of notes.

"Well?" Marcus said after what seemed an interminable length of time but which, in reality, was scarcely two minutes.

Barclay cleared his throat portentously and peered at Marcus over the gold wire frames of his spectacles. "To begin with, my lord, it appears that there never was a Mr. Bright. At least not one who was ever married to the current Mrs. Bright."

"I've already learned that much." The searing memory of the midnight tryst in the Temple of Vesta flashed through Marcus once again.

For the thousandth time he relived the glorious sensation of sinking himself into Iphiginia's hot, snug body. And for what must have been the thousandth time, he felt himself grow heavy with arousal.

He could almost feel the silken lushness of her inner thighs. The recollection of her exquisitely shaped breasts shimmered tantalizingly in his mind. Her nipples had been so fresh and ripe. They tasted like nothing he had ever known. Her beautifully rounded derriere reminded him of some exquisite, exotic fruit he had once grown in his conservatory. And the scent of her would linger in his mind forever.

Barclay's wiry brows connected in a solid line above his nose. "Begging your pardon, sir, but if you already knew that Mrs. Bright—I mean, Miss Bright—is no widow, d'you mind telling me why you sent me haring off to Devon?"

"I did not learn that particular fact until after you had left Town."

"How the devil did you discover it? I vow, no one here in Town knows."

Marcus worked to keep his answer vague. "I learned the truth about the nonexistent Mr.

Bright by using the same scientific methods I employ to discover other sorts of facts."

Barclay looked confused. "You used a telescope or a microscope?"

"I used observation and deductive reasoning." Marcus sat forward and rested his elbows on his desk. He clasped his hands together and regarded Barclay with a combination of foreboding and anticipation. "What else did you learn?"

Barclay consulted his notes. "Miss Bright was born and reared in the village of Deepford. Very small place. Finding it gave me no end of trouble, I assure you."

"Nevertheless," Marcus said, "you did find it."

"Yes, m'lord."

And if Barclay had discovered Deepford and the lack of a late Mr. Bright, others could do the same, Marcus thought. If someone else—a blackmailer, perhaps—grew curious enough to investigate her past, he would quickly learn that Iphiginia was no widow and therefore not immune to the rules Society imposed upon spinsters and innocents.

Marcus did not know which annoyed him the most, the fact that Iphiginia was so very vulnerable or her refusal to acknowledge her vulnerability.

"Continue, Barclay."

"Her parents, both of whom appear to have been endowed with somewhat unconventional temperaments, were lost at sea when she was barely eighteen years of age. She undertook the raising of her younger sister, Corina."

Just as I undertook the rearing of Bennet, Marcus thought. "How did she support herself and her sister? Was there a decent income from some inheritance?"

"No. Merely a bit from the sale of her mother's paintings and one or two pattern books that her father had produced."

Marcus picked up his wax seal and turned it in his fingers. "Not a great deal of money, then."

"No, m'lord, but Miss Bright appears to be rather enterprising in matters of finances."

Marcus got a chill in his gut. "What do you mean by that?"

"The first thing Miss Bright did after recovering from the shock of finding herself alone in the world with a young sister to support was to sell off the last of her mother's paintings and her father's pattern books. She used the money to open an academy for young ladies."

Marcus nearly dropped the seal on the desk. He stared at Barclay. "Miss Bright gave instruction to young ladies?"

"Yes, m'lord."

"Deportment, manners, proper behavior? That sort of instruction?"

"Among other things. Apparently Miss Bright's academy had an excellent reputation. A number of respectable gentry families in the vicinity sent their young girls to her."

"Good God." Marcus was nearly overcome by a crazed desire to laugh out loud. The thought of Iphiginia—notorious, free-spirited, daring Iphiginia—making a living teaching Society's grim, straitlaced rules to young ladies was dazzling.

"Her cousin, Miss Farley, came to live with her a year after Miss Bright lost her parents. Miss Farley taught mathematics and natural history, I believe."

"You say the school's reputation was excellent?"

"Yes, m'lord. As was the reputation of Miss Bright herself. You may well believe that in a town the size of Deepford, any faults, transgressions, or lapses of propriety would have been duly noted and punished."

"A single lapse would have been enough to destroy her livelihood."

"More than enough. A teacher of young ladies must maintain the highest standards. She cannot afford even the appearance of improper conduct."

"Poor Iphiginia."

"I beg your pardon, sir?"

"Never mind. Carry on. What else did you learn?"

"Let me see." Barclay shuffled some sheets of foolscap. "About three years ago, Miss Bright made another financial move which paid off rather handsomely."

"What sort of move?"

"It appears that she and her cousin formed a pool of investors. The pool was made up entirely of widows and spinsters, women who were in much the same position as themselves. They each contributed small amounts to a fund. The money was then loaned to a builder."

"A property speculation project?"

"Yes, m'lord."

"Which property?"

"Morning Rose Square."

"Bloody hell." Marcus grinned appreciatively. "She must have made a packet."

"She did," Barclay said dryly. "She used some of her profits to provide her sister with a suitable portion."

"What about the sister? Where is she?"

"Still in Deepford. Last year she married one Richard Hampton, the only son of an established gentry family."

"I see. Presumably the Hamptons are blissfully unaware that Iphiginia is masquerading as a widow here in Town?"

"Quite unaware. One can only imagine that the entire village would be horrified if the truth came out. Everyone back in Deepford, including the sister, believes that Miss Bright is still traipsing about Italy in the company of her cousin."

"I wonder what the good people of Deepford thought of Miss Bright's decision to tour the Continent?"

"You may be certain that the journey was viewed with considerable disapproval."

"But it was not considered scandalous?"

"No, although there were any number of villagers who predicted that Miss Bright would come to a bad end when she closed her academy for young ladies and took off for the Continent."

"I'll wager there were." He got to his feet and went to stand at the window. "You have done an excellent job, Barclay."

"Thank you, sir, I do try."

"I know that I can rely upon your continued absolute discretion."

"Of course." Barclay sounded deeply grieved that Marcus even bothered to mention discretion. "Not a word will pass my lips."

"Thank you, Barclay."

Barclay hesitated. "There is one other small

fact which may or may not be of interest to you, sir."

"What is that?"

"I mentioned that Miss Bright's sister, Corina, is married to Richard Hampton."

"What of it?"

"It seems that a couple of years ago there was talk of Mr. Hampton marrying the elder Miss Bright rather than Corina."

Marcus stilled. "Indeed?"

"There appears to have been some confusion on the matter." Barclay paused. "Even the elder Miss Bright is said to have been, shall we say, surprised when Hampton made his interest in Corina known."

"Is that so?"

"The villagers concluded that the elder Miss Bright's heart was broken when Mr. Hampton made it plain that he preferred Miss Corina."

The news that Iphiginia had loved another man, might still be in love with him, went through Marcus like a knife.

Did he break your heart, Iphiginia? Was that why you cast off the shackles of propriety and chose to ignore the rules? Do you still love him? Was Richard Hampton the man you were thinking of last night when you held me in your arms and whispered that you loved me?

Marcus gazed out into the garden for a few minutes. A gentle rain was falling, muting the bright hues of the flowers and dampening the verdant green of the foliage. The day had turned unexpectedly bleak.

He turned back to face Barclay. "Is there anything else I should know?"

"No, m'lord, I believe that about sums up the results of my inquiries."

"Thank you for your hard work."

"Of course, sir." Barclay heaved himself to his feet. "It was a rather hectic journey. I look forward to going home and putting my feet up in front of my own hearth."

"There is one more thing."

"Sir?"

"Tomorrow I would like you to make other inquiries for me."

"Concerning?"

"I would like you to find out who recently built an elaborate sepulchral monument to a Mrs. Elizabeth Eaton in Reeding Cemetery."

Barclay eyed him askance. "A sepulchral monument?"

"Yes, Barclay. A sort of grotto arrangement."

Barclay looked resigned. "Very well, m'lord. I shall see what I can discover. Will there be anything else?"

"No, Barclay, you may go."

Marcus waited until he was alone in the library. Then he walked slowly back to his desk and picked up the message he had received from Hannah an hour ago.

M:
Must see you. Urgent. Entrance to Dollanger Gardens. Two o'clock.
Yrs.
H.

Marcus crumpled the small sheet of paper in one hand. He was afraid he could guess why Hannah was so anxious to risk seeing him again.

At two o'clock that afternoon, Marcus got into the nondescript hackney coach that halted on the street outside Dollanger Gardens.

Hannah, heavily veiled and dressed in an unremarkable brown carriage gown, waited inside. She had closed the curtains on the windows. The interior of the coach was drenched in shadows.

She confirmed his unpleasant hypothesis immediately.

"I received another blackmail demand while you were out of town, Marcus. Another five thousand pounds." Hannah's normally soft voice was harsh with anxiety. "I was forced to pawn a lovely bracelet that Sands gave to me on my last birthday. I fear that I shall never be able to buy it back. I live in dread of the day he asks me why I never wear it."

"Where were you instructed to leave the money?" Marcus asked.

"The instructions were the same as last time. I left the money in a hackney coach in Pall Mall. Marcus, this cannot go on. I cannot continue to pawn my jewelry. Sooner or later Sands will notice."

"I suppose that it would be useless for me to try once more to convince you to tell Sands the truth."

"You know that I cannot do such a thing." Hannah raised her veil, revealing her desperate expression. "He will turn from me in disgust, I know he will."

"He is a reasonable man. Give him a chance, Hannah."

"I love him too much to take the risk. I do not expect you to comprehend my fear, Marcus. You have never been afraid of anything or anyone in your life. And it's obvious that you have never loved a woman the way I love my husband. If you had ever experienced such great depth of feeling, you would understand."

Marcus wondered if Iphiginia had loved her Richard Hampton with as much intensity and fervor as Hannah loved Sands. He pushed the notion aside. "I shall give you the five thousand pounds, Hannah. Fetch the bracelet from the jeweler's before he resells it."

She sagged back against the seat in relief. "Thank you, Marcus. You are a good friend. I shall pay you back, I swear it."

"There is no need. We both know that I shall not miss the money."

She smiled wistfully. "No, but that is hardly the point, is it? There are many people as wealthy as yourself who would not advance a friend so much as a penny."

Marcus paid no attention. "This bloody blackmailer is getting bolder. He must be stopped."

"Have you made any progress toward discovering his identity?"

"Some, not much." Marcus regarded her through narrowed eyes. "I have a question to ask you."

"What is it?"

"I seem to recall that at the time of Spalding's death you had a young woman in your employ. I met her only once or twice, but I believe she had red hair."

"Caroline Baylor." Hannah grimaced in disgust.

"What do you know of her?"

"Very little. Spalding would not allow me to go anywhere alone, not even to see my family in Hampshire. He claimed he was protecting me, but the truth was, he suspected that I would run away from him. He feared the scandal."

"Bastard."

"When I complained of being confined to the house, he hired Caroline Baylor as a companion for me. I never did care for her. She was very sly. She came from a very respectable agency and had all sorts of references, but to this day, I believe she was actually Spalding's mistress."

It would have been typical of Spalding to install his mistress in his wife's household, Marcus reflected. "Do you know what became of her?"

"She disappeared the morning after I—" Hannah's hands tightened on her reticule. "The morning after I killed Spalding. But she was not in the house that night, Marcus. She had gone out. You know that. You walked in right after I had pulled the trigger. I was alone with Spalding."

"You said that she came from a respectable agency. Do you recall which one?"

"The Wycherley Agency. It's considered the finest in London."

"Perhaps the owner of the agency will know what became of her."

Hannah's eyes widened. "Surely you do not believe that Caroline Baylor is the blackmailer?"

"Where do you think she went that night?"

"I have no notion." Hannah's mouth twisted. "Caroline Baylor was not the usual sort of companion. She came and went as she pleased. Why are you suddenly concerned with finding her?"

It was not easy to juggle so many secrets. Marcus chose his words carefully. "I have formed a theory that the blackmailer may be a paid companion. Someone who would have once been in a position to know the secrets of both your household and that of the other victim."

"And who is now blackmailing her former employers? Good Lord, I never thought of that." Hannah frowned. "I can certainly envision Caroline resorting to blackmail. But why would she wait so long to do it?"

"We do not even know if she is the one behind this. But it's a place to start." Marcus pulled his watch out of his pocket and glanced at the time. It was two-thirty. He had a three o'clock appointment with Iphiginia. "I must be on my way, Hannah. I shall see that you get the five thousand pounds as soon as possible. My man of affairs can arrange to deliver it."

"It is very kind of you to help me again after all these years," Hannah whispered. "I do not know what I would do without you."

"We are friends. There is no need to thank me." Marcus reached out to open the carriage door.

"Marcus, wait." Hannah touched his arm. "Forgive me for asking, but are you on your way to meet Mrs. Bright?"

Marcus paused. "Why do you ask?"

"Speaking as your friend, I must tell you that I have been hearing the oddest rumors. Are they true?"

"The rumors concerning me are always odd, Hannah, you know that."

"Yes, but these are different. I have heard that your new mistress is really quite extraordinary."

Marcus fought back a violent desire to tell her that Iphiginia was not his mistress, that she occupied a far more important role in his life. But there was nothing he could say at this point, not even to Hannah.

He retreated behind one of his well-known rules. *Never explain*.

"Hannah, you know that I never discuss such matters." He smiled humorlessly. "As the one who taught me how to conduct myself in Society, you would be the first to condemn me for ungentlemanly behavior were I to make any comment at all on the subject of my association with Mrs. Bright."

Hannah quickly withdrew her gloved hand from his sleeve. "I taught you how to eat with the proper fork and how to dance the waltz, but I certainly did not teach you how to become a figure of legend. You managed that on your own with your famous rules and your enigmatic ways."

"Do not concern yourself with my affairs, Hannah. I shall take care of myself."

"Yes, of course. I am sorry. I did not mean to pry. You are the best friend I have, Marcus. I cannot help but worry about you."

"It is your husband who should be your best friend now, not I." Marcus opened the door and got out of the carriage.

Adam Manwaring set his papers down on Iphiginia's library desk and took a seat. He looked intently at Amelia. "Before I give you the results of my inquiries concerning Lady Guthrie's old companion, I should first tell you that I have talked to Mr. Dodgson."

Amelia tensed. "I trust that you informed him that he is not welcome to join the investment pool?"

"I did." Adam's expression was surprisingly grim. "And I told him why."

"Excellent," Iphiginia said. She glanced at

Amelia and thought she saw a brief flicker of satisfaction in her cousin's eyes.

"I informed Dodgson that the investment pool is composed primarily of widows and spinsters, many of whom have worked as governesses and companions," Adam said. "I told him he no doubt understood why such ladies would not wish to do business with a man of his unfortunate reputation."

"What did he say?" Iphiginia asked.

Adam shrugged. "He was incensed, naturally. Claimed he had been grossly insulted and insisted on a meeting with the principals so that he could explain the misunderstanding."

Amelia looked down at her folded hands. "What did you tell him?"

"Simply that the principals had no intention of meeting with him," Adam said. "He then said that he had no recollection of any improper incident involving a young female employee in his or anyone else's household."

"Did he say that?" Amelia asked softly.

Adam raised his brows. "He then proceeded to undermine his entire defense by flying into an apoplectic rage. He said everyone knew that the sort of females who became governesses were all bent on seducing the gentlemen in the households in which they were employed. He said that they were not to be trusted."

Amelia exchanged a sharp glance with

Iphiginia. "He specifically mentioned governesses?"

"Yes," Adam said. "He did."

"Then he most certainly does remember,"
Amelia whispered.

"Obviously." Iphiginia hurried to change the
topic. "So much for that issue. Let us get on to
the matter of Aunt Zoe's companion."

Adam reluctantly returned his attention to
his papers. "As to that, I'm afraid I discovered
very little information of a useful nature. Miss
Todd died some five years ago."

"She's dead?" Iphiginia sat forward abruptly.
She was so intent on Adam's announcement
that she barely noticed the sound of a carriage
in the street.

Adam glanced up from his notes with a quizzical frown. "She was nearly seventy. Did you
know the lady?"

"No. No, I did not." Iphiginia recovered her
aplomb. "But an acquaintance of mine is under
the impression that she is still very much alive.
This news will certainly come as a surprise. Did
you learn anything else?"

Adam looked at his notes. "Miss Todd died a
spinster. She was born in a small village in Sus-
sex and worked as a governess or companion
most of her life."

"A dead end," Iphiginia murmured. "I told
him so."

Adam looked at her. "I beg your pardon?"

"It's not important," Iphiginia said. "Is that all of it?"

"Yes, other than the fact that she spent most of her career with the—"

A crisp knock on the library door interrupted Adam before he could complete his sentence.

Iphiginia glanced at the clock. One minute until three. She glanced out the window and saw the black phaeton that had halted in front of her door. Her pulse quickened. Anticipation heightened all of her senses.

This was madness, she thought. She could not allow Marcus to affect her so acutely. She struggled to infuse her voice with an appropriately unconcerned tone.

The library door opened. Mrs. Shaw appeared.

"Yes, Mrs. Shaw?" Iphiginia inquired.

"The Earl of Masters is here to see you, madam. Are you home?"

"Of course she's home. Any idiot can see that." Marcus strode into the library without waiting for the housekeeper to finish announcing him in a proper fashion. "Good afternoon, Mrs. Bright. Miss Farley."

"My lord," Iphiginia said very coolly. "You're early."

"By one minute. I trust you will forgive me." Marcus walked toward the desk, took her hand,

and brought it to his mouth. Amusement gleamed in his eyes, as though he was well aware of the chaotic condition of Iphiginia's senses.

"Allow me to introduce my man of affairs, Mr. Manwaring," Iphiginia said.

Marcus gave Adam a narrow look. "Manwaring."

"Sir." Adam rose politely. "I was just leaving."

"Were you?" Marcus asked in an encouraging tone. "Do not allow me to delay you."

Adam flushed.

Iphiginia scowled at the ill-concealed rudeness. "Mr. Manwaring has not quite finished his business, have you, Mr. Manwaring?"

Adam gathered up his notes. "As I said, there isn't anything else to add, except that Miss Todd was associated with the Wycherley Agency throughout most of her professional career."

"Damn," Marcus said very quietly.

Iphiginia looked at him, surprised by his reaction. "Is something wrong, my lord?"

"No." Marcus wandered over to the window. "Something just occurred to me, that's all."

Iphiginia turned back to Adam. "Thank you very much, Mr. Manwaring. You've been most helpful, as always. That will be all for today."

Marcus spoke without turning around. "A moment, Manwaring."

"Yes, my lord?"

"Did you inquire after Miss Todd at the Wycherley Agency?"

"Yes, I did, as a matter of fact," Adam said. "I spoke with Mrs. Wycherley herself yesterday. She has owned and operated the agency for over twenty years. She was the one who informed me that Miss Todd had died five years ago."

"I see."

Iphiginia glared at Marcus's broad back. Adam was her man of affairs, not his. "Would you see Mr. Manwaring out, Amelia?"

Amelia rose quickly. "Yes, of course."

Adam blushed. "It's not necessary. I can see myself out, Miss Farley."

"I shall be happy to escort you to the door, Mr. Manwaring," Amelia said.

"If you insist."

Iphiginia waited until the library door had closed behind the pair. Then she chuckled with satisfaction. "Those two were made for each other, you know."

"Which two?"

"My cousin and Mr. Manwaring. I have every hope that they will soon realize that they are an ideal couple. They have so much in common in terms of personality and intellect."

"What utter nonsense." Marcus swung around with an impatient air. "Do you fancy yourself a matchmaker?"

"You'll see," Iphiginia said in a very superior tone. "I have an instinct for these things."

"Rubbish. You have an instinct for creating trouble."

She glowered. "What is wrong with you today, sir? Are you still brooding about what happened at the Pettigrews'? I told you, nothing has changed. All will be well."

"No, damn it, I am not brooding about that situation. There is nothing to brood about. What's done is done."

"Then what is affecting your temper?"

He lowered his large frame onto a claw-footed chair and regarded Iphiginia with a meditative expression. "Do you believe in coincidence?"

Iphiginia gave a small shrug. "Strange things do happen. Why do you ask?"

"Because a rather interesting coincidence has just turned up with regard to our blackmail problem."

"What coincidence is that?"

"My friend, the other victim, had a companion in her employ at the time the events for which she is now being blackmailed occurred."

"Stop right there." Iphiginia held up a triumphant hand. "If you're going to tell me that the companion's name was Miss Todd and that you think she is the blackmailer, you may as well save your breath. Miss Todd has been dead for five years."

"My friend's companion was named Caroline Baylor," Marcus said evenly. "The interesting coincidence is that she was also connected to the Wycherley Agency."

Iphiginia considered that carefully. "It is not such a great coincidence, is it? After all, the Wycherley Agency has been around for years. At one time or another it has no doubt sent governesses or companions into many of the best families."

"Nevertheless, it's a connection." Marcus glanced at the clock. "It's only a bit after three. I intend to speak to Mrs. Wycherley myself this afternoon."

"But Miss Todd is dead and you said your friend's companion has disappeared. What do you hope to learn from the owner of the agency?"

"I am not certain yet, but I intend to ask a few questions concerning both Miss Todd and Miss Baylor."

Iphiginia was intrigued. "I shall come with you to see Mrs. Wycherley."

"There is no need," Marcus said easily. "I

shall report any information that I discover in the course of the interview."

"On the contrary, my lord." Iphiginia fixed him with a determined look. "We are partners in this venture, if you will recall."

Marcus contemplated her for a moment. "Very well. I suppose you'll only call on her by yourself if I do not take you with me."

"You suppose correctly." Iphiginia was pleased by the small victory. She picked up her teacup and took a sip. The trick to handling Marcus, she told herself, was to demonstrate firm resolve. He was the sort of man who naturally assumed command of a situation. A woman of weak spirit would be soft clay in his powerful hands.

"We shall deal with Mrs. Wycherley together in a while, then," Marcus said. "But first there are a few other matters I wish to discuss with you."

"What matters are those?" Iphiginia started to put her teacup down onto the saucer.

"The lack of a late Mr. Bright is the first item on the agenda."

The delicate teacup slipped from Iphiginia's grasp. It crashed against the edge of the saucer, tipped over, and spilled tea onto the polished mahogany desk.

"Good heavens." Iphiginia jumped to her

feet, snatched a gossamer white lace hankie from her pocket, and began to dab ineffectually at the spilled tea. "I thought we had already disposed of that subject, sir."

"We certainly disposed of something in connection with the topic, but it wasn't the late, unlamented Mr. Bright."

Iphiginia tried desperately to control the blush that she knew must be turning her face a bright pink. "Really, Marcus."

"Yes, really, Iphiginia." Marcus withdrew a large, sturdy linen handkerchief from his pocket, got to his feet with leisurely grace, and blotted up the tea in a single swipe. "Furthermore, having delved into the subject at some depth, so to speak, I find there is a great deal more to it than was apparent at first."

Iphiginia was seized with a sense of panic. "Such as?"

Marcus's amber eyes gleamed. "Such as a certain academy for young ladies, a village called Deepford, and a sister who is married to the son of the most important family in the neighborhood. In short, Iphiginia, I know everything."

She felt as though she'd had the wind knocked out of her. She sank slowly back down into her chair. "How did you discover so much about me?"

"That is not important. What is important is

that if I was able to learn the truth, others can and no doubt will eventually discover it, also."

Iphiginia was dazed by his blunt revelations. He had learned so much in such a short period of time. It was unnerving. "Sir, I believe you are telling me this because you are about to present me with a choice of two options."

He cocked a brow. "Two?"

"Yes." She raised her chin. "You are going to tell me that I must either leave Town immediately before anyone else stumbles onto the truth or else I shall have to consider an offer of marriage from you. Is that not right?"

"You are wrong, Iphiginia."

She looked at him with renewed hope. "I am?"

"Under the circumstances, there is only one option, not two. That option is marriage."

"Never," Iphiginia said loudly, resolutely, and so forcefully that she knew Marcus could not possibly guess that her heart was breaking. "Absolutely impossible. Out of the question. The entire notion cannot even be considered."

Marcus smiled grimly. "One of the most interesting things I have learned in the course of my scientific studies is that there are very few things which are impossible."

TWELVE

You and your bloody rules," Iphiginia said
fiercely. She leaned forward and planted
both of her hands flat on her desk. Her eyes
were brilliant with outrage. "That's what this is
all about, is it not? You believe that you broke
one of your damnable rules and therefore you
have to pay the price."

"Calm yourself, Iphiginia. You are becoming
overwrought."

"I will not calm myself and I will not be married because of Masters's Rules. Do you hear
me, sir?"

"I hear you." Marcus set his jaw and kept his
face impassive as he refolded his tea-stained
handkerchief. It occurred to him that, what
with one thing and another, he spent a great

deal of time mopping up tea in Iphiginia's study. "But I do not believe that you have given the matter due consideration."

"Do not lecture me as though I were a schoolgirl, sir. I am a rational, educated, intelligent woman, not a foolish child. Of course I gave the matter proper consideration."

She would fight him every inch of the way. Anger flared in Marcus as he realized just how difficult his task would be. "You call masquerading as a notorious widow and my mistress the action of a rational, educated, intelligent woman?"

"You were not nearly so scathing about my masquerade before you discovered that I was not a widow. In fact, if memory serves, you were quite willing to go along with the plan. You rather liked the notion of having a new and unusual mistress, did you not, sir?"

"That was before we took a midnight tour of Pettigrew's Temple of Vesta and discovered that the damn antiquity was so authentic there was still a Vestal Virgin hanging about the place."

She looked desperate now. "Marcus, that is a very minor detail. You must not let it influence your actions."

"I shall be the judge of what influences my actions."

"Damnation, sir, nothing has changed."

"That's not true. One element of this farce has most certainly changed."

"It's not a farce." She glared at him. "It was a very clever scheme which has every chance of producing results. Society still believes me to be a widow and it is convinced that I am your mistress. Every element of the plan remains intact."

"But for how long?"

"For as long as we wish," she retorted. "No one other than yourself has questioned my authenticity."

"It's only a matter of time before someone else decides to go to Devon to ask a few questions."

"Nonsense. Why would anyone bother? My lord, let us have some honesty here. The real reason you are being so difficult about this is because you feel that you broke one of your own rules."

"I am well aware that you do not think much of my rules, but I have lived by them for a long while and I do not violate them for the sake of convenience."

"Marcus, listen to me. I have a deep and abiding respect for your rules and the sense of honor that inspires them. But in this instance, you did not violate your rules."

"No? I seem to recall quite clearly that I was

the man who lay between your thighs two nights ago. Am I mistaken?"

Iphiginia's eyes widened in shock. The bright flags in her cheeks turned a darker shade of red. "There is no excuse for vulgarity," she said quite primly.

"You sound like a bloody schoolmistress."

"I *am* a bloody schoolmistress. Or, rather, I was at one time. I repeat, my lord, you did not violate your precious rules; I did. That makes all the difference, don't you see?"

"No," Marcus said.

"You're not responsible for what happened. I am."

"Don't try to twist the logic of this situation. It is perfectly straightforward."

"But Marcus, you cannot marry me and you know it."

"Why not?"

She threw up her hands in exasperation. "Because in the eyes of Society I'm the mistress of the most notorious man in London, namely you, my lord."

"So?"

"We both know that a man in your position does not marry his mistress."

Marcus flattened his hands on the surface of the desk and met Iphiginia eye to eye. "I make my own rules. Never forget that."

She blinked, straightened, and took a hasty

step back. "But surely in a matter such as this—"

"In *everything,* Iphiginia."

"I am not overly fond of rules, sir."

"That has become quite obvious."

She took another step back and came up against her chair. "I was obliged to live by the rules of others for too many years. I find rules very depressing to the spirits. I thought that you, of all people, would comprehend my desire to be free."

"Free? Christ, Iphiginia, none of us is ever truly free. We all live by a set of rules, whether it be our own or someone else's. If you haven't reasoned that out for yourself yet, you are far more naive than you pretend to be."

Her chin came up proudly. "Very well, then. If I must have a set of rules, I shall do as you do, sir. I shall make up my own."

"And, pray, just what do your rules have to say about the situation in which you presently find yourself?"

"They say that I am not obliged to marry any man. To be perfectly frank, sir, I do not see any great benefit to the married state for a female. Indeed, I do not even see the appeal of the marital embrace. From what I could deduce the other night, it is not nearly as thrilling as the poets would have one believe."

Marcus felt as though he had taken a pugilist's blow in his gut. He felt himself turn a dull red. "I told you, that was my fault. I was clumsy and hasty."

"Oh, Marcus." The fire of battle vanished from Iphiginia's eyes. She rushed around the edge of the desk. "You mustn't blame yourself for that, too. It was not your fault. It was mine."

"Yours?" Marcus stared at her uncomprehendingly as she flew toward him. It struck him belatedly that she was going to throw herself into his arms.

"Yes, of course. What happened the other night was of my instigation. I misled you. I knew all about your silly rule against getting involved with inexperienced females, but I wanted you to make love to me. I encouraged you, sir. Indeed, I practically begged you to do so."

"Iphiginia—"

Iphiginia landed against him with a soft thud. He caught hold of her and held her close before she could change her mind.

"I seduced you, sir," she whispered into his coat.

"No, you did not. I seduced you. I wanted to make love to you." His voice roughened. "God help me, even if I had known the truth, I do not think that I could have stopped myself. My only regret was that you did not enjoy my lovemaking."

"But I did." Her words were muffled against his shoulder. "At least, I did up until the very last bit. As I told you that night, I did not calculate certain factors correctly. But that was entirely my own fault, not yours."

Marcus groaned. Incredible as it seemed, Iphiginia did not blame him for his clumsy lovemaking. She insisted on taking full responsibility for the debacle in the Temple of Vesta.

Perhaps another man would have been amused by her naïveté. Marcus was both awed and deeply moved by it.

"Listen to me, Iphiginia. You are a very well educated woman and I will allow that you have no doubt studied a great many classical statues of nude men, but you do not know all there is to know of such calculations."

"But I have studied the original statues, my lord. Not just copies."

He framed her face between his palms and forced her to meet his eyes. "It will be much more pleasurable the next time, Iphiginia. I swear it."

She fixed him with a sober, searching gaze. "Do you really think so?"

"You must trust me." He brushed his mouth lightly across hers.

"I do, Marcus. Oh, I do trust you." She stood on tiptoe, threw her arms around him, and kissed him with the same joyful enthusiasm she had demonstrated since the start of their relationship.

Her mouth was soft and warm and exciting beneath Marcus's. Her breasts were crushed against his chest. He could feel the delightful curves of her thighs pressing against his legs. No other woman had ever felt so good in his arms.

More important, it was obvious that her passion for him still sparkled within her, a crystal prism that glowed with warmth and light. He had not shattered it the other night.

Relief surged through him. *She still wanted him.* His clumsy lovemaking had not dampened her sweet ardor or lessened her desire for his touch. Everything was going to be all right.

He raised his head reluctantly after a moment and looked down at her. "Then that settles the matter, does it not?"

She gave him a tremulous smile. "I am not opposed to making another attempt at lovemaking, if you truly believe it will work."

"It will." Silently he vowed to make it perfect for her.

"Does this mean that you will allow our liaison to continue?" she asked with a hopeful look.

"It means," he said deliberately, "that we will be married as soon as possible."

She stiffened. "I told you, it is not possible."

"And I told you that anything is possible."

Her mouth tightened into a stubborn line. "Marcus, will you give me an honest answer to a question I must ask you?"

"I will never lie to you, Iphiginia."

Her mouth curved wistfully. "Another one of your rules?"

"Yes."

"Very well, then, I shall ask my question. Would you be standing here today insisting that I marry you if you had discovered the other night that I actually was a widow with some experience of the marital embrace?"

He told himself he ought to have seen that trap early on, but he had not. The snare caught him unawares and he stumbled badly. "Devil take it, Iphiginia, that is completely irrelevant."

"No, Marcus, it's very relevant."

He saw the hidden pit that had opened beneath his feet. He made a desperate bid to recover his footing. "Who knows what would have happened had you been who you claimed to be? I have never met anyone like you, Iphiginia. I do not know how I would have reacted."

"If you had found me to be exactly who and

what I purported to be, you would have been content to let me continue on as your mistress. Is that not so?"

"Damn it, Iphiginia, how can I answer that? I am a man of science. I deal in facts, not fancies or conjecture or what-might-have-beens."

"Please, answer me, Marcus. It's very important."

"The answer to your purely conjectural question is that I do not know the answer."

"Well, I do," she said gently. "And the answer is no. Therefore my answer to you now must also be no."

"Bloody hell, woman, don't you comprehend the situation? You have no choice."

"If I were eighteen, unable to support myself, and concerned with the opinion of others, that might be true. But I am twenty-seven, financially independent, and I do not give a fig for Society's rules."

"Iphiginia—"

She hugged herself. "I spent too many years abiding by the dictates of a small village. I do not intend to be governed by those of the *ton*." She shuddered. "Sometimes I still awake in the middle of the night and remember how I had to bite my tongue whenever the vicar stopped by to lecture me on proper behavior."

A rush of empathy went through Marcus. "I,

too, was reared in a small village. I know how it must have been for you in Deepford."

"It never ended," Iphiginia whispered. "There were eyes everywhere. No one really approved of Mama or Papa. They were possessed of artistic temperaments, you see."

"I know."

"My parents always said that I could ignore the rude, interfering ways of others, but I was not able to do that after they were gone. I had to make a living for myself and my sister. And then Amelia showed up on my doorstep, penniless and alone."

"So there were three of you to support."

"Yes. And in order to do so, I had to submit to all the bloody petty little rules of the good folk of Deepford." Iphiginia looked out the window into the street. "Squire Hampton and his wife were always giving me advice on my conduct. Mrs. Calder, who had the cottage next to my academy, prattled on endlessly about how an instructor of young ladies must be a paragon of propriety. The vicar and his wife were forever hovering, waiting for me to trip and fall in the muck of what they considered improper behavior."

Marcus walked around the desk, reached out, and pulled her back into his arms. "I understand."

"There were eyes everywhere. I had to be so careful. All three of us depended on the income from the academy. And the academy's existence depended on the goodwill of the Hamptons and the vicar and all the other people in Deepford who made the rules by which the rest of us were forced to abide."

Marcus tightened his arms around her and breathed in the flowery scent of the soap she used to wash her hair. He realized with an odd sense of awareness that in that moment he felt closer to her than he had ever felt to anyone else in his life.

"I know what it is to be trapped by one's responsibilities," Marcus said into Iphiginia's hair. "And by other people's rules."

"A year ago, I left Deepford forever. I do not intend to ever go back except very occasionally to visit my sister. I am determined to follow your example, Marcus. If I must have rules, they will be of my own making."

Marcus moved one hand soothingly down her proud, tense spine. "I comprehend your feelings better than you know, but I cannot allow you to continue to masquerade as my mistress."

"Why not?"

He sought for a sound, unemotional argument. "It is too dangerous."

"No, it is not." Iphiginia lifted her head from his shoulder. "We are both equally concerned with identifying the blackmailer and we have both agreed that we must combine our forces in order to do so. What better way to go about the task than to allow our pretense to stand?"

He studied her pensively. He had known he would have a battle on his hands, but he had not understood just how obstinate his opponent would be until now. "One of the problems which you continue to overlook, Iphiginia, is that the pretense is no longer, strictly speaking, a pretense."

She flushed. "For heaven's sake, Marcus, if the thought of making love to me alarms you to such a degree, we shall simply refrain from such activity."

There was about as much chance of him refraining from making love to Iphiginia as there was of building a ship that could carry him to the stars, Marcus decided.

When faced with a seemingly imponderable problem, he had learned that it was sometimes best to approach it obliquely rather than head-on.

He had some time, he assured himself. How much time, he did not know. But Iphiginia had not been exposed thus far. There was no reason to suppose that anyone else would stumble onto the truth in the near future. The present situation could not be allowed to go on indefinitely, but as far as he could ascertain, no immediate threat loomed.

She still wanted him, Marcus thought. He would hold on to that knowledge, study it, examine it, analyze it. Eventually he would find a way to use her weakness for him to wear down her defenses.

The door of the library opened.

Amelia walked into the room. "Iphiginia? Mr. Manwaring reminded me that we must—" She broke off, flushing, when she saw Iphiginia in Marcus's arms. "I beg your pardon."

"It's quite all right," Marcus said. He looked down at Iphiginia. "We will finish this conversation some other time. As it happens, we were just about to leave, weren't we, Iphiginia?"

"Yes, as a matter of fact, we were." She stepped quickly away from him and gave Amelia a shaky smile. "We're off to the Wycherley Agency to see what we can learn from Mrs. Wycherley."

"Do not bother to give my regards to Constance Wycherley," Amelia muttered. "I never did like that woman."

It had been a near thing. Much too close for comfort.

Twenty minutes later, after a silent, brooding carriage ride to a small lane just off Oxford Street, Iphiginia was still feeling the effects of the quarrel.

She was in a desperate fix because of Masters's Rules and it was her own fault, she thought as she was handed down from the black phaeton.

She should have known that Marcus would likely feel compelled to marry her were he ever to discover that she was not a widow. But she had deliberately allowed herself to believe that she could deceive him.

She had convinced herself that she could fool Marcus, just as she had fooled Society. She ought to have known better.

Now she had to find a way to convince Marcus that he was not obligated by his own rigid code to wed her.

It would not be easy, Iphiginia knew. He was too much like her in too many ways. The man was too bloody stubborn and determined for his own good.

"This is Number Eleven." Marcus frowned at the darkened windows of the Wycherley Agency. "The agency appears to be closed for the day."

"How odd." Iphiginia studied the drawn curtains that blanked both windows and the door. "It is not yet four in the afternoon."

"Perhaps Mrs. Wycherley was forced to close the premises early for some personal reason."

"One would think that she would have staff to keep the office open."

"True." Marcus walked to the door and twisted the knob experimentally. "Locked."

Iphiginia looked up. The two stories above the agency premises were also dark. "I wonder if Mrs. Wycherley lives above her place of business."

"Very likely." Marcus stepped back to survey the upper stories. "But if she is at home, she is definitely not receiving visitors."

"She may be ill."

"Manwaring told you that he spoke with her yesterday. Did he mention that she appeared to be ailing?"

"No. But that doesn't mean she did not fall ill during the night," Iphiginia said. "Perhaps she left for a visit to the country."

"In which case," Marcus said with a speculative expression, "the shop and the rooms above are very likely empty."

Iphiginia gave him a sharp glance. "Are you about to suggest what I think you are about to suggest?"

"You know me so well, Iphiginia." Marcus took her hand. He glanced both ways up and down the street to be certain that no one was paying any attention to them. "Come. There is no harm in our taking a quick look 'round back."

Iphiginia did not protest as he led her to the end of the short street and around the corner into the alley. "But what do you hope to find?"

"Who knows? One of the first rules of scientific inquiry is to ask a great many questions."

"What questions are you asking right now?"

"Why a successful, long-established business would close so early in the day."

Iphiginia got a distinctly uneasy sensation. "Especially the day after my man of affairs interviewed the owner and asked her about one of her former clients?"

"Precisely."

Marcus led the way down the alley behind the row of shopfronts. He stopped in front of the back door of Number Eleven and knocked softly.

There was no response. He reached for the doorknob and tried it carefully. "This door is locked also."

Iphiginia looked at the small-paned windows that flanked the door and saw that the one on the right was ajar. "Look, Marcus."

He followed her gaze. "It appears as though someone left in a great hurry and forgot to secure all the windows."

"Yes, it does."

Marcus eased open the unlocked window,

moved the curtain aside, and peered into the interior of the shop.

Iphiginia crowded close behind him. "Can you see anything?"

"Not much. The room is rather dark. The curtains are drawn shut. Hold on a minute." He opened the window all the way and then stepped back to study the situation. "Damn. I do not think that I will be able to fit through that opening."

Iphiginia studied the situation. "I can fit through it."

Marcus looked at her. "If you think that I am going to allow you to go through that window—"

"Marcus, be reasonable. I shall simply slip through the opening and immediately unlock the door for you. You will be inside with me in no time."

"Hmm." He hesitated, clearly torn. "Very well. But don't waste a moment once you're inside. Go right to the door."

"I will." Iphiginia went to stand in front of the open window. It was too far off the ground for her to be able to simply step through it. "You'll have to help me."

"I can see that." Marcus fitted his hands to her waist and lifted her effortlessly off the ground.

Iphiginia shivered, remembering the feel of

his hands on her bare skin two nights ago. He was so strong and yet she felt so safe when she was in his embrace.

"Hurry, Iphiginia."

"Yes, of course." She shook off the hot memories and concentrated on the matter at hand.

Scrambling through the window proved unexpectedly awkward. Iphiginia was hampered by the long, ruffled skirts of her white muslin walking dress and matching spencer.

"Good God," Marcus muttered somewhere behind her. "How many petticoats do you have on under your gown? I am about to drown in them."

"It was rather chilly today." Iphiginia was intensely aware of his hand on the calf of her leg.

A few seconds later she landed on her feet inside the shadowed room. She reached out to steady herself. Her fingers brushed against a sheaf of papers that were lying on a nearby table. Several sheets of foolscap drifted to the floor at her feet.

"Oh, dear," she murmured.

"What's wrong?" Marcus demanded instantly.

"Nothing serious. I knocked some papers to the floor." Iphiginia stooped to retrieve them. She stared in amazement as her eyes began to adjust to the gloom. "Good grief. Marcus, there are papers and ledgers and such scattered about everywhere. The place looks as though a whirlwind went through it."

"Open the door. Quickly."

Iphiginia straightened and went to the back door. She unlocked it. Marcus strode into the shop and shut the door behind himself. He stood still for a moment, gazing into the shadows.

"Bloody hell," he said softly. "The place has been ransacked."

Iphiginia stared at the chaos around them. "What do you think happened here?"

"I don't know." Marcus moved toward the narrow staircase that led to the private rooms above the shop. "Wait here. I want to take a quick look around upstairs."

Iphiginia ignored him. She followed him up the stairs and came to a halt beside him in a doorway that opened onto a tiny parlor.

Here everything was in order. The folding table of the secretary desk was neatly closed. The furnishings were not tumbled about. The carpet was not littered with papers.

"This room does not appear to have been disturbed," Iphiginia said.

"No." Marcus turned and walked down the hall.

Iphiginia followed.

Together they looked into one small, comfortably furnished room after another and then they climbed the stairs to the top floor.

It was not until Marcus put his hand on the knob of the bedchamber door that Iphiginia was suddenly struck by a deep sense of dread. "Marcus?"

"I'll go in first."

He opened the door of the last bedchamber and stood very still in the opening.

Iphiginia tried to peer around Marcus's broad shoulders. She could see what appeared to be gray skirts and a pair of high laced shoes lying on the floor. "Oh, my God. Is that . . . ?"

"No doubt. Stay right here."

This time Iphiginia obeyed. She watched Marcus walk toward the body. He came to a halt beside the dead woman and knelt down to examine her.

"She was shot," Marcus said. He touched one of the fingers of a limp hand.

"She's . . . ?"

"Dead. Yes." Marcus got to his feet. "I would estimate that she has been dead for several hours."

Iphiginia's stomach clenched. She backed hurriedly out of the doorway, gasping for air.

Marcus walked out of the room. He looked at her with concern. "Are you all right?"

Iphiginia nodded hastily. "Yes. I think so."

"Come on, let's get out of here. The last thing we want is to be discovered hanging about a dead woman's rooms."

Marcus took her arm and whisked her down the staircase.

"Do you think Mrs. Wycherley was robbed?" Iphiginia asked.

"No," Marcus said. He came to a halt on the first landing and glanced into the parlor again. "If that were the case, the thief would have taken those silver candlesticks and a few other items."

"Then what happened here?"

"I'm not positive, but I can create a hypothesis which would explain what we see."

"What is your hypothesis?"

"I suspect that Mrs. Wycherley was the blackmailer and that your aunt and my friend were not her only victims. Nor were we the only people who managed to make the connection to the Wycherley Agency."

"You believe that someone else came here after Mr. Manwaring talked to her yesterday?"

"Yes. It's entirely reasonable to assume that Mrs. Wycherley was murdered by one of her victims."

"And after he killed her the victim went through her files searching for the evidence she had used to blackmail him?"

"Yes," Marcus said.

"Marcus, that is brilliant. It would explain everything." Iphiginia frowned. "It also means that the crisis is over."

"It appears that way."

She tried to feel a sense of relief. After all, Aunt Zoe's secret was safe once more.

But the blackmail problem was not the only thing that had disappeared, she realized. Along with it had gone her excuse for continuing her masquerade as Marcus's mistress.

THIRTEEN

At seven o'clock that evening Marcus sat at the worktable in his laboratory and pondered the dilemma of how to turn a mistress into a wife.

It was a problem he had never thought to encounter. By comparison, the construction of clockwork mechanisms, telescopes, and hydraulic reservoir pens seemed quite simple.

He pushed aside the leather-bound notebook he had opened a few minutes earlier, leaned back in his chair, and propped his booted feet on the cluttered table.

Glumly he contemplated the clockwork butler which he had constructed last year. It stood silent and still, a silver salver in one wooden hand. On a whim, Marcus had painted a proper black coat and a white shirt on the automaton.

He had even made an attempt to capture Love-lace's air of aristocratic disdain in the cold eyes and unsmiling mouth.

Life had seemed so simple until Iphiginia had appeared in his carefully regulated uni-verse, Marcus thought.

As though she were a shooting star flashing through the dark night, she had lit up the sky. But if he did not find a way to catch hold of her, she would either disintegrate in a shower of sparks or fall to earth with a devastating thud.

A knock on the door of the laboratory brought Marcus out of his reverie. "Enter."

"Marcus?" Bennet stuck his head around the door. "Thought you might be in here. Are you working?"

"No. Come in."

Bennet walked into the room with his new languid, world-weary stride, closed the door, and approached the worktable. Marcus glanced at him and winced. His brother was very much the stormy-eyed poet again today.

Bennet's dark hair was carefully brushed into a careless, windswept tangle. His shirt was open at his throat and he was not wearing a neck-cloth or a waistcoat.

"I trust you intend to put on a cravat before you go out," Marcus muttered. "You'll not be allowed into any ball or soiree tonight if you show up looking as though you just got out of bed."

"I have not yet dressed for the evening." Bennet went to the window and slouched against the frame, ennui personified. He stood gazing out into the garden with a moody expression.

"Was there something you wanted?" Marcus finally prompted.

Bennet looked at him with hooded eyes. "I came here to tell you that I have made a decision."

"You're going on a tour of the Continent?" Marcus asked without much hope.

"I am going to ask Dorchester for Juliana's hand in marriage."

"Bloody hell."

"Marcus, I have got to do it now. For God's sake, don't you understand? If I wait until I return from a tour of the Continent, Dorchester will have married her off to someone else."

"Only if you are extremely fortunate."

"Damn it to hell." Bennet swung around, his expression passionate. "I know that you do not care for Dorchester, but why must you also condemn his daughter? She's not at all like him."

"You think not?"

"She's a true lady. An innocent beauty whose spirit is as pure and untarnished as . . . as—"

"New-fallen snow, perhaps?"

"I warn you, I will not tolerate any of your poor jests about her, Marcus." Bennet clenched his fist. "I intend to ask for her hand, do you comprehend?"

"God save us."

"Do you know what your problem is?"

"I have no doubt but what you will tell me."

"You're a bloody cynic, that's what you are. Just because you choose to indulge yourself with outrageous little adventuresses such as Mrs. Bright, don't presume to judge a genuine innocent."

Marcus was out of his chair before Bennet even realized what was happening.

He vaulted over the table and crossed the room in two strides. He caught hold of Bennet's shoulder, shoved him hard against the wall, and pinned him there.

"Don't call her an adventuress," Marcus said softly.

"What the hell?" Bennet's eyes widened in stunned amazement. "She's merely another one of your paramours, for God's sake. Everyone knows that."

"She is my very good friend," Marcus said.

"An insult to her is an insult to me. Do you comprehend my meaning, brother?"

"Hell and damnation, yes." Bennet eyed him warily. "Yes, of course I comprehend you. I had no notion you were so touchy on the subject."

Marcus held Bennet against the wall for a moment longer and then released him abruptly. "Perhaps you had better leave. I have work to do and you obviously have plans of your own."

Bennet straightened his rumpled lapels and adjusted the cuffs of his coat. "I apologize for any offense."

"Apology accepted. Now kindly take your leave."

"You cannot blame me for mistaking the situation. Your sentiments concerning Mrs. Bright appear to be far stronger than the ones you generally entertain toward your lady friends," Bennet observed.

"You would do well to remove yourself from this chamber before I lose my patience entirely."

Bennet angled his chin. "I'm going to do it, you know. I am going to seek Juliana's hand in marriage."

Marcus shrugged. "You have made it plain that nothing I say will dissuade you."

"Will you wish me luck?" There was a tentative note in Bennet's voice.

"I regret that I cannot do so." Marcus stood looking down at the mechanical butler. "I do not believe that you will find any lasting happiness with Juliana Dorchester."

"What would you know about finding happiness with a woman?" Bennet asked bitterly. "You have made so many bloody rules for yourself that you can no longer find any joy in your life."

"Get out of here, Bennet."

"So be it. I will not ask for your good wishes, then." Bennet stalked toward the door. He paused with his hand on the knob. "Do you know something, brother? I believe that I actually feel sorry for you."

"Don't waste your sympathy on me. You will need it for yourself if you go through with this marriage to Juliana Dorchester."

Bennet went out of the chamber without a word. He slammed the door so hard that the electricity machine shuddered on its bench.

Marcus reached down and snapped the switch that released the springs within the mechanical man. Wheels and gears clanked and whirred as the clockwork butler jerked into action.

The automaton lurched blindly forward, silver salver extended.

Marcus watched the progress of the soulless creature as it crossed the laboratory. How easy it was to be an automaton, guided only by a mechanical spring.

The artificial man stared straight ahead, looking neither to the right nor to the left, heedless of what lay before it or behind it. It had no past and no future. Its present was governed by the inflexible rules of a mechanical universe.

It did not know pain.

But neither did it know joy.

"There is a small item in the morning papers concerning the death of Mrs. Wycherley," Zoe said. "No mention of her being a blackmailer, of course. Good lord, who would believe it?" She flung herself back against the elegant curve of her red velvet Roman sofa. "It is utterly astounding."

"It is the only conclusion that Masters and I were able to reach." Iphiginia picked up her teacup.

"I can hardly credit it," Zoe said. "It is simply too fantastical."

Lord Otis's bushy brows drew together in a considering scowl. "Has a certain logic to it when you think about it."

"Yes, it does," Amelia said. "It explains why Iphiginia could not discover a clear link between Guthrie's circle of friends and that of Lord Masters. There wasn't one."

"So much for all my clandestine searches for black sealing wax and a seal engraved with a phoenix." Iphiginia heaved a small sigh of regret. "I was so certain that I was on to something there."

"How positively brilliant of Masters to hit upon the notion of making inquiries into the whereabouts of our former paid companions," Zoe said in tones of great admiration.

Iphiginia rolled her eyes. "His original hypothesis was not entirely correct, you know. Neither of the companions proved to be the blackmailer."

"No, but his theory led straight to the real blackmailer," Otis observed. "Man has an excellent intellect."

Iphiginia made a face. "Yes, and he is well aware of it."

Amelia gave her one of her infrequent smiles. "I do believe that you are somewhat jealous, Iphiginia."

"Well, I was quite partial to my own hypothesis," she admitted. "Masters's notion is fascinating, however. And Otis is right, it's very logical. Just think, all those years Mrs. Wycherley was using certain governesses and companions to collect damning information about some of the best families."

"I never really cared for Miss Todd," Zoe

said. "She had eyes that reminded me of a small rat. I did not retain her for long."

"You should have let her go much earlier than you did," Amelia remarked. "She was obviously around long enough to conclude that Maryanne was not Guthrie's daughter."

"Obviously." Zoe shook her head. "One wonders how many other victims the woman had. Is every house in London infested with spies?"

"I doubt it." Iphiginia pursed her lips. "From all indications, Mrs. Wycherley was very selective and quite cautious, at least until recently. She no doubt chose her victims carefully."

"Hah." Otis's whiskers twitched. "She made a serious blunder when she undertook to expand her list of victims to include my Zoe and a good friend of the Earl of Masters, by God."

"Yes," Iphiginia said. "She did."

"Well, it's over at last, thank heavens." Zoe helped herself to a small pink cake from the tea tray. "Now we can get on with the Season. I confess I have had some difficulty planning Maryanne's marriage, what with this blackmail business hanging over my head."

Otis gave Iphiginia a shrewd look. "Masters is certain this is the end of the matter?"

Iphiginia hesitated. "He seems quite satisfied that it is."

"Well, then, that's the end of it," Otis declared.

"Yes." Iphiginia rose to her feet and picked up her white bonnet. "Amelia and I must be on our way. We have an appointment with our man of affairs. Perhaps we shall see you at the theater later this evening."

"Very likely," Zoe said cheerfully. "What a relief it will be to be able to sit in my box without wondering if a blackmailer's eyes are fastened upon me."

"There's just one more thing." Iphiginia fixed each of the other three in turn with a deliberate look. "I trust that you all realize that merely because the blackmail situation is finished, nothing else has changed."

Zoe looked blank. "Whatever are you talking about, Iphiginia?"

"For all intents and purposes, I am still Mrs. Bright so far as Society is concerned."

"Damnation," Otis exclaimed. "She's right. Cannot go changing her identity at this point. She'd be ruined."

"We agreed at the beginning of this affair that when the matter was resolved I would disappear discreetly from the scene," Iphiginia said. "But I have changed my mind."

Zoe eyed her with grave interest. "You're going to finish the Season as Masters's mistress?"

"Yes."

Zoe exchanged uneasy glances with Amelia and Otis. Then she turned back to Iphiginia. "Masters has agreed to this plan?"

"More or less," Iphiginia said airily. There was no point in telling them that Marcus had actually insisted on marriage. She feared that they would all side with him.

And Iphiginia knew that she could not possibly marry Marcus unless she could find a way to make him fall in love with her.

Discovering the identity of the blackmailer had been a simple matter compared with her new problem.

She was confronted with the daunting task of persuading Marcus to change his own rules.

Iphiginia was aware of Amelia's deep silence as they walked down the front steps of Zoe's town house. Her companion said nothing until they had each been handed up into Iphiginia's white and gilt carriage.

"Out with it, Amelia." Iphiginia settled back against the white velvet cushions and arranged her skirts. "What is troubling you?"

Amelia watched her closely. "I sensed that you hesitated when you told your aunt and Lord Otis that you were certain the blackmail matter was concluded. Something is worrying you."

The little carriage started to roll forward. Iphiginia looked out the window. It was nearly five o'clock in the afternoon. The street was filled with fashionable carriages en route to the park.

"What bothers me," she said slowly, "is that Masters and I searched Mrs. Wycherley's desk before we left yesterday."

"So?"

"So we did not discover a seal engraved with a phoenix. Nor did we find any sign of black wax in her wax jack."

"I can promise you that Constance Wycherley was many things, but she was no fool. She must have lived in constant fear of discovery. She would not have left any obvious evidence of her guilt lying about."

"That's what Marcus said. But if she was so very clever—shrewd enough to get away with blackmail, in point of fact—why did she make the serious mistake of trying to blackmail a friend of Masters? She must have known that she ran the risk of drawing him into the business."

"Perhaps she had gotten away with blackmail for so long that she had grown quite bold," Amelia suggested. "Or perhaps she got greedier. She may have needed more money to cover gaming debts or some such thing. Who can say?"

"I suppose we shall never have all the answers."

"Come, Iphiginia. You have already admitted that what is really disturbing you now is that Masters's hypothesis was the correct one."

"My own was really quite good, you know."

"It was. It just happened to be the wrong hypothesis. Now that the affair is over, what do you intend to do about your other problem?"

"What other problem?"

"I heard what you said in Aunt Zoe's drawing room, but we both know that you cannot continue to masquerade as Masters's mistress indefinitely."

"I can carry on with it until the end of the Season." Iphiginia cleared her throat delicately. "And you may as well know that it is not, strictly speaking, a masquerade."

Amelia studied her with shadowed eyes. "I was very much afraid of that."

Iphiginia gripped the strings of her white lace reticule. "Do not worry about me, Amelia."

"You are not only my cousin, you are my dearest friend. I cannot help but worry about you."

"Concern yourself with the financial arrangements for Bright Place. It will prove infinitely more profitable."

"He will discard you without a qualm when

he grows tired of you. You know that, do you not?"

"Perhaps I shall grow tired of him first," Iphiginia said lightly.

"I wish I could believe that. I do not suppose there is anything I can say that will dissuade you from continuing on with this reckless business?"

"No. But you may take heart from knowing that when the Season ends, my association with Masters will likely end also."

"What will you do then?"

"Oversee the construction of Bright Place. Devote myself to my plans for a pattern book of classical designs." Iphiginia smiled wistfully. "There are any number of interesting projects ahead of me, Amelia. I assure you that I shall not fall into a complete decline when my liaison with Masters is over."

"I am well aware of how strong you are, Iphiginia. Still, I do not want to see you hurt."

"It is too late to save me. I am determined to enjoy this grand adventure, Amelia. There will not be another one remotely similar to it, you know. Masters is quite unique."

Marcus inclined his head aloofly when he saw Hannah and her husband in the theater lobby that evening. Sands glowered at him, nodded stiffly in return, and then pointedly turned away to greet someone else. It was not quite the cut direct, but it was close.

Hannah gave Marcus a nervous smile. There was a look of near-desperation in her eyes.

The glittering throng of theatergoers acted as a hunting box blind. It allowed Marcus to get very close to Hannah for a few vital seconds without arousing Sands's suspicions.

"It's finished," Marcus whispered as he brushed past Hannah. "The blackmailer was Mrs. Wycherley. She is dead."

Hannah searched his face. "I saw the news in the morning papers and wondered what had happened." Her eyes widened suddenly. "Marcus, you did not—"

"No. I believe one of her victims did the deed."

"Good heavens."

"Come, my dear." Sands took her arm. His eyes narrowed when he saw Marcus gliding on past his wife into the crowd. "I shall fetch you a glass of lemonade."

Marcus pretended not to notice as Hannah was whisked away through the throng. He regretted the animosity that Sands felt toward him, but in truth he could not blame the man for his wary, watchful attitude. Marcus recognized that he experienced a similar sense of possessiveness toward Iphiginia these days.

He made his way through the lobby and went

up the red-carpeted staircase. It was intermission. The corridor behind the first tier of boxes was nearly as crowded as the lobby.

Gentlemen bustled back and forth, fetching refreshments for their ladies. Others ambled out into the hall to exchange gossip with their cronies or visit those in neighboring boxes. A handful of young bucks brushed past Marcus. They were obviously on their way to call upon the elegant courtesans who displayed their wares in some of the most expensive boxes.

Marcus nodded to a few acquaintances as he walked along the curved corridor. When he reached the box on the end, he pushed aside the heavy curtain and stepped inside.

Dorchester, his sharp-eyed wife, and the lovely Juliana turned to stare in astonishment.

"Good evening," Marcus said. "Enjoying the performance?"

Dorchester's start of surprise became an expression of great caution. "Masters. Didn't know you were attending tonight's performance."

"My lord. How nice to see you." Beatrice Dorchester was clearly as stunned by Marcus's appearance in the box as she would have been by the appearance of a ghost. "Juliana, make your curtsy to his lordship."

Juliana leaped to her feet as though she had

been jolted by a spark from an electricity machine. "My lord."

"Mrs. Dorchester. Miss Juliana." Marcus surveyed them both briefly. "You're both looking very fine this evening."

"Thank you, my lord." Mrs. Dorchester was almost painfully relieved by his civility. "Won't you sit down for a few moments? Pray, take the seat next to Juliana."

"Thank you. I believe I will."

He sat down carefully on one of the spindly little chairs. It groaned in protest, but it did not crumple beneath his weight. "I understand Kean is in excellent form tonight."

"Yes, indeed. The man can certainly act even when he's in his cups," Dorchester said with an air of hearty good humor.

"Just as well, as he is as drunk as a wheelbarrow most of the time, from all accounts," Marcus said.

"Yes, well, you know how it is with these actors," Dorchester murmured. "Very unstable lot."

"They're not the only ones who are unstable." Marcus surveyed the vast theater. He ignored the crowded pit and the galleries and concentrated on the tiers of boxes. He spotted Iphiginia immediately.

She glowed in a classically simple white

gown. White plumes wafted gracefully from her hair, which was parted in the middle and neatly coiled over her ears. A crystal necklace sparkled around her throat.

She was not alone in the box. Amelia sat on her left. As Marcus watched, the curtains behind the two women parted. Herbert Hoyt entered, dapper as always in a blue coat, paisley waistcoat, and pleated trousers. He held a glass of lemonade in each of his gloved hands.

Mrs. Dorchester lurched into conversation with the awkwardness of a clockwork toy. "Lovely weather we're having, is it not, my lord?"

"Yes," Marcus said.

"Juliana and I took a turn about the park this afternoon, didn't we, Juliana?" Mrs. Dorchester continued with dogged determination.

"Yes, Mama." Juliana clutched her fan as though she feared Marcus might reach out and snatch it from her. "It was quite pleasant." She brightened. "We saw your brother, sir."

"Did you?"

Juliana flinched at Marcus's tone. Mrs. Dorchester gave her husband an urgent look.

Dorchester manfully attempted to carry his share of the burden of conversation. "I trust you are well, sir?"

"Very," Marcus said.

"Excellent, excellent," Dorchester said with artificial enthusiasm. "Glad to hear it."

Marcus watched Iphiginia take a sip from the glass Hoyt had handed to her. "I am feeling in such remarkably good health, in fact, that I have decided to marry."

A stunned silence greeted that remark.

Dorchester gaped. It took him several seconds to get his jaws closed. "Thought you'd determined not to remarry, sir. Thought you had a rule about it or some such thing."

"I've changed my mind," Marcus said. "A friend of mine has convinced me that some rules are made to be broken."

"I see." Dorchester collected himself. "Well, then. My heartiest congratulations. I say, this news will certainly cause a stir."

Juliana glanced at her father and mother and then smiled tremulously at Marcus. "I wish you every happiness in your marriage, sir."

Marcus raised one brow. "Thank you, Miss Dorchester."

Mrs. Dorchester narrowed her beady eyes. "Will you be announcing the betrothal in the near future, my lord?"

"In the very near future," Marcus assured her.

Dorchester scowled. "Who is the lucky young lady, if I may be so bold?"

"I am not at liberty to announce that yet.

There are still a number of details to arrange. Settlements and the like. You understand, I'm certain."

"Of course," Dorchester said weakly. "Settlements. Very important."

"Quite." Marcus got to his feet. "Pray excuse me. I must be off. I find that I am very busy these days. Marriage plans are a great nuisance, I have discovered."

"They are?" Mrs. Dorchester narrowed her eyes.

"Yes, indeed," Marcus said. "One must completely redo one's will, for example, in order to provide for one's future wife and potential offspring."

"Offspring?" Mrs. Dorchester repeated in a numb tone.

"One must do one's duty when there is a title involved," Marcus reminded her. "And then there is the matter of adjusting the incomes of the other members of one's family."

"Adjusting them in what way?" Mrs. Dorchester asked swiftly.

"Downward, naturally," Marcus said. "The family fortune must be concentrated in the hands of my heir in order to preserve and protect it."

"I thought your brother was your heir, sir," Dorchester said.

"Yes, well, that will change now that I'm going to marry, won't it? With any luck I shall have a son of my own to inherit the title and the fortune."

Mrs. Dorchester appeared shaken. "I see."

"My brother will continue to receive a reasonable allowance, naturally. Just as he always has." Marcus pushed aside the curtain and stepped out of the box. He turned back to smile at the three Dorchesters. "Unless, of course, he marries without my approval."

"Beg pardon?" Dorchester looked stricken.

"I feel quite strongly that, for sake of his future, Bennet must find himself an heiress. After all, he will have the future of his own offspring to consider."

"Offspring?" Dorchester was clearly dazed.

"It always comes down to that, does it not?" Marcus went out into the corridor. The heavy curtains fell closed behind him.

He followed the curving corridor to the far side of the theater where Iphiginia's box was located.

Herbert Hoyt stepped into the hall just as Marcus reached out to take hold of the curtain.

"I say. Beg pardon." Hoyt hastily got out of the way. "Good evening, Masters. Didn't mean to nearly run you down. Damn crowded out here in the corridor, is it not?"

"Yes." Marcus went into the box and let the curtain fall.

"Good evening, Iphiginia. Miss Farley." Marcus took one of the small chairs without waiting to be asked.

"My lord," Amelia murmured politely. She turned away to watch the activity in the pit.

It occurred to Marcus that Amelia cut him in the same subtle manner that Sands often used. He was not a very popular person these days.

Iphiginia smiled with welcome. Her eyes gleamed with curiosity. "Good evening, my lord. I thought I saw you sitting in the Dorchester box a few minutes ago."

"I had a few words with Dorchester." Marcus extended his legs and scowled briefly. "Why the devil is it that I find myself forever tripping over Hoyt? He seems to spend a great deal of time in your vicinity."

Iphiginia gave a dainty shrug. The crystals around her throat glittered with colorless fire. "Mr. Hoyt is a friend. And he is quite harmless. You know that, my lord."

"He's a damned nuisance."

Iphiginia's brows rose. "You appear to be in a rather foul temper, sir."

"I am." Marcus glanced toward the stage as the lights dimmed. "Perhaps Kean's performance will put me in a more cheerful frame of mind."

"Let us hope so." Iphiginia gave him a quizzical glance before she turned to look down at the stage.

Kean was in excellent form in the role of Macbeth, but even his riveting skill could not shake Marcus's dark mood.

What he really wanted to do, Marcus realized, was talk to Iphiginia. He wanted to tell her about Bennet's stubborn determination to marry Juliana Dorchester.

He needed to confide his uneasiness to her, get her opinion, ask her if she thought he had done the right thing by trying to discourage Dorchester tonight.

But the ability to share his problems with another person was a skill that had gone to rust years ago. It had been so long since he had asked for advice or confessed uncertainty or simply requested another's opinion that he did not even know how to go about it.

In any event, his rules did not allow him to exhibit weakness.

In the middle of the last scene of *Macbeth* the curtain of the box was jerked abruptly aside. Bennet stalked into the small sitting area. His hands were clenched into fists at his sides. His face was a mask of fury.

"Damn you, Marcus. I shall never forgive you for this. Never. I know what you are about and it will not work. Do you hear me? You cannot stop me from marrying Juliana."

Marcus turned slowly, aware of Iphiginia's and Amelia's astonishment.

"You appear to have forgotten your manners," Marcus said mildly. "Allow me to introduce you to Mrs. Bright and Miss Farley."

Bennet cast a scathing glance at Iphiginia. "Why should I bother with good manners in the presence of your *mistress* when you cannot be bothered to exercise them in front of my future wife and the members of her family?"

"*Enough*." Marcus got to his feet. "I have warned you, Bennet. We will discuss this later."

"There is nothing to discuss. I should have known that you would try your damnedest to ruin my happiness. But oddly enough, it did not occur to me that you would go to these lengths. I understand that you plan to disinherit me."

"We will deal with this when we can be private," Marcus said very evenly.

"Do you think I give a bloody damn whether or not you cut me off? I can make my own way in the world. And Juliana knows it. She has faith in me, even if you and her father do not."

"If you are determined to make a scene, then we shall adjourn to the street."

"There is no need. I'm leaving now." Bennet's mouth curved in an angry sneer. "By the bye, allow me to congratulate you, brother. I comprehend that you are soon to announce your own betrothal."

Marcus heard Iphiginia's small, shocked gasp. He did not look at her. His entire attention was fixed on his brother. "That is correct."

"The entire theater is already abuzz with the news. You must have been truly desperate to halt my plans for marriage if you have gone so far as to break your most firmly established rule."

"Bennet, that is enough."

"But that part of your plan won't work, either. Juliana will marry me regardless of whether or not I stand to inherit your damned title. You'll see. She loves me, not the bloody earldom. Which is more than you'll be able to say about your future wife, whoever she is."

Bennet whirled around and stormed out of the box.

FOURTEEN

*I*phiginia sat very still on the black squabs of Marcus's ebony carriage. The interior lamps were unlit. Marcus filled most of the opposite seat with his large frame. He had one long leg stretched out along the cushion. The other boot was planted on the floor. There was a dangerous, morose quality about him.

He had said no more than a dozen words since they had left the theater a few minutes earlier. Most of those had been primarily commands to Dinks.

Iphiginia had not been allowed to see the end of Kean's performance. Marcus had muttered something about avoiding the crush of theater traffic, but Iphiginia knew that was not the primary reason he wished to leave early.

When he had brusquely ordered her to accompany him, she had seen the doubt and disapproval in Amelia's eyes. But Iphiginia had quietly agreed. Amelia had remained behind in Zoe and Otis's box. They would see her home.

There had been a thousand questions in Zoe's eyes when Iphiginia and Marcus had escorted Amelia to the box. Iphiginia had ignored them. She knew her aunt had already heard the rumors of Marcus's betrothal, but she had no explanations or answers to give her.

When the carriage moved into the street, Marcus finally broke the thick silence.

"I regret that you were subjected to that unfortunate scene in your theater box." He gazed out into the night. "My brother appears to be immersed in a rather melodramatic phase at the moment."

"Marcus, I think you owe me an explanation."

"Mmm."

Iphiginia waited for a few seconds. Marcus said nothing.

"Well?" she finally prompted.

"Well, what?" Marcus did not look away from the window.

Iphiginia made a heroic effort to compose herself in patience. "Well, what is the explanation for that scene in my theater box?"

Marcus hesitated, as though about to tread on uncertain ground.

"I am aware of the fact that you have a rule against explaining your actions to anyone," Iphiginia said. "But I really think that in this instance—"

"Bennet believes himself to be passionately in love with Juliana Dorchester."

"And you do not approve of the match?"

Marcus finally glanced at her. "How did you guess?"

"It wasn't difficult."

"It's Dorchester's fondest wish to shore up the family's flagging fortunes by marrying his daughter into money. Mrs. Dorchester's primary goal is to get a title into the family. Together they have contrived to hurl Juliana at every wealthy, titled gentleman in the *ton* for the past two Seasons."

"Including you?"

"Last Season I was a target for a short period." Light from a passing coach glinted briefly on the starkly etched planes of Marcus's grim features. "Dorchester went so far as to attempt to force me into a compromising position with his own daughter."

"Good grief. What happened?"

"I won't go into details. It was a shabby little plot, ill-conceived and extremely transparent. Suffice it to say, the attempt failed."

"I see." There was a distinct chill in the air. Iphiginia pulled her white lace shawl a little more securely around her bare shoulders. "I collect that you escaped unscathed."

"Yes."

"Unlike the other night in the Pettigrews' Temple of Vesta when you did not discover the truth until too late."

There was a short, brittle pause. Marcus eventually stirred in the manner of a large beast of prey seeking a more comfortable position. He leaned his head back against the cushion, narrowed his eyes, and folded his arms across his chest.

"I made it clear to Dorchester that I would not marry Juliana even if he arranged for the two of us to be discovered nude in bed together," Marcus said deliberately.

"Oh." Iphiginia did not know what else to say.

"I reminded him of my rule against marriage. Dorchester apparently took me at my word. He ceased throwing Juliana at my head, in any event. But this Season he seems to have concluded that my brother will make a suitable substitute."

"So tonight you again tried to dissuade him from his goal," Iphiginia concluded. "But this time you find yourself dealing with an additional problem. Your brother is in love with Juliana."

"My brother has succumbed to the lure of

physical attraction and the overheated prose of the Byron set. He is not in love."

Iphiginia winced at the disgust in his voice. "How can you be certain that what your brother feels for Juliana is not true love?"

"For God's sake, he's barely twenty. He's in the throes of his first fit of passion, that's all. In the typical manner of young males, he wishes to dignify his perfectly natural lust by calling it love."

"Perhaps his feelings for Juliana run deeper than you believe."

"Not bloody likely," Marcus muttered.

"What did you hope to accomplish by announcing your own fictitious betrothal this evening?"

"The betrothal is not fictitious. We are going to be married, Iphiginia."

"Let's return to that point some other time," she said. "At the moment we are discussing your brother. You think to forestall Dorchester's plans by causing him to believe that you have changed your mind about remarriage."

"I have changed my mind."

She ignored that. "You may have succeeded in persuading Dorchester that Bennet is no longer a good match for his daughter, but what about Bennet and Juliana?"

"What about them? Juliana's parents will

not allow her to marry my brother if they believe that I will cut him off. Their aim is to get their hands on a portion of the Masters fortune. I control that fortune, not Bennet."

"Marcus, I do not think it will be as easy as all that. I saw your brother's face tonight. He believes himself to be in love with Juliana."

"He'll soon discover that it will not do him any good. Dorchester will remove Juliana from my brother's vicinity and fire her off at another target now that I've manned the primary one."

"Rubbish. You and Dorchester are both idiots if you truly believe that you can control the lives of others in such a fashion. Juliana and Bennet are young, but they are adults. There is no knowing what they might do if you and Dorchester try to bend them to your wills."

Marcus watched her from the shadows. "What are you saying? That they might run off to Gretna Green together?"

"It's a possibility, is it not?"

"No. I'll admit that in his present state Bennet might be foolish enough to suggest the notion, but Juliana is a very rational young woman. She is highly unlikely to do anything so impractical as to marry a man whose financial prospects are uncertain."

"Meaning she will marry for money rather than love?"

"Precisely. Do not forget, I saw her in action last Season."

"I suspect the people you saw in action were her parents. Poor Juliana was no doubt merely attempting to obey their instructions."

"There is no difference."

"Marcus, I hesitate to mention this," Iphiginia said, "but you are not quite the great judge of human nature you perceive yourself to be. At least not when it comes to affairs of the heart."

"Affairs of the heart should be handled in the same manner as affairs of business. They should be approached with circumspection and care."

"You mean with cynicism, do you not? I understand what you are trying to do," Iphiginia said gently. "You wish to protect your brother from an unhappy marriage. But I do not think that you are going about it in the right way."

"This does not concern you, Iphiginia."

"Nonsense. You have dragged me into it. If you wanted to keep me out of the thing, you should never have told Dorchester that you were about to announce a betrothal. Now we shall both have to deal with all the annoying questions and speculation. It will make everything vastly more difficult."

"I do not see any great problem. I have a rule against answering personal questions."

"But Marcus, people will expect you to announce your engagement to one of the young ladies who was brought out this Season. Not to your mistress, for heaven's sake. Even your own brother assumes that you are going to declare yourself for one of the eligible young women of the *ton*."

"I am going to betroth myself to a young lady who is having her first Season," Marcus said. "You."

"You are the most stubborn man I have ever met in my entire life."

"You may as well get used to it because I have no intention of changing."

Iphiginia stifled a groan of exasperation. "Let us get back to the matter at hand. I advise you not to take such a hard and inflexible stand with Bennet and Juliana. I fear that by doing so you will only drive them into each other's arms."

"I do not recall asking for your advice on the subject."

"Then why are we having this discussion?"

"Damned if I know," he muttered. "It's none of your affair. Bennet is my brother and I will act as I see fit."

"Marcus, I comprehend what you are trying to do. You wish to protect him."

"What is wrong with that?"

"Nothing. I understand your desire. You

raised him. I suspect that in many ways you are more of a father than a brother to him. I was in a similar position with my sister. In some ways I was almost a mother to her."

"I'm aware of that," he said quietly.

"You and I both became parents before we had a chance to become mature adults ourselves. And we feel protective toward our charges, as any parent would feel. But as much as we would like to guard them forever, we cannot do so."

"I can and will protect Bennet from Juliana Dorchester."

"You are going about it in the wrong way."

"What do you suggest that I do?" Marcus growled. "Give my blessing to the marriage?"

"Yes."

"Never."

"Hear me out." Iphiginia leaned forward earnestly. "Tell your brother that you will give the marriage your blessing if he will agree to a reasonable period for the engagement."

"What do you call reasonable?"

"Many young couples in the *ton* are betrothed for a year. Surely you can convince Bennet to go along with such a request. You can ask for six months at the very least."

"And what happens when the engagement period is finished?"

"A year is a long time, Marcus. So is six

months, for that matter. If Juliana is the wrong woman for Bennet, there will be ample opportunity for him to discover that fact."

"Breaking an engagement is no light matter."

"True, but it can be done and it is done. You can arrange for the thing to be handled quietly."

Marcus's expression darkened. "What if Juliana succeeds in compromising herself with Bennet before the year is ended?"

"You already face that risk. In fact, the threat is greater at this very moment because the pair will be feeling desperate. If Juliana does care for Bennet as much as he cares for her, they may see themselves as star-crossed lovers. They may decide to defy family and convention in order to be together."

"Bloody hell. What you are saying is true only if I am wrong about Juliana's feelings. But if I am right, the entire matter is finished. The Dorchesters, Juliana included, will decide that Bennet is no longer a suitable marriage prospect."

Iphiginia sighed. "My lord, I doubt that you are right in your assessment of the situation. You are a man of science, probably the most intelligent man I know, but you are blind when it comes to dealing with matters such as this. Love makes people do very desperate things."

He slid her an assessing, sidelong glance. "What makes you an expert?"

She refrained from pointing out that she was a living example of the desperate lengths to which love could drive a person.

"I watched my sister fall in love," Iphiginia said instead.

Marcus's gaze became even more intent. "With the man you had thought loved you?"

Iphiginia caught her breath. "You know about Richard Hampton?"

"Yes." Marcus looked out at the street.

"You think you know everything, do you not, my lord?"

"It has been my experience that it is better to have all the information one needs before one makes a decision."

"Well, then, as you appear to be all-knowing, you do not need any further explanations from me concerning Richard, do you?"

Marcus met her eyes for an instant. Then his gaze slid back to the night-darkened streets. "Did you love him?"

"The answer would be meaningless to a man who does not believe in love."

"You're evading the question."

"I'm merely adopting your own rule against providing the curious with explanations." Iphiginia paused. "But I will make a bargain with you, my lord."

"What bargain?"

"I'll tell you the answer to your question if you will agree to answer one of my questions."

"Very well," he pounced. "But you will answer my question first. Did you believe yourself to be in love with young squire Hampton?"

Iphiginia struggled for an honest response. Odd how hard it was to recall her emotions during those days when she had thought Richard might ask her to marry him. Her feelings for Richard had been so pallid and bland compared to her feelings for Marcus.

"I believed that I could have learned to love him," she said quietly.

"You believed that you could have *learned* to love him?" Marcus scoffed. "What rubbish."

"I do not think it's rubbish. I am a bluestocking at heart. A former schoolteacher. I believe in the powers of the intellect. I am convinced that where the right factors are present and where there is determination, goodwill, and a degree of intelligence, it is possible that one can learn to love."

"The poets would laugh to hear you talk of applying rational intelligence to love."

"You are not a poet, my lord. Why are you laughing?"

"The whole bloody subject is laughable." Marcus shot her a derisive look. "You said that the right factors must be present in order for one to learn to love. Were those factors present in Richard Hampton?"

"I believe so. Richard is a good man. A kind man. Strong, gentle, and constant. Yes, I could have learned to love him."

"He sounds like a damned paragon. Do you honestly think that you would have been happy with him?"

"Yes."

"You would have been true to him?"

She frowned. "Of course."

"Even if you had met someone else after the marriage? A man who turned your blood to molten fire? A man who made you compre-hend the works of the poets? A man who tempted you to touch the stars?"

"You mean, even if I had met you, Marcus?"

He went very still in the shadows.

Iphiginia smiled wryly. "It is highly unlikely that you and I would ever have encountered each other had I married Richard Hampton. But the answer to your question is yes. Even if I had met you, I would have been true to him. I may not care for rules, but I do possess a sense of honor."

"Passion is not always subject to the dictates of will, madam."

"I disagree. And I think, deep down, you do, too. We are intelligent human beings. Temptation and passion can most certainly be controlled if one is determined to do so."

To her surprise, Marcus smiled slightly at that. "You may be right. What does that say about you and me, Iphiginia? That we lack willpower?"

"No." She unfurled her fan very slowly and then closed it. "It says that we are both free to indulge our passions and we have decided to do so. It is our prerogative, our right as unattached adults. If we were not free, honor would constrain us from giving in to temptation."

"Ah. I see. We happened to be free to allow ourselves to be tempted, so we were tempted. An interesting bit of logic."

"Perhaps we should return to the subject of your brother's passions, rather than our own. You cannot control Bennet's life, Marcus. Nor should you."

"Don't you think I know that? I don't want to control his life. I want to protect him."

"He will love whom he will. All you can hope to do is purchase some time for him to consider his actions. With any luck he will use the time to make certain that what he feels for Juliana Dorchester is genuine love and not a passing fancy."

"I still think my approach is more likely to produce the desired results," Marcus said. "I wouldn't be at all surprised if I have nipped the entire affair in the bud this evening."

"I think your approach will lead to disaster."

"Hell and damnation. I detest this sort of emotional nonsense."

"You, sir, have no patience with anything that does not conform to the laws of science."

"Things were so much simpler when Bennet was younger," Marcus said in a low voice. "He respected my advice in those days. He asked me for help when he needed it. He sought my approval before he undertook an important task."

"I understand." Iphiginia smiled wistfully. "It was the same way between my sister and myself when she was a child. But everyone grows up eventually, Marcus."

"Must they destroy their own chance of happiness in the process?"

"Sometimes."

"The cost of being wrong is too high. I cannot let him do it, Iphiginia."

Iphiginia took a grip on her fan. "Sir, I have taught students for several years. I have discovered that they do not always learn the lesson you believe that you are teaching. Too often they learn something else entirely."

"What is that cryptic remark supposed to mean?"

"You must believe me when I tell you that

your way of dealing with this situation is fraught with risk. Bennet will learn much from how you handle this situation."

"I should hope to God he will," Marcus said fervently.

"But I doubt that he will learn the lesson you believe that you are teaching. In short, my lord, when all is said and done, there is every chance that he will become more like you if this business ends badly. Do you really want that for him?"

Marcus looked at her in cold amazement. "I beg your pardon?"

"You are teaching him the things that are likely to transform him into a copy of yourself in later years."

"And just what sort of man is that?" Marcus asked in a dangerously soft voice.

"A man who lives by rules that are so rigid and so unbending that they do not allow room for love."

A terrible silence descended inside the carriage. Marcus did not move so much as an inch, but Iphiginia nearly drowned beneath the silent waves of his fury.

"My lord, I do not pretend to know much about your first marriage. I cannot help but conclude, however, that it was not a happy one."

"It was a living hell."

"I wish to claim my half of our bargain. I want an answer to this question. Could anyone who knew you at the time of your marriage have stopped you from going through with it?"

For a moment she did not think he would answer.

"No." The single word was as heavy as a stone. "Very likely not. I thought I knew what I was doing. I thought that I was in love." His smile was savage. "I believed that Nora loved me."

"Perhaps she did," Iphiginia offered tentatively.

"No." Marcus's hand closed briefly into a fist. "She needed a father for the babe she carried."

Iphiginia froze. "I did not realize—"

Marcus met her eyes. His own were cold. "No one did. I have never told another soul that Nora came to me after she had got herself with child by another man."

"Oh, Marcus. How terrible for you."

He fell silent for a while. Iphiginia could not think of anything more to say. She was stunned by the realization that he had kept the truth to himself for so long.

"Nora's family lived on the neighboring farm," Marcus said eventually. It sounded as though he were digging the words out of a grave where they had been buried for a very long time. "I had known her most of her life. I was a year older than she and I had believed myself to be in love with her since the day I turned sixteen."

"Marcus, please, you do not have to tell me this."

He acted as if he had not heard her. "She found me amusing, I think. And useful. We learned to dance together at the local assembly rooms. I taught her to fish. She was the first woman I ever kissed."

Iphiginia did not want to hear any more. "Please—"

"But I was just a simple country farmer. At the time the title was in the hands of a distant uncle. I never expected to inherit. Nora wanted more out of life than I could ever give her. And she was so very beautiful that she and her parents convinced themselves that she could look a good deal higher than a local country squire. The year Nora turned eighteen, her family took her to London for a Season."

"What happened?" Iphiginia asked, dreading the answer.

"She came home in June of that year and everything had changed. She was no longer the flirtatious, charming, happy young woman she had been when she left. She virtually threw herself into my arms and told me that she had finally realized that it was me she loved."

"I see." Iphiginia looked down at her fan. The waves of Marcus's old anger and pain beat at her steadily, unrelentingly.

"And I was so naive and inexperienced that I believed her." Marcus kept his gaze fixed on the night outside the coach window. "She told me that she had discovered that she did not care for Town life. She wanted us to be wed as soon as possible. Her parents were in full agreement. Her father took me aside and suggested we go to Gretna Green."

"No long engagement, I take it?"

"Somehow everyone came to the conclusion that there was no point in wasting the time or the money. And I was so eager for her that I did not raise any objection. Nora and I went to Gretna Green. We spent our wedding night at an inn. I couldn't wait to take her in my arms."

"I really do not think I want to hear this."

"I wanted her so much. I was determined to be as gentle as possible with her. But she cried that night. For hours, it seemed. She told me that I had hurt her dreadfully. Told me that I had the rough, callused hands of a farmer." Marcus looked down at his broad fists. "It was true. I did have the hands of a farmer. I was a farmer."

Iphiginia shivered at the memory of his hands on her. Strong hands. Good hands.

Hands that made a woman feel wanted, needed. And safe. Tears formed in her eyes.

"The next morning there was a fair amount of blood on the sheets. I learned later that her mother had provided her with a small bottle of the stuff from the kitchen the day we left for Gretna. She needn't have bothered."

"I don't understand," Iphiginia whispered.

"Even if there had been no blood, I would not have suspected that Nora had been with another man. I was the virgin in that wedding bed. I was far more ignorant than she about such matters."

"How did you learn that she had had another lover?" Iphiginia asked quietly.

"She miscarried the babe a month after we were married. I nearly went mad. I had no notion of what was happening. I thought she was dying."

"Dear heaven."

"I summoned the doctor. When it was all over he told me what had occurred. He wanted to reassure me. He assumed I was the father, of course, and that the babe was the reason for our hasty trip to Gretna. He patted me on the shoulder and told me there would be another babe soon enough."

"You did not tell him the truth?"

Marcus's mouth twisted. "Of course not.

What man would admit that he had been duped in such a fashion? And then there was Nora. She was my wife."

"And you felt you had to protect her, too, didn't you?" Iphiginia asked.

Marcus shrugged but said nothing.

"You had taken care of your brother for years. Protecting someone younger and weaker than yourself was second nature to you. What did Nora say?"

"When I confronted her with the truth, she cried again. Then she broke down and told me the whole sordid tale. She had been seduced by one of her admirers in London, a young rake who was after an heiress and who had no intention of marrying her. Nor did he hesitate to boast of his conquest."

"Poor Nora."

"The gossip ruined her. There was no hope of marriage. Her family did not have the social power it would have taken to force Nora's seducer to marry her."

"So they whisked her back home and contrived to marry her off to you?"

"They concluded that the bumbling country squire next door was unlikely to discover the truth." Marcus glanced at his hands again. "They were right. To this day I sometimes wonder if I would ever have learned what a fool I had been if Nora had not miscarried the babe."

"Surely you would have known the truth when the child was born several weeks too soon?"

"I doubt it. I told you, I knew little of such matters. I would have been informed that the infant was born prematurely and I would have wanted to believe it."

"The rumors I heard said that Nora died of a fever."

"She did. Six months after she lost the babe."

"The duel," Iphiginia whispered. "That was what the duel was all about, was it not? Shortly after Nora died, you went to London and challenged her seducer."

"He told me I was a fool, which was no doubt true. He demanded to know what possible difference it all made now that the wench was dead. I did not give him any answers because I had none."

"You defended your wife's honor even though she had wronged you. Even though she was no longer alive." Iphiginia felt a tear trickle down her cheek. "Marcus, that is so exactly like you."

Marcus scowled. "Bloody hell. Are you crying?"

"No." She gave a tiny sniff.

"I should hope not. The matter does not warrant tears."

"But it does, Marcus. I feel sorry for both you and Nora. She must have been literally terrified when she discovered that she was ruined and pregnant."

"Yes."

"She was young and desperate. She was an innocent girl who had allowed herself to be seduced. She had broken one of Society's strictest rules. She knew that she would have to pay a terrible price. So she turned to you, her childhood friend."

"The thing is," Marcus said, "I wanted her so much I would have taken her on any terms. I would have given her my name and claimed the babe as my own. If only she had not deceived me. That was what I could not forgive."

"Because whenever you think back on her deception, you feel you played the fool."

"I did play the fool."

Iphiginia felt a chill in the pit of her stomach. She, too, had deceived him. He no doubt believed that he had played the fool with her, also.

She reached out and put her gloved hand on his leg. "Nora did not make a fool of you, Marcus. No one could do that. You behaved in a noble, chivalrous fashion. You avenged her honor and you kept her secret."

"I had little choice in the matter. I could hardly reveal her dishonor without making myself appear a naive, gullible idiot."

"I do not believe that it was the thought of appearing naive or gullible which bothers you the most about the past," Iphiginia said. "I think it was the fact that you had given her your heart but she did not love you in return. You feel that she used you to save herself."

"And so she did."

"I will not quarrel with your conclusion," Iphiginia said. "Nora was little more than a girl and she was no doubt hysterical with fear at the time. Her parents must have been equally frantic and desperate to save their daughter from utter ruin."

"Yes."

"Your marriage was begun under a dreadful cloud. You say that you were the virgin on your wedding night, but I think you were years older than Nora in all the ways that truly count. You had been obliged to grow up very quickly, after all. Nora, on the other hand, was barely out of girlhood."

Marcus said nothing.

"Do you know what I think?" Iphiginia said. "I believe that if she had lived, Nora would have grown up and fallen deeply in love with you. She would have learned to love you when she was mature enough to comprehend your finer qualities."

Marcus stared at her. "For an intelligent female, you sometimes spout the most outlandish nonsense. What in the name of the devil makes you believe such a ridiculous thing?"

She smiled. "Because I know how very easy it is to fall in love with you, my lord. Indeed, I have done so myself."

*F*IFTEEN

*M*arcus felt as though the universe had shifted around him, leaving him in a different place than he had been a moment earlier. The light from the stars seemed to come from a slightly different angle. The moon had altered its position in the sky.

Iphiginia had said that she loved him.

Again.

Quite clearly.

Marcus studied her very closely. She did not appear to be overwrought as she had the other night in the Temple of Vesta when she had thought she'd murdered him.

"Marcus?" Iphiginia frowned in concern. "Are you all right, my lord?"

"No." But he could not explain what was wrong or changed or different. He could not even form a coherent sentence.

He reached out and caught Iphiginia around the waist. He dragged her off the seat and into his arms.

She uttered a small, delicious gasp of surprise and then dropped her fan when he crushed her mouth beneath his own. Her shawl fluttered to the floor of the carriage.

"Marcus." Her arms stole around him. She sighed softly and nestled close.

Without taking his lips from hers, Marcus closed the carriage curtains. The cab was filled with soft darkness.

He kissed Iphiginia deeply, hungrily, with all the consuming need that he had kept tamped down since the night in the Temple of Vesta.

She did not appear to mind his desperation or his lack of subtlety. She clung to him. Her hands moved in his hair. Her head fell back against his shoulder.

Marcus put his hand on her stocking-clad calf. He slid his palm up to her knee, past her garter, and all the way to the warm, silken flesh above. Her delicate petticoats foamed around his arm and cascaded across his legs.

He found his way to the heated place between her thighs and groaned when he discovered that she was already damp. She smelled of roses and feminine desire. It was the most intoxicating scent he had ever encountered. His whole body clenched with need.

Marcus realized that his hands were trembling. He fought for breath and control. He would not throw himself on her the way he had last time, he vowed. He would not act the rough, clumsy farmer. He would make it good for her.

He wanted to please her.

He was desperate to please her.

He had to please her.

He eased her to a sitting position until she straddled his thighs. Her white skirts pooled on the black velvet cushions. He reached down to unfasten his breeches.

Iphiginia braced her hands on his shoulders. "Marcus, what are you doing?"

"Making love to you." His erect shaft sprang free.

"In your *carriage*?" A narrow sliver of light from the crack in the curtains revealed her wide-eyed expression.

"It must be either here or on your front doorsteps. I cannot last until we find the comfort of a bed. Touch me."

"Yes. Oh, yes." Tentatively, she removed her hand from his shoulder. She took the tip of one gloved finger between her teeth and tugged. Then she went to the next finger. Slowly she eased the white satin glove off her hand.

Watching her strip the glove from her fingers

was one of the most excruciatingly erotic sights Marcus had ever witnessed.

She finished the task. The satin glove that dangled from her teeth gleamed in the strip of light. She reached down, fumbled a bit, and then gently curled her fingers around him.

"*Marcus.*" The glove dropped from her teeth.

For a moment Marcus thought he would disgrace himself just as he had on the last occasion. He sucked in his breath and wondered if he would survive.

"Marcus?" Iphiginia sounded anxious. "Are you all right? You are not about to collapse again, are you?"

Marcus nearly choked on his laughter. He smiled faintly. "No. At least not just yet. I want to be inside you, Iphiginia. But I don't want to rush you. This time you must guide me."

"Very well. But I warn you, all I know of this sort of thing is what I have learned from our last experience together and what I observed during my tour of Lartmore's statuary hall."

"It will be enough, I promise you." He cupped her with his palm and felt the moist heat that awaited him. "More than enough."

"You're certain?" She ran her thumb across the end of his shaft.

Marcus steeled himself. "Quite certain." He moved his fingers through the soft nest of hair between her thighs until he uncovered the swollen bud. He stroked gently.

"Good heavens, *Marcus*."

He felt the tremor that went through her. It was a sweet, powerful signal of her response to him. A fierce joy seized Marcus.

Her fingers tightened convulsively around him. Marcus winced and caught his breath.

"Did I hurt you, my lord?"

"You are going to be the death of me, Iphiginia."

"Oh, no, I'm so sorry. Are you all right, sir? I did not mean to do you an injury." Alarm briefly doused the sweet intensity of passion in her husky voice. "I warned you that I did not know precisely what to do."

"I was merely jesting," he assured her. He took another deep breath. "I'm nowhere near death." He continued to stroke her carefully, drawing forth the dew until his hand was slick with it. "In truth, I do not know when I have ever felt more alive."

Iphiginia's tentative, experimental caresses threatened to demolish his defenses and scatter his senses to the four winds. He was sweating now, every muscle tensed.

She moved slightly in his lap, adjusting herself. She tightened her legs. Her inner thigh brushed against his engorged shaft. His whole body clenched. Her whispered sighs and quickening breath told him of her increasing excitement.

Then, when he was beginning to wonder if she would ever finish the business, she guided him awkwardly to the exquisitely soft, hot place between her legs. Cautiously, slowly, carefully, she fitted herself to him.

She was so tight. Marcus wondered if he would, indeed, expire before he got inside.

She eased herself downward, drawing in her breath sharply at one point. Then her passage closed snugly around him. Marcus shuddered and held himself unmoving.

A distant warning bell rang somewhere in his fevered brain. He reminded himself that he must withdraw before he spilled his seed. He was not using one of his specially modified French sheep gut condoms.

And then Iphiginia began to move on him and all rational thought dissolved in Marcus's fevered brain. More demanding than any goddess from classical times, she clutched at him, whispered his name, pleaded, begged, scolded, demanded.

Marcus teased her gently, tormenting himself in the process. And then quite suddenly she shivered and convulsed in his arms.

"Marcus."

She collapsed against him with a tiny scream of surprise and pleasure.

The warning bell sounded again somewhere, but Marcus was unable to respond. He gripped Iphiginia's thighs and surged upward. He bit back the exultant shout of satisfaction that threatened to erupt from his throat.

Several moments later he sagged back into the corner of the carriage seat. Iphiginia sprawled on top of him.

There was silence. Marcus listened to it while he inhaled the unique, earthy scent of sexual satisfaction that drifted in the air of the closed cab.

The carriage turned a corner and came to a halt a few minutes later. Marcus stirred reluctantly and lit one of the interior lamps. He allowed himself a few seconds to savor the feel of Iphiginia nestled against him and then reality struck him.

"Iphiginia? We have arrived at your home."

She mumbled something indistinct and snuggled closer. Her skirts rustled softly. Marcus realized that she had fallen asleep. He smiled.

"Wake up. Hurry, my dear." He shook her gently, urging her to a sitting position. He heard the footman clamber down from the box to open the carriage door. Marcus hastily reached out to latch it.

"Iphiginia."

"What is it?" She patted back a charming

yawn and blinked with sleepy languor. Her skirts were crumpled around her thighs. One neat coil of hair had come loose. It dangled over her ear. A white plume bobbed at an odd angle. "Is it morning?"

"No, it is not." Marcus quickly set himself to rights. "It's the middle of the night and you look as though you have been tumbled in a carriage."

Iphiginia giggled. "Fancy that, my lord."

Marcus paused in the act of shoving his shirttails into his breeches. He gazed at her, riveted by her happiness.

He was responsible for this, he thought with a sense of awed wonder. He had made her happy. It was an infinitely more satisfying achievement than the creation of a clockwork butler or viewing stars through a telescope.

The footman rapped on the carriage door. "M'lord, do you wish to descend?"

"One moment, Jenkins." Marcus shook himself out of his momentary reverie. "Turn around," he muttered to Iphiginia. "The bodice of your gown is twisted and that plume looks as though it's about to fall out of your hair."

"Yes, my lord. I cannot imagine how I came to be in such disarray." Iphiginia obediently turned her back toward him and sat patiently while he fumbled with her gown.

"There, now, let me see you." Marcus turned her about again and surveyed his handiwork with a critical eye. He scowled at the loop of hair that still danced over Iphiginia's right ear. "Give me a pin."

She reached up and removed one from her chignon. "Here you are, sir. Pray do not stick yourself."

"Stop giggling. The footman will think I am tickling you."

"Yes, my lord." Mirth bubbled up inside her once more.

Marcus pinned the fallen coil into place. "With any luck that will hold until you get inside."

"I'm certain that it will, sir. You have a talent for mechanical things."

He unlatched the carriage door and shoved it open. Jenkins, waiting patiently outside, turned with an impassive expression and set down the step.

Marcus hid a smile as he watched Iphiginia descend with grand dignity just as though she had been doing nothing more unconventional than conversing about classical antiquities for the past half hour.

When she reached the pavement she gave Jenkins a smile which appeared to temporarily blind the man.

"Thank you," she murmured to the footman.

She would make a perfect countess, Marcus thought.

He walked her to her door and saw her safely inside. It took every ounce of his willpower to stay outside on the front steps. He had an almost overpowering urge to sweep her into his arms and carry her up the stairs to her bedchamber.

"You were quite correct about one thing, my lord," Iphiginia whispered in a soft, dreamy voice as he made to close the door.

He paused on the step. "What was that?"

"It was much better this time."

He grinned. "Yes, it was, wasn't it? I actually survived a second encounter. It was not even necessary to summon a doctor to revive me afterward."

Iphiginia smiled with smug satisfaction. "Obviously you are possessed of a very strong constitution, my lord."

"Obviously."

Marcus closed the door and went down the steps to where his carriage waited. He whistled softly and took a deep breath of the midnight air.

"A fine night, m'lord," Jenkins said as he opened the carriage door.

"It is indeed. Tell Dinks to take us home."

"Yes, m'lord."

Marcus vaulted up into the carriage and settled onto the seat where he and Iphiginia had made love. Pale white satin gleamed against the ebony velvet.

He picked up Iphiginia's glove. It lay as soft as a swath of starlight across his broad, muscled palm. He closed his hand very tightly around it.

Marcus went straight to the library the moment he got home. He had a long time to contemplate his decision while he waited for his brother to return from his night on the town. It was nearly three in the morning before Bennet's carriage rumbled to a halt in front of the town house.

Marcus cradled his brandy glass in his hands and waited for the door of the library to slam open.

He did not have to wait long.

Bennet stormed into the room. "Lovelace says you wish to speak to me."

"Yes."

Bennet stalked to the hearth, flung one arm out along the marble mantel, and took up a stance of sullen defiance. "Well, what is it, then? I cannot imagine what more we have to say to each other, brother."

Marcus gazed into the fire. "I regret my attempt to interfere in your plans for marriage to Miss Dorchester."

Bennet stared at him. "What did you say?"

"You heard me." Marcus took a sip of his brandy. "I should not have tried to scare off the Dorchesters. I had no right to threaten to cut you off from the family fortune, especially since I never had any intention of following through on the threat. It was a bluff."

"Marcus, what are you saying? Is this some sort of cruel jest?"

"If you choose to wed Juliana Dorchester, rest assured that you will be able to keep her in suitable style. You will continue to have full access to your income. Tomorrow I shall have my man of affairs draw up papers that will protect your inheritance."

Bennet looked completely nonplussed. "I don't understand. Are you telling me that you will give your approval to my betrothal to Juliana?"

"Yes." Marcus paused. "On the morrow I shall make it clear to Dorchester that I have no objection to the announcement of an engagement."

"But earlier this evening you implied that you would never tolerate it."

"I said a great many things earlier this evening. I regret all of them. You have my apologies."

"Your *apologies.*" Bennet sounded thunderstruck.

Marcus raised his eyes to meet Bennet's. "My only excuse is that I believed that I was protecting you from suffering a fate similar to my own."

"Juliana is not Nora, damn it."

"You are correct," Marcus said. "She is not Nora."

Bennet shook his head as though to clear it. "I do not know what to say."

"You are my brother, the only family I have. I would no more cut you off than I would cut off my right arm. In truth, I would sooner lose my arm than your affection and trust."

"I do believe you really mean what you are saying."

Marcus turned his glass in his hand and watched the firelight dance through the facets. "You may instruct Dorchester to have his man of affairs call upon mine to begin work on the marriage settlements. This sort of thing takes a great deal of time, you know. Several months is not unusual when there is so much money involved."

"Uh, Marcus, I haven't actually asked for Juliana's hand yet."

"No?" Marcus shrugged. "Well, I expect there is no great rush now that you know that there will be no objection from me."

"I shall speak to her at once," Bennet said

eagerly. "She will no doubt wish to send the announcement to the papers before the end of the Season."

"No doubt." Marcus took another swallow of brandy. The end of the Season was a month and a half away.

"Marcus, I don't know what to say." Bennet ran his fingers through his carefully tousled curls. "I was not expecting this change of heart from you."

"Neither was I," Marcus said under his breath.

Bennet frowned. "What was that?"

"I acted in haste and I have since had time to evaluate my actions. I pray you will forgive me."

"Yes, of course." Bennet hesitated. "Thank you. I cannot tell you how much this means to me. You will see that Juliana is a fine, gracious lady. She will make me an excellent wife."

"I expect you will want to set the wedding date sometime in the spring of next year?"

"Next year?" Bennet looked disconcerted. "That is a long time off."

"We might be able to manage with a six-month engagement, but a year is a more acceptable period, I'm told."

"Well, as to that, I had not really considered a proper engagement period. To be perfectly frank, Marcus, I was looking into hiring a carriage to take Juliana and myself to Gretna Green."

Marcus nearly strangled on his brandy. "I see."

"Are you all right?"

"Yes." Marcus recovered, took a breath, and then another swallow of the brandy. "Gretna is out. I'm sure Mrs. Dorchester will want to plan a fashionable wedding for her only daughter."

"No doubt. And Juliana does try to be a dutiful daughter. It is one of her many virtues."

"Indeed."

"Well, then." Bennet grinned. He looked as though a tremendous weight had been removed from his shoulders. "I shall discuss the engagement with Juliana and let you know what length of time we wish to choose."

"Of course. Your decision entirely. Just be certain to allow Dorchester's man of affairs sufficient time to confer with Barclay."

"I will. Marcus, I don't mind telling you that I find myself amazed by this turn of events."

"Do you?"

"You must admit that it is not like you to change your mind, especially on a matter such as this. You have a rule against altering a decision once it's made."

"Perhaps I am mellowing as I age."

"It is even less like you to apologize."

Another rule broken, thanks to Iphiginia. "I am aware of that."

"Would you mind telling me what brought about this sudden transformation?"

"I have had time to reflect and upon reflection, I feel I was mistaken."

Bennet eyed him closely. "What about the other business?"

"What other business?"

"Juliana said that you not only threatened to cut me off if I married without your approval, you also announced your own intention to wed." Bennet tilted his head curiously. "Was that a bluff, too?"

"No."

Bennet smiled. "I am pleased to learn that."

"Are you?"

"Of course I am. I've been telling you for an age that it is high time you remarried. I warned you that if you were to continue along your present path you would be in imminent danger of turning into one of your own clockwork automatons."

"I trust I shall avoid such an end."

"So?" Bennet gave him an inquiring look. "Who is she?"

"I am not prepared to make a formal announcement yet. There are, ah, certain details to be worked out."

"Yes, yes, I know." Bennet made an impatient movement with his hand. "If there is a great deal of business to be gotten out of the way in my marriage, I can envision how much there will be in your situation. After all, you've got the future of the title to consider."

"Yes."

"But surely you can confide in me, Marcus. I'm your brother." Bennet chuckled. "Is it the Chumley chit?"

"No."

"Elizabeth Anderson, perhaps?"

"No."

"Let me see." Bennet tapped his finger on the mantel. "I know, Henderson's daughter. What's her name? Charlotte?"

"I am going to marry Iphiginia Bright."

Bennet's mouth fell open. "The devil you are."

Marcus frowned. "You are not to say a word about this until I tell you that you may do so. Is that understood? This must remain a secret for now."

Bennet opened and closed his mouth twice before he managed to speak. "Damnation, Marcus. You cannot possibly be serious about marrying Mrs. Bright."

"But I am serious."

"She's your *mistress,* for God's sake."

"She is the lady I intend to wed. I told you that I will not tolerate any disrespect."

"But you're the Earl of Masters." Bennet slammed his hand against the mantel. "It's one thing to conduct a liaison with a woman such as Mrs. Bright. It is quite another thing to marry her."

"Give me one good reason why I should not marry her," Marcus challenged.

"One? I can give you a dozen. A man in your position is expected to marry a young lady, not a mature woman. Someone from a good family. Fresh out of the schoolroom. Unstained. Untouched. Your bride should be a respectable innocent—a virgin, to be perfectly blunt—not a notorious widow with whom you have been having an affair."

"Iphiginia Bright is just the right age for me." Marcus propped his elbows on the arms of the chair and steepled his fingers. "She is from a good family. She is respectable. You may put the word about that anyone who disagrees with me is free to do so over a pair of dueling pistols."

"Damn it to hell, Marcus, you cannot mean that."

"I find your objections to my forthcoming marriage every bit as irritating as you found mine to yours."

"But this is a different matter entirely."

"No, it is not."

"Good Lord, the woman has bewitched you."

"Do you think so?" Marcus considered that. "As a man of science, I have never believed in witchcraft."

Bennet flushed with outrage. "I would not have believed this if I had not seen it with my own eyes."

"Seeing is believing. And that, my dear brother, is the essence of sound scientific investigation. Now that you have, indeed, witnessed my decision to marry, you may believe it. And you will keep silent about it for the time being."

"You've gone mad. Marcus, you've inherited an earldom. You have certain responsibilities and duties to the title. You cannot allow passion to rule your actions."

Marcus started to smile. "I beg your pardon? Would you care to repeat that? Surely I did not hear what I thought I heard. Surely my brother the romantic poet did not just advise me to turn my back on my passions."

Bennet's mouth tightened. "You know what I mean."

"Yes, I do. You wish me to ignore my emotions and be guided by rational thought. You sound exactly as I must have sounded when I told you not to be swept off your feet by your feelings for Juliana Dorchester."

"My connection with Juliana is vastly different."

"No, it is not." Marcus gave him a hard look. "You will bear in mind that I do not wish this news to be spread about until I am ready to make a formal announcement."

"Do not concern yourself on that point," Bennet said furiously. "I am not about to humiliate either of us by breathing so much as a word about a possible marriage between you and Mrs. Bright."

"Thank you. I appreciate that."

"It is too bloody dreadful to even contemplate, let alone to discuss in public." Bennet stalked toward the door. "I shall pray that you come to your senses before you do anything so rash as to send word to the papers."

"I would not hold my breath if I were you."

"Damn it, this is abominable." Bennet yanked open the door. He turned to glance over his shoulder. "She has done something to your brain, that's what it is. I can only hope that you will recover from this strange fever before it is too late."

"You were the one who feared I might become an automaton if I did not marry soon."

"Mrs. Bright was definitely not what I had in

mind as a bride for you." Bennet stomped out into the hall and slammed the door.

Marcus sat quietly for a while. Then he got to his feet and crossed the room to the brandy table. He poured himself another glass and went to stand at the window.

He had done it, he thought. He had taken Iphiginia's advice and violated several of his own rules in the process. *Never explain, never discuss the past, never alter a decision or retreat from an objective.*

So many rules broken in one night.

Perhaps Bennet was right. Iphiginia did seem to have inspired a sort of fever within his brain.

On the other hand, Marcus thought, he no longer felt as though he were turning into a clockwork man.

SIXTEEN

*T*he following evening Zoe swooped down on Iphiginia at the Platts' ball. "I have been looking for you all day, my dear. Didn't you get the message I had sent 'round?"

"I'm sorry, Aunt Zoe. Apparently it did not reach me," Iphiginia said placatingly. In point of fact, she had ignored the message that had arrived at the kitchen door earlier that day.

"Have you heard the latest?" Zoe searched her face. "They say that Masters is going to announce his betrothal before the end of the Season."

"London is always rife with gossip, Aunt Zoe. As a connoisseur of rumors, you know that better than most." Iphiginia smiled at Herbert, who was forging a path toward her through the throng. "There is a variety of news at the moment. For instance, I heard that Masters has made it clear that his brother is free to choose his own bride without fear of being cut off."

"Yes, yes, but that hardly matters compared to this other business of his own marriage." Zoe fixed her with a pointed look. "If it's the truth, then Masters has broken one of his most firmly held rules."

"Highly unlikely." Iphiginia watched Herbert draw closer. He saw her and beamed good-naturedly. He carried a glass in one hand.

"I'm not so certain of that." Zoe pursed her lips. "There is a title involved, after all. And a great deal of money. Perfectly natural that a man in his position would come to his senses eventually and do his duty. He is only thirty-six, after all. It's not as though he's got one foot in the grave."

"The title can go to his brother."

"Yes, but it's not quite the same thing as having an heir of one's blood, is it? It was bound to come to this, I suppose. But I am so sorry for you, my dear. I know it must be very painful. It's been obvious for days that you've developed a tendre for the man. What are you going to do?"

"Nothing, for the moment." Iphiginia turned

to Herbert, who had finally reached them. "Ah, some lemonade. I need it. Thank you, Herbert. You are always so thoughtful."

"My pleasure. Whew. What a crush." Herbert gallantly handed her the glass of lemonade and then reached into his pocket for a handkerchief to mop his brow. "Bloody hot in here, is it not?"

"It is a trifle warm." Iphiginia took a sip of lemonade.

Herbert folded his handkerchief. "Evening, Lady Guthrie. Sorry, didn't see you earlier or I would have brought you a glass also."

"Quite all right. I just finished some champagne. Iphiginia and I were discussing the rumors of Masters's forthcoming betrothal."

"Aunt Zoe, please," Iphiginia murmured. "I think we've exhausted the subject."

"Heard all about it at my club," Herbert said helpfully. "The betting books are filling up all over Town. Everyone's taking a flier on this one."

Zoe frowned. "People are attempting to guess who the bride will be?"

"Yes." Herbert slid Iphiginia an embarrassed glance. "No one's got a clue. Lot of money on the Chumley chit and a good deal on Elizabeth Anderson, though. Both in their first Seasons. Quite lovely. Good families. Spotless reputations."

Iphiginia was keenly aware of Herbert's increasing discomfort and her aunt's worried gaze. She summoned up a serene smile. "If there is one thing everyone should have learned about Masters by now, it is that there is very little point in attempting to second-guess him."

"Man o' mystery, right enough," Herbert agreed quickly. "Everyone knows that. Enigma. No telling what's going on in his brain."

"It cannot be a complete secret," Zoe said. "Someone other than Masters must know the truth about this situation. After all, there is another party involved."

"You mean the bride?" Herbert's brows bounced up and down several times. "If Masters has sworn her and her family to secrecy until he's ready to announce the engagement, you can be certain they'll keep mum. Wouldn't dare defy his edict. Not if they want to pull off the match of the Season."

"I suppose not," Zoe admitted. "Masters's rules."

"Precisely." Herbert smiled at Iphiginia. "I say, Mrs. Bright, would you care to dance?"

"Yes, thank you, Herbert." Anything to terminate the discussion of Marcus's wedding plans, Iphiginia thought. She set her glass down on a passing tray.

Herbert took her arm and led her out onto

the floor just as the musicians began to play a waltz. He regarded Iphiginia with an anxious expression as he took her very decorously into his arms.

"I say, is this business of Masters's engagement oversetting you, my dear?"

"Not in the least," Iphiginia said firmly. "Masters and I are very close friends, as you know. I can assure you that the gossip about an engagement is just that. Gossip."

"Forgive me, but I am also your friend, Iphiginia," Herbert said gently. "I feel you and I are very much alike in some ways. And while I realize that I do not enjoy the sort of intimate connection with you that Masters does, I am deeply concerned for you."

"That is very kind of you. But there is no need."

"The thing is, the man is known to be quite ruthless, m'dear. He is perfectly capable of marrying this young innocent he's selected to be his wife and then continue to maintain a liaison with you on the side."

"Do not fret."

"Surely you will not countenance such a situation?" Herbert asked rather desperately. "It would be intolerable for a proud, spirited female such as yourself. It would mean that you would have to share him with his wife."

Iphiginia gave him a repressive look. "One

always shares one's friends with other people, Herbert."

"Damn it all, he's your paramour, not your friend. There's a world of difference."

"That is quite enough, Herbert."

Herbert turned a dark shade of red. "I did not mean to intrude, but everyone knows about your association with Masters."

"Do they?"

"Well, of course they do. Never been any secret. Iphiginia, I feel that I must be blunt. As your true and devoted friend, I must ask that you consider your future course of action quite carefully. You are the most elegant, most gracious, most intelligent, most admirable woman it has ever been my privilege to meet."

"Why, thank you, Herbert." Iphiginia was touched by the gallant declaration. "That is very kind of you."

"It is because you are so very estimable, such a paragon, that I feel I must urge you to think about your future. It is one thing to have an, er, exclusive connection with a powerful man such as Masters. Quite another to be kept as a bit of fluff on the side."

"A bit of fluff?" Iphiginia came to a halt in the middle of the floor.

Herbert gazed at her helplessly. "Masters will never be able to offer you marriage, madam. Everyone knows that if he has determined to violate his most cardinal rule in order to remarry, he will choose some young innocent to bear his heirs. It's the expected thing."

"You go too far, Herbert. You know that I do not discuss the details of my relationship with Masters with anyone." Iphiginia was aware of the covert stares she and Herbert were receiving from the other dancers.

"I did not mean to offend you, madam." Herbert looked thoroughly abashed. He cast an embarrassed glance around at the other couples and then took Iphiginia's arm. He hastily escorted her off the floor. "I pray that you will forgive me."

"Of course."

"I spoke out of turn. But I did so only because I am so deeply concerned about you."

"I know, Herbert." She patted his arm. "But I am not a young innocent. I am a woman of the world and I am quite capable of looking after myself."

"If you say so." Herbert withdrew his handkerchief again and dabbed at the beads of sweat on his brow. "You're a brave female, m'dear. You will always have my greatest admiration. Please remember that if there is ever any way in which I can be of service, you must not hesitate to call upon me."

"Thank you, Herbert." She smiled at him.

"Pray, excuse me. I must have a word with someone who just came in."

"Yes, yes, of course."

Herbert stuffed the crumpled handkerchief back into his pocket. Iphiginia could feel his wistful gaze resting on her as she made her way across the crowded room.

She knew that Herbert meant to be kind and that her aunt wanted to protect her from heartache, but neither of them knew the real truth. Iphiginia did not want to even attempt to explain the bizarre situation in which she found herself.

Curious eyes, most politely averted or hidden behind discreetly held fans, watched her as she headed toward the French doors. Iphiginia knew that the gossip about Masters's forthcoming engagement had crested into a tidal wave that had inundated Society.

Everyone was talking about her once more, just as they had a few weeks ago when she had descended on the Polite World. But this time they were speculating on her fate.

Iphiginia knew that no one expected Marcus to give up his mistress. It was accepted by one and all that he could and would have both a paramour and a suitable wife.

The real question as far as the Polite World was concerned was whether or not his unpredictable, independent mistress would abandon him rather than share him with a bride.

Society was titillated by the current developments, but it was not shocked. The only thing that could really stun the haute monde would be to discover that the woman Masters intended to wed was his mistress.

The *ton* would be even more astounded to learn that she had no intention of marrying him.

But no one was even speculating on such bizarre possibilities because, as usual, Society was two steps behind the notorious Earl of Masters.

Iphiginia slipped through the open doors and escaped to the cool darkness of the terrace. A handful of other people had drifted outside. They glanced at her as she emerged from the ballroom.

Iphiginia ignored the interested gazes and sought the seclusion of the far corner of the terrace. She needed a few moments of privacy. It had been a trying day and an even more trying evening.

The sound of a footstep behind her and the clearing of a masculine throat told Iphiginia that she no longer had this section of the terrace to herself.

"Mrs. Bright?" Bennet said in a very low voice.

Iphiginia turned slowly to face him. She summoned up a smile. "Good evening, Mr. Cloud."

"I saw you come out here." Bennet glanced awkwardly toward the brilliantly lit ballroom. Then he looked back at her. He squared his shoulders and took a resolute breath. The expression on his face was one of stern determination.

"You remind me of your brother when you do that," Iphiginia said dryly.

Bennet scowled. "When I do what?"

"Never mind. What was it you wanted?"

"Mrs. Bright, I will be blunt. The whole world is saying that my brother intends to marry a respectable young lady of the *ton*. But I know the truth."

"You do?"

"He told me that it is you he plans to wed," Bennet blurted. "It is a crazed notion, but I know him well and I fear that it is not beyond the realm of possibility that he would do something so . . . so . . ."

"So what?"

"So impossible as to wed a most improper female simply because he has taken a fancy to do so. He has no regard for Society's opinion or for propriety or tradition."

Iphiginia studied Bennet's earnest features. "I have heard that your brother has withdrawn his objection to a marriage between you and Juliana Dorchester."

"What in blazes has that got to do with anything?"

"Masters told me that he has many grave concerns about an alliance between you and Miss Dorchester. Yet he concluded that you were no longer a boy in need of his guidance. He feels that you are a mature man who has the right to make his own decisions."

"He should feel that way. I *am* a mature man." Bennet's gloved hands clenched and unclenched. "But my own plans for marriage have nothing to do with this discussion."

"Against his better judgment but out of respect for you, your brother has elected to stay out of your affairs. Don't you owe him the same courtesy?"

"Damnation, this is an entirely different matter. Miss Dorchester is a perfectly respectable young lady without a single blemish on her reputation. An innocent. She is above reproach. Marcus had no right to raise any objections to my intention to ask for her hand."

"You think not?"

"No offense, madam, but you are hardly in the same category as Juliana Dorchester. You are a woman of the world, if you do not mind my stating the obvious."

"Your brother is a man of the world."

"Yes, he is, but he is certainly not acting as though he were," Bennet retorted. "He appears to be smitten by you, Mrs. Bright. I vow, you have put some sort of spell upon him."

"What on earth makes you say that?"

"Why else would he violate his most closely held rule? He once vowed never to remarry. I confess, I had hoped he would change his mind. But I never dreamed he would do something so mad as to marry his mistress."

That was too much. Iphiginia was at the end of her tether. She had been under a strain for too long and now something inside her snapped.

"I am sick of hearing about Masters and his rules," she said forcefully. "He is not the only one who has chosen to live by his own rules. I happen to possess one or two myself."

"One can only speculate about the sort of rules a woman such as yourself would choose to honor. Do you have one which states that you will take only wealthy men as paramours?"

"I do not need a wealthy man to take care of me. In case you have not paid attention, Bennet, I control a rather handsome fortune of my own."

"Maybe it's the title you're after."

"I assure you, gaining a title is the least of

my concerns. I value my freedom and my rights as an independent widow far too highly to surrender them for a mere title."

"Then just what sort of rules do you abide by, Mrs. Bright?"

"There is only one that need concern you. I have an ironclad rule which states that I will never, ever marry a man who does not love me. And as your brother has never once said that he loves me, it does not require any great intellect to perceive that Masters is perfectly safe from me."

Bennet stared at her. "Mrs. Bright—"

"Begone, sir. I hate discussions of rules. I wish to be left alone." Iphiginia spun around on her heel and rushed toward the steps that led down into the garden.

She ran straight into Marcus, who had just emerged from behind a hedge.

"Ooph." Iphiginia staggered and lost her balance as she crashed against his broad chest.

Marcus steadied her while he looked at his brother. "What the bloody hell is going on here?"

Iphiginia's head came up quickly when she heard the dangerous edge of steel in his voice. " 'Tis nothing of any great import, sir. Your brother was merely concerned for your future well-being, just as you are concerned for his."

"My brother will keep his opinions on the subject to himself," Marcus said. "Is that understood, Bennet?"

"She will make a fool of you, if you allow her to do so," Bennet said savagely. "She is infinitely more clever than Nora. Can you not see that?"

"Any idiot can see it. It's one of the reasons I intend to wed her," Marcus said. "I cannot abide brainless females."

"You cannot possibly expect to turn her into a countess, Marcus. She would be a disgrace to the title."

In spite of her desire to put an end to the dreadful scene, Iphiginia took umbrage at that remark. "Now hold on one moment here, Mr. Cloud. Your brother was a farmer, a man who worked with his hands for years before he came into the earldom. He has managed very nicely with a title. I assure you I would have no trouble at all playing the part of a countess, if I so chose."

"Quite right," Marcus murmured.

"This is ridiculous," Bennet snapped.

"You are the one who is behaving in a ridiculous fashion," Marcus said. "Now take yourself off before I lose my temper."

"This is beyond anything. I can only pray that you told me the truth about your own rules, Mrs. Bright, and that you will have the decency to get out of my brother's life." Bennet whirled and stalked back toward the ballroom.

"You go too far, brother." Marcus made to ease Iphiginia out of his path. She panicked and seized hold of the lapels of his finely cut coat.

"Marcus, no. I do not want you and your brother quarreling because of me."

"Do not concern yourself, my dear. I shall deal with Bennet."

"Bloody hell, Marcus, I vow, if you go after him, I shall leave Town this very night."

He paused, frowning. "What are you saying?"

"I mean it, my lord. I will not allow you to stage a scene with Bennet because of me. He was doing no more than what you tried to do when you learned that he wished to marry Miss Dorchester. He was attempting to protect you."

"He is behaving like a pompous little prig. Who the devil does he think he is?"

"He is your brother and he is terrified that you are about to make a horrendous mistake. Does that sound familiar, Marcus? You were behaving in precisely the same manner just yesterday."

"It is hardly the same thing."

"It is precisely the same thing." Sensing that

she had won the small battle, at least for the moment, Iphiginia stepped back. "Come, my lord. Let us take a walk in the garden. I find I am in need of fresh air."

Marcus hesitated, clearly torn. He gazed at the open glass doors of the ballroom, then shrugged and took Iphiginia's arm. "Very well."

Iphiginia heaved a silent sigh of relief. Disaster had been averted for the moment, she thought, but sooner or later it would strike. She could feel it looming over her head.

She had hoped that she would have the remainder of the Season in which to savor the love of her life, but it seemed that such was not to be the case. She could not allow Marcus's relationship with his brother to be ruined because of her.

The time had come to think about leaving Town.

"What would you say if I were to suggest that we take an extended tour of America?" Iphiginia said to Amelia the following morning at breakfast.

Amelia looked up from the morning papers. "Are you serious?"

"Very."

"But there are no classical antiquities in America. Everything there is new. I have heard that the people live in little wooden houses of the most primitive sort."

"Rustic, primitive ruins can be quite inspiring, artistically speaking."

"Rubbish." Amelia folded the newspaper, set it aside, and regarded Iphiginia with a perceptive gaze. "Are you thinking of running away from this affair in which you find yourself embroiled?"

"The thought has crossed my mind."

"Need I remind you that it is not so simple as all that? We are in the middle of arranging the finances for Bright Place. We cannot deal with the details of such a large project if we are in America. It takes weeks to get a message across the Atlantic."

Iphiginia sighed. "I suppose you are right."

"If you wish to remove yourself from the situation, I suggest we retire to Deepford."

"*Never.*" Iphiginia shuddered at the thought. "The wilds of America would be preferable to the suffocating rules of Deepford. I shall never go back."

"Then you must think of another place." Amelia reached for the coffeepot. "Why this sudden panic? I was under the impression you believed that you were in control of the situation."

"Things are getting out of hand," Iphiginia muttered.

"In what way?" Amelia's eyes widened in sudden concern. "Good heavens, you aren't pregnant, are you?"

Iphiginia stilled. "No, of course not." *At least, I don't think so.* Iphiginia crossed her fingers in her lap.

Amelia frowned. "I imagine that Masters, being a man of the world, is cautious in such matters."

"Uh, yes." Iphiginia picked up a spoon and stirred her coffee very rapidly. "Yes, of course."

"Tell me, does he employ those odd French apparatuses fashioned from sheep gut? The ones the Italian countess told us about?"

"Amelia."

"I have always been rather curious to see one." Amelia looked at her with brief interest. "The countess also mentioned that a woman could use a small sponge soaked in some astringent liquid."

"I really do not want to discuss this at the breakfast table, Amelia."

"Oh." Amelia shrugged. "Some other time, perhaps."

"Perhaps." Right after she had discussed the subject with Marcus, Iphiginia thought grimly. He had never once mentioned the possibility of pregnancy. And she, heaven help her, had never given the matter much thought.

An image of herself holding Marcus's babe in her arms formed in her mind. It was such an intensely powerful vision that she caught her breath with a sense of wonder.

The infant would have miniature versions of his father's fine, strong hands. He would have his father's brilliant, intelligent amber eyes and broad forehead.

He would be beautiful and she would love him as much as she loved his father.

"Iphiginia? Did you hear what I said?"

Iphiginia blinked and brought herself back to reality. "I beg your pardon?"

"I suggested that if you are concerned about your association with Masters, we might consider removing ourselves to Bath. I have always wanted to take the waters."

"I shall consider the notion." Iphiginia set her spoon precisely on the saucer. "Won't you miss being able to work so closely with Mr. Manwaring?"

"Whatever do you mean?"

"It strikes me that matters have gone very efficiently thus far with Bright Place primarily because Mr. Manwaring is situated nearby and able to meet with us at a moment's notice. Business will not be nearly so convenient if we remove ourselves to Bath. We shall have to depend upon the post and the occasional visit."

"We managed to work quite nicely with him

during our years in Deepford." Amelia picked up the newspaper and frowned over one of the articles. "It's true that having Mr. Manwaring in the vicinity has made things go more smoothly. But I am sure we shall be able to carry on business from Bath."

Iphiginia stifled a small sigh. Perhaps she had been wrong when she had concluded that Amelia and Manwaring were made for each other.

Lord only knew that she was not nearly so clever about such matters as she had once thought. The situation in which she found herself was a perfect example of how muddled affairs of the heart could become.

Until now she had assumed that her problem was that she loved a man who could not bend his own rules far enough to allow himself to admit that he loved her.

But perhaps the situation was even worse than she had thought. Perhaps Marcus had become so chained by his own rules that he could never love any woman again.

"Damn you, Nora," Iphiginia whispered.

Amelia looked up. "What was that?"

"Nothing." Iphiginia drummed her fingers on the table. One thing was for certain. She must take care not to become pregnant. It would be the last straw, for then Marcus would surely insist on marriage. And she would have no choice but to wed him for the sake of the babe.

"Do you know something, Amelia? Being a mistress is a bloody complicated business."

"I am told that being a wife is even more difficult," Amelia said.

"Yes, I suppose that is quite true."

But if Marcus loved her, Iphiginia thought wistfully, she would take the chance.

The note was waiting for Iphiginia on the white velvet seat of her carriage that afternoon when she returned from a shopping expedition. She was seized with a sense of foreboding when she saw the folded sheet of foolscap.

She waited until the coachman had closed the door before she reached out to pick up the note. She saw with relief that there was no sign of black wax or a phoenix seal.

Slowly she unfolded the note and read the contents.

My Dearest Pandora.

If you wish to open the box and discover the truth about the past, present, and future you must come to Number Nineteen Lamb Lane off Pall Mall tonight on the stroke of midnight.

Come alone. Tell no one and all will be made clear.

If you do not come, or if you fail to come alone, someone you care about will suffer the consequences. Your sister, perhaps? Or will it be Lady Guthrie, your aunt?
Yrs.
A Friend

Iphiginia's fingers trembled as she carefully refolded the note.

Your sister.

Your aunt.

The words seemed to burn straight through the paper. The threat was not the least bit subtle. Whoever knew that she possessed a sister and that Zoe was her aunt, knew everything, Iphiginia realized.

My Dearest Pandora . . .

Iphiginia quickly reopened the note and studied the salutation. Pandora was a clear reference to the Greek tale of the lady who had given in to temptation to open the magic box and in so doing had unleashed chaos and woe.

Iphiginia felt a kinship with Pandora at that moment.

Whoever had sent the note had apparently noted the similarity.

Iphiginia had given in to the temptation of an affair with Marcus and trouble was now abroad in her world.

SEVENTEEN

*G*as lights had not yet been installed in Lamb Lane. The narrow street, lined with small shops, huddled in the shadows. The pale glow of a fitful moon provided just enough illumination to reveal that the hackney which carried Iphiginia was the only vehicle in the vicinity.

The coach came to a halt with a clatter of wheels and harness. Iphiginia started when the coachman rapped on the roof to announce their destination.

"Number Nineteen Lamb Lane," the man called loudly.

Iphiginia gathered her dark cloak around her and pulled the hood over her head. She opened the carriage door and cautiously descended to the pavement.

"Do not forget," she said to the man on the box. "I have paid you to wait for me."

"I'll be waitin'," the coachman muttered in a surly voice. "But there'll be an extra fee if ye bring any of yer clients back 'ere."

"I beg your pardon?"

"Ye heard me. If yer thinkin' o' usin' me coach fer a bedchamber tonight, ye'll 'ave to pay me a fair rent. I'll give ye the usual hourly rate I give the other girls."

Iphiginia felt herself turn hot with embarrassment and anger. "What on earth do you think I am about, my good man?"

"Same as what most of the other wenches are about at this time o' night in this part o' Town. Business. Go on, now. Just keep in mind that I'll be wantin' me fair share if ye use me coach."

She did not have the time to deliver a scathing lecture to a drunken coachman. Iphiginia turned away, disgusted, and studied the darkened entrance to Number Nineteen. There was just enough moonlight to make out the sign over the door.

Dr. Hardstaff's Museum of the Goddesses
of Manly Vigor
Learn the Secret and Authentic
Invigorating Powers of
the Goddesses of Antiquity

It appeared that her curiosity about Dr.
Hardstaff's museum was about to be satisfied,
Iphiginia thought.

A glance over her shoulder assured her that
the coachman was still waiting in the street.
She saw that the carriage lamps burned with a
reassuring glow.

Iphiginia went toward the darkened premises of Number Nineteen. She wished Marcus
were with her. Or even Amelia or Zoe. Anyone
at all, for that matter.

She was far more anxious this evening than
she had been the night she paid the visit to
Reeding Cemetery. The threats contained in
the note that she had found in her carriage had
jarred her nerves as nothing else could have
done.

When Iphiginia got close to the sign for Dr.
Hardstaff's Museum, she noticed a painted
hand at the bottom. The pointing finger urged
visitors to go down the narrow walkway between two buildings.

Iphiginia peered hesitantly into the thick
shadows of the tiny alley. She could just make
out a flight of steps that led to the upper story
of the building.

With one last glance at the hackney,
Iphiginia started down the alley.

She climbed the stairs as quietly as possible,
her pulse beating more rapidly with each step.

Every squeak, every groan of the treads sent a shiver through her. The darkness seemed to grow more and more dense around her.

She should not have come here alone.

But there had been no choice.

At the top of the stairs she paused and studied the closed door in front of her. Another sign, this one barely discernible in the shadows, indicated that this was the entrance to Dr. Hardstaff's Museum.

The rumble of carriage wheels in the street jolted Iphiginia just as she put her hand on the knob. The hackney was abandoning her.

"No," she gasped, and turned to rush back down the steps.

The lights of a second carriage appeared. Iphiginia halted, one foot on the landing, one on the first step. Her hackney had not left, she realized. Another one had arrived.

It rolled to a halt near her own. Horses stomped their hooves. Voices echoed through the shadows.

"Wait for me," a man ordered crisply.

"Aye, m'lord. Take yer time. Brung a gennelman here last week what spent most of the night." The new coachman chuckled heartily. "Dr. Hardstaff's goddesses give quite a cure, they tell me. Wonder if it works."

"I shall not be long," the newcomer said.

Footsteps sounded on the paving stones.

They paused briefly. And then, to Iphiginia's horror, they started toward the narrow alley where she hovered at the top of the stairs.

Fear ripped through her. In a matter of seconds the man who had gotten out of the second hackney would come down the alley. It was obvious he was en route to Dr. Hardstaff's Museum. He would surely see her as soon as he mounted the stairs.

She could not go back down the staircase without running straight into the stranger, so Iphiginia did the only thing she could do. She turned the knob that was pressing into her lower back.

The door opened with only a small squeak of its hinges. Intent on watching the staircase, Iphiginia backed through the door into a darkened hall. She closed the door very carefully.

A man's arm came out of the intense shadows of the hall. It wrapped around Iphiginia's throat.

She was dragged against a broad chest as a rough palm clamped over her mouth. Her incipient scream was cut off before it could escape.

"Bloody hell," Marcus muttered. "Iphiginia?"

She nodded wildly. Relief rushed through her, draining her.

"What in the name of the devil—" Marcus took his hand away from her mouth.

"Someone's coming up the stairs, Marcus," she whispered frantically. "He'll be here any second."

"Damn." Marcus released her and grabbed her hand. "This way. Hurry. Don't make a sound."

She needed no second urging. The newcomer's footsteps thudded on the stairs outside.

Marcus yanked Iphiginia down a dark hall, opened a door, and tugged her into a large room that was dimly lit by a single wall sconce.

"What in the world?" Iphiginia gazed about in astonishment. "What is this place?"

The lamplight revealed the most oddly furnished chamber Iphiginia had ever seen. Exotic drapery hung from the ceiling in the style of a Turkish tent. A large bed dominated the center of the room. It was decorated with gauzy hangings and an extraordinary number of pillows. It was surrounded by erotic statuary of the sort Lord Lartmore favored.

The walls were decorated with huge murals depicting classical gods and goddesses from various mythological tales. The deities appeared to be nude. The men were all in a state of extreme sexual arousal. The female figures were voluptuous to the point of being ludicrous.

"Welcome to Dr. Hardstaff's Museum,"

Marcus said as he pulled her across the chamber. "One night in the therapeutic bed is guaranteed to cure impotence."

"Marcus, what are you doing here?"

"An excellent question. I intend to put the same one to you as soon as we have an opportunity. In the meantime, we must get you out of sight."

"Good heavens." Iphiginia stared at a painting that featured several woodland nymphs cavorting with three overly endowed satyrs. "These are the most perfectly dreadful copies of classical antiquities that I have ever seen."

"I regret that your scholarly sensibilities have been affronted." Marcus took hold of the edge of a heavy red curtain that stretched the length of the chamber. "You can take it up with Dr. Hardstaff later."

"What are we going to do now?"

"You are going to get out of sight and stay out of sight." Marcus jerked aside the floor-to-ceiling curtain and pushed Iphiginia through the opening onto a small stage. Several Greek urns and a scrolled pedestal occupied the platform. There was a narrow door in the side wall behind the curtain.

"But Marcus—"

"Go through that door and hide in the hallway behind it." Marcus caught her chin on the edge of his hand. His eyes were grim. "Do not come out until I tell you. And whatever you do, don't make a single sound. Do you comprehend me?"

"Yes, but—" She broke off as she heard the outside door on the landing open. Her mouth went dry. "Oh, Lord."

"Hush." Marcus yanked the curtain back into position, concealing Iphiginia from the view of anyone who might enter the chamber.

The heavy curtain cut off the glow of the wall sconce. Iphiginia found herself in near darkness. She started to grope her way toward the small door and struck her toe against the pedestal. She swallowed a grunt of pain.

The door of the outer chamber slammed open. Iphiginia went still, not daring to move for fear she would crash into another object.

"Damnation, Masters." The stranger's voice was raw with fury. "It's you. I didn't believe it when I got the note. I told myself that it was all a terrible joke. But it seems I've been both a fool and a cuckold."

"Good evening, Sands." Marcus's tone was cool to the point of indifference. "I didn't realize that someone else also had an appointment with Dr. Hardstaff this evening. I specifically requested a private treatment."

Iphiginia realized that the man who had entered the chamber was the husband of the mysterious Lady Sands.

"Where is my wife, you bloody bastard?"

"I have no notion," Marcus said quietly. "As you can see, I'm quite alone. I confess I'm disappointed by that fact. I had hoped there would be a bit more to Dr. Hardstaff's famous therapy than a few bad paintings and some equally poor statuary."

"You arranged to meet Hannah here, didn't you?" Sands asked in a seething voice. "That's what the note said."

"The note?"

"Someone knows what you're about, Masters. A note was left in my carriage this evening telling me that if I wished to discover the place where you and my wife carried on your assignations, I should come to Number Nineteen Lamb Lane."

"Someone has played an unpleasant practical joke on you, Sands. Whoever it was undoubtedly knew that I had an appointment here tonight."

"An appointment with my wife, damn you."

"No."

Iphiginia started when she heard the side door open. She peered anxiously into the shadows and saw a figure emerge from a dark hall. The woman carried a candle in her hand. The flame illuminated her pretty features, blond hair, and extremely low-cut, diaphanous gown.

She halted abruptly when she spotted

Iphiginia. Then she put her hands on her hips and glared.

" 'Ere, now, what do ye think yer doin'?" she demanded in a loud tone. "This is my night to be the Classical Goddess o' Manly Vigor."

There was a sudden silence from the other side of the curtain.

Iphiginia stared at the woman and desperately tried to think of what to do next. "I'm sorry," she managed in a thin whisper. "There's been a mistake."

"What's going on back there?" Sands demanded. Footsteps echoed on the floor as he strode toward the heavy scarlet curtain.

"I believe the performance is about to begin," Marcus said dryly.

The blond woman gave a small, disgruntled screech and turned toward the curtain. "What's this? There be two of 'em out there?"

"Uh, yes," Iphiginia murmured.

"Don't ye dare touch that curtain," the blonde yelled. She turned to Iphiginia. "Hardstaff didn't say nothin' about there bein' two gennelmen gettin' the classical treatment tonight. What's 'e think I am? A genuine goddess?"

Marcus spoke up quietly. "If I were you, Sands, I would not interfere."

"What the devil is happening here?" Sands sounded confused.

"I said, don't ye dare touch that curtain," the blonde roared. She peered at Iphiginia. " 'Old on. Is that why yer 'ere? To handle the second gennelman?"

"Uh, yes," Iphiginia whispered. "Yes, I believe so."

"Well, I suppose that's all right, then. Get yer cloak off and we'll give these gentry coves their money's worth. I'm Polly. What's yer name?"

"Uh, Ginny." Iphiginia slowly removed her cloak. She put it on top of the pedestal.

"Ye new at this?" Polly surveyed Iphiginia's delicate white evening gown with a critical gaze. "Yer overdressed."

"I'm sure I'll get the hang of this quickly," Iphiginia said. "I am an excellent student."

"Enough of this nonsense." Sands started toward the curtain. "Come on out here, you two. I have some questions to ask."

"Stop," Polly yelled. "Got rules against anyone comin' back 'ere before the performance, y'know."

"Now see here," Sands growled, "I do not intend to be ordered about by a cheap whore."

"This is a theater, damn yer eyes," Polly snarled back through the curtain. "And we're bloody actresses, we are, not whores. And we ain't cheap. Ye'll do us the favor o' treatin' us with some respect or ye can just plain forget about gettin' any o' Dr. Hardstaff's special treatment tonight."

"I am not here to see your damned show," Sands snapped. "I'm here to find someone."

"Ain't no one backstage 'ere except us professional actresses. Now either sit down to enjoy the performance or get out o' 'ere."

"The lady has a point," Marcus said. "I would very much appreciate it if you would remove yourself, Sands. I paid good money to be entertained this evening."

"Entertained?" Sands sounded disgusted. "You call this entertainment?"

"I was told it was somewhat amusing," Marcus replied. "Inspirational, even."

"We're about to start the bloody show," Polly announced through the curtain. "If ye two fine gennelmen want to get the treatment together, that's yer affair. But I warn ye, it'll be double the price."

"Unless you're willing to pay your share, Sands," Marcus said, "it's time to leave."

"I am not leaving," Sands said furiously. "Not until I can deduce what in blazes is going on here."

"If yer stayin', ye can make yerself useful," Polly snapped. "Put out the lamp near the door."

"I believe I will do that," Sands said coldly. "Let us see just what is going on behind that curtain." His footsteps rang out once more as he turned and strode back toward the door.

"About time. No respect fer professional work anymore." Polly bent down to light a row of lamps on the stage. They flared to life.

Then she reached out and hauled mightily on a long, heavy cord.

The heavy red curtain moved to the side, leaving a very thin muslin drape in its place.

"Bloody hell," Marcus muttered.

Iphiginia realized that the lamps on the stage were producing strong silhouettes of both herself and Polly against the gauzy curtain. She stilled.

"Interesting," Sands said laconically. "How much did you say you paid for this, Masters?"

"Too much," Marcus said. "I fear I may have been fleeced."

"They're all critics at first, y'know," Polly said. "The whole lot of 'em. But they change their minds soon enough." She straightened and frowned at Iphiginia. "Get yer urn. 'Urry up, now."

Iphiginia took a deep breath and forced herself to move. She picked up one of the large urns that had been positioned on the stage. It was surprisingly light. "Now what?"

"Strike yer pose. Don't ye know anythin' about this business? Dr. Hardstaff gets right cranky if the patients don't get their money's worth." Polly picked up her urn and struck what she undoubtedly believed to be a classical pose.

It finally dawned on Iphiginia that she and Polly were performers in a transparency show.

The transparency curtain acted as a veil, concealing the details of her features while it revealed the clear outline of her figure.

The lamps, strategically situated behind the two women, produced a ghostly scene.

Iphiginia had seen a handful of such productions, but they had all been of an educational nature. The last one, which she had attended with Amelia, had featured an extremely edifying tableau illustrating the classical ruins of Herculaneum.

But the scene staged by herself and Polly tonight was clearly designed to be of a much less elevating nature. Iphiginia had a horrible suspicion that her gossamer white silk skirts afforded little or no modesty. The flaring lamps were placed so as to render Polly's attire virtually transparent.

Iphiginia clutched her urn more securely and held it directly in front of herself. She prayed that it was large enough to cover a goodly portion of her torso. With any luck only a hazy view of her legs, head, and shoulders would be visible through the gauzy transparency screen.

"The goddess on the left isn't bad," Sands

drawled with icy sarcasm. "But the one on the right is a bit slender for my taste. What do you think, Masters?"

Iphiginia flushed as she realized that she was the goddess on the right.

"I've never been fond of transparency shows," Marcus said. "If I had realized that Hardstaff's famous production consisted of something this tame, I would have found other ways to amuse myself this evening."

Iphiginia looked helplessly at Polly.

Polly winked. "Don't ye worry. We'll impress 'em." She altered her pose to one that displayed her ample bosom to better advantage. "Personally, I'm real fond o' the job," she whispered. "Much easier on a girl than workin' flat on her back."

"I can imagine," Iphiginia muttered.

"Give 'em a few good poses and they'll go off 'appy as larks." Polly shifted her urn slightly, arched her back, and thrust her bosom upward. "They always do."

Iphiginia did not dare move. She kept her urn positioned firmly in front of herself.

"Seen enough, Sands?" Marcus asked. "I have. My curiosity is satisfied. Dr. Hardstaff's miracle treatment is not nearly so entertaining as I had been led to believe."

"I've seen more than enough," Sands said roughly. "Now it's time for a few answers."

Footsteps sounded on the other side of the curtain again. Sands was coming toward the stage.

"*Damnation.*" Marcus's bootsteps thudded on the floor behind Sands. "Don't touch that curtain. You'll upset the actresses."

"Do you think I give a damn about these wenches? I want to know why someone sent me here tonight. I'm through playing games."

Iphiginia saw Sands's hand appear at the edge of the gauzy curtain. He grabbed a fistful of the fine fabric and yanked hard. The delicate transparency curtain ripped loose from the hooks in the ceiling.

Iphiginia and Polly were fully revealed.

"See 'ere now," Polly scolded, outraged. "What do ye think yer doin'? Yer goin' to pay fer that curtain, not us."

Sands ignored her. He stared at Iphiginia, astounded. "*Mrs. Bright.* What the devil are you doing here?"

She smiled weakly. "Good evening, Lord Sands. I don't believe we've been introduced."

"Rest assured I know who you are, madam," Sands said grimly.

Iphiginia blushed. "Yes, well, as you have no doubt guessed, I am part of the treatment Dr. Hardstaff designed especially for Masters."

"His *treatment?*" Sands shot a scathing glance at Marcus, who raised his brows slightly but said nothing. Sands turned to Iphiginia. "Forgive me, Mrs. Bright, but I find that a little difficult to believe."

"But it's true," Iphiginia said quickly. She cast a quick, urgent look at Marcus, who offered no assistance. "Dr. Hardstaff stated that the results would be more immediate and far more dramatic if I assisted in the treatment."

"Hardstaff is a damned quack," Sands said. "Everyone knows that."

"I didn't," Iphiginia said. She gave Marcus another urgent look, but he appeared bored by the entire affair. She began to grow annoyed.

"Come now, Mrs. Bright," Sands said. "Every gentleman in Town is well aware that Hardstaff's so-called treatments for impotence are nothing more than titillating transparency shows. They are staged by pretty little whores who make themselves available after the performance."

"'Ere, now," Polly snapped. "That's a bloody lie, it is. I'm an actress."

"That's certainly one word for your profession," Sands agreed.

Iphiginia concluded that, in the absence of any assistance from Marcus, she had no choice but to take an aggressive tack. "How would you know whether or not Dr. Hardstaff's treatments were legitimate unless you'd taken one, my lord?"

"Aye, that's a bloody good question," Polly said. "And I ain't never noticed you in this chamber o' the Goddesses o' Manly Vigor before. Stands to reason ye don't know what yer talkin' about."

"Quite right," Iphiginia said staunchly. "You've been forming your opinions on hearsay, sir."

"It's common knowledge that the treatments are at best a fraud," Sands retorted furiously.

"Nonsense," Iphiginia insisted. "We have every hope of a cure, don't we, Masters?"

Marcus gave her a dangerous look.

Polly put her hands on her hips and glowered ferociously at Sands. "I know lots o' fine gennelmen who was miraculously cured by one o' these treatments."

Sands narrowed his eyes. "Is that a fact?"

"Aye, it's a fact, all right." Polly lifted her chin proudly. "I've seen gennelmen come in 'ere what 'adn't been able to raise the flag fer years. When they left, they was as stiff as a poker."

"There, you see?" Iphiginia said brightly. "A testimonial from one who should know."

"Enough of this nonsense." Marcus finally deigned to intervene. He drew a handful of notes out of his pocket and thrust them into Polly's hand. "You've given us a fine performance, madam. You may take your bows and leave. We won't be needing your services any longer."

Polly snatched the notes from him. "Are ye certain?"

"Quite certain," Marcus said.

"Well, all right, then." Polly smiled cheerfully at Iphiginia. "Nice workin' with ye, Mrs. Bright. Ye've got some potential, in me 'umble opinion. With a bit o' practice, I 'ave a 'unch ye'll get the 'ang o' this actin' profession."

"Thank you," Iphiginia said politely. "I shall work hard to perfect my craft."

"Reckon I'll be on me way, then." Polly sauntered to the side door.

Iphiginia, Marcus, and Sands watched as she let herself out of the chamber of the Goddesses of Manly Vigor.

A short silence ensued after the door closed.

Marcus broke the strange spell that seemed to have settled onto the chamber. He stepped onto the stage and walked along the row of stage lamps, turning them off one by one. "As the evening appears to have degenerated into a complete farce, I suggest we take our leave, Mrs. Bright."

"Yes, of course." Iphiginia set down her urn.

Sands scowled at Marcus. "I don't understand any of this."

"I think it's safe to say that we have all been

the victim of an unpleasant joke, Sands." Marcus left the last lamp burning.

"It makes no sense." Sands shoved his hands into his pockets and began to pace the chamber. "Who would do such a thing?"

"Someone who knows that you are suspicious of my long-standing friendship with your wife, naturally." Marcus propped one shoulder against the wall, folded his arms, and contemplated Sands. "There are any number of people in this world who take great delight in stirring troubled waters. You know that as well as I do."

Sands gave him a cold look and continued to pace. "But what did the villain expect to happen when I arrived here tonight and discovered that you were playing games with Mrs. Bright rather than Hannah?"

Iphiginia flushed. "We were not playing games, sir."

Sands's mouth curved derisively. "You may call this nonsense whatever you wish, madam. It is entirely your affair."

Marcus studied Sands's pacing figure. "I expect whoever sent you here was hoping that you would spread the tale of this night's events far and wide."

"What do you mean?" Sands demanded.

"I suspect that the real target of the jest was

not you, but my friend Mrs. Bright," Marcus said in a very soft voice. "I intend to see that the culprit pays for it."

Iphiginia stared at him. It was obvious that Marcus was very serious.

Sands paused abruptly. He swung around and considered Iphiginia intently. "You believe that someone wished to see Mrs. Bright humiliated?"

"Yes."

"But why?" Sands asked.

"Because whoever it is does not want me to marry her," Marcus said simply.

"*Marry her.*" Sands stared. "You're going to marry Mrs. Bright? Your, uh, very close friend?"

"Yes." Marcus looked at Iphiginia. "We have not yet made a formal announcement, however, so I trust you will remain silent for the time being?"

Iphiginia opened her mouth to argue but closed it again when she realized that any protest would only cause Sands to ask more pointed questions.

Sands frowned. "I had heard the rumor that you were going to announce your engagement. But I naturally assumed you would offer for one of the young . . . ah, er, never mind." He coughed discreetly and inclined his head at

Iphiginia. "Please accept my best wishes, Mrs. Bright."

"Thank you." She glowered at Marcus, furious with him for forcing her into the awkward situation of verifying the marriage. "Let us hope that Dr. Hardstaff's cure takes effect before we celebrate our wedding night."

Sands grinned. He suddenly looked much younger and a good deal more likable. "I shall wish you the best of luck in that regard, also. By the bye, you need have no fear that I will tell anyone about this evening's events."

"I appreciate that," Iphiginia said.

"I doubt anyone would even believe me. Whole thing is too bloody outrageous." Sands started toward the door. "Do you know something? I believe the two of you were made for each other. Now, if you will forgive me, I'll be on my way." He cast a derisive glance at the paintings on the walls of the chamber as he opened the door. "Unlike yourself, Masters, I do not have any need of Dr. Hardstaff's therapeutic treatments."

"How very fortunate for you," Marcus said.

Silence fell once more as the door closed behind Lord Sands.

Iphiginia and Marcus listened to his receding footsteps as he went down the hall and opened the outside door.

A moment later they heard the door close.

Iphiginia heaved a sigh of relief and then she rounded on Marcus. "You should be ashamed of yourself. Lord Sands will be waiting for the notices of our marriage to appear in the papers. How could you?"

"I supplied him with the only answer that was guaranteed to distract him."

"But what will he think when he never sees the formal announcement? He's bound to wonder if you lied to him. Perhaps he'll conclude that he was duped."

"I shall worry about that later. In the meantime, I have a more pressing problem on my hands."

"Oh, really?" Iphiginia planted her hands on her hips. "And just what might that be, pray tell? Perhaps you would care to explain what you're doing in this very odd chamber, my lord?"

The side door opened, cutting off Iphiginia's tirade. She stared at the newcomer in shock. She had never been properly introduced to Lady Sands, but Zoe had once pointed her out at a ball.

Hannah, covered from head to foot in a dark cloak, walked out onto the stage. She smiled at Iphiginia with sad apology.

"I believe Marcus is referring to me, Mrs.

Bright. I fear that I have been a nuisance to him for some time."

Before Iphiginia could respond, the chamber door swung inward with a small squeak. Lord Sands walked back into the room. He carried his shoes in one hand.

"As long as Masters is going to explain matters," Sands said in an icy voice, "he may as well explain them to all concerned. And when he has finished, he can explain them again to me at dawn over a brace of pistols."

Hannah stared at him as though she were seeing a ghost. "Dear God, no." Her hand went to her mouth. And then she crumpled to her knees, sobbing.

"Lady Sands." Iphiginia hurried toward her.

"Hannah." Sands dropped his shoes and started toward his wife.

"One would think," Marcus said to the room in general, "that one would be able to get a simple medical treatment done with some degree of privacy."

E IGHTEEN

"L ady Sands, please, you mustn't carry on so."
Iphiginia pulled a hankie out of her little
white satin reticule. She bent down and thrust
it into Hannah's shaking fingers. "Everything
will be fine."

"Thank you." Hannah blew her nose and
risked an anguished look at her stony-faced
spouse. "I'm so sorry, Mrs. Bright. I never
meant for this to happen. Marcus was right. I
could not conceal the truth forever from my
husband."

"What truth? What the devil is going on
here?" Sands looked at Marcus, his face
twisted with rage and pain. "And don't give me
any more rubbish about taking one of Hardstaff's treatments, damn your eyes."

"Hannah is the only one who can tell you the

truth," Marcus said. "I have given her my word that I would keep her secrets."

"What secrets do you share with my wife?" Sands exploded. "Did you trick her into coming here so that you could seduce her in that brothel bed over there?"

"No," Marcus said calmly.

"Of course he did not do any such thing." Iphiginia straightened and glowered at Sands. "Really, sir, that is beyond anything. Masters would never seduce another man's wife."

Sands turned on her, his face still tight with fury. "How would you know?"

"Because I know him very, very well." Iphiginia patted Hannah's shoulder. "He is incapable of that sort of unprincipled behavior."

Marcus gazed at her with an unreadable expression.

Sands eyed Iphiginia intently. "How do you come to be here tonight, Mrs. Bright?"

"I received a note, just as you did, sir," Iphiginia said. "I arrived only moments before you and hid behind the curtain." She swept a hand out to indicate the bed, the erotic paintings, and the statuary. "Obviously, someone intended that I discover Masters together with Lady Sands in a compromising position. I suspect you were meant to do the same."

"Someone staged this entire affair?" Sands set his jaw. "Is that what you're saying?"

"It's the only logical assumption, is it not, Masters?"

"Yes." Marcus regarded the small group thoughtfully. "Hannah and I both received notes, too."

"They could not have come from the black-mailer," Iphiginia said. "Mrs. Wycherley is dead. Besides, there was no demand for money in this night's work. Some other malicious person is behind this."

Sands stared at each of them in turn, more frustrated than ever. "What blackmailer?"

Hannah raised her head with sad dignity. "Someone blackmailed me, my lord. We believe it was Mrs. Wycherley from the Wycherley Agency. She also blackmailed an acquaintance of Mrs. Bright's. She was murdered by one of her other victims."

"That was our initial conclusion," Marcus said.

"Good Lord," Sands whispered. He glanced at Marcus and then strode toward his wife. He pulled Hannah up into his arms. "Tell me everything, Hannah. For God's sake, the truth can be no worse than what I have been forced to imagine for the past fortnight."

Hannah's eyes filled with tears. "You will turn from me in disgust."

"Never," Sands vowed. "Never, my love. You cannot have done anything that will give me a disgust of you. The only way in which you could break my heart would be to turn to another."

"Oh, Edward, I killed him." Hannah pressed her face into his shoulder. "I shot him dead. And I do not regret the murder. I only feared your discovery of it."

"Who did you kill?" Sands moved his hand gently on her shivering back.

"Spalding," Hannah blurted.

Sands frowned. "Your first husband?"

"I killed him one night when he came home drunk and started to beat me. I could not endure any more of his rages." Hannah sobbed heavily. "I could not take the never-ending fear. The cruelty. I feared for the life of any child I might bear. Oh, Edward, I was always so afraid. Only Marcus discovered the truth."

Sands looked at Marcus over the top of Hannah's head. "Masters? How are you involved in this? The old rumors always labeled you as the killer."

"I walked in five minutes after she had shot him," Marcus said evenly. "I got rid of the body for her. Tossed it into the river. Made it appear as though he had been killed by a footpad."

"That was the least of what he did." Hannah sniffed back tears. "He also bore the brunt of the suspicions and the gossip afterward. Everyone believed that Marcus profited from Spalding's death. But the truth was, my husband had cheated him and many others. The investment pool they had formed was on the verge of bankruptcy."

"I came to London that day to confront Spalding with the facts of his deceit," Marcus explained. "I arrived late in the evening and went straight to his house on Fulston Street. I discovered Hannah with the pistol still in her hand."

"I was in a state of near-collapse." Hannah looked at Sands. "Panic-stricken would be a better word. I was relieved that Spalding was dead but terrified of what would happen next. Masters took care of everything."

"I see." Sands gave Marcus a speculative look. "You kept quiet not only about Hannah's involvement in Spalding's death, but also about the financial state of the investment pool, did you not?"

"I had little choice," Marcus admitted. "There was too much at stake."

Hannah pushed a strand of hair back behind her ears. "If word of the instability of the pool had gotten out, there would have been panic. The investors would have sold their shares at a terrible loss. So many people would have been ruined." She smiled wistfully. "Marcus took charge of the investment pool and salvaged everything."

"And got very rich in the process," Sands observed neutrally.

Marcus shrugged but offered no further explanation.

"Oh, Edward, I am so dreadfully sorry that you had to learn the truth this way," Hannah whispered. "Marcus insisted I should tell all. He claimed it was the only way to remove the venom from the blackmailer's fangs, but I was afraid to confide the truth to you. I loved you too much to risk turning you against me."

"I always suspected what sort of man Spalding was." Sands gripped her arms gently and pulled her against him. "I heard the rumors. But you know how such things are ignored by Polite Society."

"I know," Hannah mumbled.

"Listen to me, Hannah. I am glad that you shot him. Do you hear me? I only wish that I had had the privilege of doing so myself. If I had been acquainted with you then, I would have done so."

"Edward." Hannah held him more tightly.

"I told you, Hannah, there is nothing on the face of this earth that could turn me away from you except to learn that you loved another."

"*Never*," Hannah vowed. "You are the only man I have ever loved. The only one I will ever love."

Sands touched her hair. "Then from now on, will you also trust me?"

"Yes." Relief and joy were mingled in Hannah's voice. "I am so sorry that I did not tell you everything long ago."

Sands looked at Marcus. "It would appear that I am in your debt, sir. Not only for helping Hannah that night, but for shielding her from all the questions and suspicions that ensued."

Marcus shrugged. "It was nothing."

Iphiginia smiled proudly. "That is Masters for you, Lord Sands. A gentleman to his fingertips."

"It was Hannah who made me into a gentleman." Marcus thrust his legs out in front of him and leaned back against the seat of his coach. He stared out the window into the night and thought about the past. "She taught me everything I needed to know so that I could move confidently in Society."

"One cannot make a silk purse out of a sow's ear," Iphiginia said. "Lady Sands may have given you a polite polish, but the truth is, you must have been born with the proper instincts for noble behavior."

Marcus glanced at her, amused. "I was born a farmer, Iphiginia."

She dismissed that with an airy wave of her

gloved hand. "What has that got to do with it? You would be a true nobleman if you fished for a living or sold vegetables out of the back of a cart."

He was touched by her naive faith in him. He tried to hide it behind a blandly derisive expression. "How very democratic of you. You sound like an American."

"As far as I am concerned, the title of gentleman belongs to those who earn it, not to those who happen to be born into the right families."

"That is not a commonly held view."

Her mouth curved in the shadows. "I rarely hold common views."

Marcus grinned briefly. "I am well aware of that. It is one of your more endearing qualities."

"Only a man who also holds uncommon views would appreciate such a quality in a female."

"No doubt." Marcus went back to his brooding contemplation of the night. It was a relief to be freed from the burden of Hannah's secret, he thought. Normally such things did not bother him, but he had not liked having to keep the truth from Iphiginia. She was the first woman with whom he had ever wanted to be completely open.

Having a confidante was a new experience for him. It was a simple pleasure but a profound one.

"Marcus?"

"Yes?"

"What are we going to do now? Mrs. Wycherley is dead. She could not have sent those notes tonight. Who is behind this new trouble?"

Marcus brought his thoughts back to the issue at hand. "I don't know yet, but I have a theory that whoever killed Mrs. Wycherley may have found her list of blackmail victims."

"And that person has decided to carry on where she left off?" Iphiginia asked.

"It's possible."

Iphiginia frowned in concentration. "It makes no sense. By forcing the four of us into a confrontation tonight, he risked ruining the scheme. Hannah revealed her secrets to her husband. She can no longer be blackmailed."

"Both you and Sands saw Hannah and me in a thoroughly compromising situation tonight, Iphiginia."

"Yes, but I knew immediately that you were not guilty of seducing Hannah. And Sands did not believe it for very long, either."

"No one," Marcus said very deliberately, "least of all the kind of person who is willing to pick up where a blackmailer left off, could have predicted that outcome."

Iphiginia stared at him in surprise. "Whatever do you mean? Oh." She wrinkled her nose. "You think that the villain assumed Lord Sands and I would believe the worst?"

"Yes."

"Well, he was quite mistaken, was he not?"

"It was an assumption that most people would make," Marcus said softly.

"Nonsense. Only those who do not comprehend connections based on mutual respect, intellectual affinity, and true love would be so idiotic."

"This may come as a surprise to you, my dear, but I would venture to guess that ninety-nine percent of the populace in general, and one hundred percent of the *ton* in particular, fails to consider that such connections between men and women are even remotely possible."

"Is that so?" Iphiginia's gaze was startlingly direct. "How would you have reacted if you had walked into that chamber tonight and discovered me attempting to conceal the fact that a man was hiding behind the stage door?"

"I would have been bloody furious."

"But would you have believed me if I had told you that I was innocent?"

Marcus thought about it. It came as something of a shock to realize that he would no doubt believe even the wildest explanation rather than face the possibility that Iphiginia had betrayed him. "Yes."

Iphiginia smiled with smug satisfaction. "I knew it. You do trust me, sir, do you not?"

"Yes, but I still would have been bloody furious. Pray, do not take a notion to put the matter to the test."

"I still do not understand what the villain hoped to achieve by throwing us all together tonight. Any way you look at it, he was putting his future income at risk."

Marcus was silent for a moment while he examined the conclusion he had reached earlier. "Perhaps we are now dealing with someone who gets a thrill out of malicious mischief. Whoever it is may not need the money he could make by blackmailing Mrs. Wycherley's victims."

"But he may enjoy exposing their secrets?"

"It's possible. Society breeds too many dangerously bored people, any number of which might find it titillating to use the information from Mrs. Wycherley's files to wreak havoc in the *ton*."

"Good heavens. What a terrible notion."

"Not a pleasant one, I'll grant you that." Marcus had no intention of explaining the rest of his hypothesis.

What really worried him was that he had sensed a personal element about the mischief that had been produced tonight. It was almost as though someone had wanted vengeance.

Iphiginia's eyes widened suddenly. "Aunt Zoe's secret may be at risk again. This villain may choose to expose her past in order to create a furor."

"It's possible," Marcus agreed.

"I must warn her."

"There is nothing we can do now to stop the revelations, if that is what the villain intends."

"Yes, I know, but poor Aunt Zoe. She will be devastated if her secret is revealed."

"We shall see if we can locate her tonight and tell her what has happened. But it's entirely possible the villain will take no further action for a while," Marcus said. "He may wait to see if he achieved the desired effect from tonight's little scene before he goes to the trouble of planning another such elaborate production."

"Tonight's work did take planning, did it not?"

"A considerable amount of it, I should think. Iphiginia, I'm beginning to have a few doubts about our earlier conclusion that Mrs. Wycherley was the blackmailer."

"But Marcus, that makes no sense. It must have been her."

"Perhaps. But in the morning I shall attempt to do something we have been unable to do until now."

"What is that?"

"Obtain some further facts which may establish her guilt."

"What sort of facts?"

Marcus contemplated a passing carriage. "I shall ask my man of affairs to look into a few matters."

"Such as?"

"Such as who owns the premises used by the proprietor of Dr. Hardstaff's Museum."

Iphiginia blinked. "Surely Dr. Hardstaff owns it or rents it, whichever the case may be."

"I believe it's safe to say that Hardstaff is very likely a *nom de guerre* of sorts," Marcus said dryly. "It is a most uncommon name."

Iphiginia frowned. "It is rather unusual."

"A bit too appropriate for his line of work."

Iphiginia looked momentarily disconcerted. "Hardstaff. Yes, I see what you mean."

"In any event, I think it's time to dig a bit deeper."

"What do you hope to find?" she asked.

"I do not know yet."

Iphiginia fell silent for a few minutes. Marcus assumed she was mulling over the night's events. He was contemplating the instructions he intended to give Barclay in the morning when she interrupted his thoughts.

"Marcus?"

"Yes?"

"Did you think that the Goddess of Manly Vigor on the right behind the transparency screen was a bit too thin?"

Marcus gave a crack of laughter. He reached out and pulled Iphiginia into his arms.

"Not in the least. I believe that she is precisely the tonic I require to maintain my manly vigor."

They located Zoe at the Crandals' ball. She and Lord Otis were just leaving the dance floor. They were both flushed from a lively waltz.

" 'Evening, Iphiginia. Masters." Otis's eyebrows bobbed. "Didn't know you were planning to attend this crush."

Iphiginia looked at Zoe. "We must speak to you immediately."

Zoe's smile of welcome dissolved into an anxious expression. "What is it? What's wrong?"

"Whoever killed Mrs. Wycherley appears to have acquired some of the information on her victims and is amusing himself by revealing their secrets," Iphiginia said quietly.

"Oh, my God." Zoe put her hand to her throat.

Otis gripped her arm in a supportive manner. "Calm yourself, m'dear. We can deal with this."

Marcus took charge. "Let's go out into the garden, where we can talk about this with some degree of privacy. There really is only one solution to this situation, you know."

"We must tell the truth to Maryanne." Otis's whiskers twitched. "I told Zoe as much weeks ago when it all started. Chickens always come home to roost, I said."

"But our precious Maryanne," Zoe whispered in a shaky voice. "What will she say? What will Sheffield say? What about the marriage plans?"

"We shall get through this, m'dear," Otis murmured as he guided her toward the doors. "From the very beginning we knew that someday we might have to face the thing."

An hour and a half later, shortly before two-thirty in the morning, Marcus walked into his laboratory, poured himself a glass of brandy, and settled into the chair behind his worktable.

He surveyed the chamber by the light of the single lamp that he had lit. He needed to think and he always did his best thinking in this room.

He propped his boots on the table, leaned back, and took a sip of the brandy. It was his habit to let his thoughts drift aimlessly for a few minutes before he began to concentrate. The technique helped him to focus his attention.

He reflected briefly on the conversation in the Crandals' garden an hour ago. He knew Iphiginia was anxious about her aunt's situation, but Otis had seemed quietly satisfied with events. Marcus thought he understood. After eighteen years of being forced to play the role of a doting friend, Otis would now be able to claim his daughter.

By the end of the discussion, Zoe had seemed resigned to the inevitable, perhaps even relieved that the secret was about to come out.

It remained to be seen how Maryanne would respond to the news that Otis was her real father. Her wedding plans were unquestionably in jeopardy, but who knew how it would all fall out? Marcus thought. Sheffield was an independent-minded young man with a will of his own. If he really loved Maryanne, he might not give a bloody damn about the gossip.

If he really *loved* Maryanne?

"Bloody hell." Marcus's mouth turned down in disgust. He was starting to think like one of those idiot romantic poets. Obviously he had been spending too much time in the company of his brother and Iphiginia. Their distorted, overly romanticized views of the relations between men and women were having an insidious effect on him. He would have to take care that he did not allow them to influence him unduly. He was a man of reason, not a poet.

He had learned his lessons the hard way, formulated his rules so as to protect himself from the pitfalls of naïveté and romantic inclinations.

A knock on the door of the laboratory interrupted Marcus before he could refocus his thoughts.

"Enter."

"Marcus?" Bennet walked into the room.

Marcus glanced at him. "What is it?"

"Nothing." Bennet hesitated. "Lovelace said you were in here. I was on my way upstairs to bed. Thought I'd say good night."

"I came in here to do some thinking." Marcus looked down at the glass in his hand. "Have a brandy with me?"

"Thanks." Bennet seemed relieved by the invitation. He crossed the room to the brandy table and poured himself a measure.

Marcus waited.

Bennet cradled the brandy glass and looked down into its depths. "I saw you with Mrs. Bright an hour ago."

"At the Crandals'?"

"Yes."

"I didn't see you."

"It was an awful crush," Bennet said. "The ballroom was packed."

"Yes, it was."

Bennet cleared his throat. "Have you made plans for your wedding yet?"

"Mrs. Bright has not yet consented to be my bride."

Bennet's head came up swiftly, his expression one of amazement. "What did you say?"

"She is not precisely leaping at the opportunity to become my wife." Marcus smiled ruefully. "She claims that although she is rather, ah, fond of me, she is not terribly keen on the notion of marrying me."

Bennet choked on his brandy. "She must be mad." In spite of his opinion on the subject, it was obvious that he was affronted by the news.

"I shall take that as a compliment," Marcus said. "But in truth she is far from mad. She is spirited, proud, independent, and very much an Original, but she is not mad."

"How could she not want to marry you? You're an earl, for God's sake. And wealthy into the bargain. Any woman in her position would kill to marry you."

"Mrs. Bright is quite comfortably well off, thanks to her own judicious investments. Nor does she seem overly impressed with my title."

Marcus smiled faintly. "She has a remarkably egalitarian notion of what constitutes a gentleman. I believe she has read a bit too much of Locke, Rousseau, and, very likely, Jefferson."

Bennet was incensed. "She has not questioned your right to the title, has she?"

"No."

"I should hope not." Bennet scowled. "Are you telling me that she might actually refuse your offer?"

"I am telling you that I shall have to put forth considerable effort in order to convince her that I would make her a suitable husband."

"Hellfire," Bennet breathed. "This is amazing. I do not know whether to be cheered by the news or insulted by her nerve."

Marcus turned the glass in his hand and watched the lamplight dance in the crystal. "It was Mrs. Bright who convinced me to withdraw my objections to your plans to become engaged to Juliana Dorchester."

Bennet glowered at him. "I don't believe that. Why would Mrs. Bright get involved in my affairs? Why should she give a damn whom I marry?"

"She cares about a great many odd things. And a number of people."

"Marcus, do you actually mean to say that you changed your mind about my marriage plans because of something your good friend Mrs. Bright had to say on the subject?"

Marcus smiled ruefully. "Does that surprise you?"

"It astounds me."

"I confess, you aren't the only one. I was somewhat taken aback myself."

"I cannot imagine you allowing anyone, least of all one of your paramours—" Bennet broke off abruptly when Marcus narrowed his eyes in warning. "I mean, one of your female acquaintances to influence you. Devil take it, I've never known you to alter your views on a subject once you've made up your mind."

"That's not entirely true. I've been known to change my mind when new facts are introduced which warrant a new conclusion."

"Bah. That almost never happens because you almost never make up your mind before you have investigated all aspects of a matter quite thoroughly."

"Suffice it to say that Mrs. Bright succeeded in causing me to alter my decision regarding your plans." Marcus took a swallow of his brandy.

"Damnation."

"It concerns you that I have allowed her to influence me?"

"Yes." Bennet's mouth tightened ominously.

"Yes, it does, even though in this instance I have been the beneficiary of her interference. This is not like you, Marcus."

"No, it's not." Marcus studied the clockwork man in the corner. "I have always made it a point to order my life along a few simple, straightforward principles."

"You certainly have done so since I was a boy," Bennet agreed sourly.

"Mrs. Bright has caused me to bend, and in some cases break, several of my own rules. Barring the possibility that I have, myself, gone mad, what do you suppose it all signifies?"

"No offense, brother, but it strikes me that you have allowed your passions to rule your head."

"I once accused you of the same thing."

"Yes, you did." Bennet looked bleak. "You really do intend to marry her, do you not?"

"Yes."

Bennet sighed. "Would you mind telling me why you feel you must marry this particular female, Marcus?"

Marcus gazed broodingly at the clockwork man. "When I am with her I do not feel as though I am made of gears and springs."

Barclay examined the notes he had just finished making. He pushed his spectacles more firmly onto his nose and considered Marcus

through them. "What, precisely, do you hope
to discover, sir?"

"I am looking for some sort of link between
the Hardstaff museum operation and the person who is constructing the sepulchral monument."

"I don't understand. What possible connection could there be?"

Marcus smiled thinly. "That is what I am
paying you to learn, Barclay."

"Yes, my lord." Barclay groaned as he
heaved himself out of the chair. "I shall get to
work on it at once."

NINETEEN

"We told Maryanne directly after breakfast. She was very quiet for the longest time." Zoe sniffed into a hankie. "I was terrified that she would hate us forever. She started to cry."

Iphiginia, seated behind her desk, exchanged a glance with Amelia. Amelia raised her brows but said nothing. Neither of them interrupted the tale.

"And then—" Otis blew into a large handkerchief—"she looked at me and said 'Papa.' After all these years, she finally said 'Papa.' She threw herself into my arms."

"I vow, it was the happiest moment of my life." Zoe burst into more tears.

"And of mine, my dearest." Otis went to her and put his arm around her. "You cannot imagine what it means to me to be able to openly acknowledge my own dear daughter."

"We should have told her immediately after Guthrie died last year," Zoe said to Iphiginia. "Only think of the trouble it would have saved."

Iphiginia folded her arms on her desk and frowned. "What about the marriage to Sheffield?"

"Maryanne insists upon telling him the truth," Otis said, not without a touch of pride. "May as well, since the blackmailer will no doubt do so, anyway."

"I expect he'll cry off." Zoe sighed. "There's no help for it. The Earls of Sheffield have always been very high in the instep. Pity. It was such a fine match. But Maryanne is so lovely and charming that I am convinced that we'll find another equally suitable husband for her."

"I shall make it public knowledge that I intend to settle an inheritance upon her," Otis said stoutly. "Always intended to do so, of course, but planned to keep it a private matter. Now we can be open about it. That should help produce a good selection of candidates."

"Very true." Iphiginia picked up her pen and fiddled with it as she considered the situation. "Do you know, it strikes me that there might be an even simpler way of brushing through this entire affair."

"What's that?" Zoe asked.

"If you and Otis were to marry," Iphiginia said, "Maryanne would become Otis's step-daughter in the eyes of the law."

"*Married?*" Zoe stared at her. "Married? But Otis and I are so happy the way we are. Isn't that so, Otis?"

"You have always been the delight of my life, my dear," Otis said gallantly. "You know that. You will continue to be my heart's truest friend regardless of whether or not we are wed."

Zoe smiled tremulously. "Otis, I do love you so."

"The thing is," Iphiginia said briskly, "If Otis were to marry you, there would be no need to make the true facts of Maryanne's parentage public."

"Iphiginia is right," Amelia said.

Zoe frowned. "I do not comprehend."

Otis's brows formed a bristly hedge across his nose. "I say, she has a point, y'know."

Iphiginia saw the new light in his eyes. She smiled. "If you and Otis were to wed, he would become Maryanne's stepfather. She could call him Papa and no one would take any notice. He can refer to her as his daughter and people will merely assume that he has a genuine pater-nal affection for her."

"Which is no particular secret, anyway,"

Amelia pointed out. "Furthermore, the legalities of the situation settle rather nicely into place with regard to both the Guthrie money and the Otis fortune."

"Precisely," Iphiginia said. "Maryanne will no longer be a young lady with a respectable portion, but a great *heiress*."

"No one will think to question the situation," Otis murmured. "Perfectly natural that I would provide for her."

"Good Lord." Zoe was clearly struck by the possibilities. "She would have her pick of husbands."

Otis took her hand and kissed it. "And I would have the great pleasure at last of not only claiming my daughter without a scandal, but of being able to claim you, my sweet, as my wife."

"Oh, Otis." Zoe looked up at him. "You have always been so good to me. You were the only thing that made my life bearable while Guthrie was alive."

"It was my greatest pleasure," Otis said. "And if you wish to continue our liaison as it is, I shall be honored to do so. But I want you to know that nothing would make me happier than to be able to call you my wife."

Zoe's eyes glowed. "How can I say no? I thought never to marry again after being freed

of Guthrie. But in truth, you are the only man I
have ever loved. The father of my child. My
dearest friend."

"I shall obtain a special license this afternoon," Otis said. "We can be married tonight."

"Something tells me that Maryanne will be
delighted," Amelia said.

Iphiginia tapped her pen against a sheet of
foolscap. "And a bit more venom has been
leeched from the blackmailer's fangs. I begin to
perceive that Masters was right all along. He
said the easiest way out of this situation was to
call the villain's bluff by unveiling the secrets."

"It would, indeed, appear that he was correct," Amelia agreed.

"He very often is," Iphiginia muttered.
"What is worse, he knows it and does not hesitate to make one aware of that fact. I vow, it is
vastly annoying at times."

"I suspect you feel that way because you are
so accustomed to being correct most of the
time yourself," Amelia said.

Iphiginia wistfully recalled her plan to solve
the blackmail problem by discovering the
owner of a phoenix seal and some black sealing
wax. "I have never met a man who is right
more often than I am. It is rather unnerving,"
she admitted.

It was even more unsettling to know that she
was in love with a man who was convinced that

he was intelligent enough to learn anything except how to fall in love again.

"What is Masters's latest hypothesis, Iphiginia? Who does he believe is behind this nasty attempt to reveal everyone's secrets?" Amelia asked as she and Iphiginia walked up a flight of stairs that led to Adam Manwaring's office.

"He does not know the new villain's identity yet," Iphiginia said. "His most interesting theory is that Mrs. Wycherley may not have been the villain in this piece, after all."

Amelia shot her a startled glance. "Really? But who else could it have been?"

"As I said, Masters does not yet have a new suspect, merely a few doubts about the old one." Iphiginia reached the landing and started down the hall to Adam's door.

"What do you believe, Iphiginia?"

"I no longer know what to make of the events. I am still stuck on black wax, phoenix seals, and the fact that whoever sent that first note to Aunt Zoe knew that Masters would be out of Town for an extended period of time."

"I know how difficult it is for you to abandon your own notions. Well, I'm certain that Masters will soon get to the bottom of this."

Iphiginia wrinkled her nose. "Goodness, such faith in his intellect and talents. There was a time not so long ago when you spent a great deal of energy warning me off him."

"I still think that he will break your heart, but in the meantime, perhaps he will also solve the puzzle."

"You are always so very practical, Amelia. It is one of your most endearing qualities."

They came to a halt in front of the narrow door. Iphiginia raised her hand to knock and then noticed that the door was ajar. A man's voice, raised in blistering rage, boomed through the opening.

"I demand to meet with the principals of this venture, d'ye hear me, Manwaring?"

Iphiginia opened the door quietly.

A large, thickset man was leaning over Adam's desk. His face was contorted with anger. Adam sat quietly, his own expression one of cold disgust. Neither of them saw Iphiginia and Amelia in the doorway.

"I have told you, that is impossible," Adam said.

"I insist upon it," the stranger roared. He slammed his meaty fist down on the desk with such force that the wax jack and pens shuddered. "I insist upon being allowed to speak with them. I won't take no for an answer."

Iphiginia heard Amelia's soft, choked cry of dismay.

"Amelia?" Iphiginia touched her cousin's arm. "Are you all right?" she whispered.

Amelia did not answer. She stood stock-still, her attention riveted on the man who was pounding on Adam's desk.

"I've told you that the principals behind this speculation venture are not interested in including you in the pool, Dodgson." Adam got to his feet, his jaw set as solidly as that of a bulldog. "And I told you the reason why."

"Lies. All lies told by a slut of a governess," Dodgson howled. "I cannot believe men of the world would listen to the creature."

Amelia took a step into the room. Her shoulders were rigid. "They are not lies. You are a nasty, vicious man, Dodgson. You know it and I know it."

Dodgson whirled around. "Who the devil are you?" he demanded.

"Don't you even remember me, Dodgson? I'm Amelia Farley. At one time I worked as a governess. But now I make my living in a much different fashion."

Dodgson's eyes glazed with the shock of recognition. He stared at Amelia, mouth agape. "It's you. You're the one who told the principals that I could not be trusted. How dare you? Why would anyone listen to you?"

"Miss Farley is one of the principals of the

investment pool," Adam said with grim satisfaction.

"I don't understand." Dodgson's heavily
jowled face swung back and forth between
Amelia and Adam. "This is impossible."

"No, Dodgson," Adam said evenly. "It is far
from impossible. You will not be allowed to
join the investment pool."

"On the word of this . . . this pinch-faced
little lightskirt?" Dodgson bellowed. "You cannot be serious."

Adam rounded the edge of his desk, drew
back his fist, and slammed it straight into
Dodgson's unsuspecting face.

Dodgson shrieked with pain, surprise, and
fury. He reeled back against the wall, clutching
at his nose.

Adam advanced on him with clenched fists.
"One does not speak to a lady with such disrespect in my office."

"Damn you." Dodgson examined the blood
on his hands with horror and disbelief. "Damn
all of you. This is a nightmare. I am to be
ruined because of the whim of a silly little governess who should have been grateful that
some man was willing to tumble her."

"I have news for you, Dodgson," Adam said
softly. "Financial ruin is not all you face. You
will meet me at dawn tomorrow morning in the
park. Name your seconds."

Amelia gasped. She gripped the handle of her parasol with such force that her knuckles went white. Iphiginia stepped closer to her.

"Seconds?" Dodgson appeared dazed. "You're issuing a challenge because of that ridiculous creature? This is insane."

"I shall expect to see you at dawn," Adam said. "Or all of London will know you for the coward you clearly are."

"If you have not already chosen your own seconds, Manwaring," Marcus said calmly from the doorway, "I would be honored to act as one of them."

"Marcus." Iphiginia turned quickly. A rush of relief went through her at the sight of him.

Marcus filled the doorway. His broad shoulders nearly brushed the sides. He was so tall that he'd been obliged to remove his gray, curly-brimmed hat.

He studied the scene in the office with his usual unruffled air, but there was an ominous gleam in his amber eyes.

Adam inclined his head brusquely in Marcus's direction. "Thank you, sir. I shall take you up on your offer to act as a second."

"Masters?" Dodgson stared first at Marcus and then at Adam. "Have you both gone mad?"

"No," Marcus said. "But we are in danger of becoming quite bored. I suggest that you take your leave."

"An excellent notion," Amelia said. "My friends and I have some matters of business to discuss."

Dodgson turned to her with a desperate look. "Amelia, for God's sake, you cannot do this to me. There is too much at stake. Please, my dear, you must allow bygones to be bygones."

"Get out of here," Adam said.

Amelia looked at Dodgson. "You heard Mr. Manwaring. Remove yourself from these premises immediately. The very sight of you makes me ill."

"Amelia." Dodgson went toward her as though to take her hands in his. "I cannot believe you would be so hard-hearted. You were once such a sweet creature."

"Do not touch me." Amelia stepped back quickly. "Do not ever touch me, Dodgson."

"You heard Miss Farley." Adam came up behind Dodgson, grabbed him by the collar, and propelled him toward the door.

Marcus politely got out of the way.

Adam shoved Dodgson out into the hall and slammed the door.

He turned and looked straight at Amelia. "I regret that you were obliged to come face-to-face with the bastard, Miss Farley. I assure you, it will be the last time."

Amelia stared at him. "Mr. Manwaring, you must not meet him tomorrow at dawn. I forbid it."

Adam gave her a crooked smile. "Think nothing of it. As it happens, I am a rather good shot. Hobby of mine, you know."

"But you might be injured. Even killed. Dodgson is a liar and no doubt a cheat. There is no telling what he might do in a duel. You cannot trust him."

Marcus stirred. "Do not concern yourself, Miss Farley. As Manwaring's second, it will be my privilege to keep an eye on Dodgson. There will be no cheating."

"No," Amelia blurted. "You must not do this, Mr. Manwaring." She dropped her parasol and ran toward him. "You cannot risk your life."

She hurled herself into Adam's arms.

"It's all right, my dear," Adam said. He held her close. "I do not mind in the least."

"If it's any comfort to you, Miss Farley," Marcus said, "I believe that I can say with some certainty that Dodgson is highly unlikely to appear for his dawn appointment. I expect he will be halfway to Scotland by then."

Amelia raised her head from Adam's shoulder. "Do you really think so?"

"Yes." Marcus smiled. "I really think so."

"I'd rather he showed himself," Adam said. "I quite relish the notion of lodging a bullet in him."

"That is very gallant of you, sir." Amelia blotted tears from her eyes. "But I fear I would be devastated if anything were to happen to you."

"Do you truly mean that?" Adam asked.

"Yes." Amelia gave him a tremulous smile.

The two gazed deeply into each other's eyes, oblivious of Iphiginia and Marcus.

Iphiginia smiled to herself. She glanced at Marcus. *I told you so,* she mouthed silently. *Made for each other.*

He raised one brow in silent acknowledgment.

It suddenly occurred to Iphiginia that he had no business being there.

"What are you doing here, sir?" she asked in a low tone.

"What do you think? I came to request that I be allowed to purchase shares in the investment pool that is being formed to finance Bright Place."

She gazed at him in amazement. "You know about the pool?"

He gave her a smile of superiority. "Of course."

"You know that Amelia and I are the principals?"

"Naturally."

"You think you know everything, don't you?"

Marcus's eyes were brilliant with amusement. "I believe in keeping myself informed on a wide variety of topics."

"He thinks he is so very clever," Iphiginia grumbled an hour later as she and Amelia got out of the white and gilt carriage. "Quite arrogant about it, in fact."

"Who?" Amelia cast her a distracted glance as they went up the steps of the town house. "Masters?"

"Yes."

"Well, he is quite clever. What do you expect him to do? Conceal his intelligence? You rarely bother to hide yours."

"He could practice being a bit more discreet about it."

Amelia nibbled uneasily on her lower lip. "Personally, I pray that he is correct in his belief that Dodgson will flee rather than confront Mr. Manwaring at dawn."

Guilt swept through Iphiginia. Here she was complaining about a minor annoyance while poor Amelia was burdened with a very genuine fear. It struck her that if she were in her cousin's shoes, she would have been hysterical.

"I'm sure Masters has the right of it," Iphiginia said soothingly as Mrs. Shaw opened the front door. "As I was just telling you, he is *always* right."

"Yes, I know." Amelia seemed to take heart from that. Her face brightened a bit.

Iphiginia smiled at her housekeeper. "Good afternoon, Mrs. Shaw. All is well?"

"Aye, Mrs. Bright. Oh, that very nice Mr. Hoyt called while you were out. He returned a book he said you had lent to him."

"Grayson's *Illustrations of Classical Antiquities,* yes, of course." Iphiginia untied her bonnet and handed it to Mrs. Shaw. "Anything else of import?"

"No, madam. Everything has been very quiet."

"Excellent. Would you please send a tray of tea into the library?"

"Immediately, Mrs. Bright."

"Thank you." Iphiginia paused at the door of the library. "By the bye, you may expect both Mr. Manwaring and his lordship, the Earl of Masters, shortly before five o'clock. They will be calling to take Amelia and myself driving in the park."

"Very good, Mrs. Bright." Mrs. Shaw smiled and went down the hall toward the kitchen.

Iphiginia followed Amelia into the library. She glanced at the copy of *Illustrations of Classical Antiquities* on her desk as she sat down. Then she turned her attention to Amelia.

"Try not to worry too much, Amelia. I trust Masters to know about these things. If he feels there will be no duel, then there very likely will not be one."

Amelia clasped her hands in front of her and stared out the window into the street. "I cannot believe that Mr. Manwaring actually challenged Dodgson because of me."

"I can. I have known for some time that Mr. Manwaring was quite enamored of you, Amelia."

Amelia slanted her a wryly amused glance. "As I noted a moment ago, you can be just as arrogant in your conclusions as you say Masters is."

Iphiginia chuckled. "Masters and I do have a great deal in common, do we not?"

"Yes." Amelia's smile faded. "What are you going to do about him, Iphiginia? You know very well that you cannot go on forever as his mistress."

"I know."

The clatter of carriage wheels interrupted Amelia's reply. The vehicle came to a halt in front of the town house.

"I wonder who that could be," Iphiginia said.

"It is only three o'clock. Masters said he and Mr. Manwaring would not come by until five."

Amelia peered out the window. "I do not recognize the carriage. I cannot see who is getting out."

Iphiginia and Amelia waited expectantly as Mrs. Shaw responded to the knock on the front door. There was a murmur of voices in the hall.

A moment later the library door opened.

"Mr. Bennet Cloud is inquiring to see if you are at home, Mrs. Bright," Mrs. Shaw said.

"Good heavens," Iphiginia muttered. "Marcus's brother. I wonder what he wants. You'd better send him in, Mrs. Shaw."

Bennet, his expression grim and intent, appeared in the doorway. "Good afternoon, Mrs. Bright. Thank you for seeing me."

"Come in, Mr. Cloud." Amelia gave him a reassuring smile. "This is my cousin, Miss Farley."

"A pleasure, Miss Farley." Bennet nodded stiffly at Amelia.

Amelia stirred. "Perhaps you would prefer to speak in private."

"If—if you don't mind," Bennet stammered. "I do not wish to be rude, but my business is of a personal nature."

"Of course." Amelia walked out of the library and closed the door quietly behind her.

Iphiginia folded her hands on top of her desk. "Won't you have a seat, Mr. Cloud?"

"What? Uh, no. No, thank you." Bennet began to pace restlessly in front of her. "This is very awkward for me, Mrs. Bright."

Iphiginia sighed. "Allow me to make it easier for you. You no doubt wish to give me a long lecture consisting of all the many and varied reasons why I should not marry your brother. Rest assured, Mr. Cloud, that I am already aware of all those reasons."

"No."

Iphiginia blinked in surprise. "I beg your pardon?"

Bennet stopped his pacing and swung around to face her. "I am here to tell you that I wish to withdraw all of my objections to the marriage."

"You do?"

Bennet grimaced. "Not that my brother would give a damn whether I objected or not. He always does as he pleases."

Iphiginia stared at him with sudden concern. "Are you feeling well, Mr. Cloud? My housekeeper will be bringing tea any moment now. Perhaps a cup will revive you."

"Damnation, I do not need any tea. You must marry my brother, Mrs. Bright."

Iphiginia eyed him warily. "Why?"

"Because I believe that he needs you."

"He needs me?"

"Devil take it, how can I explain?" Bennet resumed his fevered pacing. "Mrs. Bright, I have known my brother all of my life."

"Obviously."

"But I have never fully understood him. Perhaps I never tried to understand him. He didn't seem to require understanding, if you see what I mean."

"No, I do not."

"He was always there." Bennet moved his hand in a vague, all-encompassing motion. "Rather like a mountain or the sea or some other force of nature. Oh, he can be bloody stubborn and quite set in his ways. And he insists on living by his own damnable rules. But he has always seemed so strong."

"Being strong does not mean that one doesn't need a bit of understanding from others now and then," Iphiginia said gently.

"I have recently begun to comprehend that." Bennet reached a wall of bookcases, turned, and started back across the room. "Last night I realized that Marcus has depths that I have not, until now, even suspected existed within him. I recognize that he has certain needs. Needs which he believes only you can fulfill, Mrs. Bright."

"Masters told you this?"

"In a manner of speaking. I gained the impression that he wants you very badly."

"In the same way that you want Juliana Dorchester?"

"Good Lord, no, of course not." Bennet scowled. "The feelings that I bear for Miss Dorchester are really quite extraordinary. I am in love with her, Mrs. Bright. And she is in love with me."

"I see."

Bennet was momentarily overcome by his favorite subject. "Our mutual affection is characterized by sublime emotions and a truly metaphysical communion of the senses."

"How nice for you."

"There is a noble grandeur to our love that leaves me floundering for words."

"I had not noticed."

"She engenders within my breast the most elevated of passions."

"Quite understandable."

"Frankly," Bennet concluded, "it is difficult to speak of Miss Dorchester's exquisite sensibilities, her refined mind, or even her gracious manner without resorting to poetry."

"Your feelings are, indeed, extraordinary. You do not believe your brother capable of such emotions?"

"If he was ever capable of the more delicate and exalted emotions, his experience of marriage destroyed all such inclinations within him." Bennet shrugged. "To be perfectly truthful, I am not certain he was ever the sort to surrender to the higher sentiments. His is an intellectual nature, you understand."

"Yes." Iphiginia propped her chin on her hand. "Forgive me, sir, but your change of heart on the subject of your brother's marriage has left me somewhat confused."

"It is important that you marry him, Mrs. Bright. Please believe me. I would not be here today if I did not think that it was a necessity. I think it should be a quiet wedding. Special license, preferably. You will not want a formal engagement of the sort that Miss Dorchester and I intend to have."

"You've asked Miss Dorchester for her hand?"

"I've spoken to her about it. I'm pleased to say that we have agreed to announce our betrothal at the end of the Season. We shall be married in the spring. Miss Dorchester and I wish to spend the next few months becoming better acquainted with each other. And there are so many plans to be made, you know."

"Yes, of course." Marcus would be relieved, Iphiginia thought. He had at least bought some time for Bennet to make certain that he was doing the right thing.

"She was willing to elope with me," Bennet confided proudly. "During that brief span of time when she thought I would have nothing, she said that she would go to Gretna Green with me. She loves me as much as I love her."

"I believe she does. I have met her, you know."

"Have you?"

"Yes. And I found her quite charming." Miss Dorchester really was a nice young lady, Iphiginia thought, even if her parents were a trifle overambitious.

Bennet glowed with enthusiasm. "She is most charming, indeed. Very likely the most charming woman on the face of the earth."

Marcus would require some convincing of that fact, but Iphiginia had a hunch that all would be well between Bennet and his beloved Miss Dorchester.

"Our situation is quite different from your own, however," Bennet continued. "You and my brother needn't bother with a long engagement. No offense, Mrs. Bright, but it's not as though you were a young chit fresh out of the schoolroom. And God knows my brother is not getting any younger."

"True."

Bennet frowned. "Cannot ever remember my brother being young. Even when I was a lad, he seemed something of an antiquity. But that's neither here nor there. The important thing is your marriage."

"I appreciate your concern, Mr. Cloud. However—" Iphiginia broke off frowning at the sound of another carriage halting in the street. "More visitors?"

The knock on the front door was followed by the sound of familiar voices in the front hall.

"Good grief," Iphiginia whispered. "Corina and Richard. And Aunt Zoe and Lord Otis. What is going on here? Pray excuse me, Mr. Cloud."

She leaped to her feet, dashed across the room, and flung open the library door before Mrs. Shaw could announce the new arrivals.

"Iphiginia," Zoe exclaimed. "You will never guess who has just arrived in Town."

Corina, dressed in a charming blue gown that nicely complemented her golden hair and blue eyes, turned toward Iphiginia with an expression of grave concern on her lovely face.

"*Iphiginia*. Are you all right? What is going on?"

"Good afternoon, Corina. Richard."

Richard Hampton, his handsome features set in lines of worry, inclined his head. "Good afternoon, Iphiginia. We set out for London the moment we received the message."

"What message?"

Corina shuddered. "The strange one that said you had become the . . . Well, never mind. It is too dreadful to repeat. I knew it could not be true, of course. But I had to find out what was going on. We arrived an hour ago."

"And came straight to my house." Zoe gave Iphiginia a wry, apologetic look. "Otis and I told them that they must ask their questions of you, not us."

Richard's warm, brown eyes were deeply troubled. "I shall be blunt, Iphiginia. We received an extremely alarming message informing us that you had become the paramour of the Earl of Masters."

Zoe rolled her eyes.

"Richard, really, must you say such things aloud?" Corina flushed. "We are in mixed company, you know."

"I apologize, my dear, but we must get to the bottom of this," Richard said with considerable determination. "This is no time to be mealy-mouthed or delicate."

Bennet came up to stand behind Iphiginia. "What you have heard is a damned lie."

"Who are you?" Richard demanded.

"Bennet Cloud, Masters's brother. And I am pleased to inform you that Mrs. Bright is not my brother's mistress. Far from it. She is his fiancée."

Chaos erupted in the crowded hall. Everyone tried to talk at once.

"*Fiancée,*" Corina gasped. "Iphiginia, do you mean to tell me that you are engaged?"

Richard looked startled. "To an earl?"

"I say," Otis murmured. "Hadn't heard about this development. Congratulations, m'dear."

Zoe rounded on Iphiginia. "Good Lord. So Masters has decided to do the proper thing by you, has he?"

"Yes, he has," Bennet said staunchly. "The problem is that Iphiginia does not wish to marry him."

Amelia appeared. "That is perfectly ridiculous. She will most certainly have to marry him."

"Of course she will," Corina decreed. "If my sister's name has been linked to Masters's in a fashion which has cast even the smallest shadow over her reputation, she has no choice but to marry him."

Richard nodded soberly. "Quite right. If he fails to come up to scratch, I shall call him out."

"Call Masters out?" Otis looked at him with alarm.

"*Silence.*" Iphiginia raised her hand to get everyone's attention. "I said, silence." When that failed, she made a fist and pounded loudly on the wall. "If you please."

Silence finally descended. Everyone looked at her.

"Now, then," Iphiginia said quite forcefully, "let us be clear about this matter. My connection with the Earl of Masters is no one's business but my own. And his."

Zoe sighed. "You may as well be realistic about this, Iphiginia. If he has made you an offer, you will have to accept it."

"And be grateful for it," Corina added bluntly. "Especially if your reputation has, indeed, been sullied."

"Quite right," Richard said.

"*Enough.*" Iphiginia put her hands on her hips and glowered at the lot. "I will say this once and for all. I have absolutely no intention of marrying a man who, as Mr. Cloud here has just pointed out, is incapable of the higher sentiments."

"What higher sentiments?" Amelia asked.

"What on earth are you talking about?" Zoe demanded.

"Man's got a fortune and a title," Otis pointed out logically. "Should think that would compensate for any number of elevated feelings."

"My brother will make you an excellent husband, Mrs. Bright," Bennet said loyally. "Shouldn't think the more refined emotions would be very important in your marriage. After all, you and Masters are both of an intellectual nature."

"Bloody hell, what does that matter?" Iphiginia could have wept, she was so angry and overset. "Listen to me, all of you. I will not marry a man who has a rule against falling in love."

A short, stark silence fell.

And then a large, familiar figure moved in the doorway.

"You have taught me to break most of my other rules, Iphiginia," Marcus said quietly. "Teach me to break this one, too."

Everyone turned, dumbfounded, toward Marcus. They had all been so busy arguing that none of them had heard him come up the steps and open the front door.

Iphiginia met his eyes. A rush of longing went through her. She loved him so much, she thought. She had always known that they had been meant for each other.

She had to believe that he could learn to love her.

"Oh, Marcus."

She flew toward the doorway and sailed into his arms.

Marcus caught her close and held her very tightly.

TWENTY

The news that Dodgson had slithered out of town shortly after dark went unremarked by virtually everyone except Amelia. She wept with relief.

The truly riveting news, as far as the Polite World was concerned, was the engagement of the Earl of Masters to his notorious mistress, Mrs. Bright.

Word of the betrothal and the plans for a speedy marriage by special license flew through the *ton*. The curious and the amazed as well as a number of genuine well-wishers lay in wait at every point along the park paths that afternoon.

Perched boldly atop the high seat of Marcus's sleek black phaeton, Iphiginia met stare after stare with a cool smile and a regal inclination of her head. She and Marcus dealt with the comments and veiled questions with bland civility.

That evening the inquisition began anew at every ball and soiree.

Herbert came up to Iphiginia at the Binghams' ball.

"Cannot blame them, y'know," he said, slanting a glance at two turbaned matrons who had just finished quizzing Iphiginia. "Word of your engagement took Society by surprise. I confess, I was rather startled, m'self."

"So was I." Iphiginia smiled at Herbert, relieved to see a friendly face. Zoe and Otis had disappeared a few minutes ago and Marcus, who had been helping her deal with the curious, had gone off to fetch some champagne.

Herbert gave her a kind, supportive smile, but his normally cheerful gaze was troubled. "No offense, m'dear, but are you certain you know what you're doing? I realize that Masters is rich and there is the title. But marriage is a very serious proposition."

"I assure you, I am aware of that."

"Speaking as your friend, one who knows you infinitely better than Masters does, I beseech you to give the matter more consideration before you take any irrevocable steps. There are rumors that you intend to wed by special license. Surely you can wait before you rush into this?"

Iphiginia looked at him in surprise. "What makes you think you know me better than Masters does?"

Herbert gazed out over the crowded room. "I have felt that way from the beginning, Iphiginia. You and I have much in common. More than you realize. In a way, I believe that we are two of a kind."

"I know that you wish to be a good friend to me and I very much appreciate it." Iphiginia touched his sleeve. "But you must not concern yourself on my behalf. I know what I'm doing."

"Do you?" Herbert looked at her. "I hope you are right, m'dear. I shall miss you."

"Miss me?"

"I fear that once you are wed to Masters, I shall see a great deal less of you."

"Mr. Hoyt, you are acting as though I am about to be locked away in a convent."

"A harem, I believe, would be a better description," Marcus said from just behind Iphiginia's left shoulder.

She turned quickly to smile at him. "There you are, my lord. I did not see you return from the buffet table."

"I know." Marcus thrust a glass of cham-

pagne into her fingers, but his gaze rested on
Herbert. "You were deep in conversation with
your good friend Mr. Hoyt."

Herbert inclined his head in a stiff nod.
" 'Evening, Masters. I was merely giving Mrs.
Bright my best wishes on her forthcoming mar-
riage."

"Thank you, Herbert," Iphiginia said gently.

"My pleasure." Herbert took her gloved
hand in his and kissed the back of it. "Whatever happens, Mrs. Bright, I want you to know
that I shall treasure the friendship we have
shared."

Marcus took Iphiginia's arm. "I think it's
time we moved along to the Wilkersons'. It's
nearly midnight and we are expected to put in
an appearance."

"Yes, of course." Iphiginia gave Herbert a
farewell smile and allowed herself to be led
away through the crowd.

"I grow increasingly weary of stumbling over
Hoyt in order to get to you," Marcus said.

"I regret that he annoys you, but he is my
friend, Marcus. I am quite fond of him."
Iphiginia gave Marcus a repressive glance as he
led her down the steps to the waiting carriage.
"I expect you to be polite to my friends after
we are married."

"Of course, my dear," Marcus said with un-
characteristic and rather suspect meekness.

Iphiginia scowled at him. "What was that nonsense about locking me away in a harem?"

"A harem of one, my sweet. I assure you that you will be the only occupant."

"That sounds interesting," Iphiginia said.

"It certainly struck me that way."

Iphiginia was exhausted by the time Marcus finally escorted her home at three in the morning.

The town house was quiet, Amelia and the staff having long since retired to bed. Marcus and Iphiginia went quietly across the hall and walked into the shadowed library.

Marcus closed the door, loosened his cravat, and lit the candle on Iphiginia's desk.

"Good heavens, what an exhausting evening." Iphiginia stripped off her white kid gloves and flopped into the chair behind her desk. Her white sarcenet and satin skirts fluttered around her. "One would have thought you had announced your intention to marry a female who possessed two heads. I have never seen so many curious eyes or heard so many gasps of amazement."

"The worst is over."

"I certainly hope so." Iphiginia frowned at her white skirts. "The first thing I am going to do after our marriage is purchase some new gowns. I am dreadfully bored with white."

"It served its purpose." Marcus helped himself to a small glass of brandy.

"I suppose it did."

"It was an extremely daring and rather shrewd notion."

"Thank you, my lord. I was rather pleased with the notion myself." Iphiginia tried to summon up a casual smile.

In truth she felt anything but calm tonight. The enormity of the step she was about to take was having a deeply unsettling effect on her nerves.

Teach me to break this rule, too.

Had Marcus really meant that he was willing to learn how to love again? Iphiginia wondered. Or had he offered her the challenge, knowing that she would be unable to resist?

He could be so bloody clever, she thought.

"Speaking of our marriage," Marcus said.

"Yes?" Iphiginia watched as he began to prowl the room, brandy glass in one hand.

Marcus paused in front of a statue of Aphrodite. "I intend to procure a special license in the morning. We can be married tomorrow afternoon."

Iphiginia caught her breath. "So soon?"

He looked at her over his shoulder, his intelligent gaze shuttered and brooding. "There is no need to delay the event, is there?"

It dawned on Iphiginia that, in his own way,

Marcus was as ill at ease as she was tonight. How odd that, having been through so much together, they should suddenly find themselves nervous around each other.

"No," she said.

Marcus nodded once, satisfied. "I shall make the arrangements."

"Very well."

Marcus took a swallow of brandy and moved on to study the statue of the Roman centurion. "I thought we managed quite nicely this evening."

"People are amazed that you are going to marry your mistress, you know."

"You are not my mistress." Marcus set his glass down on a nearby table. "You are my fiancée. The gossip will vanish once we are wed."

Iphiginia glanced at the copy of *Illustrations of Classical Antiquities* on her desk. "Are you certain?"

"Quite." Marcus smiled without any humor. "Marriage fixes everything, you see."

Iphiginia recalled the circumstances of Marcus's first marriage and winced. "Yes."

"It silences scandal before it can flower. It renders titillating gossip of an affair into extremely dull tea conversation. In short, Iphiginia, once we are married, we shall become a very boring subject so far as Society is concerned."

Iphiginia gazed at him very steadily. "Is that the reason you wish to marry me, sir? I would sooner return to Deepford than be wed in order to silence the threat of scandal."

"No," Marcus said. "It is not why I wish to marry you. I wish to marry you because you are the only woman I know who can keep me from becoming a clockwork man."

"*Marcus.*" Iphiginia was shocked at the analogy. "You cannot mean that."

"But I do mean it." He hesitated, as though gathering himself to jump off a cliff into a roiling sea. "I need you to keep me from becoming a victim of my own rules, Iphiginia."

Iphiginia felt the talons of his deeply buried torment as though it were her own flesh they pierced. She knew without a trace of doubt what his admission had cost him.

Another rule broken, no doubt, she thought.

She got to her feet and went around the corner of her desk. She stepped into his arms and framed his hard face with her hands.

"Marcus, pay close attention. You are in no danger of becoming an automaton. You are a warm, passionate man with extremely refined sensibilities."

"Do you think so?" The dark intensity vanished from his voice. He grinned briefly. "Well, in that case, it would probably be best not to delay our marriage. I'm not at all certain my

refined sensibilities could withstand the strain
of waiting."

"No." Iphiginia stood on tiptoe to brush her
lips against his faintly curved mouth. "We
would not want to stifle your warm, passionate
nature any longer than necessary."

"Or yours." Marcus folded her into an un-
shakable hold and kissed her thoroughly.

He deepened the kiss until Iphiginia sighed
softly and went limp in his arms.

"I love you, Marcus," she murmured against
his throat.

She was not certain he had heard her, but
when he raised his head a moment later, his
eyes were the color of ancient amber. "I shall
come for you at three tomorrow. I trust you
will be ready."

Iphiginia smiled. "Should I wear white?"

"You may wear whatever you wish." Marcus
moved reluctantly away from her to scoop his
hat up off her desk. "Or nothing at all. Good
night, Iphiginia. I shall look forward to tomorrow night. Do you realize that it will be the first
time we will be able to make love in a bed?"

"How very convenient should you suffer another collapse after the event, my lord."

"Adam will be coming by again today at five
o'clock to take me for a drive in the park,"
Amelia announced at breakfast the following

morning. "What do you think I should wear, Iphiginia?"

Iphiginia frowned over the gossip column in the morning paper. The article she had been reading featured a very recognizable "Mrs. B" and an equally obvious "Lord M." The news of the impending nuptials had been related in arch prose.

The Polite World is agog this morning to learn that Lord M. has reportedly broken his most infamous rule . . .

"What did you say, Amelia?"

"I said, will you help me select something to wear for a drive in the park this afternoon?"

Iphiginia looked up and saw the hopeful anticipation in her cousin's eyes. She smiled.

"You and I are very near the same size," Iphiginia said. "You shall wear my saffron yellow walking gown and the pale yellow pelisse that goes with it. The color will be perfect on you."

Amelia's eyes widened. "But you have not yet had an opportunity to wear that gown and pelisse yourself."

"It is yours with my blessings." Iphiginia refolded the newspaper and set it aside.

"Very kind."

"Think nothing of it. We must both go shopping as soon as possible. You need some brighter gowns and I am weary of white."

"It is very becoming on you."

"Thank you, but white attire grows exceedingly dull after a while. I do not know why the ancients favored it." Iphiginia paused. "You look very happy, Amelia."

"I am happy." Amelia smiled slowly, as though surprised by the fact. "Do you know, I have not felt this . . . this *unburdened* in years. To think that I was always terrified of coming face-to-face with Dodgson again. Yet when it actually happened, I experienced nothing but acute loathing and disgust."

"And rightfully so. It was extremely satisfying to see his expression yesterday when he learned that you had the power to deny him entry into the investment pool."

"Do you think that it is wrong of me to take such satisfaction from my revenge?"

"Don't be ridiculous. You exacted retribution and justice. You are entitled to a sense of satisfaction."

"Adam says that Dodgson will probably not be able to recover from his recent financial reverses," Amelia confided. "Apparently he is too far under the hatches to crawl back out on his own."

"I shall certainly not waste any sympathy on him. And I cannot tell you how delighted I am to know that you care for Mr. Manwaring. He has been attracted to you since the moment you met, you know."

"I think I did know. I always felt a certain warmth toward him. But for some reason I could not allow myself to admit it. Then, yesterday, after I confronted Dodgson and watched him go down in defeat, I suddenly felt free to turn to Adam." Amelia smiled. "Oh, Iphiginia, I do feel glorious today."

"Excellent. Then you can help me deal with what I believe may be an extremely nasty case of wedding nerves."

"Nerves? You? Iphiginia, are you telling me you are anxious about this marriage to Masters?"

"Yes, I believe I am. Remind me to take a vinaigrette with me to the preacher's this afternoon. I would hate to humiliate myself by fainting at Masters's feet."

"I am astounded. I do not know what to say. You always seem so certain of yourself. I have never known you to suffer from nerves."

"I have never been married," Iphiginia reminded her. She smiled wryly. "But Marcus has. If I am anxious, only think what he must be going through."

.   .   .

Half an hour later, feeling restless and more anxious than ever, Iphiginia wandered into her library with the intention of distracting herself.

She sat down behind her desk, opened a drawer, and removed several sheets of foolscap. She closed the drawer and reached for her pen.

Inspiration did not strike.

She took up a penknife and fiddled with the nib of her quill for a while. Then she put down the pen and contemplated several pieces of the statuary she had brought back with her from Italy.

It was no use. All she could think about was how her life was about to be irrevocably changed by a special license.

Teach me to break that rule, too, Iphiginia.

Marcus had as much as asked her to teach him how to love again. She had been so certain that she could do it.

But what if she was wrong?

Iphiginia got to her feet and started around her desk with no particular goal. She just felt the need to move.

The copy of *Illustrations of Classical Antiquities* caught her eye. Having nothing better to do, she picked it up to place it back in its proper place on a library shelf.

Idly she thumbed through it, seeking favorite scenes.

The tiny blob of black wax was stuck to page two hundred and three. It had obviously been dropped onto the volume by accident. It had dried there and gone undiscovered.

Iphiginia stared at the small bit of wax for a long time. *Someone who knows everything and everyone in Society.*

Then, at last, inspiration finally did strike.

"You're certain of these facts, Barclay?" Marcus sat forward behind his desk and forced himself to be patient. Sound scientific investigation had to be done carefully and thoroughly. He must not allow emotion and enthusiasm to rush him into a false conclusion.

He had allowed Iphiginia to persuade him to abandon a few of the rules which had governed his personal life until recently. That did not mean he had abandoned the sound, sensible rules of scientific experimentation.

Nevertheless, Marcus could feel the familiar thrill of discovery and satisfaction welling up inside. It all made perfect sense, he thought. It was logical. With this bit of information all the rest of the pieces began to fall into place.

He could not wait to tell Iphiginia.

"Yes, yes, quite certain." Barclay shuffled his papers and peered at his notes through his spectacles. "The original Dr. Hardstaff, whose real name was William Burn, sold his premises to the same individual who built the sepulchral monument in Reeding Cemetery. That man's name is H. H. Eaton."

"And he is the son of the Elizabeth Eaton who is buried in that monument?"

"Yes." Barclay looked up. "He appears to have dropped his last name when he entered Society two years ago. That was why it took me so long to discover his connection. Indeed, if you had not suggested that I look into the ownership of the museum, I would never have gotten to the bottom of the thing."

A knock on the library door got Marcus's attention. He glanced toward it with an impatient frown. "Enter."

Lovelace opened the door. Iphiginia, dressed in a white morning gown and a flower-trimmed chip straw bonnet, bobbed up and down behind him.

"Mrs. Bright to see you, sir," Lovelace said, just as though Iphiginia were not waving madly to get Marcus's attention.

Marcus grinned. "Send her in, Lovelace."

Lovelace stepped aside. Iphiginia rushed past him into the library. She was carrying a massive leather-bound volume.

"Marcus, you will never believe what has happened. I think I know the identity of the blackmailer. I found a bit of black wax on this book that I lent to—"

"Herbert Hoyt?" Marcus asked politely.

"Good Lord." Iphiginia came to a halt and gazed at him in astonishment. "How did you guess?"

"I never guess, my dear. I form scientific hypotheses."

It was quite dark in the narrow alley. There was barely enough moonlight to see the rear window of Number Two Thurley Street. Marcus hefted the length of iron in his hand and fitted it cautiously between the window and the sill.

"Be careful," Iphiginia whispered. She glanced back down the length of the alley to be certain they were still alone.

"I am being careful."

"Marcus, are you annoyed?"

"Oddly enough, I had not planned to spend my wedding night breaking into Hoyt's lodgings." Marcus pried the window open with a judicious jerk of the iron bar. The frame gave with gratifying ease. "I had envisioned more interesting entertainment."

"Hurry." Iphiginia pushed back the hood of her cloak. The unlit brass lantern she carried gleamed in the moonlight. "I am certain that we shall find the black sealing wax and the phoenix seal somewhere in his rooms."

"This is a complete waste of time." Marcus

swung one leg over the sill. "We already know that he's the blackmailer."

"But we need proof. The wax and seal will give us solid evidence."

Marcus swung his other leg over the sill and dropped into the shadowed room. "We are not doing this to obtain evidence. We are doing it solely because you want to prove to me that your hypothesis was as sound as mine."

"It is sound. I know that I would eventually have found the blackmailer on my own." Iphiginia caught up the hem of her cloak and her skirts in one hand and put a stocking-clad leg over the edge of the sill.

Marcus wistfully contemplated the graceful limb and thought about how it would look tangled in the white sheets of his massive bed.

Later, he promised himself. Iphiginia was his, that was the important thing. He could relax. She had belonged to him since they had exchanged vows earlier that day in front of a preacher.

She was his wife.

Satisfaction surged deep inside as he caught her by the waist and lifted her through the window. Offhand he could not think of any other female who would have demanded to spend her wedding night rummaging through a blackmailer's desk, but Iphiginia was nothing if not an Original.

Marcus had concluded that he could afford to indulge her now that he was certain of possessing her.

In truth, he had not been particularly keen on the scheme to search Hoyt's lodgings, but Marcus had convinced himself that the plan was not unduly risky. Hoyt, after all, was a creature of Society. He was out until dawn every night. His servant, Marcus had learned, had formed the habit of spending the evenings at a tavern.

"Close the curtains," Iphiginia ordered softly as she lit the lantern.

Marcus obligingly drew the curtains. He turned to survey the room by the light of Iphiginia's lantern. It was a comfortable chamber, quite suited to a single gentleman of modest means. There was a desk in one corner and a row of bookcases along one wall. A wingback chair stood before the cold hearth. The table next to it held a half-empty bottle of brandy and a glass.

"Hoyt does not appear to have invested his ill-gotten gains in his living quarters," Marcus observed.

"No, but he orders his coats from Weston and he recently purchased his own carriage. You know what that costs." Iphiginia explored the desk quickly. "And there is that building he purchased from the original Dr. Hardstaff. That must have cost a great deal."

"And that monument he built in Reeding Cemetery." Marcus opened a drawer in a bureau and saw a stack of freshly laundered and starched cravats.

"It is difficult to credit that a man who is nasty enough to commit murder and blackmail would be the sort to build such a striking memorial to his mother." Iphiginia sucked in her breath. "Ah-hah."

"What does *ah-hah* mean?"

"It means that the desk is unlocked." Iphiginia began rummaging around in the top drawer.

Marcus moved across the room. "I hate to mention the obvious, but if the desk is not locked, it is no doubt because there is nothing of any great import inside."

"Nonsense. One cannot conclude that. It simply means that Herbert does not consider the wax and seal dangerous."

"Then he is not quite as intelligent as I had assumed." Marcus frowned as Iphiginia opened the wax jack. "Well?"

"Red wax," she said, disappointed. "But perhaps there is another wax jack about somewhere. And the seal must be here, too."

But after twenty minutes of diligent searching, neither black wax nor the phoenix seal came to light.

"I do not understand it." Iphiginia stood in the center of the room and tapped her toe in evident frustration. "They must be here."

"Not necessarily." Marcus was impatient to be gone. It was all very well to indulge one's bride, he thought, but enough was enough. "He may keep them on his person or in a safe that we have not discovered. There are any number of places where one could conceal items as small as a wax jack and seal."

"I know where he would keep such items." Iphiginia's eyes widened with excitement. "Dr. Hardstaff's Museum of the Goddesses of Manly Vigor."

Marcus groaned. "I really don't believe that there is much point searching the museum. What if one of Dr. Hardstaff's patients is receiving a treatment?"

"It is certainly worth a try." Iphiginia turned down the lantern and started toward the window. "Don't dawdle, Marcus. We do not have all night, you know."

"Thank God." Marcus glanced quickly around the shadowed room, making certain that they had not left any obvious sign of intrusion. "I would very much like to spend some portion of this night in bed."

Iphiginia scooped up her cloak and skirts and put one leg over the windowsill. "Must you grumble? We have the rest of our lives to spend in bed."

Marcus cheered at the notion. The rest of his life with Iphiginia. . . .

The alley behind Number Nineteen Lamb Lane was as shadowed and empty that night as it had been the other evening. The stairs that led up to the back door squeaked and sighed beneath Marcus's weight. He climbed them ahead of Iphiginia, treading warily.

For some reason he felt now a sense of unease that he had not been aware of earlier in the alley behind the Thurley Street lodgings.

Marcus reached the landing and tried the door. It opened easily, just as it had the other night. The fine hairs on the back of his neck stirred.

"Marcus?" Iphiginia paused on the step and looked up. "Is something wrong?"

"Stay here. I'll go in first." Marcus removed his coat and slung it over his shoulder. The night air came straight through the fine lawn of his shirt, but he paid no attention. He had a sudden wish to feel less encumbered. "Let me have the lantern."

"But Marcus."

"Wait here, Iphiginia. I mean it."

To his infinite relief, she obeyed. Marcus lit the lantern and moved into the darkened hall.

The corridor was eerily silent. Apparently none of the Goddesses of Manly Vigor was giving a performance this evening. Marcus went down the hall to the chamber that contained the bed and the stage.

He opened the door cautiously.

The interior lay in deep shadow. The light from the lantern revealed the torn transparency curtain in front of the stage. It had not been repaired since Sands had ripped it from the ceiling hooks.

"Do you see anything?" Iphiginia asked softly from the doorway.

Marcus spun around. "Damn it, Iphiginia, I told you to wait outside."

The scrape of a boot on the wooden floor of the hall sent a cold chill through him.

"Iphiginia, *move*." Marcus put the lantern down and launched himself toward the door.

He was too late.

A man's arm came out of the shadows from behind Iphiginia and caught her by the throat. Iphiginia gave a soft shriek that was cut off almost immediately.

"Not another step, Masters." Herbert held Iphiginia in front of him as a shield as he moved into the chamber. The lantern light glinted on the barrel of the pistol in his hand. "Or I will shoot you."

"Let her go, Hoyt." Marcus came to a halt. He took a reluctant step back and stopped next to the lantern. "This has all gone far enough. It must end tonight."

"I agree." Herbert smiled bitterly. "But as I have written most of the other scenes of this play, I will write the ending. I fancy something melodramatic that will make an interesting tidbit for the *ton*. What do you think about having the notorious Lady Masters kill her husband when she discovers him at Dr. Hardstaff's Museum on their wedding night?"

TWENTY-ONE

"What happens to Iphiginia in your little play?" Marcus asked.

"I regret that my good friend the former Mrs. Bright—or should I say *Miss* Bright, of Deepford in Devon—will suffer an unfortunate accident on the rear stairs. She will break her neck as she flees the scene of her crime of passion."

"You will never get away with this," Iphiginia vowed. She was clearly frightened, but still self-possessed. "You'll hang, Mr. Hoyt. If not for this, then surely for the murder of Mrs. Wycherley."

"You reasoned that out, did you?" Herbert smiled his jovial, ingratiating smile, but his eyes were as hard as glass. "Very clever, madam. I always did admire your intellect. So much so that I tried to keep you out of this, but you would not be warned off."

"It was you who locked me in the sepulchral monument in Reeding Cemetery, was it not?" Iphiginia demanded.

"I thought a good scare might persuade you to mind your own business, but I was wrong."

Marcus kept his coat hooked over his shoulder. "Why did you kill Mrs. Wycherley?"

"Ah, yes, Constance Wycherley," Herbert said in a musing tone. "She was the one who began it all. Her little blackmail business operated quite innocuously for years. In exchange for a plump fee, she convinced any number of the governesses and companions she placed in certain households to give her interesting items of information concerning their employers."

"And then she blackmailed those people?" Iphiginia asked.

"Yes. It was a rather brilliant scheme, but I saw at once that Mrs. Wycherley lacked the vision to make it fulfill its true potential. She kept her demands very modest and stuck to blackmailing only the lesser members of the *ton*. She was afraid to pursue the more powerful names on her list."

"For fear that they would discover her identity and take action to stop her?" Marcus asked.

"Precisely. She didn't care to take chances,

you see. Very conservative type. But I insisted
that we broaden the scope of the business. She
was quite nervous about it." Herbert shrugged.

"How did you convince her to take you on as
an accomplice?" Iphiginia asked.

"I merely threatened to expose her. Actually,
we worked together rather well for a while, although she became increasingly anxious. Unfortunately, after Iphiginia's man of affairs
called to make inquiries about a certain Miss
Todd, she panicked and demanded we halt the
scheme entirely. I was forced to kill her before
she ruined everything."

"And then you ransacked the place in order
to make it appear that she had been murdered
by one of her victims?" Iphiginia asked.

"Or a thief. I was not particularly worried
about what conclusion was drawn. After all, no
one could connect her death to me."

"How did you learn of her blackmail
scheme?" Iphiginia asked.

"My mother was a governess. She sold information to Mrs. Wycherley for years and in exchange the Wycherley Agency kept her
employed in some of the best homes." Herbert's mouth twisted bitterly. "Until my mother
was seduced by one of her employers, that is. A
fine gentleman of the *ton* got her pregnant. She
was turned off immediately, of course."

"And Mrs. Wycherley refused to place her in

any more posts after that," Iphiginia whispered.

"How did you know?" Herbert's voice, which had been almost jovial until that moment, suddenly rose in fury. His arm tightened around her throat. "Bloody hell, how did you know that?"

"It was merely a hypothesis," Iphiginia whispered.

Marcus tensed. "You're hurting her, Hoyt."

"Don't move." Herbert kept the gun pointed at Marcus. "You are correct, Iphiginia. Mrs. Wycherley wanted nothing to do with a governess who'd been so stupid as to get herself pregnant by one of her employers. My mother was forced to fend for herself."

"You were the babe she carried, were you not?" Iphiginia asked with surprising gentleness.

"Yes. I was her bastard son. The son of a viscount, but a bastard, nonetheless. Mother had some money, thanks to the fees Mrs. Wycherley had paid her for information over the years. And she was clever. She set herself up as a widow in a small village in the north. No one ever learned the truth."

"How did you learn it?" Marcus asked.

"Two years ago on her deathbed, my mother told me the entire tale. I came to London to find Constance Wycherley."

"And your father?" Iphiginia asked very softly.

Once more Hoyt's expression turned violent. "He was *dead,* damn his soul. He broke his neck in a phaeton accident five years ago. I never even got the chance—" Herbert stopped abruptly and took several deep breaths. "I went to the Wycherley Agency and introduced myself to the old bitch."

"I see you've expanded your business empire from blackmail to fraud," Marcus said.

"Yes." Herbert indicated the premises of the museum with the nose of the pistol. "You would not believe how much money certain gentlemen of the *ton* will pay to regain their manly vigor, especially those who have not yet managed to produce an heir."

"I suppose there is a certain irony in your choice of business enterprise," Marcus said. "The illegitimate son of a titled gentleman engaged in defrauding other gentlemen."

"They are always so bloody concerned about begetting their legitimate heirs, are they not?" Herbert asked. "Their bastards can rot, of course. It's only the legitimate offspring who count."

Iphiginia stirred in his grasp. "Mr. Hoyt, please listen to me."

"*Silence.*" Herbert's arms tightened ominously once more around her. "At one time I had hoped that you and I might become more than friends, my dear Iphiginia. We had so much in common. I wanted you to comprehend that, but you never did."

"What on earth do you mean?" Iphiginia asked.

"You and I are two of a kind, m'dear. Oh, yes. Yes, indeed. I realized that from the first moment we met. You were so utterly outrageous. So clever. I knew I had to find out more about you. Your close friendship with Lady Guthrie was the clue, of course."

"All you had to do was examine Mrs. Wycherley's files to discover that she had two nieces, one named Iphiginia Bright and one named Amelia Farley," Marcus said.

"Mrs. Wycherley kept excellent files," Herbert said. "Once I realized that Iphiginia was her niece, I knew she was also a fraud. One thing led to another and soon I had it all sorted out."

"What made you think we had a great deal in common?" Iphiginia demanded.

"It's obvious, is it not? We had both carved out a place for ourselves in the highest levels of Society by virtue of our own cleverness and determination. We had deceived the Polite World, convinced it to accept us as one of its own. I thought that we were made for each other, m'dear. But you insisted on setting your sights on the Earl of Masters."

"You thought she had entered Society in order to form a connection with me?" Marcus asked.

"I did not discover that she was trying to find her aunt's blackmailer until the night she went to Reeding Cemetery. Until then, I thought it was you she was out to snag. I could not blame her for aiming high. Indeed, I admired her nerve. But I feared it would not end well."

"You intended to be there when her grand schemes came to naught, is that it?" Marcus asked.

"Yes. Damn you. Who could have foreseen that the legendary Masters would abandon all of his rules to marry his mistress?"

"You tried to destroy our attachment the night you sent her here to discover me with Lady Sands, did you not?" Marcus kept his gaze on Iphiginia, willing her to ready herself.

"Everyone, including Lord Sands, I think, believed that you and Lady Sands had been conducting a quiet affair for years. I expected I could convince Iphiginia of that, also."

"But why did you send Lord Sands here that night?" Iphiginia asked.

Marcus raised his brows. "Hoyt no doubt

hoped that Sands would kill me when he found me with his wife."

Herbert gave him an approving look. "Quite right. Sands is inordinately fond of his lady. My congratulations, sir. You really are as intelligent as everyone says."

"Thank you."

Marcus dropped his cloak over the lantern, plunging the room into darkness.

"Bastard," Herbert yelled. "Do not move." He shrieked in startled pain. "Damnation, you bit me, you little bitch."

An audible scuffle ensued.

Marcus slipped to the right in hopes of avoiding a bullet. He went in low and fast toward his quarry. He could see nothing. He was forced to rely on sound to guide him.

Herbert's pistol roared. The sparks from the explosion momentarily illuminated his face. His well-fed, normally pleasant countenance appeared demonic.

An instant later, Marcus slammed into him.

They both went down, rolling on the floor. The pistol fell with a crash. Marcus heard Iphiginia's footsteps as she groped her way toward the covered lantern. He sincerely hoped she would reach it before his coat caught fire.

Herbert yelled and clawed at Marcus, his rage imbuing him with surprising strength. He thrashed free for an instant. Marcus heard him stagger to his feet.

Iphiginia got the coat off the lantern at that moment. Light flooded the chamber.

Marcus came up off the floor in one move. He used the sudden gift of visibility to aim a blow at Herbert's midsection. Herbert sagged but did not go down. Instead, he reeled toward the lantern.

He kicked out savagely at the flaring lamp.

Glass shattered. Oil spilled. Flames leaped to follow the path of the fuel.

"My God," Iphiginia shouted. "The bed."

Out of the corner of his eyes Marcus saw her grab his coat and begin to beat at the flames.

"Get out, Iphiginia," he shouted.

"If the flames reach the bed or those ceiling hangings, this whole building will become an inferno."

Marcus knew that she was right. And if the building went up in flames, there was no telling how much damage might be done or how many lives might be lost. There were bound to be several families sleeping in the rooms above the many shops in Lamb Lane.

Herbert seized the opportunity created by the distraction. He lurched toward the door. Marcus instinctively went after him.

He reached the door and heard his quarry's

footsteps pound down the darkened hall. A second later the outer door opened. A weak shaft of light illuminated Herbert's bulky figure.

Marcus ran the length of the hall. He reached the outside landing just as Herbert started down the shadowed steps.

"You're not getting away, you little bastard." Marcus grabbed the railing with one hand and reached out to snag Herbert by the collar.

"Goddamn you, Masters." Hoyt swung out wildly to ward off Marcus's arm.

The frantic motion caused the panicked man to lose his balance. He fell against the rail, spun around, and toppled backward down the steps.

Hoyt's short, anguished scream was cut off abruptly when he hit the pavement below.

Marcus looked down at the unmoving body. There was just enough light to see that Hoyt's neck was twisted at an unnatural angle. The man was dead.

"Marcus," Iphiginia called. "Help me."

Marcus whirled around and raced back down the hall. He ran into the chamber and saw that Iphiginia had nearly succeeded in dousing the flames. There was a single ribbon of fire left. It was eating its way across the carpet.

"Stand back." Marcus grabbed the edge of

the carpet and rolled it, swallowing most of the flames whole.

Iphiginia quickly smothered the rest with the coat. Darkness descended once more.

"Thank God. Marcus, are you all right?"

"Yes. Hoyt is dead. He fell down the steps."

"Dear heaven."

Marcus lit the wall sconce and surveyed the chamber. The fire had done surprisingly little damage. He looked at Iphiginia.

She met his eyes, his still-smoking coat clutched in her hands.

Marcus searched her soot-streaked face. "Did you get burned?"

"No."

Marcus sniffed the stench of burned wool. He suddenly remembered something. "Let me see that."

He snatched the coat from her hands and groped inside one of the pockets. His hand closed around his new, improved hydraulic reservoir pen. He winced when he felt the crumpled length of metal. It was hot. "Damn and blast."

"What's wrong?"

"Nothing important. It appears I must return to my drawing table."

It was nearly dawn before Marcus opened the door of the bedchamber that adjoined his own and walked into the room. A single candle burned beside the turned-back bed.

The bed itself was empty.

Iphiginia waited for him near the window. She turned when she heard him enter. She was dressed in a white, lace-trimmed nightgown of softest lawn. A ruffled nightcap was perched on her head. Her glorious smile of welcome made Marcus catch his breath.

"Iphiginia." He could not think of anything else to say.

He opened his arms and she ran into them. He scooped her up, carried her to the bed, and fell with her into the clean, sweet-smelling sheets.

He felt whole and right inside, no longer a man made of smoothly oiled wheels and gears.

"I love you, Marcus."

Marcus pulled her close and kissed her fiercely, passionately. He cradled her hip in his hand and took a taut, sweet nipple into his mouth. She was so perfect, he thought, awed. It was as though she had been made especially for him.

He had been waiting for her all these years, he realized.

"Hold me, Iphiginia. Don't ever let me go."

"Never."

Marcus was not certain that he recognized the emotion that swept through him a short time later when he sheathed himself within Iphiginia's warm, tight body.

He rather thought that it might be joy.

Iphiginia awoke to find herself alone in the rumpled bed. Early morning sunlight streamed into the bedchamber and splashed across the sheets.

She closed her eyes and stretched slowly, savoring the aftereffects of Marcus's lovemaking. Memories drifted through her, warming every inch of her body. She closed her eyes and recalled the wonderful feel of her husband's strong, exciting hands on her breasts, her thighs, between her legs.

An odd ticking sound broke through her reverie. It was accompanied by the distinct rasp of gear and wheel.

Chunkachunkachunka.

Iphiginia opened her eyes and saw that the door between the bedchambers was open. Marcus stood there, one shoulder propped against the jamb.

He was garbed in a black silk robe. His dark hair was still tousled from the pillow. He crossed his arms and studied her with his brilliant amber eyes.

"Good morning, Iphiginia."

"Good morning. I was wondering where you

had gone." Iphiginia pushed herself up against the pillows. "What on earth is that odd noise?"

Then she saw the clockwork man coming toward her across the carpet. She watched in amazement as its legs jerked back and forth, propelling it toward the bed. One arm was outstretched. The wooden hand held a silver salver.

On top of the salver was a small folded sheet of paper.

Iphiginia watched, fascinated, as the automaton reached the bed and found its path blocked. Its innards continued to grind and its legs went on churning uselessly, pushing its face into the side of the mattress.

Iphiginia reached down to pick up the note on the salver. She opened it carefully and read the message inside.

I love you

"Oh, Marcus." Iphiginia threw back the covers and scrambled out of bed.

She ignored the clockwork man and ran, barefoot, across the room to where Marcus waited in the doorway. She halted directly in front of him.

He smiled.

"Do you mean it?" she asked.

"With all my heart."

Happiness inundated her in a sparkling waterfall of light. "I knew we were made for each other."

He laughed, swept her up into his arms, and carried her back to the bed. "You were right."

"As usual," Iphiginia said.

10/94

3/03 -31

Q Quic
Quick, Amanda.
Mistress